WEHR WOLFF CASTLE

The Wehrmacht's Mutante Wolf Program

The Wehr Wolff Chronicles, Book One

B. Bentley Summers

Published by
NineStar Press
PO Box 91792
Albuquerque, New Mexico, 87199
www.ninestarpress.com

Print ISBN # 978-1-947139-45-9
Cover by Natasha Snow
Edited by Jason Bradley

During the rise of Nazi Germany, Hagen Messer joins the Royal Air Force as an American soldier who specializes in tracking. He's attached to British commandos and given a seemingly simple mission—to find a captive and destroy a dam—but everything goes awry. Hagen's plane crashes into Germany's Wehr Forest and he has to use his extrasensory abilities to track the captive to nearby Wehr Wolff Castle, a secret Nazi base where vile experiments are being conducted.

Hagen and his surviving team members must sneak into the castle and devise a way to destroy the experimental labs creating diabolical creatures. Hagen is horrified to find Nazis and scientists with no scruples, and at the most inconvenient time, he learns that he may be in love with one of his teammates, an Irishman named Liam. In order to protect his love and his friends, Hagen must feign nonchalance amidst pure degeneracy and suspicion. Hagen soon discovers, though, that he is in over his head.

What may not only redeem him, but also save his lover and friends, is a childhood past and a darkness lurking deep inside him, just waiting to be engaged.

*This book is dedicated to my mother who has been my most avid
book reader from book one till now. Thanks, Mom!*

Acknowledgements

Wehr Wolff Castle is a work of fiction. Certain items, such as clothing, planes, and weapons are accurate for that time period. A few real persons are presented in this book, though the main characters of this story are entirely fictional and of my imagination. Lastly, for the purpose of the plot, I have altered some historical timelines and events.

I would like to acknowledge my editor, Jennifer Collins, who has been helping me with writing projects and to become a better writer. As well, I would like to give special thanks to NineStar Press for their dedication to LGBT literature and making this manuscript shine.

One: Hagen

May 10, 1940
Somewhere over the border of Switzerland & Southern Nazi Germany

THE WIND WHISTLED through the shattered window and into the airplane's cabin. The draft had a cold bite, the air a metallic smell. A tremble spasmed through Hagen, and he crossed his arms over his chest and shivered.

On the row of seats facing him, blood spatter spread over the chairs and over the remaining wall. The engine nearest him sputtered.

This time, it'll surely stop.

He rose from his seat and looked out through a nearby window to the wing. Black smoke poured from the spinning propeller but then cleared, and the engine roared back to life, setting into a steady thrum. He stared past the wing to the mountain range below. The plane passed through a heavy white cloud, and he sat back down in his seat.

One recurrent thought plagued him. *If we crash, will it hurt? Breathe. Just breathe.*

Raising his hands, he stared once again at the blood that had partially dried on them. Not his, thankfully. He wiped them on his shirt-front, which was soaked with blood, then reached for his forehead and winced as his fingertips dusted his wound.

Shouting from the cockpit drew his attention.

Lt. David sat in the one-man cockpit and turned so he could shout up to the white-haired pilot assistant, Alan Hodges. Hodges stood close to the pilot's chair, holding onto a map and yelling down.

Someone grabbed Hagen's knee and shouted at him gruffly. He met Sgt. Collins's gaze. The man's short salt-and-pepper stubbled face had specks of blood in it. The large man sat back on his haunches, his belly protruding over his belt. He peered at Hagen's forehead and nodded with approval.

"Cheers, Kraut, received your first war wound." Sgt. Collins leaned in and touched Hagen's paratrooper jacket. "That blood yours?"

Hagen shook his head, licked his lips, and then asked, "We on the right course, Sarge?"

Sgt. Collins cupped his hand to his ear and furrowed his brow.

"Are we on the right course?" Hagen shouted.

Sgt. Collins glanced up at the front of the plane, where Lt. David and Officer Hodges argued, then brought his eyes back to Hagen.

"Have no bloody idea, Kraut. All I know is that I hope we don't land in Hitler's front lawn."

Hagen nodded and clenched his fists. The sergeant shouted something else at him, but Hagen stared over his shoulder at the woman on the other side of the airplane. Roesia. He barely knew her, but it was comforting to see a survivor from the onslaught. So many had died. Her face was pasty white, and she had a vacant stare.

Sgt. Collins snapped his fingers in front of Hagen's face, gaining his attention once again.

"Bloody hell, you're completely out of it!" Sgt. Collins said, patting Hagen's chest and sides, looking for any wounds. "Nothing. You're lucky, Kraut."

Sgt. Collins stood, went toward the tail, and yelled down to the lower gun turret. "O'Malley, say something, you Irishman!"

"Me arse is killing me, Sarge!"

A smile formed on Hagen's face at hearing his friend's voice.

The sergeant moved toward the tail and yelled up to the upper gun turret. "Kirby, keep your wits about you! If those bandits come at us, you take as many of them as you can."

Corporal Kirby yelled something unintelligible. Hagen shifted in his seat and stared down as a viscous red fluid ran across the floor. A photograph lay near his foot. Reaching down, he plucked it off the ground—the one of him and his father from a year or so ago. Except half of it was now bloodstained and he could only see himself. He studied the broad-shouldered striking nineteen-year-old with a full-face grin that made him radiant. The picture could easily have been of one of those Hollywood actors, but it was of himself.

He leaned his head against the chair as his teeth chattered and his eyes became impossibly heavy.

Seems like so much has happened since then. But I arrived in England just two days ago? That's it? Just two days?

A slap of metal caused his gaze to shift to the other side of the plane. A commando by the name of Commander Ford picked up the assault rifles and opened each ammo clip to check the bullets inside. Once satisfied, he laid them on top of a tarp that had turned a dark maroon from the blood-drenched floor. A second commando sat in a seat next to him, twirling a serrated knife in one hand.

The spinning knife mesmerized Hagen and helped him ignore the macabre scene around him.

Yes, it was. Two days ago, I rode into Shoreham Royal Air Force Base.

A freshly trained paratrooper from America with no war experience. While my brother's mortally wounded body lay in front of me years ago, it was nothing like this.

Memories of the last couple of days reeled through his mind.

Two: The Irishman and the Night Angel Crewmembers

Shoreham Royal Air Force Base, England
Two Days Earlier, May 8, 1940

THE ARMY TRANSPORTATION truck pulled around the bend, its left tires dropping into the potholes pocked across the asphalt road. The back of the vehicle stood open, and the young men sitting in the rear gripped the ledges to keep their balance as they jostled from side to side.

The transport came to an abrupt halt at a sentry point manned by two guards. Beyond sat a bustling airfield. Hagen waited in the truck with other young men, some with partial beards while others were smooth-faced like him. He studied the photograph he'd been holding for the last few minutes. It was from one year ago when he attended university. His father, a man never known for being affectionate, had draped his arm around Hagen's shoulder and offered a thin-lipped smile to the camera. Unlike the crew cut he had now, Hagen's thick hair was combed to the side and a few strands hung down over his forehead. A full grin spread over Hagen's tan face, showing off white even teeth and, as his mother had been fond of saying years ago before she died, making his handsomeness shine.

The engine revved as the truck headed into the camp, then ground to a halt. The men rose at once and started to unload. Hagen placed the picture into his pocket, picked up his duffel bag, and hopped to the ground, while taking in his surroundings. Off the main airfield was an expansive Victorian stone mansion with three spires across the front.

Even though he'd been told the Royal Air Force headquarters was opulent, he still gazed at it with awe.

As he had been told to report there, he headed in its direction, admiring the building on his stroll and noticing a couple of blonde young women who were ogling him from nearby. Both of them snapped their gazes away. One woman with glasses put her hand over her mouth and giggled into her palm. She glanced back at Hagen but was pulled forward by her friend and hurried toward the house that he presumed to be the main headquarters.

His name was shouted from behind him.

"*Hagen Messer!*" The name was repeated. Hagen returned to the area where he had been dropped off. In a section of the field that was partitioned off with large tents, a skinny older man wearing thick-rimmed glasses held up a slip of paper.

Hagen raised his hand. "Yes, sir."

The man creased his brow. "Private Hagen Messer?"

Hagen nodded. "Yes, sir."

The man handed him a piece of paper. "Your new orders. You're with Lieutenant David's outfit now. Oh, and welcome to England, Private."

Hagen looked down at the order in his hand, then back up. "Is this in communications?" He pointed to the Victorian home.

The older man adjusted his glasses and gave Hagen a quizzical look. "No, Private." He shook his head as he pointed toward the edge of the airfield, where there stood several mammoth-sized bombers and a row of hangars. "Hangar five."

A few moments later, Hagen walked past the parked bombers that had eighty-foot wingspans and two engines on each wing. A ruckus of cheers caught his attention. A group of men were gathered close to hangar five, making a circle around two others who were bare-chested. Both wore boxing gloves, hands held up in front of them. One was an athletic, well-built man with a blond beard. The other was thickset with black and gray stubble on his face and a belly that stuck out over his waistband.

The crowd roared, "Collins, Collins, Collins."

The blond-bearded man swung, and though the thick, stubbly-faced man did not look fast, he moved with speed, dipping under the hit and executing two uppercuts, which he finished with a hard hook. The blond-bearded man staggered back, wobbled, and fell to the ground.

The cheers grew in intensity as the group shouted the victor's name. "Collins! Collins!"

A long tube sock lay near Collins's foot as he took his gloves off, and he picked it up. A couple of crumpled bills spilled from the lip, and he plucked them from the ground and stuffed them back inside. He pivoted toward a man holding a fistful of money and took the cash with a half grin.

Hagen moved past the fight and came to hangar five, where a smaller bomber with one engine on each wing sat. A profile portrait of a pretty blonde woman had been rendered near the nose of the plane. She was dressed provocatively in a_black dress that was transparent along the bottom, showing off the side of her thigh. A rifle was slung over her shoulder while she stood in front of a full moon. Red lettering painted underneath declared her the *Night Angel*.

Two men in overalls hoisted a gun turret near the belly of the plane. A mechanic worked on the engine, the cover raised as he leaned forward, twisting a ratchet.

Someone spoke by Hagen's shoulder. "American, not English."

Hagen turned to discover a mechanic wiping his greasy hands on a rag. Hagen shook his head in confusion. "I'm American."

The man chuckled. "A Yankee, eh?" He pointed to the plane, drawing Hagen's attention in that direction. "No, I meant she's American. Not a beaut like the Lancaster Bomber, but she's blooming fast."

Hagen turned to face the mechanic once again, uncertain what to say, and finally managed, "Looks sturdy."

"A Lockheed Hudson. A light bomber with two 14-cylinder Wright engines. Has a nineteen-hundred-mile range. Needs a crew of five. She's fast and might just survive if you come across them dodgy Nazi Messerschmitts."

Hagen pointed to the men who were pulling the hoisted gun up into the belly. "They replacing the old gun?"

The mechanic stuffed his greasy rag in a pocket. "These gems don't come off the American assembly line with a belly gun turret. That's where the bombs typically go, but the Night Angel is getting a special gun there. Hear she's going deep in Germany on a special mission." The mechanic clapped Hagen on the shoulder. "Cheers." He then returned to the plane.

Men's voices reached Hagen, and he turned toward them. Two men approached, one man he recognized as the victorious, obese, and stubbly faced boxer.

Collins? Yes, that was the name.

Collins had a few folded bills in his hand and change in one palm. He placed it all in the small worn cotton sock he still carried in one hand. The second man was in his early thirties, had a stout build, chubby red cheeks, and a corporal insignia on his shirt. Collins pulled a light green shirt over his sweaty torso, and Hagen observed that his insignia showed a sergeant status. Neither had noticed him yet.

Collins told the smaller-framed guy, "He's a lucky bugger that I held back."

The corporal asked, "How much you make?"

Sgt. Collins rattled his sock. "Enough to get pissed this weekend. And—" He stuck his hand inside his sock, rummaged, and pulled out a couple of lighters. "—these will fetch a pretty quid in Brighton."

Sgt. Collins glanced at Hagen and stopped talking, scanning him up and down. He scratched his salt-and-pepper whiskers and addressed the other man. "You see what I see, Kirby? An American uniform?"

"Yes, sir." Hagen coughed into his hand. "I'm looking for a, uh, Lieutenant David."

Corporal Kirby scratched his chin and grinned from ear to ear, showing off a row of yellowish stained teeth. "What's a Yank doing all the way over here in little ol' England? Thought you boyos had cold feet, letting us take care of Hitler."

Hagen made no immediate response, but finally managed to say, "I trained in paratrooper school at Lawson Army Airfield in Fort Benning, Georgia, got to Brighton last night—" Hagen stared at Sgt. Collins in bewilderment; the man had cupped his hand up to his ear.

Sgt. Collins straightened and rubbed his ample belly. "Bloody hell, is that a Kraut accent?" He squinted accusatorily at Hagen.

"I'm American," Hagen protested, his voice rising and his hands closing into fists.

Sgt. Collins smirked and pointed at Hagen. "You sure? I heard those Germans have blond hair and blue eyes like that. I bet they could put your picture on every Nazi pamphlet recruiting new bloody Nazi soldiers."

"I'm American," Hagen repeated, gritting his teeth.

Corporal Kirby's red cheeks grew redder and his foolish grin wider. "Sounds like a bloody Germ to me. Can you do the goose walk they talk about so much?"

A crisp voice called from the other side of the hangar. "Collins. Kirby. Enough." The two men flinched and did a half-face pivot. A man sauntered toward them, wearing an officer's hat, his face hidden by the shade. As he came closer, it became apparent he had a long nose, pronounced dark eyebrows, and a scar that ran from his left ear, down his neck, and under his leather officer's jacket.

"You're the American volunteer? Messer, right? I'm Lieutenant Graham David."

Hagen went to attention and saluted, saying, "Private Hagen Messer, sir. Reporting for duty."

A smile curved on Lt. David's mouth, though he didn't return the salute. "At ease. Lieutenant will suffice once we're on our mission tomorrow."

The sergeant and corporal looked at each other, concern written on their faces. The sergeant mouthed, "*Mission?*"

"How long you been in the army, Private?" Lt. David asked.

"Completed paratrooper training camp a week ago, sir," Hagen answered, handing his papers over. "Was supposed to be sent to communications."

Lt. David grunted and read his papers.

Sgt. Collins and Corporal Kirby glanced between Hagen and the lieutenant. The sergeant asked, "Sir, why do we have a Kraut coming with us? And a boy with barely any fuzz on his face?"

Lt. David handed the papers back to Hagen and smiled at the sergeant, saying, "Sergeant Collins, our friend here is an American citizen, not German."

Sgt. Collins looked over at Hagen and wiped his mouth with the back of his hand. "Yes, sir."

Lt. David jabbed his thumb to the two men, and asked Hagen, "I see you met Sergeant Brady Collins and Corporal Brian Kirby?"

Hagen gave the men a dubious look. Sgt. Collins was scratching his whiskered chin, his attention focused on Hagen.

The lieutenant patted the front of his jacket, searching for something. "But to answer your question, Sergeant, Messer will be vital to a secret mission that has been pushed to tomorrow. Cannot do it tonight—there's a storm front in France."

"Mission, sir?" Corporal Kirby asked, his pitch rising. "I thought we were on R&R tomorrow through Sunday."

"Cancelled, Corporal. We've been asked to take on a mission for His Majesty."

The men looked at one another. Lt. David asked the mechanic working on the propeller, "Ted, when is she going to be ready?"

Ted wiped his brow. "Nineteen hundred, tops."

Hagen stepped up, speaking in a low tone. "Sir, what mission?"

Lt. David raised his eyebrows and met Hagen's gaze while he removed a small silver case from his inner pocket and opened the lid. His fingers dug out a cigarette from the row lying inside.

"Sir," Hagen said, "I was supposed to be assigned to Communications. Interpreting intercepted radio signals."

The lieutenant placed the cigarette between his lips then returned the case to his pocket, his brow furrowed.

The corporal brought a matchbox from his pocket, and the lieutenant's eyes brightened. "Ah, Corporal Kirby. On point as always." The corporal blocked the wind as he lit the cigarette.

Lt. David drew in smoke, blew it out, and ignored Hagen's comment, instead asking Sgt. Collins, "Say, Sergeant. Isn't that where I recruited you from? Communications?"

"I bloody well didn't interpret German. I interpreted French."

The lieutenant made a short laugh. "Come to think of it, Sergeant, I never have heard you speak French."

Sgt. Collins's face turned red. "Don't speak it worth shite, sir. I just translate it. Grandmother, God rest her soul, was French and helped raise me."

Lt. David smiled. "Right-o. Oh, and Sergeant, I've heard reports there was another boxing match on premises. Believe I even heard cheers, in fact. Is that true?"

Sgt. Collins balked. "Well, sir, uh..."

Lt. David puffed out smoke. "Sergeant, at least do it somewhere off base. And make blooming sure you don't fight anyone that buggers me out of one of my crew."

Sgt. Collins shook his head. "Bloody unlikely that could happen, sir."

Lt. David raised his brow, then turned to Hagen. "Messer, we need someone who speaks German, and, well, can track. I understand you received high merits for your tracking skills?"

Hagen gave one perceptible nod. His commander had told him he was going to Communications, and the new assignment jarred him.

Lt. David leaned against the side of the airplane. "Understand you emigrated from Germany when you were a child?"

Hagen glanced to the men and back to the lieutenant. "I was barely thirteen. My father took us to Pennsylvania."

"At thirteen? You are quite fluent in English."

"My pa spoke it, but he hired a tutor when we were kids. His dream was to go to America, and he made good business with his trade."

Sgt. Collins chuckled, and asked, "And what'd he do, shine shoes?"

Corporal Kirby covered his mouth, but a snicker slipped between his fingers.

Hagen stiffened. "He designed high-powered telescopes. He was good enough that he now works for the American Navy."

The lieutenant gave Corporal Kirby a reproving look and blew a puff of smoke up in the air, asking, "Lived near Konstanz, was it?"

"Konstanz? That by Berlin?" Corporal Kirby asked, scratching his thinly haired scalp.

"Not even close, Corporal," Lt. David answered. "Germany's a big place. It's in Southern Germany."

Hagen's palms sweated. *Is this vital to his mission? I barely lived in Konstanz.* "Yes, sir. But barely three years. I grew up far into southeast Germany, close to Czechoslovakia." *Right near the Bavarian Alps.*

The lieutenant nodded. "And you speak fluent German, Messer?"

"Of course, sir."

A handsome young man, about nineteen years old with red-brown hair, came running into the hangar. His riveting green eyes immediately went to Hagen for a cursory moment, then back to Lt. David. A distinguished-looking man with a gray mustache, wearing an officer's hat, strolled into the hangar a moment later.

"Ah, O'Malley." Lt. David smiled. "You bring me those maps I asked for?"

O'Malley slapped his forehead and spoke with a thick Irish accent. "I'm a crikey eejit, Sir. I'll go back and get them."

"Hodges," Lt. David said, "can you tell me what you both have been doing?"

O'Malley didn't let the older man, Hodges, answer. "Blimey, craziness is what we've seen, sir. There's a lass who is going to parachute into Germany."

Sgt. Collins rolled his eyes. "God save us."

Corporal Kirby shook his head and honked out a laugh. "A bloody woman parachuting? The RAF has gone completely loony."

Hodges tweaked the end of his mustache and said, "Born and raised in Germany, but half French. She was a professor at Humboldt University in Berlin before she took a boat over here and defected."

Sgt. Collins furrowed his brow and crossed his arms so that his shirt lifted up and his hairy belly was displayed. "A bloody spy, no doubt."

Lt. David tapped his cigarette, and ashes swirled down as he stared in contemplation. After a moment, he turned to Hodges. "Right, introductions would be proper. Pilot Officer Alan Hodges, meet our new recruit, Hagen Messer." Lt. David held hand out to the Irishman introducing him. "And this is…"

The Irishman interrupted, offered a crooked grin, and stuck out his hand. "Liam O'Malley. Airman Second Class." Liam flinched, then said, "Oh, sorry, sir."

Lt. David flapped his hand and gestured it didn't matter, his partially smoked cigarette still between his fingers.

Hodges spoke. "And, sir, I heard some officers say France feels concern they may be flooded with Nazis any day now."

Hagen asked, "What do you mean, France is going to be flooded with Nazis?"

Sgt. Collins grumbled, "Any day now, France is to be invaded by Nazis. Damn French. Make bloody fine wine but have a worthless air force, or army, for that matter." He held his thumb to his chest. "Everyone leaves it to us Brits. And there's only so much we can do."

Hagen's gaze flitted over to Liam, who had already had his attention on Hagen. They both smiled and looked back to the lieutenant.

"Okay, gentlemen," Lt. David said. "Prayer services tonight at eighteen hundred for Marcus Cross. Be there on time. Report to the briefing room tomorrow at twenty hundred for our operation. O'Malley, show Messer the latrines and grub."

Liam nodded. "Yes, sir. And he can bunk with us."

Hagen turned to Lt. David. "Lieutenant? Who was Cross?"

"They're coming back!" shouted Hodges, tweaking the end of his mustache as he stepped out of the hangar and looked up into the sky.

The steady buzz of a multitude of engines reached Hagen as everyone moved closer to Hodges. A fleet of fighters were coming in to land.

Lt. David peered upward and answered Hagen. "Cross was one of our crew. KIA on a mission into Germany. We took only two bullets, and one bugger managed to strike the poor chap in the head. Sometimes, it's only a matter of luck, or in Cross's case, the lack of it." Lt. David took his cigarette from his mouth, scratched the scar by his ear, and brought his attention to Hagen. "Sometimes, you have it or you don't."

Sgt. Collins sighed, placed both hands on his hips, and walked farther from the hangar. "Blimey, isn't that breathtaking?"

Hagen looked up once more, then glanced around, searching for Liam. He was standing a few feet away.

Liam stepped closer to Hagen. "They've been conducting practices every day." He nudged Hagen with his elbow, led him from the group, and glanced over his shoulder to Lt. David and the other crewmembers who were enraptured by the landing airplanes, and then spoke in a hushed voice. "Say, you ever have a Guinness? We have a pub not far from the base. We'll have time tomorrow to get one, if you fancy."

"That'd be great! But Lieutenant David doesn't care?"

Liam laughed and socked Hagen in the arm. "Don't be a complete muppet!"

Hagen frowned. "What?"

Liam grinned and his face shone. "Means don't be a dope." He put a finger up to his lips. "If no one knows, we'll be fine. Bloody better than afternoon tea. Brits are so stuffy."

Hagen heaved his bag over his shoulder and followed Liam to their bunks.

"How you like England so far?" Liam asked.

Hagen rubbed the back of his neck. "You all use strange words."

Liam laughed. "Me words are strange? Bloody listen to yourself, why don't you?"

Lt. David yelled from behind them. "O'Malley. Messer. Report back here, gentlemen, tomorrow. And report at nineteen hundred."

Three: The Mission

AFTER A MORNING of grueling physical training, Hagen and Liam were given a brief period of free time. The Irishman took Hagen on a hike from the airfield to a local hole-in-the-wall Irish pub as promised and bought both of them a Guinness, along with fish and chips.

Hagen bought them a second round. Liam got them a third.

Hagen and Liam returned from their beer and meal, both of them tipsy from one too many pints. They walked close to one another as Liam spoke of his home and the girls he'd slept with or turned away. The Irishman was a natural storyteller, and Hagen laughed several times at the clever turn of words he chose. Liam's thick accent had a calming rhythm, though Hagen did get distracted when he used peculiar words for commonplace items. Hagen had to explain that Americans referred to breakfast pork as sausages, not bangers; and that it was kiss, not snog; nude rather than nip; and Americans said trunk, not boot.

Reaching the edge of the airbase, Liam suggested they climb up onto a hangar that was in disuse and watch the planes fly overhead. On the rooftop, Liam pulled his shirt over his head, and Hagen gazed at his flat stomach with a trail of light-colored hair extending from his waistline to his chest. Hagen looked away as Liam glanced at him and followed Liam's lead by removing his shirt as well.

Liam lay down, but his attention was fixed on Hagen; he patted the surface next to him. "Come on, boyo."

Liam did not have the pale white skin like the English. It was olive, and he'd tanned recently. He had a well-formed chest; his hands were under his head and his biceps bulged. Hagen lay down next to him, and Liam's emerald gaze met Hagen's.

A crooked smile formed and Liam said, "I'm zonked after that beer. You?"

Hagen chuckled and gazed up in the sky. "I have no idea what zonked is, but if it means anything like being sleepy, then yes."

Liam did not say anything so Hagen glanced over. Liam stared at him with intensity, and some emotion lurked deeper. What, Hagen did not know. But it reminded him of a hungry man who just spied a fragrant pot roast.

The corners of Liam's mouth curled up. "Your eyes. They're peculiar."

"How's that?"

He rolled onto his back and closed his eyes, speaking in a soft voice. "They're like the Irish Sea on a stormy night. An ocean-green one moment, then blue the next. Very peculiar." He then fell asleep, and Hagen stared at him for a few more moments before lying on his back and taking his own afternoon nap.

Upon waking, they went to dinner. Hagen was surprised by the uncertain new feelings that he'd noticed during the afternoon. He wanted to spend more time with Liam and listen to that soothing accent. He didn't want the time to end, and wished to postpone whatever mission was coming.

After dinner, Liam said it was time, so they grabbed their gear from their bunks and headed to the hangar to be briefed on their mission. It occurred to Hagen that, within a few hours, he would be flying over the English Channel and on to some mission that would take him into Germany. The hangar was vacant when they arrived, and the Night Angel faced them with the belly gun turret having been completely installed.

Liam took a cigarette from his pack and offered Hagen one, but he hesitated. *Father would disapprove.* He looked at Liam's face and took one, though, and Liam lit both.

"You have any girls back home?" Liam asked, his jade gaze aimed at him, his lips pursed over his cigarette.

Hagen drew in smoke, coughed, and shook his head; his eyes watered and he said, "Dated a couple. But no takers." Hagen put his arm up to his mouth, feeling another fit of coughs coming.

Liam leaned against the hangar door and stared up into the sky. The sun was starting to set. "Broke a couple lasses' hearts meself. A couple of them had some knockers." Liam looked over to Hagen and laughed. "Oh, right, you call them boobs." He inhaled and spoke after exhaling. "And please, Jaysus, I hope I never put one up the pole."

The ends of Hagen's mouth turned down, and he slid his hand through his blond hair. "The what?"

Liam chuckled and took a drag on his cigarette. "Oh, you Yanks say *pregnant*."

"Oh, right."

"Yeah, I don't want to be foostering away my time and fall in love. Any day might be my last—just ask Cross. Good fella, he was."

Liam stared out at the airfield, his expression suddenly serious. Hagen found himself staring hard at Liam but then turned away.

Liam slapped Hagen's arm. "Say, when we get back, I'll take you to Dublin and show you the local pubs. Then take you to me hometown in Arklow. You think *I* talk funny..."

Hagen smiled. "That'd be excellent." He drew on his cigarette, then bent over in response, hacking with tears wetting his cheeks.

"Bollocks," Liam said. "You ever smoke before?"

Hagen shook his head.

Liam guffawed. Between breaths, he said, "Me first time to meet a Virgin Mary."

Hagen straightened, wiping the wetness from his eyes, a smirk on his face. "I'm not a virgin."

"*Right*. And they don't smoke in America?"

"Like chimneys. But my pa forbade it. Said it broke his concentration when he worked."

"What's he do?"

"Now he designs telescopes and binoculars for the American Navy. Has his own lab in the house, too. Sent me to university, but I quit and joined the army against his wishes."

Liam removed the cigarette from his mouth and regarded Hagen with a fresh face. "Oy, a college fella. Not met many of them." He slipped his cigarette back in his mouth and inhaled, then puffed out the smoke. "That's a bit more interesting tale than my own. Me father was a fisherman and vanished in the Irish Sea when I was a wee boy."

"Oh, I'm sorry," Hagen said as he straightened and leaned back against the hangar, not meeting Liam's gaze.

Liam shrugged, his eyes vacant. "A bugger, death is. It was me mom and me other three brothers after he left us."

"My mom died. I was five. My father was on a work assignment and wasn't around when it happened. Ivan and I were with our English tutor when it occurred; we found her outside. She was making a birdcage and had fallen—she looked like she was asleep. She never woke up, though.

Five years later, it was my brother who d—" A lump formed in Hagen's throat as he stared out at the airfield. *Ivan. I haven't thought of him in years.* "Sorry," Hagen said, "I don't know why I told you all that."

Liam faced Hagen, asking, "What happened? Your brother?"

Hagen shook his head. "I don't know."

Liam gave him a bewildered look.

"I mean, it was an accident. But I have blanks around what happened."

"You liked your brother a lot?" Liam asked.

Hagen nodded, unable to speak, shifting his gaze away from Liam. He felt tears starting to build up.

"I can tell," Liam said. "Me gormless brothers are absolutely worthless." He chuckled and looked up into the sky. "Jealous blokes. They call me the pretty one. I suppose they have a point. Growing up, I could get any girl. A different story for me brothers; they're all ogres. I think we had different parents." Liam sighed. "But I suppose they had their moments."

Hagen put the cigarette to his mouth and barely drew in the smoke before he bent over, hacking once again.

Liam plucked the cigarette from Hagen's fingers and stomped on it. "Grand first start, ya dope." Liam then grabbed his sleeve and pulled at him. "Come on, I'll give you a tour of our tin can."

Liam led Hagen into the hangar, then inside the aircraft and pointed to the rear area where a ladder went down to the turret. "Kirby goes up there. Brits call those guys arse-end Charlie."

He led Hagen to the middle of the cabin, which had a narrow staircase leading down to the belly gun. He pointed. "Me post is down there. Not much to see right now. I'll grab you when we're up in the air and show you the sight." He smiled, then asked, "Aye, you ever see the channel at sunset?"

Hagen shook his head.

"Oy, me grandmother would call it *aoibhneas.*"

"What?" Hagen asked, but Liam was past him, going to the one-man cockpit where there was another staircase going down to the nose.

Liam said over his shoulder, "Alan Hodges, the one with the mustache, sits here. He helps with navigation, and the old man knows a thing or two about being a medic. Good fella, he's been like a father to me since I came on." Liam sat down in the chair and looked up at Hagen, scooting over and patting the seat next to him. "Come on."

Hagen stepped down, trying to figure out how he was going to sit down in the cramped spot, then just squatted. His butt ended up in Liam's face, who smacked at his rear end and laughed hard. "Get your bum down before ya break something."

Hagen wiggled down next to Liam, his calf crossed over Liam's shin. He observed the twin gun barrels under the cockpit, extending out from above him.

Liam said from his side, "Lieutenant David operates those."

Hagen nodded, staring out, the entire airfield in front of them. Several fighters were scrambling and then taking off from the airstrip.

Liam repeated that strange word with an awed tone. "Aoibhneas."

Hagen glanced at Liam, their gazes meeting. "*EEV-nass*. What is that you're saying?"

Liam smiled. His fingers threaded through his coarse hair as he explained. "It's Gaelic. Me grandmother used to say it all the time."

"But what's it mean?"

Liam put his arm on the back of their chair behind Hagen's shoulder. His fingers dusted Hagen's arm on the outside and met his eyes. "When yea are overfilled with joy and beauty."

Hagen didn't speak for a moment, lost in those green eyes. Liam's smile faded, becoming serious, but he did not look away. Hagen felt a blend of feelings. Something intense. *What is this?* Excitement did not quite catch it.

Hagen shifted in the seat, and asked, "You mean, like it takes your breath away?"

Liam removed his arm from the back of the chair and clapped Hagen's knee. "That's it, boyo."

They didn't speak for a moment but kept each other's gaze again. Liam's hand tightened over Hagen's knee, and he leaned forward. Someone came to the top of the stairs, and Liam shifted in his seat and pulled away from Hagen as if they had been deep kissing. Hagen looked up to see a slender blonde woman, dressed in Army fatigues and wearing a leather jacket. Hagen exchanged looks with Liam.

Liam smiled. "Say, lass, you lost? The bunking area for secretaries is at the main house."

The woman came down the stairs in a crouch and shook her head. She stared out the window, not speaking. In her late twenties, the woman had striking hazel eyes, high cheekbones, and silky-smooth skin. She seemed mesmerized by the view of the airfield as well.

Finally looking down at them, she asked with a German accent, "What's it like? To see the channel at night?" She met Hagen's eyes and Hagen shook his head. *My second time to be asked that question.*

"I've never flown over it, ma'am," Hagen answered.

Liam answered enthusiastically. "It's bloody great."

The woman smiled. "I didn't mean to intrude, but I heard you say the word aoibhneas. That's a word my aunt used often."

Hagen turned a little more in his seat and held out his hand. "Hagen Messer."

"Roesia Caron."

Liam waved up at her. "Everyone calls me Irish or Liam." Then Liam asked, his pitch rising in disbelief, "Oy, you're not that bloody crazy woman we were talking about yesterday, are you? You can't be—you're too pretty."

Roesia laughed, blushing, then bit on her lower lip as if she had heard that line before. "What were you saying?"

"We heard—" Hagen began, but Liam interrupted.

"Some lass was going to *parachute* into *Germany!*"

She laughed, gave an awkward smile, and crossed her arms over her chest. "Well, then, I guess that's me. I've been training with the British paratroopers."

Liam and Hagen simply stared at her. Then Liam murmured, "*Blimey,* a woman jumping. What will they let them do next?"

"Say, this is the Night Angel, right? Lieutenant David is the captain?" Her tone sounded vexed.

Shadows moving at the opening of the hangar caught Hagen's attention. Lt. David came into the area, followed by Officer Hodges, Sgt. Collins, and Corporal Kirby. Today, Sgt. Collins had on a clean light-green shirt with fatigue pants, and carried a leather jacket over one arm and a bag over his shoulder.

Hagen pointed. "That's Lieutenant David there."

"Well, come on then, Miss, and meet the Night Angel crew." Liam led the way out of the plane, calling out to everyone. "Look, fellas! We get the lass who's bloody jumping!"

Sgt. Collins and Corporal Kirby stopped in place. Sgt. Collins shook his head and grumbled, and Corporal Kirby whined petulantly, "Lieutenant, this can't be right. She doesn't even look like a paratrooper!"

Hodges's eyes were wide, but he only tweaked his mustache and gave a short bow before he took her hand and pressed his lips to it. "Well, ma'am, my pleasure. Alan Hodges, Pilot Officer."

"*Doctor* Roesia Caron." Roesia slid her hand away from Hodges.

"Oh, you're a medical doctor?" Hodges asked.

"Professor," Roesia said, her tone clipped.

"A professor?" Hagen asked, glancing at everyone. He'd never met a woman professor before. The university he'd attended had only male instructors.

"Yes, in engineering," Roesia said.

Liam and Hagen glanced at each other, questioning, then Liam asked, "Like a train engineer?"

Lt. David answered, "Structures, gentlemen."

"Architectural engineering, specifically," Roesia said.

"Well," Hodges said, "This is the first time the Night Angel has had a woman on board. A pleasure."

Corporal Kirby volunteered from the side, "Not a first, sir. We had a couple over last weekend."

Sgt. Collins sniggered.

Lt. David gave the men a reproachful look. "Everyone, take a seat in the briefing room."

Hagen stepped away as the lieutenant apologized. "Excuse my men. They are not around many educated women, or any proper women, for that matter. I don't know about a woman paratrooper, but if it's for His Majesty, then it's surely for the best..."

Hagen headed through the doorway into the briefing room with Liam, Sgt. Collins, and Corporal Kirby at his heels.

Sgt. Collins growled, "We just need one of Stalin's men and it'd make this a perfect bloody grand trip."

Corporal Kirby shoved Hagen's shoulder. "Just don't do anything daft and get us killed, Kraut. Like sending SOS signals to Hitler."

Hagen turned with clenched fists, but Liam grabbed his arm, saying in his ear, "Hagen, never mind their blather."

Sgt. Collins jabbed his finger at Liam. "And you, Irishman, I've seen you with this Kraut all day. I took you for a lady's man. You better not be no poof."

"Poof on this, Sarge," Liam said and grabbed his crotch. Sgt. Collins chuckled at Liam's banter and glanced back to Hagen, his eyes narrowing. Hagen turned and followed Liam to a seat.

Hagen glanced over his shoulder, noting Sgt. Collins and Corporal Kirby leaning against the far wall and speaking in low, conspiratorial voices. The corporal looked over at Hagen, and he gave a *Heil Hitler* salute. Sgt. Collins broke out in laughter.

Hagen's face flushed and he started to rise from his seat, but Liam put a hand on his shoulder. "Hagen, they're just acting the maggots."

Hagen sat back down, shrugging off Liam's hand. Lt. David, Officer Hodges, and Roesia came through the far doorway, and Roesia took a seat behind Hagen.

Sgt. Collins joked from the side, "There, that's perfect, a Kraut barely out of diapers and a mum—we'll terrify the enemy."

Liam leaned over to Hagen and Roesia, whispering, "Corporal is from some small country town, a bit thick." Liam tapped his head. "And Sarge, not even sure how he knows French. They ne'er took to me at first either." Liam paused, thinking, then continued with a smirk on his face. "You know, can't really say we've ever had a cup of tea together."

The room hushed as Lt. David took his place at the front, a cigarette dangling from his mouth. Two men came into the room dressed in black commando uniforms with berets on their heads. One, who held everyone's focus, walked briskly down the aisle. He was in his mid-forties—well-built, with a buzz cut, his chiseled face and cleft chin covered with gray whiskers.

Lt. David dropped his cigarette in an ashtray, stubbing it out, and then held his hand out to indicate the commando. "Gentlemen, and"—he nodded to Roesia, sitting behind Hagen—"lady, we want to get out, so keep your mouths shut and listen up. This is Commander Ford. He's with a newly formed special commando unit, which has been attached to us on this mission. Commander."

Commander Ford gave one sharp perceptible nod to the lieutenant and directed everyone's attention to the map with his slender wooden pointer, aiming close to the border of Southern Germany.

"My team of commandos, accompanied by our tracker, Private Messer, and our explosive consultant, will parachute into northern Switzerland. We will meet up with a resistance group who will then help us sneak through the southern enemy lines. Our target is a primary munitions plant close to the Swiss border. We'll be blowing up a major dam nearby that will aid in destroying the plant."

Sgt. Collins peered around the room, and asked, "Where is there a qualified bloody explosive consultant? I see a lass and two lads barely done sucking their mothers' teats."

Lt. David's face reddened, as he nodded his head to Roesia. "That would be Dr. Caron. She's qualified because she had a hand in the bridge's design."

Corporal Kirby held up his hand, not waiting for anyone to call on him, and blurted out, "Why not just bomb the whole lot?"

"Corporal," Commander Ford said, his gaze steely. "Interrupt me one more time and there will hell to pay. But for your knowledge, we also have a secondary mission."

Commander Ford shifted his gaze and met Hagen's gaze. "Colonel Frank, your commanding officer and a friend of mine, said of your tracking skills, and I quote, 'He's phenomenal, seen nothing like it.'"

Hagen gave one perceptible nod, unable to speak. Liam stared wide-eyed at him.

Commander Ford's attention shifted, focusing toward the back of the room. Footsteps caused everyone's head to turn. A bald-headed stodgy man with a commanding presence came forward. He had a round face with a determined expression and wore a buttoned black overcoat.

Hagen recognized the man immediately. *Winston Churchill.*

Lt. David stood erect and introduced the man. "Gentlemen, and uh, lady, our First Lord of Admiralty, Winston Churchill. Sir, meet the crew of the Night Angel."

Churchill's eyes narrowed as he swept over the room with his gaze, and then he addressed the group. "I know you men have served His Majesty bravely. And I've heard one of your crew perished as well." He nodded sympathetically to Lt. David. "I will get right to the point of my being here. I was given latitude by the Prime Minister to form a group of specially trained soldiers whom I have come to call commandos."

Hagen's gaze turned to Commander Ford, whose expression reflected no emotion.

Churchill paced the room as he spoke. "Besides this munitions plant, we have intelligence that a British prisoner is being held at a base close to this dam by the SS Gestapo—a man by the name of Euan Hartley. Hartley is a businessman who was lured there by the Nazis and captured. Hartley's blood is being used in an experiment by a Nazi scientist by the name of Till Mengele to give the Nazis an upper hand in fighting this war. I cannot say anymore."

Churchill straightened as he said, "I can say this. Either retrieve this prisoner or confirm he is dead. Godspeed on your mission."

Four: Nazi Attack

May 10, 1940

THE NIGHT ANGEL was delayed in taking off, and it was clear to see that Commander Ford was vexed at the hold up.

The glass on the newly installed belly turret had cracked and needed to be replaced. Midnight passed, and early morning came. Sgt. Collins grumbled, Corporal Kirby whined, and the numerous commandos were restless. Lt. David ordered a pilot to take the plane up and test it, saying he didn't want one of his crewmembers falling through.

Hagen stayed close to Liam, going over the details of the mission in his head. After Churchill spoke, Commander Ford had completed the briefing and handed Hagen a couple of personal items that belonged to Euan Hartley, to aid his tracking.

Hagen held a light blue handkerchief in his hand.

"What is that?" Liam's eyes were drowsy, and Hagen presumed he was talking to stay awake.

Hagen looked to Liam, then glanced at Lt. David as he told the commander their flight would be slower than normal due to the weight and they might be parachuting in daylight; he asked the commander if he wanted to postpone. Commander Ford frowned and moved to speak to his second in command.

Hagen then answered Liam. "I've had this ability since I was a kid and never thought about it much. But, you know when you let a bloodhound sniff something and then it tracks it down?"

Liam massaged his head, messing his hair, and nodded.

Hagen held up the handkerchief. "This belonged to that prisoner, Euan Hartley."

"You're fecking joking." Liam was suddenly more awake, eyeing the cloth in Hagen's hand. "You have a bloody scent in your nose?"

Hagen shrugged. "Well, I see images. They're Euan's memories. There are smells involved. One, in particular, stands out." He turned to

Liam, "It reminds me of the chemicals they made me use when I cleaned the toilets back in training. I have this picture of a laboratory, then there's this man with slicked-back hair."

Hagen neglected to tell Liam about the other feeling he'd had when he touched the handkerchief. Earlier when he held the handkerchief and focused, he'd experienced fleeting memories from Euan. Then without warning, he'd felt Euan transforming into something beyond human. A dark powerful energy had pumped through Hagen's body, but in a flash, it had vanished. Hagen wanted the sensation to return, although so far, it hadn't. His fist tightened over the cloth. That force he felt was something he wanted to return. Hagen put the cloth back in his front pocket.

Liam regarded Hagen with a spooked expression.

Hagen gave him a nervous smile and asked, "What?"

"You looked—" Liam said, with a sigh. "I don't know. For a second there, you looked like a complete loon."

"Loon?" Hagen said. "Crazy?"

Liam nodded.

Hagen wanted to change the subject and asked, "You know that word, aoibhneas?"

"What about it?"

"When I saw some of Euan's memories, I saw another chap who smelled of lavender and had a pink tie. But I had this feeling he had this dark human core. He was with the Nazis. He was watching, uh, watching a spectacle." Euan had been transforming into a beast, but Hagen did not want to broach that subject. "The man had his hand over his mouth, and said a German word, *atemberaubend*."

"It means aoibhneas?" Liam asked.

"Well, no. It means breathtaking. It's just peculiar. The man was evil, but in that second, he was spellbound and truly awed." Hagen watched Commander Ford and Lt. David having an argument.

"Hagen?"

Hagen turned, giving Liam his attention.

Liam smiled and said, "Your mind is up in the bloody clouds. I asked if you know who this Euan is."

Hagen shook his head. "No. A British businessman. He was in France, trying to help their banks when he was kidnapped in an ambush and taken to that dam. I get this feeling, though, that he's no longer there."

Lt. David announced from across the room, "The Night Angel is ready. Commander Ford, what do you want to do?"

The Night Angel would take off at 0300.

TWO HOURS LATER, Hagen sat inside the Lockheed Hudson. His eyes had fallen shut on several occasions, but he was startled awake as their plane lurched and whined. He glanced out the window, although it was still too dark to see. The plane stabilized, but Hagen sat on the edge of his seat and rubbed his hands together. Sgt. Collins told them their jump would take place in less than two hours. Butterflies swirled in his stomach, and he did his best not to focus on the whole mission in front of him, just making his jump without breaking a leg.

According to Sgt. Collins, they were flying somewhere over southern France.

Hagen and most of the commando paratroopers had taken off their parachutes, as the gear made it too difficult to sit or maneuver easily in the cabin. Roesia had left hers strapped on. Each of them had an oxygen mask attached to their suit, but they'd been told they would not be necessary, as their plane was not going above 10,000 feet.

The hold was indeed crammed with fourteen commando soldiers sitting silently side by side, across from Hagen. They stared vacantly ahead while one twirled a serrated knife in his hand. He had a bent nose; Hagen thought his name might be Ness.

Roesia was sitting closest to the cockpit, her arms crossed and her face ashen. It appeared her teeth were chattering.

The engines roared and drowned out conversations around Hagen. Lt. David sat in the cockpit. Sgt. Collins was in a chair near the cockpit, wearing headphones, a jumbo-size radio box near his feet. Corporal Kirby was out of sight, in the rear gun turret. Liam was in the belly of the plane, manning the gun there, while Hodges was down in the nose of the plane, helping with navigation.

Hodge's gray hair appeared as he came up the steps from the airplane's nose. The man made his way over to Roesia and squatted down in front of her, delicately taking her hand. He appeared to ask her a question. In response, her face scrunched in confusion. Hagen could tell she'd asked him to repeat himself. Hodges's words were unintelligible to Hagen over the engine noise. She nodded and got up, and Hodges guided her down the stairs.

I wonder what it looks like from that vantage point.

Movement from across the aisle. Liam had come partially up the stairs, his oxygen mask hanging close to his chin, and he waved to Hagen to come down.

Ness had his knife in his hand, twirling it while focused on this repetitious movement; a few commandos were in conversation, not paying Hagen any attention. In three strides, Hagen was at the narrow walkway and heading down.

Liam crouched close to Hagen and leaned toward his ear, then pointed down. "Go, take a look."

Hagen scooted past Liam, came to the ledge where the turret was, and observed the hard-to-get-into chair. He wondered if Liam wanted him to sit. *Is this a good idea?* Liam was at his back, pressing up against him, a couple of his fingers curled over his waistband. His cold fingertips pushed up against his upper buttock.

Liam's lips brushed against his ear as he spoke loudly. "Just kneel. I'll hold ya."

Hagen knelt down and peered over the ledge through the turret. The sun had risen, and he stared, mesmerized, at the treetops of a lush green forest on rolling hills. Liam squatted behind him; his hands held onto Hagen's belt as he leaned into him.

The plane lurched, causing Hagen to fall backward and land on top of Liam. The plane dropped and bucked several times. Hagen found himself looking up at the metal interior, his heart beating fast. He closed his eyes and breathed. *Turbulence.*

Liam laughed close to his ear, his arm wrapped around Hagen's chest and his mouth close to his ear again. "Turbulence, boyo. It's okay."

Hagen relaxed and moved back up into a kneeling position and peered down again. Liam tapped his shoulder and Hagen looked up.

Liam jabbed a thumb up toward the cabin. "Okay, probably should go back up before the lieutenant takes me arse."

Hagen nodded but glanced once more through the glass, and his breath caught. There was a city sprawled out below them. A river wound through the town, and homes were nestled together in several pockets of the city. Billows of smoke rose from several areas. A plane zipped past their window.

Liam pulled on his shoulder and tried to shove past him, yelling to Hagen, *"Jaysus! Go, go!"*

The plane dipped, and Hagen fell into the turret cockpit. He scrambled, getting his hands up onto the ledge as Liam pulled up under his arms and hauled him out. Liam jumped into the belly turret, wiggled into his seat, and put on his earphones. As Hagen knelt on the lip of the turret and the plane dove, he extended his arms out to both sides, placing his palms on the walls and staring through Liam's window.

A consecutive series of pings sounded out above from the main cabin, followed by shouting. Their plane rolled to the right.

Liam yanked back on a lever. "Shite, shite!"

A single-engine fighter with a black cross near the tail flew into view.

"Bugger to hell!" Liam pulled his trigger, and staccato bursts of gunfire thundered in the enclosed space, the handle in Liam's hand shaking. Tracers sped out but came nowhere close to their target.

The German fighter flew out of view; Liam let up and touched his headphones. Hagen started to turn but stopped short. Through the turret window, a plane spiraled out of control into the forest below, smoke drifting from its engine. *Someone got him.*

Hagen yelled, *"Look, he's going down!"*

Liam vigorously shook his head. *"No, there're more!"* Their plane dove and rolled right. A series of the pinging noises once again erupted in the cabin above. Hagen fell, almost landing on Liam. His upper body was poised over the turret, and he spread his legs wide, flexing his muscles to keep from falling on top of Liam.

Liam jabbed his finger up the ramp. *"Get fecking strapped in!"* Liam turned back around and pulled his trigger; the gun shook in his hands. Tracers flared out of his gun muzzle, and his rounds zeroed in on the enemy's tail. A few clipped it, debris spewed in the air, and the plane went into a corkscrew.

Liam thrust his fist up and shouted out a *hurrah*, his hand hitting Hagen's side. Liam glanced up at Hagen and pointed to the cabin. "Hagen! What are you doing? Get the feck up there!"

Hagen headed up the stairs but stopped. One of the commando soldiers was standing at the top, his hand held over his neck as blood sprayed from between his fingers. The man's mouth yawned open as more poured profusely over his bottom lip. He fell face-first and tumbled toward Hagen. The plane dove and screeches of metal were audible around them. Hagen was jerked off his feet by the movement and landed on top of the commando, the body breaking his fall.

A deafening roar erupted from Liam's gun, the noise cutting through the air. Hagen crawled over the body and into the cabin. The plane shuddered as he got to his feet. Sgt. Collins was yelling into a microphone. The man's face was pasty; his widened eyes reflected the fear that certain death was near. Sgt. Collins looked up at him and jabbed his finger violently close to the cockpit. Hagen looked down to see someone crawling on the floor behind Lt. David.

Sgt. Collins yelled, *"Help her!"*

Roesia. She had to have scrambled back up from the nose.

Hagen moved to her, clutched her bicep, and lifted her from the floor. Her face was white, and a steady flow of blood came from her nose. He shoved her into her seat and fastened a seat belt over her lap. The plane jerked and he staggered backward, then turned to get into an empty seat. The plane rolled, and he was thrown off of his feet again.

Blackness.

A shrill voice was calling his name. *"Hagen, Hagen."* His lids flew open. Roesia was screaming down at him, frantically grabbing at her belt, trying to take it off. He rolled to his stomach, pushed up on his hands—liquid rushed over them. Someone grabbed him by his arm. He looked up to see Commander Ford, who pushed him to a seat.

The commander returned to his seat, four spots away, and yelled over his shoulder, "Fasten your belt, lad."

Liquid streamed down Hagen's face, he wanted to wipe the wetness away, but his hands froze in midair. They were drenched in dark red. He stared down at the floor, which was covered in blood. The plane jostled and caused him to reach for his seat's bottom, blindly searching for the seat belt. His hand was engulfed in something squishy. He glanced over to see the commando soldier next to him. Half of the soldier's face was gone.

Hagen whipped his head around, taking in the entire cabin as he became aware of the multitude of bullet-hole perforations in the fuselage. The plane banked sharply left and he came partially out of his seat. The clasp of the seat belt was in his sights and he reached out quickly, then yanked it across his body to snap in place over his lap. His gaze came up as the entire body of the plane whined and every nut and bolt rattled. Roesia had her head down and her thumbs hooked around her belt.

Hagen quickly scanned the commandos seated near Roesia. They appeared to be asleep. Their heads were down, and their bodies bobbed and bounced with the planes movements. At the end nearest the tail sat a commando, his chair dribbling blood at a steady pace. The soldier was slumped over, his hands touching the floor. One soldier, near the front, looked alive, although he had blood smeared over his face and stared vacantly.

At the rear of the plane, the machine gun Kirby manned came alive. Their plane nosedived at a steep angle.

Sgt. Collins roared, *"Brace yourselves!"*

The plane's hull shrieked and the entire cabin vibrated wildly. It pulled up from its dive. Hagen chanced a glance over his shoulder, out the window. They were flying in and out of a cloud. Tips of snowcap mountains came into full view below.

How close are we?

Sporadic gunfire erupted from the rear gun. An enemy fighter moved in and out of Hagen's view, and a thick line of smoke came off one engine.

Hagen turned around and undid his seat belt, then advanced toward the cockpit where he froze. His breath halted. The peak of a mountain was approaching fast, and they were going to hit it.

At the last minute, their plane zoomed up over the peak and Kirby yelled down, "Bloody yes!"

Lt. David pulled the aircraft so the tip of the mountain they just missed was visible.

Dark black smoke rose into the air from the rocky face where the enemy plane had crashed, and a distant thunderous noise rumbled.

Collins pumped his fist in the air. *"Bloody fucking nice flying, Ace!"*

Their plane climbed for several more minutes before it leveled out. Hagen's breathing was uneven and his hands trembled. His gaze met with Roesia's terror-stricken expression; she didn't seem to register seeing him, or anything for that matter.

Sgt. Collins stared over at Hagen, shouting, "You okay, Kraut?"

Hagen nodded. The sergeant turned to Roesia and asked, "You, prof?"

She vigorously nodded her head.

"Commander Ford?"

Hagen looked over and saw that Commander Ford had gotten out of his seat and was staring in shock at his men, many of whom appeared to be dead. He didn't respond but came up to a man two seats from Hagen, unbuckled the man's seat belt, and helped him to the floor. The man was breathing heavily; red mist came from his mouth, his back arched. A gory wound showed where a bullet had exited. His hand clasped Commander Ford's as his breathing grew more labored, the whites of his eyes showing. The man breathed out a raspy breath, and then his chest deflated and did not rise again.

Commander Ford gently closed the man's eyes and placed his hands to his side. Ford then rose and went to the man nearest the front who looked to be alive, grabbed his shoulder, and asked questions. This commando was the one with the bent nose, named Ness.

Ness met Commander Ford's eyes, then unbuckled his belt and started to help the commander check the other men.

Hodges came up the stairs from the plane's nose, looked immediately over at Roesia, and sighed in relief.

His fingers threaded through his disheveled gray hair and he shouted to the cabin, "Last bugger face-planted in a mountain—" He froze, staring at the carnage inside the cabin. His mouth was open, but no words came out.

"Hodges, my radio has been shot to bloody hell. Check on O'Malley and Kirby," Sgt. Collins said.

Hodges nodded and stepped partially down the stairs leading to Liam. Hagen's heart soared to hear Liam calling back up from the belly turret.

Hodges came out of the staircase and called to Commander Ford. "One of your men is over there by O'Malley!" Hodges went to the rear of the plane and returned a minute later and gave a thumbs-up to Sgt. Collins.

Commander Ford stood by a kneeling Ness. They both lifted one man from the floor into a sitting position.

Ness felt over the unconscious soldier. "Benton has no wounds. I think he just hit his head." He looked up at Ford. "It's just you, me, and Benton, sir."

Commander Ford regarded Hodges and Sgt. Collins. "What's our status?"

Hodges answered, "Damaged engine. We're trying to navigate to the nearest French base at, uh, let's see, Mulhouse. But I've lost my bearings, and the cloud coverage is hurting us."

Hagen regarded the cabin. A couple of shattered windows were allowing cold air to stream through. One side was riddled with bullet holes. They had gained more altitude, but the mountaintops were still very close. The plane went into a white cloud and Hagen felt queasy, his body trembling from the cold and sheer terror.

"Where'd those fighters come from?" Ness asked.

Hodges shook his head as his fingers pulled at his hair, getting it even more ruffled. "An air raid. We're lucky they were at the tail end of their squadron..."

Commander Ford gave Hodges a stern glare. Hagen glanced down at the corpses and back up to Hodges, the commander's face clearly expressing that not everyone had been lucky.

Hodges looked away, then called out to Sgt. Collins, who was standing behind Lt. David, yelling down at him.

"Bollocks, Sarge, what are you blubbering on about?"

Sgt. Collins turned to Hodges and spoke loudly. "I got emergency transmissions on my radio before it was destroyed. The Germans are invading France."

"Oh, bugger to hell, Sarge," Hodges said. "Deception. Jerries do it all the time."

Commander Ford frowned, his hard-set chin working as he ground his teeth.

He cupped his hands over his mouth and asked, assuming the intercepted messages were spoken in English, "German or French accent?"

Sgt. Collins's jaw worked before he answered. "It was all in French. Which I know. And on all frequencies." Everyone took in this revelation, but no one said anything. Hodges played with his mustache.

"I believe that the invasion of France is under way!" Sgt. Collins yelled.

Hodges nodded, took in this information, and went down into the nose of the plane. Sgt. Collins's shoulders sagged, and he sat down heavily in a seat.

Commander Ford and Ness moved several of the corpses onto the floor, toward the tail of the plane. The man who had been knocked unconscious, Benton, had opened his eyes and looked around him. Ness came to him, asking questions, and the man nodded—his expression reflected disorientation.

A biting cold wind whipped through the cabin. Hagen sat back, listening to the hum of the engine. Clink-clink-clink noises became noticeable, and he looked around to find them before realizing his own teeth were chattering.

The image of his mortally wounded brother came to Hagen without warning. He crossed his arms over his chest and stared with vacant eyes. *Ivan.* Once in a while, he looked out the window across from him and observed the partial fog. He felt someone was watching him, though, and turned, catching the professor's eye. Neither of them glanced away from the other's gaze until Roesia finally looked down.

The right engine choked and sputtered a few times. Hagen stared out the window closest to him, seeing thick black smoke blow from the wing and then thin. The engine roared back to life. The sergeant came to check on him and then left. Hagen shifted in his seat and rested his head back, his eyes heavy and closing. The seat vibrated under him, cold whipped around him, and he entered a dazed lull, recollecting the last couple of days.

"Kraut!"

Hagen's eyes popped open and he sat up, getting his bearings. Sgt. Collins stood near the cockpit. Hodges was leaning against the wall, a map at his feet and a second in his hands. Commander Ford was to one side of the aisle, staring at him.

"Kraut!" Sgt. Collins waved impatiently at him, saying, "Bloody hell, Kraut, move your arse."

Hagen went to Sgt. Collins and found the lieutenant wrestling with his wheel, which wrenched from side to side. The cloud coverage had lessened, and though there were mountains below them, he could thankfully not discern every minute detail.

"Messer!" the lieutenant shouted, handing him binoculars while keeping his attention forward. He pointed out the window. "I need to take the lass down. You recognize this area? I was looking for Kreuzlingen, which is southwest of Konstanz, Germany. But I think we're too far south, and we've had to pass it."

Hagen brought the binoculars up. A castle came into view as he twisted a knob. It was dilapidated and set on a snowcapped peak; its outer wall had crumbled long ago and half the parapet was gone. A grand statue of a horseman was perched high on a podium; his hands held axes that were extended over his head. Hagen brought the binoculars down.

He turned to Roesia who was still sitting in her seat but stared through her. He muttered, "Earl Groscz Castle."

She leaned up, cupping a hand to her ear. She undid her seat belt and came closer. Lt. David called his name. Sgt. Collins gripped Hagen's arm, yelling, "Answer the lieutenant. We need to land."

"You know the area?" Lt. David asked, his tone exasperated.

Roesia was beside him, snatching the binoculars from Hagen's hands, and she asked, "Where are we, Hagen?"

His mouth was close to her ear, and he shouted, "Wehr Forest!"

She straightened and looked through the binoculars. "That statue. Lt. David, we are in Germany."

Sgt. Collins shouted over the wind and engines. "That's not possible. We'd be dead, flying in this tin can with its smoke, and not to mention tooting and parping for everyone to hear."

Hodges put his map down and spoke with an incredulous tone, agreeing with Sgt. Collins. "He's right. We would have at least hit anti-aircraft munitions or run into the Luftwaffe."

Commander Ford was at their back. "Cloud coverage and they're conducting an invasion at this very moment. Their forces could be allocated to the front. Could be perfect timing."

Hagen spoke loudly. "We are in Germany! That's Earl Groscz Castle."

Lt. David was curt. "Sergeant, get Liam and Kirby into the main cabin; everyone strap in." The sergeant barked orders and walked through the cabin, shouting down to Liam. Liam climbed up a moment later, grabbed a blood-soaked seat, and put on his belt. Corporal Kirby came down and was doing the same. Their plane angled toward the treetops.

Hagen turned to stare out the window one last time before taking his seat as well. The tops of the green trees became more detailed and a nearby pond came into view. He noticed a road that ran through the forest, a worn hut, and deer darting through the woods. His breathing became heavy, and he hurried to his seat, strapped on his seat belt, and braced himself for the crash.

Then everything went black.

Five: The Castle Beyond

Hagen's Dream of Childhood, 1930

TEN-YEAR-OLD Hagen inched through Wehr Forest and peered around a spread of thick branches. He crept to a clearing, knelt, and brought his rifle's stock to his shoulder.

Ivan was close to him, and whispered, "Remember, breathe."

Hagen brushed his finger against the trigger, took a full breath, and squeezed. A sharp crack erupted. The deer jerked upright and galloped away.

Hagen lowered the weapon. "It was a clean shot."

"Come on." Ivan moved in front of him. "It won't go far then."

Hagen advanced but soon lost sight of his brother. He focused on his senses like his father had taught him. A *drip-drip-drip* noise reached him, and he discovered thick blood dripping off a flat leaf. He avoided a tree, sensing death ahead of him. It was not a scent an average person would catch, but something he had been keen to since he'd been a young boy.

He pushed on, and after a few moments, he was at the edge of the forest in a field covered with waist-high weeds, trees with knotty trunks dotting it. Up ahead, his brother squatted. Hagen approached to stand at his side, resting his rifle on his shoulder. Ivan was close to the wounded deer. Hagen crouched at the creature's head as its eyes opened and closed, its breathing labored. Sadness came over him, and he felt guilt. He petted the soft pelt, and his eyes watered. His father would be proud—the fur was very valuable—and Hagen would be allowed to keep the funds made.

Ivan turned to him, his voice edged with annoyance. "You going to put it out of its misery? It's suffering."

Hagen shifted the rifle on his shoulder and nodded but didn't move. He stared down at the helpless creature's eyes. It was in pain. He'd see those eyes over and over in his dreams.

Ivan shook Hagen's shoulder, and said, "Okay, Hagen. It's mercy to put it down. It's in pain."

Hagen shook his head and said, "I—I can't."

"Father would tell you to put him out of his misery, Hagen," Ivan said.

The corners of Hagen's mouth worked, and his jaw quivered. His brother rose to his feet, picked up his weapon from where he'd laid it against a tree and aimed down. Hagen jumped when the loud shot erupted and turned to his brother.

Ivan stepped close and messed Hagen's hair. "You did good, brother. It's never easy to kill. Father would think you did well."

Ivan removed his hand as Hagen stared down at the deer but remained nearby for a short period, and then moved away through the brush. Hagen did not follow, and when he finally looked up, Ivan was nowhere in sight.

"Ivan?" Hagen stood up and took in his surroundings. In front of him was the old and abandoned Earl Groscz Castle, which was said to be haunted. The decrepit façade had multiple holes where stones or large chunks had fallen. Dark clouds covered mountain peaks on the horizon. He and Ivan needed to get their father and come back to clean this kill and then leave.

Hagen waded through the tall weeds. The air was musky, and a steady misting rain had set in. In front of him was a four-foot stone wall. He wheeled around.

His brother was close by—he sensed him and shouted, "Ivan!"

"Hagen," his brother called from somewhere ahead. Hagen groped along the wall's ledge and hoisted himself up. From on top, he searched the area. The wall had been built long ago, he surmised, as several places had gaps where the stone had crumbled and weeds taken over.

"Hagen!"

Hagen turned toward the castle where he finally located his brother. Ivan stood on the sunken ground of what had probably once been a cobblestone road, which had since been overgrown by wiry brush. At his heels was a wide moat, no longer spanned by its drawbridge.

Several moments later, Hagen reached Ivan, scolding him, "I've been calling you."

Ivan pushed his fingers through his thick black hair, smiled, and patted Hagen's cheek condescendingly. "Don't be such a whiner."

Hagen swatted his brother's hand away. "We need to get Father so we can clean my kill. We wandered too far as it is."

Ivan turned away, though, ignoring him. "This is it. Earl Groscz Castle."

Hagen regarded the decrepit castle. One spire had fallen inward, and several crows were resting on the debris. A statue of a horseman stood high, two axes crossing over his head.

"Mad Groscz," Hagen whispered.

Ivan nodded. "He held house parties for nearby villagers. They went missing. Women and children. Hid them down in the dungeon is where they went. Did unspeakable things. Raised his children to be—what's the word Father said?"

"C-cannibals," Hagen whispered.

"Yes, that's it."

Hagen swallowed and shook his head. "It's haunted in there, Ivan."

Ivan slapped Hagen's arm, put his rifle on his shoulder, and skipped forward. "Let's find out."

"What? Where are you going?" Hagen's voice rose in pitch. Ivan was clambering down the trench, though, not paying him attention. He reached the rocky bottom and went to the far side.

Hagen followed him, scaling down. He dropped his rifle, which skidded down the remaining few feet to the bottom. He picked up his gun, dusted off the dirt, and scrutinized it to make certain it was not damaged.

Ivan disappeared over a ledge. Hagen hurried up the side of the incline and approached his brother, who was gazing at the castle door and into the dark interior. A great hall was before them, which had probably once been decorated in splendor but was now barren. Ivan stepped inside, and Hagen followed, leaning his rifle on his shoulder. Pillars stood around them; the walls were deteriorated, faded drawings on them of gigantic wolves with long fangs, eating people.

"Ivan. *We need to go.*"

A child's whiney cry echoed off the walls and filled the vast room, then was gone as quickly as it came. They both stood stock still, leaning against each another. Neither moved until his brother finally tugged at his hand and Hagen budged from his spot.

Ivan led them toward a stone spiral staircase, but Hagen pulled back, demanding in a hushed voice. "*Ivan, stop!*"

Ivan leaned down and spoke with the same tone. "We'll just go up and come right back down."

Ivan started up the stairs, his hand clutched around Hagen's as he pulled him. A pleading yelp echoed around them, and Ivan moved faster. They circled around several loops, ascending, and then stopped at a top floor—a large bare room opened in front of them.

Hagen breathed heavily as his brother squeezed his hand hard. "Oww."

Ivan looked down at their interlocked fingers, seeming to only then realize they were holding hands. He opened his hand, meeting Hagen's gaze for a moment with large and frightened but excited eyes, and then looked out into the room. They were in the topmost part of the tower, which looked out over the edge of a cliff.

A vast mountainous valley opened before Hagen, and a region of high mountains lay beyond it, covered by dark stormy clouds that roiled over the peaks. A light rain was coming down, and sunlight suddenly shone through several of the clouds. They parted and revealed a monumental castle that sat high up on a peak.

Ivan set his rifle down and stared out at the surreal scenery. Despite the rain and cloud coverage, there was good visibility. Ivan grabbed at his satchel, rummaged in it, and pulled out a telescope.

"Ivan," Hagen whispered in a harsh tone, "you took Father's lens? He'll have your arse."

"Quiet," Ivan said and dropped his satchel next to his feet. "Father has made several of these. He won't miss it."

Ivan brought it up to his eye and twisted a knob. "Aww, you should see this."

Hagen leaned his weapon against the wall and held his hand out to Ivan, demanding, "Let me see."

Ivan handed the device over, and Hagen viewed the castle. A ray of sun shone down on the magnificence high on the edge of a cliff. A winding road twisted from a large gate, descending the mountain. Wolf statues were set on top of the wall's ledge.

Ivan grabbed at the binoculars. "Give it here."

"Wait." Hagen turned his body away. The clouds drifted back over the structure, hiding it from sight. The ray of sun was gone, and thunderclouds cut visibility. Ivan got a grip on the binoculars, and they both tugged on them until the equipment flew from their hands. The binoculars whirled end over end, plummeting down the castle's side into an abyss.

They both stared in horror, and then Ivan grabbed the front of Hagen's shirt, shaking him. "You stupid oaf. What the hell is wrong with you? I'm going to—"

A high-pitched howl pierced the air—it was not coming from outside but echoing inside the building.

"I-Ivan. Let's go."

"Yeah." Ivan pushed on Hagen's chest, saying, "Go." Hagen stumbled backward toward the door leading to the staircase, then glanced back to Ivan.

"What was that, Ivan?"

Ivan picked up the satchel he had dropped and shook his head. He started toward the door. "There's tales of beasts. Part man—"

There was a harsh grating noise, and Ivan's eyes widened. Puffs of dust blew up from under his feet. He made as if he was going to sprint forward, but the floor crumbled away from below him and he was gone. A cloud of dust hung over a hole.

Hagen screamed, "*IVAN! IVAN!*" He ran to the hole in the floor and peered down. His brother grasped the edge and dangled in the air, gaping up at him.

Hagen reached for his brother, but the stone floor below him rumbled, and Hagen was falling, too.

HAGEN WOKE UP with a scream and stared around him in confusion. The vivid dream was fading. He was lying in a bed in a small room with a nut-brown dresser on one side and a window at the end of the bed, letting in bright sunlight. He searched his memory for where he was.

He heard familiar voices coming from the open doorway.

A heavyset man with gray whiskers came to mind. Sgt. Collins.

The sergeant grumped, "Rubbish."

The memory of the plane wreck returned with full force.

Six: The Keeper of Wehr Forest

Region near Earl Groscz Castle, Germany
May 10, 1940

HAGEN WAS STILL in a strange room—he had not moved from the bed. The covers were pulled up to his chin, and he drifted in and out of sleep; it felt good not to move. But now he felt an urgency to get up, although he couldn't quite make himself follow through. *How did I get here?*

He recalled being inside the airplane, seeing Earl Groscz Castle, and then blackness.

Sgt. Collins's gruff voice reverberated through his room once again. *"Shut your cake hole. She's a bloody spy?"*

Commander Ford's voice broke in. "The mission was for you to drop us off, not crash land in Nazi Germany. You weren't going in, and you didn't need to know."

Roesia? Is that who they're speaking about?

Hagen pushed the covers down to his waist and found that someone had removed his clothes and placed ratty drawers on him. The room had worn wooden flooring, and a handmade dresser along with a table stood next to the bed. At the foot was a full-length oval mirror with decorative edges. Dreary light leaked in from a single window.

The handkerchief! Where is it?

Hagen sat up on the side of the bed, both feet on the cold floor and—there on a small table at his side was the handkerchief. It was next to his utility belt, knife, and binoculars. He snatched it and brought it to his face, then focused. The dark energy did not fill him, though. After a couple of seconds, he crumpled it in his hand, annoyed, and stood up, but soon the room rotated around him. He leaned against the cot and touched his forehead at the dizziness he felt. His fingers slid over a dry smooth surface instead of skin. He stepped up to the mirror and examined himself. Close to his hairline was a yellow-brown paste that had been smeared over his wound. His hair was a mess, his face paler than usual, and specks of dried blood were on his chest and abdomen.

He did have a bruise on his upper chest over his pectoral muscle. He slid his hand over his abdomen and flinched. He found a small cut on his side, the same paste spread over it, and raw cuts on his shoulder. He flexed his right arm and discovered a purplish bruise on his bicep.

Liam entered the room. "You're awake."

Hagen turned toward the door. "Liam."

Liam wore his fatigues, and a smile replaced his previous expression, fraught with worry.

"What happened?" Hagen croaked. "How long have I been out? Where are we?" Hagen stepped forward and lost his balance.

Liam caught him. "Whoa, boyo. Not all at once." Liam led him back to the bed, and Hagen sat down heavily.

"Water," Hagen said.

Liam turned back to the door, then said over his shoulder, "Don't move."

Liam returned moments later, carrying a tin cup that he handed to Hagen. Alan Hodges accompanied him, walking with a limp and fussing with his short gray hair. He smiled down at Hagen, tugging on the end of his mustache. "Good to see you made it, lad."

Hagen gulped the water down as Hodges placed a steadying hand on the cup.

"Not too fast," he suggested, then took the cup once Hagen was finished. Hodges placed his hands on both sides of Hagen's face and turned him so that he was facing him.

Hagen's eyes wandered to Liam, though.

"Look at me," Hodges said.

Hagen noticed for the first time that Hodges had crystal blue eyes, which set off his silver-gray hair and mustache. Hodges pried Hagen's eyes open farther, one after the other.

"Where's everyone?" Hagen asked.

Hodges didn't answer but scrutinized his hairline.

A familiar woman's voice answered. *Roesia.* "They're in the next room."

Roesia came in and placed some clothes on the bed.

Hodges said, "Never mind her, lad. Stand up."

Hagen stood, though his face felt hot. Hodges asked him to touch his nose and the top of his head, then walk in a line. The line-walking was a bit difficult.

Hagen sat back down and Hodges asked, "Your name, rank, birthday?"

Hagen answered the questions.

"Who's the prime minister?" Hodges asked.

Hagen shook his head. "Churchill—no, Chamber-something. I'm not British. Franklin Roosevelt is the president in America."

"What do you remember?" Hodges asked.

"Just coming in for the landing—that's it. We were close to Earl Groscz Castle."

"A small concussion," Hodges informed Roesia and Liam. "But I think he's okay." He clutched Hagen's shoulder, saying, "Bump on the ol' noggin. Not too bad, given all the deaths that happened on the Night Angel." He wore a sorrowful expression and seemed about to say more, but instead promptly left the room.

Roesia leaned close, peering at his head, carefully parting his hair. "The old woman put a couple of stitches up there. They're under the hairline, so you can't even see them." She pointed at his forehead. "She said that stuff keeps it from swelling or getting infected."

Hagen licked his cracked lips, then turned from Liam to Roesia. "What old lady?"

Roesia straightened. "She's in the other room. After we landed, this woman came out to greet us. You may know her."

A long-ago memory tugged at Hagen's mind, but he didn't recall an old woman. He shook his head. "We've been here before, but we lived farther away. My father brought us here several times to hunt. I was told my mother had family who grew up here."

Roesia nodded. "Well, the woman's name is Justine."

"Why do you think she knows me?"

"Liam and Lt. David carried you from the plane, and she looked over at you, several times." She shrugged. "It was like she knew you. And she is not your typical white German."

"What?" Hagen asked.

"She's got a wee touch of something else in her. Reminds me of the Orientals I've seen in London, but she don't have the eyes." Liam placed an index finger on the corner of each eye and made them slanted, to indicate what he meant, as he finished speaking.

Hagen stretched his legs and asked Roesia, "You recognized this place from the air... How?"

"She's a bloody spy, Hagen!" Liam announced excitedly.

Hagen regarded Roesia. "I thought you might be."

"You knew?" Liam asked, his tone sharp and surprised.

Hagen shrugged. "Not for certain. Just instinct."

Roesia ignored Liam. "When I was at Humboldt, I spied for the British. I didn't rub shoulders with major players in the Nazi sphere. But I had one particular source that was part of a secret Nazi group called the Vril Society. It was from him I gathered intel on the original genetic experiments they started in a castle. He has flown close to this base and told me about the statue with the crossed axes."

Liam glanced between Hagen and Roesia. "She was arse over elbows in Nazis. And bloody get this—she studied to impersonate a Nazi woman!"

"You were going to impersonate someone?" Hagen asked.

Roesia sighed. "Well, if the mission had gone as planned, we were going to meet with a small German resistance group. They were going to coordinate an ambush on a visiting Nazi, Gunda Lawerenze. She has been in Austria and was going to the dam to visit. But I guess that won't happen now."

"Professor," a male voice interrupted. Corporal Kirby stood at the doorway. He glanced toward Hagen for a second, and then told Roesia, "Commander Ford wants you."

She rose and nodded to the clothes on the bed. "Put those on and come out."

Liam said, "I'll wait for him."

Hagen placed the handkerchief beside him, took the coarse pants, and turned them in his hand. Looked like they would fit.

"Still have that bloody rag?"

Hagen lifted his leg and glanced up at Liam, who watched him. Liam offered a grin that lightened Hagen's heart.

"It's for the tracking," Hagen said. He stood and pulled the britches up to his waist. He put on a green button-down shirt, then picked up the cloth and put it in his front pocket. He buttoned as Liam spoke.

"Aye, but we were all worried about you. Well, maybe me more than everyone." Liam's face flushed.

"Everyone else okay?"

Liam nodded. "You should have seen it. Lieutenant David made a grand landing, but we hit a bloody stone wall covered up by grass. Who puts a feckin' wall in the middle of a field anyway? Once we hit it, everything went arse-ways. The poor lass is smashed up."

"The lass?" Hagen asked.

Liam smiled and playfully socked Hagen's arm. "Plane, you dope. After the crash, Sergeant Collins was KO'd. We carried him away, and he came to an hour later. Only three commando fellas left and they grabbed the explosives. Lieutenant David was dizzy for a bit. I got most of your parachute equipment, though you're off your nut to think it's of any use now. We were bleedin' lucky. Hodges twisted a leg, and that fella, Ness, cut his arm. That's it."

"And I hit my head...again."

Liam shook his head. "Don't think so. You were strapped in tight. Think you just passed out; you were mumbling. Yer head hurt?"

Hagen touched his head. "Aches." He massaged the side of his head, and then his knees buckled. Liam grabbed him, arms around his waist.

"Thanks." Hagen smiled into Liam's light green eyes, but an argument broke out in the other room that wrecked the spell they were under.

"How long was I out?" Hagen asked.

Liam let him go. "Four hours."

Four hours! That long?

Liam led him down a short, plain hallway. They came out into the main room where everyone was scattered around a table, a map lying between them. Roesia and Commander Ford were arguing.

The others were sitting in chairs or leaned against the wall, watching the heated debate. A savory smell filled the room, and his nose followed the scent. An old woman with thick graying hair tied at her nape was standing in a small kitchen, stirring a pot. This had to be Justine. She turned toward him. Indeed she did have darker skin than most Germans, and he had met enough mixed Chinese and Caucasians in Philadelphia's Chinatown to recognize someone of blended race.

Justine didn't smile but seemed to be gauging him and then spoke in perfect German, with a flawless southern dialect. "Guten tag. Bist du hungrig?" It took him a second to register his own childhood language. *Good afternoon. Are you hungry?*

Quietness settled on the room at hearing the elderly woman speak. Hagen felt several pairs of eyes turning to look at him and the woman. His gaze, though, was fixed on the pot that was releasing that delicious smell.

His stomach growled, and he nodded to the woman. "Ja. Danke." *Yes. Thank you.*

Lt. David came to him and touched his arm, glancing over at Justine, who was focused back on her stew. "How are you, boyo?"

Hagen shrugged and touched his head. "Throbs."

Lt. David handed him a cup of hot water with sweet smelling spices mixed into it. "Old woman's brew. I was starting to fade and now I'm wide-awake. Maybe it'll help?"

Hagen sipped. It had a fruity taste. He jabbed his thumb over his shoulder toward where Roesia and Commander Ford had been arguing. "What is that about?"

Lt. David glanced over his shoulder. Commander Ford had gone outside and Roesia was standing by the window, staring through it. He turned back to Hagen.

"Commander Ford wants to plan a route to our original mission. But it has to be 290 kilometers away. Roesia seems to think the Nazis have another secret base nearby that's not on any of the maps. Commander Ford says we have a mission we were ordered to do."

Lt. David shook his head and rolled his eyes, then shrugged as if to say, *Women, what can you do?*

Hagen massaged his head. "Does she think the secret base is at Earl Groscz Castle?"

"*Kraut!*" Sgt. Collins called from across the room.

Hagen turned to Sgt. Collins as he sauntered forward, rubbing his fingers over his gray whiskers. His untucked shirt was unbuttoned at the bottom, hairy belly visible.

Hagen gritted his teeth. The name Kraut really got under his skin. "You still think I'm some sort of spy, Sarge?"

"Maybe a bit dodgy. No spy, though."

Hagen's annoyance went up a notch. "Dodgy, now? And why's that?"

Sgt. Collins chuckled. "Well, seem like you're a bit naive. Could be some act, but bloody deserves an award if it is. You're probably just some poor wee sprog."

Hagen furrowed his brow in confusion.

"A new air boy, Kraut," Sgt. Collins growled and shook his head. He thumbed to the old woman. "Now, you want to prove you're with us? Ask the old biddy how we can get us some transportation. Then get the best route to this dam so we can blow it to kingdom come, rescue this damn miserable businessman or kill him, and then get out of Nazi-land. You can stick behind if you like; I'm sure you feel right at home. Myself, I'd like to get back and have myself a bevvy."

Corporal Kirby came over, stared at the woman's stew with a greedy expression, and then regarded Hagen. "And ask the old ninny when dinner is ready." Kirby nodded over at Roesia, across the room, and asked Lt. David in a hushed voice. "Is she barking mad?" He twirled his finger by his head.

Roesia spoke with a stern voice that carried a definitively crisp edge. "I am not crazy." She returned to the table.

"This Vril Society I encountered in Berlin was interested in many things. But the program I am telling you about, it was top priority. Hitler and his followers were pushing a top-secret program forward that could change everything—a secret weapon. The Nazis built a base that was inside a castle way before Hitler declared war on anyone. The experiments were moved to this dam for the energy it produced."

Corporal Kirby spat out. "Please, woman. Why did Churchill not mention it?"

Roesia said, "It was classified. You were need-to-know."

Commander Ford came up. "She's telling the truth. Like I said before. You did not need to know because your mission was to let us parachute out, not tag along. There is some large secret base related to our current mission. But the mission was to focus on the dam—a satellite base where they are keeping this Euan Hartley and using electricity to conduct experiments."

Hagen swallowed and asked, "But the main secret base couldn't be at Earl Groscz Castle. It's a complete shambles. I'm surprised it's even standing."

Commander Ford spoke sternly. "Never mind this castle. We have a mission. That includes getting Euan Hartley."

Hagen touched his front pocket and plucked out Euan's handkerchief. He stepped away from everyone and brought it to his nose. Images flitted through his mind. A huge fire at the dam. A convoy that headed toward an immense castle that sat up high on a peak, fog covering the base. He knew this place, and it was not Earl Groscz Castle. A white room flashed in his mind—a young man with greased black hair was crouched down next to Euan, taking his blood. A horrific reek of chemicals stung his nose. The image changed, and Euan was huddled inside a dark room with iron bars. The stench of sweat and fecal matter dominated the room.

Hagen focused. He wanted that feeling again. The memories swirled. Then it came. Euan was transforming, and that depraved but formidable energy surged through Hagen and filled him up. Hagen fell forward.

Lt. David moved fast and squatted down with Hagen, breaking his fall. Hagen stuffed the cloth into his shirt pocket.

"Hagen!" Roesia spoke, alarmed.

Hagen stared up at Lt. David's face. "Euan's not at the dam anymore. There was a fire there. They've moved him. He's being held nearby. N-not at Earl Groscz Castle either."

"How do you know that?" Lt.David asked, seemingly befuddled.

Hagen shook his head. "I just do."

Liam knelt down beside Hagen. "He's like a bloodhound that tracks scents down." Liam turned to Hagen. "Tell them, Hagen."

Hagen nodded. "It's true."

Sgt. Collins roared, "You got to be bloody fucking joking!"

"Where? Is he at the main secret base?" Roesia asked.

Justine came over, pulled up on his shoulder with one hand so he sat up, and offered him a tin cup with steam rising from the top. She touched her head. "Kopfschmerzen Heilung." He took the cup and mulled over the thick southern dialect Justine had just spoken. She got back up and returned to the kitchen. The words came to him. *Headache cure.*

Hagen took a sip, tasting sweet berries. When he looked up, everyone's attention was focused on him. Commander Ford studied him.

Hodges limped over, a pipe dangling from his mouth, and then knelt down. "Well, lad, the suspense sure has been heightened, hasn't it? Let's deflate it, shall we? Where is Euan?"

Hagen met everyone's eyes, and he said, "He's at a castle that's not far away. They've called it many things over the years. But I've always known it as Wehr Wolff Castle."

Seven: Rumored Nazi Experimentations

JUSTINE SERVED STEW to Hagen and everyone else, and the room became peacefully quiet for a short period. Even Sgt. Collins and Corporal Kirby were too busy stuffing food in their mouths to harass anyone. Commander Ford and Commando Ness sat together in the living room, eating, but Benton had been sent outside with his own meal and told to keep guard while a few others sat on the front door porch and ate.

Ever since Hagen disclosed that he'd sensed Euan Hartley at Wehr Wolff Castle, only Sgt. Collins and Corporal Kirby had grumbled, but no one else made a peep. That sensation he'd had when he touched Euan's handkerchief was back. Euan had been changing into something, and though there was the reek of terror and fear, there was also something more in that transformation. It felt liberating. He wanted to partake in the experience again.

Hagen sat at the table with Justine across from him. Roesia was at the end, and Liam sat at Hagen's side. Hagen tipped the succulent stew into his mouth, chewed a morsel of meat, and for the first time, considered his surroundings with more scrutiny.

A table was set near the entrance to the living room, on top sat a framed black-and-white photograph of a young woman and a large broad-shouldered man with a black beard that was braided at the bottom. The woman was a younger version of Justine, and the man he presumed to be her husband. A second photograph had been taken by someone who must have been rock climbing, a picture of the rock face that went down far below the photographer, into an abyss.

On the far wall were two curved swords and a lever-action rifle leaned close to the sink. On one side of the room were pulleys and ropes used for rock climbing. But most peculiar was a crystal ball perched on a wooden mold atop the far window ledge.

Justine brought a spoonful of steamy broth with vegetables to her mouth and blew on the contents. Hagen had no idea how old she was, but the woman barely had any wrinkles except at the corners of her eyes and the pronounced frown lines around her mouth. On her forearm, there was a tattoo of a crescent moon impaled by a sword.

Hagen could not help but stare as an image flitted through his mind without warning. A mysterious robed figure, a dark crypt, blood splattered over a stone column. He was no longer in the present moment. He was a ten-year-old boy again. A day later, a man with a black beard with a braided end told his father the dire news of his brother, Ivan. His brokenhearted father handed over a gold medallion.

Hagen set his spoon down and wiped his mouth with the back of his hand, unnerved by the sudden surfacing of repressed memories.

He asked in German, "Have we met?"

Justine glanced up at him, and the corner of her mouth turned upward. Liam and Roesia were quiet. Hagen felt several pairs of eyes staring at him.

Justine dabbed her lips with a ragged cloth and stared down at it. She told him in perfect German, which his mind was translating in real time. "My best linen has long been sold. For that matter, the china, too. Most of it for silver."

Hagen furrowed his brow.

Why did she purchase silver with the money she made? That image of Euan changing was back in his mind, and he swallowed.

Justine got up, collected bowls from the table, and took them to the sink. She started to speak, but not in German—in English, and with a thick accent. Lt. David and Hodges stepped inside the house and came to the kitchen area.

"I am a descendant of the Wehr Wolff family. For a long time, I have been the Keeper of Wehr Forest. I protect those who inhabit these forests, make sure no harm comes to them, and also, I make certain they remain in this realm. My husband died two years ago, killed by the Nazis along with one of my children. I've sent my daughter away for her own protection. But, alas, I'm unable to protect my children of Wehr Forest from these ruthless new invaders. These Nazis have decimated too many to count and captured many more. I have failed them all. This Euan Hartley, I have heard the rumors; he was held at this dam. His blood is being used to create a new weapon. A fire broke out at the base, and the

Nazis had to move Euan to this castle you speak of. Euan may be dead by now. I do not know. But you must go there, and do what you may, for if these Nazis accomplish what they desire, the balance of the world is at risk."

Justine was focused on Hagen. He shifted in his seat, uncertain what she meant by "children of Wehr forest." Movement at the corner of his eye caught his attention. The sergeant and Corporal Kirby huddled close to the archway to the dining room. Justine seemed unaware to their presence.

"In this castle, they conduct inhumane experiments. This Wehr Wolff Castle was once a symbol of peace; there's nothing but evil there now. The children of the Wehr Forest are their victims."

Sgt. Collins shook his head, lines creasing in his forehead, and his crass voice broke the peaceful woman's rhythm. "Who in the hell are these bloody forest children? Sounds like a bunch of Irish squatters in England, calling it their country."

Justine met his eyes. "They are called the wehrwolf of Wehr Forest."

"*Werewolf?*" Corporal Kirby squealed, then covered his mouth as he chuckled into his hand.

Justine straightened and shook her head once. "Not a werewolf. W-e-h-r-w-o-l-f. They are not the same as the mythical werewolf who changes from beast to man at will."

"What is it?" Hodges asked, awed by the prospect, "A new wolf species?"

Justine's expression had confusion written over it, and Hagen translated in German.

Justine nodded, and said, "Ah, yes, yes. A very new kind of wolf species never seen before. Long ago, a man who you would call a werewolf bred with indigenous wolves of this forest. The interspecies breeding bore a new kind of animal that was neither a pure wolf nor a pure werewolf. They came to be called...*wehrwolf*. They do not change at will from man to beast like the werewolf. Many could, from the first generations, and every now and then, I have witnessed one who has done it, but most can't or don't want to, or don't know how to."

Sgt. Collins grumped in a low voice, "Are you all barking mad? You can't be serious, blimey, listening to this bint? She's mad as a bag of ferrets. We go into that castle; we might as well paint a bleeding *X* on our arses, because we'll be buggered to hell. I say we go with our first mission and shite on that dam with the explosives we hauled with us and bugger out of Nazi-land."

Lt. David held his palm up to Sgt. Collins. "Sergeant, enough. Let's hear this out."

Roesia asked, "They use subjects for their experiments? Uh, prisoners?"

Justine answered, "Thousands of people go in, but never come out. Villagers. Prisoners of war. German countrymen of all ages, from children to old men and old women."

Liam joked, "Sounds more bloody likely they're eating them?"

The old woman looked over at Liam, and a small smile cut across her face. "Ja. Many are fed to the new creatures they have created."

Liam's expression grew somber.

Hagen asked, "Do you know what creatures they are creating?"

"Ones of pure blasphemy, o'course." Justine looked around the room at everyone.

Lt. David coughed and stepped close to Corporal Kirby. "What, uh, what creatures of blasphemy are you speaking of again, your lady, uh, Justine?"

Justine shrugged, and said, "A mutante werewolf, o'course."

Sgt. Collins and Corporal Kirby's mouths dropped open, and they turned to each other. Sgt. Collins rubbed his head, his cheeks reddening. The room was dead silent for two whole seconds. Sgt. Collins was the first to break the silence with boisterous, earsplitting laughter. He leaned back, guffawing.

He managed between breaths. "Mutant werewolves? M-mutant *werewolves*?" He clapped Corporal Kirby on the back, cackling.

Corporal Kirby was laughing as well, shaking his head, saying over and over, "Bloody hell, bloody hell..."

Hodges and Lt. David appeared amused, but Liam seemed fearful and doubting. Commander Ford worked his way into the kitchen area and leaned against the wall. His aristocratic face with high cheekbones and squared jaw was similar to a statue of a long-lived nobleman that betrayed no emotions. Roesia's expression held determination, her eyes focused, her lips pressed together, and her jaw set.

Someone grabbed Hagen's shoulder and whipped him around. Sgt. Collins's reddened face was in his. Hagen could smell copious amounts of downed whiskey. Sgt. Collins's amusement had been replaced with fury.

He snarled in a low tone, "Tell this old cuckoo we want to know how to get to that bloody dam and back to England. I don't give two bits for whoever this Euan is; our mission was the dam and that's where we're going."

Justine was speaking fast now to Roesia, but no longer in English—in German. Hagen couldn't concentrate on the words Justine was saying with the sergeant in his face. Sgt. Collins grabbed Hagen's shirt and lifted him out of his seat. His chair clattered to the floor as his back hit a wall. Sgt. Collins shook Hagen, making his teeth rattle in his head.

"Listen to me, Kraut. Ask her, or I'll put ya over my leg and flog ya with my belt. I want out of this Nazi cesspool. You hear me? I don't care none about cuckooey werewolves and goblins."

"Sgt. Collins," Lt. David said, his voice stern and sharp-edged. *"Let Messer go this moment."*

Sgt. Collins glanced over his shoulder and frowned, appearing abashed. He released Hagen's shirt, then backed away to stand next to Corporal Kirby, who was staring at Hagen through slitted eyes.

Lt. David waved to the sergeant. "Commander Ford is in charge of this expedition and I'm next in command. Then it's Officer Alan Hodges. You're not calling the shots here. First Admiral Churchill wanted this businessman found and didn't tell us why, fine and dandy. We weren't parachuting in, but now we're here. Hagen Messer was also selected for his tracking skills. Churchill was won over by his reputation, and Private Messer believes Euan Hartley is now inside Wehr Wolff Castle. We will consider this information and the rest, however ridiculous it may sound. *Go outside, Sergeant. Get some air."*

The sergeant waved his hand in disgust, slugged Corporal Kirby's arm, and nodded his head to the door. "Come on." On their way out, Sgt. Collins and Corporal Kirby grabbed the short-barreled automatic rifles leaning close to the front doorframe. Collins slung the small rifle over a shoulder, bent close to several parachutes, and picked up a machine gun with a long barrel, which had a clip that came out from the top. Hagen recognized the weapon—a Bren Light Machine Gun.

Hodges clapped Hagen's shoulder and leaned in, asking with a concerned voice, "You okay, lad? Sergeant is just under a lot of stress is all. We all are."

Hagen nodded. "Y-yes, sir."

Justine spoke to the room in English. "You must kill this blasphemy, or the world faces a horrid doom." She turned to Hagen, and spoke in German. "You coming today is no accident." Hagen opened his mouth, then closed it, not sure what to say, uncertain what that meant.

"Lieutenant, Commander Ford," Hodges said, "you think we should be getting on our way? We've been here a long time. Maybe it's time to find this dam or somehow infiltrate this castle. If anyone saw us coming down, it's already over, but we may still have time."

Lt. David rubbed his chin. Commander Ford pushed off the wall, came to the table, and rapped his knuckles on the surface, his face in contemplation.

Roesia stood up and said assertively, "You can go to your dam. I'm going to Wehr Wolff Castle to do what I can. I'll ask for a portion of explosives."

Lt. David eyed Roesia, then turned to the old woman, who was watching them both. Lt. David shook his head, and his tone rose in pitch. "Mutant werewolves?"

Commander Ford spoke. "You were on a need-to-know basis. I will tell you this. In our briefings, we learned about a Nazi's genetic experiment on a new wolf species. They called it the Wehrmacht's Mutante Wolf Program. We were told the Nazis had found a never-before-seen indigenous beast in a forest, one that is believed to have a clear link to a human gene. We had no idea where the main base was, though, but learned they had moved the experiments to this dam. We were under the impression that, if we destroyed the dam, we would stop the experiments. The dam was set up to produce electric voltage from a slick hydraulic system they designed. We heard that Euan Hartley was held there, and we were told he had genetics important to the Nazi's experimentation design."

Justine pointed at Commander Ford, her face set hard. "His genetics come from the family called the Wehr Wolffs. The most renowned werewolves to've lived over the last four centuries."

Commander Ford nodded, keeping his attention on Justine. "That's right. We heard that, too. The one thing our intel never told us was that the experiments originated in the castle, and maybe never stopped."

Hodges raised his hand, reminding Hagen of a boy in Sunday school. "Excuse me, sir, I'm confused. May be all the stress. But then, this Euan was a werewolf since birth?"

Commander Ford shook his head and rubbed his forehead. "No, no, he's a descendant of the Wehr Wolff family. Has their genes."

"Who are these bleeding Wehr Wolff chaps?" Liam asked.

Justine answered in German, staring straight at Hagen. "The Wehr Wolff family are the kings of werewolves. But just because you carry the Wehr Wolff blood does not mean you can change to a werewolf; you must be bitten first. But once bitten, your full potential can be fulfilled."

Hagen translated for everyone.

Lt. David considered Commander Ford with a surprised look. "If you knew this could be true, why were you even arguing with Roesia earlier? You both have more in common than any of us; you have all the information."

Commander Ford shrugged. "I didn't know at the time that the dam had been reportedly destroyed or that Euan had been relocated." He fixed his gaze on Hagen, then looked at everyone. "Look, Messer here believes this Euan is at this castle. I could give two damns what the First Admiral thought of Hagen, but Hagen's commander in America trusted him, and so do I. If this Euan carries the Wehr Wolff blood, the Nazis could conceivably create a new fighting force of mutant wolves, the likes which have never been seen."

Roesia spoke, her voice quiet as she glanced outside to where Sgt. Collins was. "While Sgt. Blockhead was having a tantrum, Justine told me the creatures they have made don't look anything like the wehrwolves from the forest. They're aggressive and have been trained by the Nazis to kill on command."

"What do they look like?" Hagen and Lt. David asked at the same time.

They didn't get an answer because Justine tensed, her hands drew into fists, and she spoke in clear English. *"Nazis."* She grabbed two worn leather rucksacks from the floor, strode to the window, and removed the crystal ball from the sill. She placed her palm underneath and peered down into it. Seconds later, she set it inside a bag.

Everyone looked at one another, expression distressed.

"I'm sorry, but did she just say Nazis?" Hodges asked.

"Repeat that?" Commander Ford demanded.

Justine commanded, "Bring those white packs by the porch."

"Packs?" Liam asked, and looked to Hagen. "The parachutes?"

Hagen's mind was racing, and he spoke the next word without thinking, asking, "Fallschirm?" *Parachute?*

Justine was moving to another room and nodded. "*Ja. Go!* The Nazis are close."

Commander Ford turned to Commando Ness and ordered, "Go check on Benton."

There was no need. Benton was at the door, breathing hard. "Germans, Sir. An entire unit. And they have a tank."

Justine came out of the room and shouted, "Laufen Sie wie die Hölle zum Schloss Groscz."

Hagen was barely listening; he was moving to the door, her words resonating in his mind.

"What did she say?" Lt. David asked.

It was Roesia who answered. "She said to run like hell to that castle."

Eight: Mutante Wolf

HAGEN, LIAM, AND Roesia each grabbed a rifle and scrambled to the front door. Hagen stopped and looked back, but Justine was nowhere in sight. Lt. David shoved him forward.

"Go, Messer."

Sgt. Collins and Corporal Kirby were crouched by the front of the house, alert.

Sgt. Collins muttered, "About bloody time—I finally get to kill Nazis."

The commandos had weaved out into the woods, searching for a path to lead them, and had told Lt. David to wait there.

Corporal Kirby stared at the corner of the house, his rifle raised, and asked, "Which way, Lieutenant?"

Lt. David pointed to the left side of the house, saying, "Commander Ford went that—"

Hagen cried out, interrupting the lieutenant. "Liam, what're you doing?"

Liam answered over his shoulder. "She said to grab the parachutes."

Lt. David barked, "Never mind those, O'Malley—"

Lt. David never finished. The log wall of the house exploded outward, and fragmented wood spewed over Hagen; he fell, dropping his rifle to the ground, and rolled to his side, staring in shock around him. Another explosion came close to the house, and he ducked down while debris fell close by. His ears were ringing as he crawled toward his gun and stopped. There were soldiers with crosses on their helmets coming straight at him through the trees, but they didn't seem to have seen him yet.

A soldier popped up in front of him from a bush, brown whiskers scattered on his face, probably only a couple years older than Hagen. They stared at one another.

A German soldier came up fast behind his comrade, breaking the moment. He yelled, *"Schieben! Schieben!" Shoot! Shoot!*

The young German soldier acted first, bringing his gun up to his shoulder and sighting on Hagen. The air erupted in a cacophony of firepower to the left of Hagen, and the young German soldier in front of him was hit. His shirt frayed in multiple places from the rounds that hit him, and he stumbled back, falling into the brush. Sgt. Collins stepped up, discharging his weapon in more short bursts. The other soldier took aim at the sergeant, but he was mowed down in a hail of bullets. The helmet flipped off the soldier's head, droplets of blood splattering over the leaves of a nearby tree.

Gunfire erupted in front of Hagen, several yards from the house, and a couple of rounds ricocheted close by. Something zinged by Hagen's ear.

Sgt. Collins grabbed Hagen's arm, dragging him backward, his cross voice boomed in his ear.

"It's war, Kraut. Get fighting, or get dying." Sgt. Collins shoved him back toward Lt. David.

Hagen turned toward the German soldiers that had just been slaughtered. Their bodies were not visible, hidden by brush. Two more German soldiers popped up close to the carcasses, then crouched down. Divots appeared in front of Hagen. Lt. David and Sgt. Collins opened fire. The end of Sgt. Collins's muzzle jiggled up and down, and the two troopers flailed their arms and fell while others behind them took cover. Lt. David stepped next to Hagen in a crouch, his rifle stock supported against his shoulder, firing short bursts.

He grabbed Hagen's arm and yanked him back, saying, *"Move back, Private."*

Hodges opened fire from the other side of the house. He took a pin out of a grenade and tossed it, then ducked down, yelling, "Grenade." A deafening explosion followed.

On the ground close to Hagen's feet were two pinned grenades. Hagen picked up one, unpinned it, and tossed. It exploded in trees several yards away; two soldiers flew up into the air.

Lt. David yelled, "This way, this way."

Hagen shouted over his ringing ears. "Where's Liam?"

Liam hurried toward him. He had his rifle slung over a shoulder and was hunched down, carrying several white parachutes. Liam slid to a stop in front of Hagen, his eyes huge and expression terrified.

Lt. David's gun clicked empty, and Hagen stepped up, cocked his rifle, and aimed. He sighted on a soldier sprinting for cover before he fired. The soldier fell.

Liam grabbed Hagen's shoulder. "Messer, Prof, let's move."

Hagen turned, and behind him was Roesia. She squatted down to pick up a couple of parachutes, then came up next to Hagen, her head bent, flinching at each shot fired.

Hagen moved into the woods first, Roesia close behind him. He headed toward a large steep ridge that led toward Earl Groscz Castle. Hagen glanced over his shoulder. Sgt. Collins was giving them cover.

The small German unit was advancing, the air filled with the sound of automatic rifle fire. Hagen slung his rifle higher over his shoulder. He'd just passed a cord of stacked wood when new shots opened up behind them. Hagen glanced over his shoulder in time to see the enemy caught in crossfire, and within seconds, they were mowed down. The three commandos stepped out from behind trees, heading toward their group.

Commander Ford was at point. He jabbed his finger to Hagen's left, and yelled, "Follow her!"

Hagen turned and saw that Justine was several feet in front of them. She gave a frantic wave. Hagen didn't wait but ran. Liam was at his side. They both carried parachutes, and though his mind was in panic mode, he nonetheless had a notion of what they were to be used for. Sgt. Collins's thunderous rifle resonated behind them, and then a whistling noise and an explosion sounded several yards away. Hagen fell to a knee but was right back up.

More whistles became audible, and Liam screamed, "Mortars."

The trunk of a tree disintegrated not far from him, and he fell on his back. Hagen rolled onto his stomach, Liam stood close by, screaming his name. Roesia was several feet away, lying on the ground. A thick brush was in front of them, and Hagen had the vantage point of seeing two pairs of feet showing beneath it.

Hagen yelled, "Get down!"

Liam obeyed, falling flat on the spot. Hagen stood up and saw two German soldiers, both with their sights in Liam's direction, which gave Hagen the advantage. Hagen opened fire, and the first one went down; the second soldier swiveled his aim to Hagen. Someone fired, and the soldier jerked, a gaping hole opening in his neck. He collapsed. Justine stood several feet away; she brought a Winchester lever-action rifle down from her shoulder, smoke rising from the muzzle, and waved for him to move.

Ear-splitting explosions reverberated near them, and Lt. David's voice boomed, "Move it, damn you, move!"

A high-pitched whistle that was not a mortar fire came, and Hagen glanced at Justine through a thicket of bushes. She removed her fingers from her mouth. She wore a backpack and carried a satchel over her shoulder.

Behind Hagen, the others were following closely. A blast blew several yards from them. Pieces of wood flew high in every direction, some peppering Hagen's face before he had a chance to turn away.

Corporal Kirby was close to him now, yelling, "Where the hell is she going?"

Hagen shook his head and simply followed her. She came to the embankment of the ridge.

Sgt. Collins said, out of breath, "Bloody hell, she's trapped us."

Justine bent over, pulled hard on a line of rope, and lifted. A hidden door came up, dirt that had covered it tumbling away. Justine jabbed her finger down into the darkness where a narrow staircase was visible. Roesia went first, Liam second, and then Hagen.

Clouds of dust clogged Hagen's nostrils as they descended. He reached the bottom of the spiral staircase and bumped into Liam, as they moved forward against a damp, slimy wall. Roesia was barely visible, several feet in front of them or so he thought. Hagen touched the wall, and when he felt Roesia's hand, he flinched.

"This must have once been part of a battlement connected to Earl Groscz's castle," she said.

The interior of the tunnel was partially lit by the opened door, and their escape route tunnel was made of stone and had wooden beams as supports along the sides.

Lt. David was down in the tunnel now; he came close to Hagen and peered into the darkness in front of them. The silhouette of one of the commandos moved down the stairs. Everyone's breathing was quite audible, and when the door above them slammed shut, blackness encroached.

Corporal Kirby spoke in a hushed voice. "What the hell we do now? Where'd she bloody go?"

"Damn witch," growled Sgt. Collins.

"Quiet," ordered Lt. David. "We need to line up and make a buddy system."

A scraping noise came from the ground close to Hagen and sparks spewed in the air. Someone was trying to light a flame. Everyone hushed. Another acute scratch of something solid striking a hard surface and a spark ignited. There was a burst of flame.

The old woman held up a torch and said, "*Folgen.*"

She hurried forward into the darkness.

Hagen and Roesia obeyed the woman. They both translated over their shoulder at the same time, "*Follow!*"

Justine was at point. It was too dark to know for certain, but Hagen was under the impression that the commando soldiers had taken up the rear. The tunnel went on for a great distance and finally came to a dead end before it took a right angle turn. Far down the direction they had come, there was the shouting of German voices. They had found the entrance. A mixture of growls and low-bass barks echoed off the walls.

A high, piercing howl carried to them, driving a chill up Hagen's spine.

Corporal Kirby whined, "They're sending dogs on us."

Justine said over her shoulder, "Sie sind nicht Hunde."

Hagen's mind wheeled as he deciphered her thick German accent.

"What'd she say?" Sgt. Collins asked.

Hagen answered, "I think she said those aren't dogs."

"Benton!" Commander Ford shouted.

Hagen and everyone slowed, except for Justine. Hagen turned around. Benton was barely visible, but he had taken a satchel off of his shoulder and waved for everyone to continue.

"Go! I'll blow the tunnel. I'll catch up."

Captain Ford touched the man's arm and then hurried forward. They were jogging now, when gunfire melding with horrific shrieks erupted and echoed off the walls.

Justine shouted, "*Hier!*"

A small staircase was in front of Justine. She climbed without looking back with Roesia on her heels and Hagen following. A high-impact explosion thundered from deep in the tunnel behind them, the ground quaking around them in response. Chunks of stone toppled to the ground inside the tunnel; it was collapsing. Hagen reached the top and fell to his knees onto smooth stone. Liam jumped out and slid close to him. Sgt. Collins and Corporal Kirby were out of the tunnel then. A billow of dust spewed up from the hole into the air and enveloped everyone. Lt. David and Hodges stumbled out of the gap, coated with thick dust and grime.

Hagen was up on his feet, wiping the dust from his face and looking around. They were inside the castle, in what once had probably been a great hall, complete with the splendor of antiquities and priceless pieces, but it was nothing but cold emptiness now.

Commander Ford stepped to a window, brought his binoculars to his eyes, and shouted, "They're coming. Let's go."

Hagen brought out his father's binoculars, peered out a nearby window, and observed the approaching tank. Not far away was the Night Angel, its ruins lying out on the field. The tank reached the stone wall, slowed, then crawled forward, and knocked into the barrier, the stone crumbling away. Several soldiers were crouched on the other side of the tank, and advanced in a stoop. A transport truck stopped in front of the wall and soldiers unloaded.

Three jeeps approached; each hauled a trailer. A man stood in the back of one, wearing a cap. He was waving his hands at the soldiers, shouting orders, and then he took off his hat and mopped his face with his sleeve. Hagen zoomed in on the man. He was bald-headed with a hooked nose and plump cheeks.

The bald-headed officer glanced back to the jeeps and signaled with his arm. Several large, hairy wolflike creatures burst out of the trailers and charged the castle. Hagen brought his lens down and stepped backward. Lt. David and Alan Hodges were kneeling on the ground, coughing.

Commander Ford barked orders, and Ness took a position at a window, rifle stock held to his shoulder before he fired single shots.

Ness yelled, "Something's coming. And they're not going down!"

Liam held the three parachutes over an arm and spoke frantically, but Hagen did not hear the words. He felt something incredible about to happen.

Hagen pushed Liam forward and pointed to a hallway, telling him, "Go. Take the lieutenant." Liam grabbed the front of Lt. David's shirt and pulled him toward the entrance. Roesia followed them.

Hagen hastily tucked his binoculars in the pouch attached to his belt. He started to pass a dilapidated spiral staircase when he caught Sgt. Collins's eye as he helped Hodges forward.

Hagen grabbed a wandering and dazed Corporal Kirby, and shouted, "Kirby, hurry, they're right behind us!"

The staircase exploded into fragments, and the concussion wave knocked Hagen to his side. The cannon fire from the tank echoed in the air. Liam had been in the hallway, thereby avoiding the brunt of the explosive impact, he raced out of the corridor to Hagen. He hunched down at Hagen's side, grabbed his wrists, and dragged him into the hall entrance. Lt. David was hunkered down next to the wall, his face between his knees. He was wheezing.

Liam let Hagen's wrists go, yelling, "Get your arse up, Hagen!"

Hagen was in a stupor, dizzy, but he rose shakily up to his feet. Liam picked up the parachutes at his feet.

Justine was in front of them. The lever-action Winchester rifle slung over her shoulder, she pulled on Hagen and said, *"Hilf deinen Freunden."*

Hagen's mind was sluggish, and it took him a second. He translated to Liam. "She says to get the others."

Liam handed over the parachutes and was gone. Justine took one of Hagen's hands and led him and Lt. David to a large room where a cool breeze buffeted his face. Hagen fell to his knees and tried to make sense of what was before his eyes. The wall in front of him had collapsed, and a stone floor extended beyond the gaping hole, serving as a plank over what appeared to be a drop into an abyss. He recalled from his recent dream and memory that this abyss went down to God knew what.

Justine placed a worn leather satchel over his neck and shoulder and spoke too fast. He realized she was saying to put on the parachute.

Gunfire erupted from somewhere in the castle. There was shouting. He shook his head and said, "I have to help the others."

She cawed, "Nein, Nein. Zieh es an. Ich werde sie bekommen." His mind got it... *No. No. Put it on. I'll get them.* She left the area.

Hagen helped Lt. David into the straps. Lt. David's eyes were squinted shut, tears running from the corners, and one ear had blood dripping out of it.

Hagen got his own parachute into place just as Justine returned, Liam at her heels, Roesia in tow. Sgt. Collins had Corporal Kirby's arm over his shoulder, his face white. Roesia dropped the two parachutes she was carrying.

Justine hurried from the room again, yelling, this time in English, "Put on your packs!"

Hagen observed that Sgt. Collins was no longer carrying his large machine gun, only having the commando rifle slung over a shoulder. The sergeant helped the professor put on a parachute pack and was about to help Corporal Kirby when harsh yowls came from a nearby hall.

Hagen faced the door, unable to move, memories of his past coming too fast, overloading him. Three hairy *things* came out from the hallway entry. Mutant werewolves. They were crouched on four legs. Each had a sparse coat of scraggly brown fur, blotches of white human skin showing in several places over their bodies. Their faces, it seemed, were filled with sharp teeth, saliva dripping from their fangs. One had human fingers extending from its paws, razor sharp nails coming out of several fingertips. Corporal Kirby staggered out of the room, moving into a back corridor, and vanished. One beast sprinted away and gave chase.

Sgt. Collins brought his small automatic rifle up and fired at a creature. Blood splattered onto the floor. The mutant beast yelped and fell back as the second one leaped into the air. It came down on the sergeant; he stumbled and fell onto his back. The creature was on top of Sgt. Collins, its jaws locked on his rifle.

Rage filled Hagen, and he took one stride, aimed his gun, and pulled the trigger. Machine-gun fire exploded, acrid smoke filling his nostrils. The rounds pounded into the creature. Several thwacks were audible, blood sprayed over the floor and the beast sidled off the sergeant, bearing its teeth at Hagen.

Liam stepped up, and he and Hagen fired simultaneously at the mutant werewolf that had attacked the sergeant. The bullets shredded it, and the creature jerked back and forth where it stood. Their guns clicked empty, but the pulverized creature was still standing. The mutant werewolf that had been the first to be hit by Sgt. Collins was back up, growling, its fangs showing as it came alongside its wounded comrade.

Two sharp gunshots boomed from the corner of the room, with only a short pause between. A single round struck one beast's head, and it collapsed. The second beast's mutant eye became a gory hole, and it dropped to its side.

When Hagen turned, Justine had her rifle's stock to her shoulder. She nodded at him, then to the makeshift plank outside, and said in English, "Go, child."

Hagen gave a perceptible nod and went through the breach; a gust of wind hit him as he peered over the edge. A layer of fog clouded his vision so he couldn't see what was below. Roesia tugged the lieutenant's hand, and headed out over the ledge. Hagen and Liam were behind her.

The sergeant barked from behind them, "Jump out and count to two, then yank hard on that string. Pray you jump far enough, and you don't get blown back into the cliff."

Hagen met Roesia's gaze. She touched his hand and said, "See you at the bottom." Then she ran to the ledge, jumped, and disappeared.

"Go," Hagen ordered Liam.

Liam shook his head. "You first."

Lt. David grabbed Liam's arm, his eyes streaming, and croaked, "Bloody hell, lads, let's get off this rock."

Liam went to the ledge, looked to Hagen, and leaped.

Hagen turned to Justine. She had gone to the other side of the vast room, reached a column, and knelt down. More mutant creatures flew out of two different hallways.

Sgt. Collins was backing up, fire spitting out of the end of his gun. He roared, "Lieutenant, Kraut, move your arses!"

Lt. David took three large strides and jumped. Hagen glanced once again at Justine. She had a rectangular blasting box on the floor at her knees; her hands were on a black lever that was in an upright position. Black and red wires stuck out of the back end of the box and wound over the floor and into the wall. She met his eyes and nodded, then pressed down on the handle. A series of booms reverberated far away, and large blocks of jagged stone plunged down in a nearby hallway. A cloud of dust blew out of the exit. The mutants whirled in confusion and cowered to the ground.

A series of *kabooms* drew closer and closer—the entire structure quaked. Hagen widened his stance, losing his balance.

"*Jump!*" Sgt. Collins shrieked.

Hagen looked back as Justine slipped out of the shadows and hurried to a stone staircase built inside the wall that was barely on the precipice. Dust blew out, and he could see nothing. He leaped and fell toward a layer of fog. Whiteness embraced him for a second, and then he caught sight of a vast forest and a winding river straight below. A sheer cliff was at his back. The tops of unfurled parachutes came into view where his friends glided through the air, down to the forest. Hagen yanked on his cord, and there was a loud *thumpff*. He was jerked in the air as he pulled down on his brake lines, attempting to steer himself into the trees below, but a breeze caught him. He twirled around until he faced the rock wall where an avalanche of castle rubble plunged down the steep cliff.

Treetops approached quickly. Hagen yanked harder to slow his descent. This created more surface with his chute, and he was successful to some degree. Branches whipped at him, audible cracks and snaps followed, and he jolted to a stop in the air, then swayed back and forth. Below him, the ground was a mere five feet away. He took out a knife, and after a few moments of cutting, he dropped to the ground and began a search. It took a good half hour before everyone was grouped back together.

Hagen and Liam gathered the parachutes and buried most of them under twigs and brush. They were unable to get Lt. David's, as his had been caught high up in branches, and it had taken a good deal of patience just getting him down safely. Their group was now made up of only six people: Sgt. Collins, Roesia, Hagen, Lt. David, Hodges, and Liam. Except for Hodges who twisted his ankle and Sgt. Collins's bites, no one else was injured.

Everyone not with them was presumed killed. Sgt. Collins said that, before he'd jumped, Commando Ness had been wounded, and Ford had been nowhere to be seen. Had Ford gotten away?

What about Justine? The image of Justine darting out of the shadow and moving toward a spiral of stone stairs came to Hagen. He didn't tell anyone about what he'd seen. Why? He had no earthly idea how she could have gotten out. But he remembered the photograph of the cliff face, and presumed she had taken it.

Hagen pushed this from his mind, though, and focused on survival. He led the group deep into the woods, getting distance from the Nazis.

Nine: The Medallion

May 10/11, 1940
Wehr Forest, Nazi Germany

THE DAY HAD come and gone, and the night and a chill had set in. Several hours had passed since Hagen and his fellow companions escaped Earl Groscz Castle. A near full moon bathed the Bavarian Alps and forest that surrounded them. Hagen was in point position, a rifle slung over his shoulder, as he led the other five people through the woods. He had tried to make a good distance from the castle ruins, though the trudge was slowed by Hodges's sprained ankle.

Hodges hobbled along on his bad ankle and mumbled incoherently, but Lt. David, who was much more able-bodied and coherent now, helped pull the man forward. Hodges's twisted ankle was one challenge they could handle—the inhalation of the prolific amount of dust back when Benton had destroyed the tunnel was the primary issue. Lt. David and Roesia conjectured that Hodges was having an allergic reaction, which was causing his delirium.

"Ma, I'll be up in a minute."

"Jesus, let my boy live."

"The pond is up ahead, Pa."

The sergeant appeared to be more sluggish; he winced several times. Hagen reached up to touch his shoulder. Sgt. Collins pushed forward, though, and didn't complain, but they all had to stop a few times when fits of coughs caused Hodges to double over. They at least had canteens of water and drank from them at their stops.

How far had they gone? *Fifteen kilometers?* Hagen was uncertain, but even after his physical training at boot camp, blisters were forming on his feet from their long march. Hagen kept touching his breast pocket, making certain he had not lost the handkerchief. He wanted to take it out and concentrate, and let that dark energy flood him. But there was no time for that, so he sucked in a deep breath when that thought came, and pushed it back.

Hagen tried to distract himself by recalling those mutant creatures attacking them earlier. A deep breath should have helped, but it didn't. His mind wouldn't cooperate and instead conjured up faded memories of when he'd been a youth and was helpless and vulnerable. *Ivan.* A flash of a memory came to him. He was knelt down by his brother, who was bloodied and not far from death.

Hagen massaged his head and tried to focus on the task at hand. His brother's voice whispered in his ear. *"Put him out of his misery."* Hagen shook his head.

He paused and glanced over his shoulder. No one was there. He focused and sensed Liam and the others were not far away, then doubled back and found a small clearing where he stopped to wait and rest. Moments later, Roesia came up, with Lt. David close on her heels. A snap of limbs and the sergeant came into view, helping to carry the hallucinating Hodges. Profuse amounts of sweat fell from Sgt. Collins's brow, and a rancid scent wafted from the man. A smell that no one seemed to notice but Hagen.

Liam trailed everyone and, when he saw Hagen, asked, "Bugger to hell, where'd you go, Hagen?"

A noise got Hagen's attention and raised his hackles. He held up a hand, cutting Liam off, listening. *What was that noise? Barking?*

"What is it?" Roesia whispered.

The barking noises grew louder, and everyone cringed.

"A-are those blimey weremutts?" Liam whined.

Hagen put his finger to his mouth. Something howled, and everyone tensed.

Hagen listened for a couple of moments and then said, "No, those are dogs."

That piece of news didn't appear to provide anyone any relief. Shouts from German soldiers drew closer, and Lt. David said crisply, "Go, Hagen."

Hagen pushed forward. The barks grew louder, though, and the yelling soldiers were dangerously close. The men were excited, and one yelled, "Diesen Weg!" *This way.* They were right on their trail.

Hagen stopped, hunched over, his hands on a tree as perspiration beaded on his forehead. His clothes were wet with sweat even though there was a bitter coldness to the air. Roesia came up to him, out of breath. Leaves rustled, and Liam took over for Sgt. Collins, pulling Hodges forward. The shouting of soldiers drew closer.

Lt. David shook his head and ordered, "Messer, O'Malley, Professor. *Go.* Sgt. Collins, you're in command. Get as far as you can. I'll stay with Hodges."

Hagen shook his head and opened his mouth to protest, but stopped. The German soldiers' systematic shouts had become chaotic. They were shouting orders unintelligibly. The barking grew to a crescendo.

One word became clear. "*Feuer!*" Fire. Screaming ensued. Eerie cries of agony and high-pitched yelps echoed through the forest. A chill wound up Hagen's spine. German soldiers were shouting over each other. One recurrent scream was, "*Hilfe!*"

"What do they keep saying?" Liam asked in a whisper.

"Help," whispered Roesia.

The shrieks and gunfire of the soldiers filled the shadowy crevices around them; no one spoke. At long last, a weight of dead silence hung in the air, and Hagen's group stood frozen in the eerie quiet.

Lt. David broke the spell. "Hagen, we should move," he said in a hushed voice.

Hagen nodded and started forward. Everyone followed closely for another hour until Hodges could no longer bear his own weight.

"We'll stay here," Lt. David said when they found a small clearing. They huddled close together shivering, their coats pulled close.

Lt. David sat hard on the ground and nodded to Hodges and Sgt. Collins as they sat close to him.

Roesia and Liam cozied up close to Hagen, but no one spoke. Minutes later, Liam leaned on him, his head resting on Hagen's shoulder. He was soon fast asleep.

The noise of engines drew Hagen's attention an hour later.

Roesia spoke in a hushed voice. "I think a road is nearby."

"It's less than a quarter kilometer away," Hagen said, and shifted his body. Liam slumped even harder against Hagen, his arm hugging Hagen's slim waist. Hagen turned and spoke to her. "You think we have any chance getting into the base now?"

She had her head bent back, taking in the scene above them, and said, "That's breathtaking."

Hagen followed her gaze and viewed the starlit night sky through the myriad of leaves and branches above his head. The moon was in full view, close to being full.

"Aoibhneas," Hagen whispered to himself.

Roesia turned to him. "I don't know, Hagen. Let's sleep on it. I may have been too brash before. My passion getting the best of me. Maybe we're better off sneaking back into Switzerland—try to find a contact and relay a message to England. Now at least we know where their main base is located. If we die trying to infiltrate the castle, then no one will ever know. Could you get us back across the border?"

Hagen nodded. "I could." He slumped against the tree, his hand resting on the crest of Liam's neck, his fingertips touching his earlobe. He looked down to his breast pocket, making certain Euan's handkerchief was there. It was. The urge to touch it was overwhelming. Even so, Hagen kept his hand on Liam's neck.

HE WOKE WITH his chin on his chest. Roesia leaned against him on one side, asleep. Hodges was mumbling somewhere close by. The sergeant made wheezing noises on the other side of the clearing and the lieutenant made short snorts.

Liam's head had settled on Hagen's lap, his arms wrapped completely around Hagen's waist. Hagen brought his hand up, hesitated, and then let his fingertips dust Liam's cheek. He did not bring his hand away, but stroked his face. Fantasies danced in his mind of Liam waking up, and sitting on his knees, and leaning in and kissing his mouth. He wanted to be lost in that lustful kiss and embrace Liam, and never let go. There was a knot in his throat, and he swallowed. Roesia coughed and shifted away from him. He glanced around him in guilt, but everyone was sleeping. He'd had such fleeting thoughts in the past of other guys but had never acted on them. For the first time, it felt urgent and palpable.

Liam's back rose, then fell. A feeling he had never experienced crept up hard. It was a need to protect. He put an arm over Liam's shoulder. Hagen's eyes closed. Sleep came quickly.

SNAPPING SOUNDS CAME from his left, and he startled awake. There was a snort of air from nostrils. Hagen turned and gasped; an enormous wolf stood in front of him. A decapitated head dangled from its mouth, and it dropped it on the ground and rolled it into his leg. Vacant eyes from the severed head stared up at him; Hagen was looking down at Ivan.

Ivan's mouth opened, and a dry, dull voice spoke. "Why did you let me suffer? Why didn't you put me out of my misery, Brother?"

HAGEN'S EYES SNAPPED open, and he shouted. He looked around him and rubbed his face, the nightmare fresh in his mind. The feeling of being helpless to luck and happenstance pervaded him. In the first year after Ivan died, the nightmares had been relentless; sometimes he put his brother out of his misery, sometimes he watched him die. Over time, the nightmares had lessened. But the feeling of being helpless was always the same when he startled awake. Hagen poked his fingers inside his breast pocket and touched the cloth, wanting to experience that surge of power again. He wanted that darkness to fill him. One thing he felt certain of—that force that had flooded through him was impervious to helplessness. He took his hand away, though, and scratched his head, considering his surroundings.

The night had receded and sunlight filtered through the treetops from above. Liam's head was still on his lap, and Roesia's eyes were opening, likely at hearing Hagen's shout. The lieutenant was awake, peering out into the woods. Sgt. Collins and Hodges were curled up and in deep slumbers.

Hagen heard it first: the rumble of engines. Lt. David glanced back to Hagen, and Hagen whispered, "A convoy. They're close by."

Hagen nudged Liam, who sat up as Hagen rose.

Hagen said, "I'll check it out."

Lt. David opened his mouth and appeared as if he was going to protest but then merely nodded.

Liam was up and volunteered. "I'll go with him."

"Both of you keep out of sight," Lt. David ordered. "Just recon."

Hagen hurried away, saying, "We will."

Several minutes later, they reached a high ridge covered with trees and overlooked a dirt road below. Hagen took out his pair of binoculars and stared down at the road. A convoy of jeeps and trucks came crawling around a bend, over a bridge, then passed in front of him. Hagen crawled back, deeper into the shadows.

"Well?" Liam whispered from his side.

Hagen held his hand up for silence and raised his glasses, then zoomed in. One man was riding in the passenger seat of the jeep, his hat off. Hagen recognized him as the bald German leader from yesterday.

Another jeep came into view that was towing a trailer with barred walls and ceiling. He zoomed in and observed the occupants of the cage. One man appeared to be unconscious, his face bloodied as he lay on the floor of the trailer. Commando Ness? The second person sat hunched over in the corner, his arms crossed over his chest and his face pale. The man looked up for a second, and though Hagen knew the man couldn't see him, their eyes seemed to meet. Corporal Kirby. The convoy moved around a curve and was out of sight.

Hagen brought his binoculars down and tucked them inside the case. "Saw Kirby. Maybe Ness, too, I'm not sure. He looked like he had been knocked unconscious."

"Commander Ford?" Liam asked.

Hagen shook his head and turned around, heading back into the forest. "No, didn't see him. Sgt. Collins said he disappeared. Maybe he escaped?"

Sgt. Collins was awake and sitting up against a tree, his face pale, and the scent of sickness wafted from him.

Lt. David hunched close to the sergeant, examining his shoulder. He lifted the collar and scrutinized a wound, which had soaked his clothing in blood. Roesia was at their side, watching them, but she looked up as Hagen came forward.

Hagen reported his finding. "Looked like the same soldiers from yesterday. They had Kirby, and I think Ness."

The lieutenant nodded, wiped his brow, and returned his attention to the sergeant's wounds.

Liam nodded down at the sergeant. "How's he doing?"

"He was bitten," Lt. David said.

The sergeant spoke, his voice hoarse. "Been better, Irish. Been bloody better. Guess I had this coming since I didn't believe in that loony story of goblins and mutts."

The lieutenant looked up at them. "Now that we have the blooming sun, I can see what we're dealing with. He has a few lacerations on one side. And a deep bite mark on his shoulder. I need some medic supplies."

"Didn't Hodges bring some from the airplane?" Liam asked, puzzled.

Hagen looked around them. Roesia asked, her pitch rising in alarm, *"Where is Hodges?"*

Lt. David was up on his feet, his eyes wide as he spun in a full circle. He pointed to a tree. "He was right there." He turned to Roesia accusatorily. "You were with him a second ago."

Roesia shook her head and looked around, baffled. "I-I don't know. We need to find him."

A male voice sounded from behind Hagen, coming from the direction of the road. Hagen made out Hodges's voice. *"Demons!"*

Hagen and Liam's eyes met, then in sync, they moved. Hagen pushed leaves and branches out of his way as he hurried, shortly leaving Liam behind. He came to the ridge and looked down.

Hodges was on the dirt road below, staring into the dark forest on the opposite side of the road, shouting, "I see you, Demons."

Hagen slid down the ridge, hurried across the road, and came up beside Hodges. The man had his rifle up to his shoulder and was pulling the trigger over and over. Nothing happened. He had not undone the safety.

"Officer Hodges," Hagen said, putting his hand out and touching his arm.

Hodges spun around, his weapon's muzzle aimed at Hagen's forehead. "Demons, I see them."

Hagen swallowed.

Liam yelped from the ridgetop. "Hodges! What the bloody hell?"

Hodges's eyes widened, the muzzle of his rifle lowered, and he spoke in a low tone. "They're out there. Demons. I saw them."

"Okay," Hagen said, nodding.

The deep-throated noise of motors caught Hagen's attention, and he whirled around. He wanted to run, but glanced over his shoulder; Liam was at the top of the embankment. He waved for Liam to fall back. The engine noise grew. A couple seconds later, two jeeps followed by a sedan rolled around the bend; a truck with a canvas top came into view next. They slowed down. The driver in the point jeep looked up over his shoulder to the soldier manning the machine-gun turret. He shouted up to the man. The words carried to Hagen. He'd asked where the two other transport trucks were. The turret man was not listening to the driver, though; he was jabbing his finger at Hagen. The driver turned and sat agape at seeing Hagen and Hodges.

Hagen grabbed Hodges's shirt, about to pull him into the nearby woods, but he hesitated. Liam was attempting a crabwalk down the incline, but the incoming convoy had distracted him and his foot slipped; he tumbled to the bottom. A dust cloud rose in the air where he rolled and landed. The driver in the first jeep gunned the engine, coming to a quick stop close to Liam. A bowl of dust blew over him.

A soldier on the back of the jeep had his rifle trained on him, and shouted for him to disarm, *"Entwaffne dich!!"*

Terror seized Hagen's heart, and he shouted, "Throw your gun down, Liam, and lay down!" He yelled in German, *"Nicht schießen… Wir geben auf."* *Don't fire. We surrender.*

Liam tossed his gun and put his hands up. Hagen stepped away from Hodges, tossing his weapon down in front of him.

What are we going to do? He looked into the nearby woods, his instinct being to run, but he held fast.

The second jeep pulled close to Hagen. The German's words being shouted were taking a second for his mind to translate.

The soldier standing up in the jeep's rear screamed down at Hodges. *"Entwaffne dich!"* *Drop your weapons.* Hodges continued to hold his rifle in his hands, the barrel lowered to the ground.

Several soldiers were jumping out of the back of the truck and hurrying forward. They were not wearing regular soldier uniforms, but black with red bands over their arms decorated with swastikas on them.

Hagen held his hands up high and spoke to Hodges. "Hodges, throw your gun down." Hodges did not do anything, though. He continued to stupidly hold his rifle and stare at the soldiers coming from the truck, their guns trained on their group. His eyes were no longer wild and distant, but focused.

He muttered, Hagen barely catching the words. "My God, the SS Gestapo."

Hagen didn't know how Hodges could tell the difference between regular soldiers and SS Gestapo. He had heard rumors of the Nazi secret police from friends and officers, but only rumors.

Liam was dragged across the road and pushed next to Hagen; both of them were then forced to kneel on the roadside. Two approaching soldiers were shouting for Hodges to drop his weapon; one butted the stock of the rifle into Hodges's stomach. Hodges grunted and fell to his knees. A second man snuck up on Hodges and knocked him on the back of his head; Hodges duly dropped his weapon and fell onto his side.

The back door of the sedan opened and a pair of slender legs appeared before a tall woman emerged. She had auburn hair, wore a black pants, sunglasses, and held a cigarette between thin fingers. The chauffeur got out, closing his door, then withdrew a cigarette and lit it. The woman stepped up and regarded each of them, finally reaching Hagen.

"*Wer bist du?*" she demanded. Hagen had difficulty thinking, and then realized she wanted to know who they were.

Hagen shook his head and opened his mouth. His heart pounded, and it was difficult to form any coherent thought. His instinct had been to run, but now he was frozen in place, unable to move or speak. Something flitted at a distance, and he glanced up. A figure dropped from the bottom of the truck onto the ground, rolled into a crouch, and sprinted out of sight. No one had seen that but Hagen.

The woman repeated her question, asking who they were. Hagen brought his attention back to the woman and shook his head as if he didn't understand what she was saying.

A man limped toward the woman; his insignia denoted him as a German officer.

He smiled down at Hagen. "General Wagner and Dr. Mengele will be pleased to know we found some spies. They have the look of Brits, don't you think?"

The woman raised the cigarette to her mouth, the corner curving up. "*Tommies*. It will be nice to show these trophies to the Führer when he comes to the banquet."

The officer turned to his men, ordering a few to split off and search the area for more. A German soldier called out to the officer, Hagen rolled the words around in his head. The convoy had two other transport trucks that had been with them but were now missing.

The officer waved his hand in what seemed to be anger. "*Finde sie.*" *Find them.*

Roesia's voice called from the ridge above them, *"Hallo, Jungs."* *Hello boys.*

Hagen, the SS woman, the SS officer, the SS Gestapo soldiers all snapped their eyes to the top of the ridge where Roesia stood. Hagen tried his best to comprehend what he was seeing. She was wearing her fatigue pants, but her top was undone and her breasts filling her bra were on complete display.

The officer in front of Hagen reacted first. He brandished a semiautomatic pistol and began to take aim at Roesia. The back end of the truck suddenly exploded into a ball of fire, a concussive wave hitting the men closest to it, throwing them in the air. The strong wind from the blast knocked into Hagen and he fell backward. The woman and officer fell. The chauffeur was lying facedown, a smoldering piece of metal impaled the back of his head. Gunfire erupted from the ridge as a second concussive bang sounded out. An SS soldier near the jeep was thrown into its side and fell to the ground, motionless. Hagen glanced up at the ridge. The silhouettes of Lt. David and Sgt. Collins spread out, and started firing. Hagen was frozen, unable to move.

A single-fire pistol was being fired. Hagen looked up at the sound, shocked to see Commander Ford moving down the road in a slow walk. His Browning semiautomatic held in one hand. He gun fired again and the report was deafening. A round hit a soldier's face, causing brain debris to shower the ground. Ford's pistol bucked in his hand—a sharp thunderclap, followed by a blend of four more shots. An SS trooper grabbed his neck, dropping to his knees, while another staggered backward, his rifle firing randomly in the air. Soldiers scrambled for cover. A few shot at him. Rounds hit the commander but did not stop him.

Short bursts of gunfire continued to come from the top of the ridge. Hagen gaped at the action in front of him. Five soldiers moved into the forest toward Lt. David and Sgt. Collins. The two were suddenly swept off their feet and disappeared into the woods; the other men were gone just as quickly, and then amber eyes looked at him from the shadows.

Hagen crawled past Liam, reaching for one of the dropped rifles just as the SS officer got up on one knee. The hooked-nosed SS officer brought his pistol up and aimed it at Hagen's forehead, but Hodges jumped and knocked into Hagen, pushing him out of the way. A sharp crack sounded, and Hodges fell to his knees, holding his stomach as he wavered. The SS officer fired point-blank at Hodges's face. Blood and chunky, fleshy debris splattered over Hagen's clothes.

Liam rolled to a dropped German automatic rifle, came up one on knee, and sighted. He screamed out loud and fired. A series of ear-splitting bangs erupted from the weapon; the front of the hook-nosed SS officer's shirt tore open in several places, and the man stumbled and fell.

Liam did not let up on the trigger. The barrel pulled upward, and Liam's rounds streaked sideways and hit the woman. She too was mowed down. He fired at the nearby jeep where soldiers had taken cover, the window shattered as sparks spewed up around the radiator and sharp *pings* resounded. He didn't release the trigger until the gun clicked empty. He had managed to miss both soldiers, who in turn stood and aimed at Liam. Hagen shoved Liam to the ground, the officer's pistol in his hand, but he never fired.

The men were shielded by the side of the jeep. However, both men's eyes widened as a force struck them from behind. They jolted forward and rammed into the side of the door, then fell out of sight. Shrieks followed, which turned to cries of horrid pain. The noises then grew faint as the men seemed to be dragged out into the forest.

A round from somewhere ricocheted off the jeep, hitting close to Hagen. A divot popped up from the road a couple of feet away. Hagen clutched Liam's shirt and humped it to the forest for cover. He tripped, fell, taking Liam with him, and they rolled down a slope onto the lush leaf-littered ground. When Hagen sat up, two soldiers were in pursuit of them, coming off the road into the forest. Liam was struggling to rise, but Hagen hurriedly pushed him down, face-first into the leafy layered ground. Hagen lay on his back and waited for the shot that never came. After a few moments, he got up on his elbows and looked around him, but the soldiers were gone... *Not quite.* One soldier's thrashing feet were visible at the base of a bush and then, in the next moment, were pulled inside, a thick trail of blood left behind.

Liam sat up, pulling wet leaves out of his mouth, and asked in a high-pitched tone, "Which way—"

Hagen put a hand over his mouth, and told him, "Shhh, there's something in the forest."

What's worse? The forest or the road?

Hagen gripped Liam's hand and crawled up the slope to the road; the firefight had subsided. The jeep smoldered from the radiator, riddled with bullet holes. Hagen crouched, trotted to the side of the sedan, and knelt down with Liam to his side. Hagen realized he had left the pistol where he'd fallen. He peeked over the hood to discover the last two soldiers facing Commander Ford.

An SS soldier with blood seeping from a head wound staggered in a zigzag fashion on the road, holding his rifle with both hands and heading toward Commander Ford. The commander was in the middle of the road, hunched over, one hand pressed against his side, his teeth bared in pain. Blood drooled from his mouth. Hagen glanced up and saw Lt. David take aim with his rifle, yet he never fired. He stared down at his gun with a bewildered look and removed the clip. He had to be out. He patted his side, searching his pocket for more ammunition. Hagen returned his attention to the scene before him, helpless.

Commander Ford brought his pistol up, but it clicked—empty. The SS soldier raised his rifle as Roesia's voice announced in German, "*Fick Hitler!*"

The SS soldier started to spin, but it was too late. Roesia opened fire; the man staggered backward, his body crumpling to the ground. The firefight was over.

Hagen stared at the corpses littering the road. Lt. David and Sgt. Collins made their way down the slope at a steady pace. Roesia continued to hold her rifle to her shoulder and gawked at the man she had just killed. Hagen moved over to the elegantly dressed Nazi woman who had been shot. Blood streamed from the corner her mouth and she gulped at air, her eyes open and reflecting a sense of dread. Liam came beside to him and knelt next to Hodges's body, which lay facedown. Liam placed a hand on the back of Hodges's head, then sat down and cried into his knees.

Sgt. Collins called out. "O'Malley, you shot?"

Lt. David was trotting forward in front of Hagen, and yelled, "O'Malley, Messer. You okay? Sergeant, see to Commander Ford."

Hagen barely paid them attention, shifting his focus to Commander Ford who stumbled toward him. Hagen hurried forward, catching him as he fell. He laid him gently on his back. The commander's breathing was raspy and uneven as he gripped Hagen's hand, pushing an object into his palm as he focused on him.

Commander Ford's eyes fluttered closed as though he fought to keep them open for a moment longer. "A-a spy from Wehr Wolff Castle helped me. S-said he is one of the few Wehr Wolff left. The M-mutante Wolf Program is not the worst. Hagen, you must go to the castle. You must... You must... defeat... Adolf. *I don't know how.*"

"*Who?*" Hagen asked.

The commander's gaze grew distant, "S-somehow, the spy showed me a vision of what happens if Adolf isn't stopped. He will gain world power, and then all of humanity will be turned to..." His eyes became glassy.

Hagen let Commander Ford's head down gently and stood. Roesia had been behind him but stepped aside and spoke with a concerned voice. "Hagen?"

Hagen walked past Lt. David in a daze.

"Hagen, you okay? You shot?" Lt. David asked.

Hagen shook, his throat constricting. "N-no, sir." He opened his fingers and looked at what Commander Ford had placed inside his hand. A sizable gold medallion lay in his palm, a golden necklace attached to it. Hagen closed his fingers over it as a memory flashed through his mind. His father, long ago had a similar piece of golden jewelry when his brother died—but his memory of that period of time was fuzzy.

Although what rattled him was not Commander Ford's death, disturbing as it was, or the flash recall of his father having been given a similar medallion.

No—for the briefest of moments, when the commander had placed that cool metal in his hand, he'd had that sensation of pure unadulterated adrenaline coursing through his veins. A darkness so pure and addictive filled him for the briefest of spells.

Hagen gripped the medallion tightly in his trembling hand. He so wanted that sensation to return.

Ten: Time to Don the Nazi Uniforms

Somewhere in Wehr Forest

HAGEN STOOD AT the edge of the small canyon close to the bridge. The transport truck Commander Ford had blown up had turned from an inferno to smoldered ruins. After rolling several feet backward with the initial explosion, half of the tail end had stopped on the bridge. The tires positioned on the bridge were melted to the structure. He glanced over his shoulder and observed Lt. David hauling a corpse toward him to pitch over the side.

Hagen stared down into the ravine where he too had been helping to haul the Nazi corpses. He could not see to the bottom—jagged rocks jutted out and blocked his view. It was unfitting to dump the bodies of Commander Ford or Hodges with the Nazi corpses, so they'd placed them on the back of the charred truck's ruins; the scent of burnt flesh was now palpable. Hagen tore cloth from his shirt to tie it over his nose and mouth, but the stench still became a taste in his mouth that made him want to vomit.

Hagen stared across the chasm and reflected. The brutal shootout that had led to Officer Alan Hodges's demise, and the sudden appearance of Ford and then his end, had left a deep mark on not just Hagen, but everyone. Liam appeared to be crushed by Hodges's death. He had not spoken since the shooting ended. Hagen recalled that Liam had told him Hodges was like a father to him.

Lt. David came to his side and said in a breathless voice, "Grab the legs, Hagen. I'm getting tired." Hagen bent over, grabbed the ankles, and they flung a body over the side. The corpse rolled down the rocky incline and vanished into the gap.

Lt. David rested with his hands on his knees as he stared across the bridge to the road on the other side. He grumped and said, "Where did they blimey go? I didn't tell them to go past the bend."

Hagen had related to Lt. David what he'd overheard the driver say about missing transport trucks. The lieutenant had become alert and mumbled something about wishing he'd known about that sooner. He'd ordered Sgt. Collins and Liam across the bridge to see if they could find anything around the nearby bend.

New fear gripped Hagen. He remembered the amber eyes and soldiers being dragged away.

"Sir." Hagen swallowed, his voice gaining Lt. David's attention, his gaze questioning. Hagen felt his stomach tighten with regret for not telling Lt. David the additional information sooner.

Roesia came up behind them, dragging a body. She let the legs drop to the ground, and then as she came abreast of Hagen. She sat down hard. "I need some water."

Lt. David handed over his canteen.

Roesia took it, and said, "Thank you, Graham."

Lt. David turned to Hagen. "What is it, Messer?"

Roesia interrupted them. "Here they come."

Hagen whipped his head around and sighed in relief.

Sgt. Collins and Liam had appeared around the bend farther down the road and were approaching the bridge at a trot.

Lt. David wiped his brow and muttered, "Well, thank God. What were you going to say, Messer?"

Hagen shook his head. "Nothing, sir." He did not want to disclose what he'd seen yet, though he didn't know why. He touched his shirt close to his chest, where the medallion hung from his neck.

Lt. David looked down at the corpse Roesia had been towing and observed, "These gents aren't regular soldiers. Their uniforms are SS. The Waffen?"

Hagen nodded. "Hodges said they were Gestapo. But they're Waffen-SS?"

Roesia confirmed Hagen's observation. "SS Gestapo are the secret police. These guys are almost certainly the Nazi combat unit known as the Waffen-SS. Regular soldiers are just young men from local towns and farms. These guys are nothing but hired thugs with few scruples."

Liam and Sgt. Collins passed the burning vehicle, then stopped in front of them. Sgt. Collins was hunched over, and then he knelt to try to catch his breath. Liam was not breathing as hard, but his face had blanched.

Lt. David brought the silver case from his pocket, dug out a cigarette with a shaky hand, and placed it between his lips. After pulling out a match, he managed to light it, then drew on his cigarette and asked in a faraway voice, "What'd you see, boyos?"

"Dead Nazis, sir," Sgt. Collins answered.

"Beg your pardon?" Roesia asked with a puzzled expression.

"The trucks are not far back around the bend," Liam said. "A tree fell in front of one, and I think they stopped to move it. The lot of them were grub…"

"Grub?" Lt. David asked, sounding annoyed.

"Bloody Nazis," Sgt. Collins said. "Whole lot of them been someone's grub. Severed arms and legs everywhere."

Hagen did not meet anyone's eyes and kept his mouth shut.

Lt. David stared out into the forest with newly appreciative eyes. "Whatever it is, they have not attacked us, and I assume it's the same thing that killed that Nazi party that was hunting for us last night. We've been fortunate so far, coupled, no doubt, with some teamwork."

Liam looked at Roesia, and for the first time since Hodges died, his eyes lit up. "Say, lass, or, uh, Roesia. Well played earlier with your show. Saved our arses."

Lt. David nodded in agreement as he puffed out a cloud of smoke. "We've shown we are quite formidable working together. It's why we're still standing."

Sgt. Collins spoke from the ground, "Blimey! Let's pat each other's arses later, Lieutenant. I say we commandeer the one good jeep with a couple of shots in it and the sedan with its crack in the window. Then give them fickin' Nazis our prodigious middle finger and skedaddle."

Roesia said, "I agree. We can push this truck off the bridge along with the inoperable jeep and head south. I think I saw some duffel bags in the jeep with some soldier uniforms sticking out of them?"

Liam's eyes lit up. "Some fancy ones, at that."

Roesia nodded. "Hagen and I could probably provide cover if we encounter anyone on the way and manage get us through. We could be close to the southern border by nightfall and sneak into Switzerland. We can hopefully find a way to relay a message to England, tell them we located a main secret base where the Wehrmacht's Mutante Wolf Program is being housed."

The bridge crackled and whined next to them, causing Hagen and Roesia to move away from the groaning structure. Sgt. Collins was up on his feet in a flash, as well. Suddenly, one side girder snapped and the bridge tilted, which caused the entire truck to jostle up and down.

Lt. David yelled, "Move back!"

The end of the bridge buckled and, a second later, collapsed. The truck came down on its bottom frame and teeter-tottered. Then the entire bridge fell. A cacophony of noise reverberated around them as the structure plunged down into the ravine and smashed to pieces. Roesia covered her ears from the harsh sounds. The transport truck teetered for another moment on the ledge, and then it too tipped and was gone, crashing below.

No one spoke for several moments as the metal and other bridge debris battered down the ravine until it finally grew quiet.

Sgt. Collins tossed his hands up in the air, and hollered, "Just brilliant! Dog bollocks! What's bloody next?"

Lt. David's shortened used-up cigarette was clenched between his lips, as he stared over the cliff. He flicked it away, rubbed the back of his neck, and muttered, "*Shite*."

Hagen swallowed. "We have to go to Wehr Wolff Castle." Everyone turned to him. "C-commander Ford said I must. He knew something."

Sgt. Collins grumbled and coughed up phlegm. "Look, Kraut, not sure if you were asleep, but we actually made a botch job here; we're lucky to be breathing. Sorry, Lieutenant. But pure luck. Luck wasn't with Kirby, Commander Ford, or those other blokes. You may have made me a believer in them queer mutants, but I'm glad the professor got her senses finally. How in the bloody fecking hell are we going to get into this Wehr Wolff Castle? Not to mention I feel right buggered. I'm zonked. And no offense to you, lass, or Kraut, or you, Irishman, or you, Lieutenant, for that matter, but our best fighters have all come to a sticky end."

Liam coughed and said quietly, "We have the explosives again from Commander Ford." Commander Ford had indeed been carrying the explosives that they'd brought with them and left them on the side of the road near the destroyed truck." Liam shrugged. "And maybe these guys were going to Wehr Wolff Castle? We could slip inside and destroy their base."

Roesia spoke in a hushed voice. "I know they were going to the castle. This woman that was killed. S-she was Gunda Lawerenze." Hagen, along with everyone else, turned to her. She swallowed. "I don't see how this is possible. But this is the woman I was supposed to impersonate when we went to the dam. I have to say this is either a stroke of good luck or quite a coincidence."

"Who was Lawerenze?" Lt. David asked.

"She was formerly a surgeon," Roesia answered. "But she later changed her focus and specialized in genetics, and she had a fascination with the occult."

"Genetics?" Hagen asked.

Lt. David answered, "Heard about genetics on the BBC. It looks at how parents pass traits to their children through biological means."

"In this case, though," Roesia said, "Lawerenze, I think, was looking at how to pass specific traits of a certain species to humans."

"Dammit, woman, the point," Sgt. Collins growled. He nodded to the bend in the road close to the torched truck. "Anyone could be coming around that corner, and bullets can travel just fine without a bridge."

Roesia pursed her lips and continued, "The descendants of the Wehr Wolff family have been living in this castle for generations."

Sgt. Collins shook his head. "Not this blooming conversation again."

"And the Wehr Wolff family are werewolves, or neah? I was confused after yesterday," Liam questioned.

"Most of them." Roesia nodded.

"*Most?*" Sgt. Collins asked. "You daft woman, what does *most* mean? It's you can, or you can't."

"I don't know every detail," Roesia said. "Some members of the Wehr Wolff family could turn themselves into a werewolf. They bred with normal humans, though, no interbreeding. This means their children could carry a passive gene. Like Justine said, just because you carry the Wehr Wolff blood doesn't mean you can change."

Liam scratched his head. "It doesn't?"

"No," Roesia said. "You need to be infected by a werewolf first. Any of us could be turned to one, but members of the Wehr Wolff family are said to have genetics that make them into the strongest werewolf known. And some even had powers in human form, like seeing the future, controlling people's minds, staying young, or even showing other people visions of the future." Roesia rubbed her cheek and stared out at the canyon. She wiped at specks of blood on her face, but instead smudged them and made a mess.

"So the Nazis," Lt. David said, "obviously wanted to seize someone with this family line to conduct experiments with them and harness these powers."

"Yes," Roesia said. She took a breath and met Lt. David's eyes. "The Nazis seized Wehr Wolff Castle sometime in the mid-1930s, long before war was declared. The Wehr Wolff descendants inside fled. The Nazis caught only a few servants and guards. Apparently, there is now a spy in the castle. Outside of the castle, as Justine told us, the Nazis seized the wolves of Wehr Forest, or, uh, wehrwolves, I guess. And then the Nazis got lucky, and caught this Euan Hartley."

Lt. David stared at the bend of the road. "I hate to interrupt this narrative, but I have to agree with the sergeant. We probably should be moving soon before someone finds us here."

"Right," Roesia said. "Well, simply put, the Nazis have borrowed research from Lawerenze, who was working with apes. I don't know what their end goal is. But her being here probably means they are closer to their end."

Liam asked Lt. David, "So you think these, uh, wehrwolves, are the ones who attacked the Nazis in the forest last night?"

Lt. David shrugged. "Makes the most logical sense to me." He glanced at Roesia.

She too shrugged. "The Nazis were quite methodical in capturing everything. Maybe they missed some. I would think the wolves of Wehr Forest would be fearful, though, and not come out of hiding to kill armed men. There doesn't seem to be a shortage of food."

Silence ensued for a few seconds. The lieutenant broke the quiet. "Why do you think we should go in, Hagen?"

Hagen licked his cracked lips. "Someone talked to Commander Ford and helped him here. I have a feeling the Nazis are close, and we should at least reconnoiter the area. Commander Ford felt there was something worse to fear than the Nazis' program."

Sgt. Collins grumbled, but Lt. David put his hand up, gesturing for him to remain quiet.

Hagen gazed out at the mountain range. There were dark clouds that swirled around a peak, but a colossal-sized castle was partially visible. "And we're close."

Lt. David asked, "How many explosives do we have?"

Roesia answered. "Probably enough to demolish a well-built dam."

"What about a castle built hundreds of years ago?"

She answered, "The pressure from the water helps destroy a dam, but gravity could do the same to this castle. My source showed me the schematics of a castle where the experiments started. I presume it's the Wehr Wolff Castle. I would need to observe the area first."

She looked up at the distant castle and spoke, a renewed conviction in her voice. "Hagen and I could get inside. I can impersonate this Dr. Lawerenze and inspect the area. Like Hagen said, I can at least reconnoiter the area and we can leave at nighttime."

The lieutenant rubbed his chin. "We might be captured or killed going south; if we do this, then at least we may do something that could help win the war. And you think this Dr. Mengele or anyone else in this castle has never met this Lawerenze?"

She shook her head. "In the original mission, when I was going to impersonate her to gain access to the dam, the answer was no. Lawerenze was in Austria. The program is headed by a General Wagner, and Lawerenze has only been in Germany a few times over the last year, and mostly in Munich. This Mengele stays in his labs, doesn't like to go out. Wagner likes to go to Berlin, so it's possible they met. But we do look similar."

Hagen spoke up. "I don't think she or that officer met anyone there. Before the truck exploded, they made it sound like they were meeting everyone at Wehr Wolff Castle for the first time." Hagen looked between Liam and Lt. David. "And Lt. David, you can't stay back here. There's something in the forest."

"What?" Lt. David asked. Hagen told him and the others about the Nazi soldiers being swept off their feet and dragged back in the forest.

Sgt. Collins shook his head, and muttered, "Bloody hell. That's comforting news."

"They have not tried to hurt us," Roesia pointed out.

Lt. David nodded and sighed. "If there's Nazi uniforms, we'll go with you. When we get there, get us out of sight so we don't need to talk to anyone."

The sergeant sighed, muttered unintelligibly, and rolled his eyes. "So, any of you blimey idiots carrying a machine gun armed with silver bullets? That's the myth, isn't it? Kill a werewolf with silver?"

"Actually," Hagen said, "I have silver bullets."

The sergeant's eyes widened. "I was bloody joking."

Hagen stuck his hand inside the leather satchel hanging on his shoulder. He brought out a Smith and Wesson six-cylinder revolver with one hand. He dipped his other hand into the bag and removed a number of silver bullets, displaying them in his palm.

"From Justine. There are lots of rounds in here, too."

Sgt. Collins narrowed his eyes. "That old cuckoo gave you those?"

Liam looked down at the bullets and back up to Hagen. "You think it really takes silver to kill one of those?"

Sgt. Collins answered, "Well, boyo. We shot a buck full of lead in them bugger mutants last night, and they kept attacking. But ol' witch of Wehr Forest shot them one time before they keeled over. A pound says she had silver bullets."

"And," Hagen said, "she put this in here." He brought out a wrapped stick of dynamite.

Lt. David's eyes widened. "Let me see that." He turned the explosive in his hand. "How many?"

"Two," Hagen said. "I was going to put the dynamite somewhere more secure than this bag."

"Good idea," Lt. David said. "Look in the sedan's boot. I saw a few suitcases in there earlier when I was looking for more ammunition. Plastic explosives are not volatile, but dynamite is another story."

Roesia closed Hagen's fingers over the bullets lying in his palm. "And let's hope we don't need those."

As Lt. David and Liam walked down the road toward the vehicles, Lt. David commented, "We'll see if we can push that jeep off the bridge."

Roesia started away, and then said over a shoulder, "I'm going to see what clothes this Dr. Lawerenze brought."

"Kraut," Sgt. Collins said. Hagen met the sergeant's eyes. The man scratched the scraggly whiskers on his chin and nodded to the revolver in Hagen's hand. "I shall turn into one of the things now that I'm bitten?"

Hagen shrugged and lied. "No, it's not certain."

Sgt. Collins grunted. "Rubbish. Kraut, I hope you do better lying at this castle." He poked Hagen's chest. "Be sure to put one of those in me if I turn into one of those things."

Hagen didn't answer as Sgt. Collins turned away, but he didn't have to. Hagen brought his gaze to their distant goal. Fog swirled at the base of the castle, and the massive building went in and out of sight.

He had not mentioned his real reason for wanting to go. Hagen pulled the medallion out from inside his shirt and laid the gold piece in his palm. The handkerchief was one doorway to that feeling of power. But this golden jewel had brought on that sensation of pure lustful darkness. He wanted to bathe in that.

Darkness thundered through him without warning and beckoned him. He tightened his fist over the medallion and swallowed. He wanted to quaff down that...that pure vitality. The feeling was gone in the next moment. Hagen desperately wanted it to return and gripped the medallion harder, but nothing came.

He brought the handkerchief that belonged to Euan out of his pocket. He closed his eyes and concentrated. The image of a dark cell was in his mind, and there was a sharp pain in his lower extremities. He focused. The memories of the past few weeks flitted through his mind. Then he felt it again. It was faint, but it was something. Euan was transforming into a werewolf. A surge of power flooded through Hagen's body. In the next moment, it was gone, and he felt the helplessness of the situation around him.

Hagen swallowed and put the cloth back in his pocket. He kept the medallion in his hand and stared down at it.

He had to go to Wehr Wolff Castle.

He jumped at Roesia's voice. "What's it say? Oh, sorry, didn't mean to scare you."

Hagen shook his head. "It's okay." He looked down at the piece. There were two types of inscriptions on the back. One in a language he didn't know, and the other was symbols. "I don't know. It's not English or German."

Roesia touched his hand and focused on the inscription. "It's Latin. Says 'Die or live, live for your heart.'" Her finger brushed the hieroglyphics, and she said, "This, though, is something much, much older than the other inscription. I'm no historian, but it makes me think this is some kind of Egyptian relic."

Hagen furrowed his brow. "Egyptian?"

"I don't know if it is," Roesia corrected. "But when I did my research, I learned the Wehr Wolff lineage began long ago in Egypt." Her finger brushed the hieroglyphics once more. "I wonder, who was this spy?"

Hagen had no answer.

Roesia continued her queries. "And I overheard him say Adolf. He meant Adolf Hitler? Adolf Eichmann?"

Hagen shook his head in puzzlement. "I've heard of Hitler, but Adolf Eichmann?"

She grimaced and looked out toward the bridge. "He's head of the SS Gestapo, and before I left for England, I heard he'd orchestrated German Jewish citizens to be sent to a ghetto."

Sgt. Collins called to Roesia, but she turned and walked away. Hagen tucked the medallion back inside his shirt and took a soothing breath.

Several moments later, Roesia bent over the trunk of the sedan to take out a black blouse that had two bright red bands with swastikas on the upper sleeves. Hagen assumed it had belonged to Gunda Lawerenze. A second suitcase had clothes for the Nazi officer who had been killed. She found documents that confirmed him as a Colonel Brose. Roesia told everyone she had learned from her sources that Lawerenze and Brose were regular travel companions. Brose had been a man of power before the war and had amassed more wealth by liquidating assets from Jewish people. Roesia guessed Lawerenze used Brose for her purposes, and he used her for his own needs.

Brose's clothes were large and would be a good fit for the sergeant. Hagen gave them to him as Sgt. Collins observed, "He sure was a big Nazi."

Hagen started toward the sedan, noticing no one had carted the chauffeur's body off to the ravine. He turned the corpse over and avoided staring down at the dead man's face. The chauffeur was the only one who had not had been killed with bullets, which meant Hagen did not have to worry about having blood-soaked clothes touching his body, but there was a foul smell of shit. Hagen removed the shirt and jacket, and rummaged in the trunk and found some pants that were the colonel's and too large. He would have to cinch them shut with a pin.

He stood next to the trunk, used it as cover to change, and removed his filthy pants. He pushed out of his drawers that were even worse, and put on the pants. He stupidly held the waistband with one hand and stretched it out as far as possible. They were over three times the size of his waist.

Liam came around the trunk's end, holding clothes under his arm. Hagen pinched the waistband closed with one hand so they would not fall off. Liam wore a German uniform, a cap on his head. He looked like a true Nazi. Hagen noticed Liam had green fatigues tucked under one arm. Liam stared down at Hagen's pants, and then hooked a couple of fingers over the waistband; his fingers brushed against Hagen's abdomen, and he pulled the waistband loose as he leaned over, taking a peek.

Liam brought his green gaze up and smiled as he said, "Might need some drawers; nethers may get frosty. These might fit." He handed over the clothing with a grin.

Hagen took them, his face hot, and nodded. Liam made his way toward Lt. David where he helped push the nonfunctional jeep toward the fallen bridge.

Hagen let the over-sized pants drop and quickly pulled on the drawers, then the pants Liam had brought him. A much better fit, but still loose. He pulled the belt off the dead chauffeur and put it on. He then grabbed the man's wrists and pulled him down the slope, then into the forest. He froze before going too far, scanned the forest, then decided to pull the body only a short distance farther.

He lugged the dead body past a few trees, where a snapping noise caused him to glance up. Two wolves were watching him. They were the largest he had ever seen—the words *aoibhneas* and *breathtaking* echoed in his mind. He had hunted in these forests as a lad with his brother, but had never come this far afield. *Maybe that's why I have never seen them?*

Hagen didn't move, though his heart hammered against his chest. The wolves' ears were up and their eyes alert. Then two more came to flank the others. More underbrush was disturbed close by, and other wolves joined the group, but none moved closer. Hagen let the dead man's wrists go, stepping back at a slow pace. He touched his waist to find he had left his weapon by the car.

He kept his gaze fixed on them as Roesia's voice called into the woods, "Hagen?"

He stepped backward, and his heel hit a solid mass, causing him to trip and fall onto his arse. He quickly scrambled to his feet, keeping the wolves in sight. They had not moved. He glanced down to see what he had stumbled over and saw the body of one of the soldiers who had been dragged into the woods. Except the man was not dead; his eyes were pleading as blood bubbled past his lips. The memory of the deer came to mind and his brother whispered, "Put him out of his misery." Hagen was frozen, though. He brought his attention back to the wolves, which had multiplied and were watching him.

Roesia's called again more urgently. "Hagen?" Underbrush crackled behind him, and still, Hagen couldn't move or speak until the wolves spun suddenly and melded back into the shadows.

"Hagen?" Roesia came through the brush to his side. "What's—" She drew in breath, a hand over her mouth, when she discovered the wounded soldier.

"G-gun," Hagen stammered, holding out his hands for the rifle she was carrying. She handed it over, and Hagen brought it up, aiming it at the man's head. The gun shook as he took a breath and whispered, "Look away." He was not certain who he actually meant to turn away. Roesia? The man? Himself? Roesia wheeled around just as he pulled the trigger. The report echoed through the forest as Hagen turned and stomped out of the forest with Roesia at his back.

Lt. David was trotting in their direction as Hagen came to the road. "Everything alright?"

Hagen nodded. Roesia leaned against the car, brought her hand shakily to brush her cheek, and in a numb voice said, "Sgt. Collins is in the car already. Feels sick. I'm going to splash some water on me, change, and then we should go. I'll do my best with the makeup while we drive."

Hagen nodded, then picked up the chauffeur's cap and brushed it off. After surveying the woods once more, he opened the driver's door and sat hard on the seat.

Hagen removed Euan's handkerchief from his pocket and focused. A dark brooding energy surged through him, and he no longer felt helpless and vulnerable. Best of all, he forgot about that man reaching up to him.

Eleven: Dr. Mengele, General Wagner, and Georg Martz

OVER AN HOUR later, Hagen drove the sedan down a dirt road that was surrounded by a sea of tall spruce trees on both sides. He glanced at the sergeant in the seat next to him. He was fast asleep, his chin resting on his chest. He wore the SS colonel's hat, and though Sgt. Collins was a husky man, the colonel's clothes still fit him loosely. Hagen glanced up in the rearview mirror. Roesia stared out the window and wrung her hands in her lap. Behind them, Lt. David and Liam drove the jeep.

As they went up an incline and came to the crest of a hill, the specter of Wehr Wolff Castle seemed to fill the windshield. It was surreal, settled on top of a mountain ridge as it was. Unlike the dilapidated Earl Groscz Castle, several towers reached into the air to the sides of the vast stone structure. A misty fog clung to the upper portions.

Hagen straightened, staring down the road at an upcoming sentry post. "Roesia."

She leaned forward and stared between the seats and through the windshield. A small guard tower was set off the road, with stone pillars supporting a metal gate arm that crossed over the road. Two small houses were nestled in the trees. A barbwire fence ran from both ends of the tower, out into the forest. Hagen looked out toward the forest and observed that soldiers were walking down the fence line.

Breathe, Hagen. Hagen nudged the sergeant's shoulder. He jerked awake, straightening in his seat. He looked around him, and his eyes widened upon seeing the sentries.

Roesia said from the back, "Pretend you're sleeping, Sarge."

Sgt. Collins mumbled and put his chin back down on his chest.

Roesia took a deep breath and said, "Hagen, just remember, keep it short. Don't offer any information."

Hagen nodded.

He pulled to a halt in front of three guards who were standing in the road, each of them holding a rifle. A watchtower was behind the gate on one side. At the top, a soldier manned an MG42 machine gun that was pointed down at their vehicle. A weapon, which Hagen knew, could fire 1,800 rounds per minute.

Hagen rolled his window down as the guard approached. Hagen faced forward and tapped on the steering wheel, trying his best to display an impatient manner. Gravel crunched as the guard came up to his door. He sighed, scooted his hat up on his head, and turned to the guard, pursing his lips. The man was not looking at Hagen, though, but gawked over at Sgt. Collins, no doubt registering the SS officer uniform. The guard quickly peered back at Roesia. Hagen looked into the rearview mirror and saw she was staring out her window with a relaxed posture.

A soldier behind the first guard whispered, *"Es ist ihnen." It is them.*

The guard swallowed and nodded, then said in a low tone, *"Identität."*

Hagen spoke German with his best impatient tone. "We have had a long journey, comrade. This is Dr. Gunda Lawerenze. You have her on your docket, don't you? She is to meet with Dr. Mengele and General Wagner."

Hagen jerked his thumb to indicate the sergeant. "If he wakes up, I'll let you deal with him."

Roesia asked from the backseat, "Is there a problem? General Wagner awaits our arrival. And I want to get out of this car."

Hagen said over his shoulder, "No, Doctor. No problems." He met the guard's gaze who peered back at Roesia, no doubt hearing every word she said. He leaned in. "You do know that General Wagner does not like to be kept waiting. Or we to be kept here any longer?"

The guard shook his head and stepped backward, waving his hands in front of him. *"Nein, nein, du bist klar."*

He yelled over his shoulder to raise the gate. The metal arm went up. The guard brought his right arm up in a salute, and shouted, *"Heil, Hitler!"*

Hagen said in a low tone, "Heil, Hitler," and pushed on the gas. He looked up at his mirror, holding his breath. Lt. David followed him in the jeep without incident. Liam saluted the guard with the Nazi salute for good measure. They rounded a curve and the sentry was no longer in sight.

The sergeant asked in a low voice, "We clear?"

"Yeah," Hagen said.

The sergeant looked up and raised an arse cheek as a loud fart blurted out. The air in the car instantly smelled like a carton full of rotten eggs.

"Bloody hell," the sergeant said with an exasperated tone. "I didn't think I could hold that much longer."

Roesia's hand covered her face. Hagen could not roll his window down fast enough. A cool breeze whipped through the car and the fresh scent of spruce woods thankfully filled it.

"Pull over," Sgt. Collins demanded, his face pale. Hagen pulled to the side of the road, and the jeep stopped a few paces behind them. The sergeant didn't wait for the sedan to stop, but was out the door and hurrying into the forest.

Hagen's stomach was knotted, his hands sweaty, and his nerves frayed from all the attacks. Hyper-alert to the situation, he suddenly became aware that they faced the possibility of death by following through with this.

He glanced at the rearview mirror and said, "I hope this works. You said your source showed you schematics of the base?"

Roesia nodded. "It wasn't much detail. He had to take them back, but I got a look, yes."

"You said on the way here that there was an airbase on one side of the castle? Why wouldn't Dr. Lawerenze just fly in?"

Roesia stared out her window before finally answering. "I don't know, Hagen." The passenger door opened, and the sergeant sat heavily into the seat. Hagen looked over at him; the sergeant glanced back.

"Let's go, Kraut, and have tea with your Nazi friends."

Hagen pulled out, gritting his teeth at being called Kraut again. On their way, they passed one more sentry station, but no one asked for identification, simply letting them pass. Sgt. Collins pulled out three rectangular objects from his front pocket, sifting them in his palms.

"What are those?" Hagen asked.

Sgt. Collins held one up. It was a fancy lighter with a red swastika on the front. Sgt. Collins opened the lid and a tiny flame blazed. He flicked his wrist and the top closed over the flame.

"Well, Kraut, I'll tell you. I hate these bloody Germans, but they can make something like this. I took several of these from our recently dead friends. Sell them for a handful of quid when we get back."

Sgt. Collins tucked one in Hagen's front pocket. Sgt. Collins patted his chest and said, "Merry Christmas, Kraut. Christmas came early."

Hagen nodded and muttered, "Thanks."

He drove through a covered bridge and came out onto a narrow road. The trees gradually thinned until they wound their way up a bare mountainside with a sheer cliff dropping to one side of their vehicle. Eventually, they came to the gates of the castle and drove over a stone bridge that spanned a wide canyon.

Their sedan went under an archway with statues of wolves sitting atop it and staring down. They crawled over a winding cobblestone road along which were several stone houses that were probably for servants, or now a garrison of soldiers. The car came around a corner and the castle in its entirety was in front of them. From far away, it had looked large; up close, it was titanic. Hagen tried to take in the full scope of the facade, but he couldn't discern the top through the fog.

They came to a roundabout drive that passed alongside the front door. A bald man wearing a butler's suit waited near a large arched doorframe with double wooden doors. A young man with a black beard, dressed in servant uniform, stood close to him. Two statues sat on either side of the door: one of a man carrying an axe and the other a woman dressed in medieval garments.

Hagen put the car in park and breathed. His breathing came in hitches, though.

Roesia fiddled with the front of her shirt, then, taking a steadying breath, said, "I'll do the talking. We just need to get the sergeant and the other two out of sight as quickly as we can."

The butler approached the car, and Roesia leaned forward, whispering, "Just stick to the plan. We'll leave by midnight."

Hagen stepped out of the sedan, cutting off the butler's path, and performed a quick *Heil Hitler*.

The butler returned the salute as Hagen informed him that Officer Brose was ill, pointing to the passenger seat where Sgt. Collins sat. Roesia's intel had said that Brose was unknown by General Wagner or Dr. Mengele. They all hoped that the intel was correct.

Lt. David and Liam had parked the jeep behind them, then trotted forward and opened the passenger door to help the sergeant out. The sergeant muttered unintelligibly. Hagen wiped his hands on his pants and observed the sergeant. He was held up between Liam and Lt. David.

Sgt. Collins was making an excellent production of things, when Hagen realized that this was not a true stage performance and the sergeant really was ill.

Sweat trickled down the middle of Hagen's back as he darted to Roesia's door and opened it. She breezed out, wearing a full black uniform, with red bands on each upper arm, and black gloves. She had taken some time during their journey to style her hair into a double-bun. She held an impressive persona, stepping sharply to the butler.

The butler gave a curt bow. "Dr. Gunda Lawerenze?"

Roesia gave him an impatient glare and opened the lid of a cigarette case. "Who else might I be?"

The butler nodded his head vigorously, and said, "R-right. It's a great honor. O-Otto Abel, at your servi—" Roesia gestured with her hand for him to be quiet. She took out a cigarette, placed it in a holder, and put the end to her mouth. Hagen came up, removed the cigarette lighter the sergeant had given him, and flipped open the lid. He took a moment to admire the fact that he did not have to continually press down on any button for the flame to light. The flame licked over the end of Roesia's cigarette, turning it red.

She drew on the cigarette, puffed out the smoke, and grimaced, waving a hand in front of her nose before she spoke in flawless German. "That smell, it's putrid. *What is that?*"

Otto appeared abashed. He cowered an inch lower and stammered, "S-sorry, Doctor, it comes from the dungeon. The wind is stagnant right now, making it more noticeable. I assure you that you'll not notice it in a few moments."

Roesia's eyes narrowed on Otto as she clipped out her next words with a knife-edge. "I think that unlikely, Herr Otto." She took off a glove and swatted Otto on the chest with it. "I have had an arduous journey. We were under gunfire on the way. Very horrible. And as if that wasn't enough, this brute of a man..." Roesia jabbed her thumb to Sgt. Collins, propped up between Lt. David and Liam, his chin on his chest. "Has been deathly ill for the last half of the trip, making my journey quite unbearable. Why was I not allowed to use the airbase?"

Otto backed away. "I-I don't know, m-madam, I mean, Doctor. They w-were making excavations, I think, for the Führer. He's coming in two days."

Roesia lifted her chin. "Well, no matter then. I expect to be leaving that way. Herr Otto, must I get my own luggage?"

Otto's mouth dropped open at the quick change of topic; he wheeled around and spoke to the bearded young man standing close by. "Rolph. Grab their luggage. And take Officer Brose and these men to their room. We will send for a doctor." The young man obediently headed toward the trunk.

Roesia hurried toward the front door and stopped in the middle of the porch. She wheeled around to face Otto, bristling with impatience. Otto jogged up the steps and yanked the door open for her. She zipped through.

Hagen trailed Roesia through the double doors of the castle; Lt. David, Sgt. Collins, and Liam were a few paces behind.

Hagen stopped, his hands interlocked in front of him, as he stood behind Roesia in a vast foyer. She barraged Otto with more information regarding the discomfort of her journey, making quite a dramatic scene, while managing to ask pertinent questions in between her ranting.

"How many troops are at the castle?"

"When will I meet Dr. Mengele?"

"How many people do I know here?" She adeptly gathered a great amount of intel in a short time. She told Otto she needed adequate time to bathe, and suggested she would even need to stretch her legs before she met with anyone and would like to walk the grounds of the castle.

Hagen observed his surroundings. He stood on oatmeal-colored marble tile; oil paintings set upon the walls. The room held antique furniture and a winding staircase with dark polished wooden balusters and handrails. Hagen glanced over his shoulder. Liam and Lt. David continued to bolster the slack sergeant between them. The sergeant's face was pale and a string of drool hung off his bottom lip. Lt. David gazed briefly over Hagen's shoulder, and at the same time, Otto's tone became even more submissive. "Dr. Mengele, General Wagner, the guests have arrived."

The air reeked of chemicals.

Dread filled Hagen as he turned to face four men who had stepped out of a nearby room. The lead person was a wiry man with full cheeks, dark eyes, and thick black hair combed back with a liberal amount of grease applied over it. He smelled of repugnant chemicals. *Ammonia*, Hagen thought as he was finally able to place the stench. Hagen had seen photographs before embarking on their trip, and recognized the man. This was Dr. Till Mengele.

A second man had high cheekbones, a narrow face with thin lips, and a slender nose that seemed to go on and on. He wore an officer's SS uniform. *General Wagner?*

Dr. Mengele stepped up, stroked his hair, and shakily took Roesia's hand. He appeared uncertain what he should do next. "I-I'm so grateful you could come. It will be such a great pleasure to show you the specimens—"

The slender-nosed SS officer coughed behind Dr. Mengele. "Perhaps, we should make introductions first, Dr. Mengele?"

Dr. Mengele stammered, "O-oh, of course, General Wagner."

Wagner's thin lips formed into a smile that made Hagen's stomach turn.

Dr. Mengele let Roesia's hand go and gestured to the SS officer. "This is Lt. General Karl Wagner of the SS."

Wagner stepped forward and delicately took Roesia's hand, his thin lips peeling back to show even white teeth. "My pleasure. They said you were striking." He expertly placed his snakish lips to the back of her hand while gazing straight into her eyes. He nodded. "It is certainly my pleasure."

Wagner reluctantly released her hand. "I apologize we had to drive you here. We have an airbase that is still being finished. Heads have rolled, I assure you. The Führer is expected for the banquet in two nights' time, and his plane requires a specific runway length. Not to mention, his entourage is coming in an airship."

Roesia waved her hand in dismissal. "Thank you, General Wagner. I'm flattered."

"It has not helped," Wagner continued, "that we have just invaded France. But I'm pleased to let you know that Wehrmacht has marched steadily forward in Southern France; I'm sure they will fall in a matter of weeks, if not days."

"Oh, how splendid," Roesia said.

Wagner smiled, his white teeth gleaming. "Yes, it is. They are making wonderful progress. I hope you did not come across anything horrible on your journey. There was an encounter with some insurgents the other day."

Roesia opened her mouth to speak, but Wagner had already turned to the two other men who stood waiting. He indicated a handsome blond young man with broad shoulders who was dressed in an SS officer uniform and clutching his officer's hat under his arm. "Major Quintin Becke. He is visiting from Berlin."

Becke was just as charismatic as Wagner, but more graceful. He brushed his blond bangs from his face and offered an easy smile.

"Striking is an understatement," he murmured, and mimicking General Wagner, he kissed her hand too. "It's a pleasure, Dr. Lawerenze."

The sensation of being watched became palpable, and Hagen wheeled around. Rolph, the black-bearded servant, had his gaze locked on Hagen. His beard covered his youthful face, hiding any emotions. Rolph shifted his attention, and Hagen swallowed the knot that had formed in his throat.

Something was behind that stare.

The room had grown quiet. Hagen startled to find that Wagner and Becke were waiting for him to respond to...what? Roesia's white face turned a hue of red; she appeared to be tongue-tied.

What'd I miss?

Hagen wasn't sure if he was supposed to speak.

Roesia found her voice. "They asked your age?"

His mind had gone blank. They had agreed Hagen would be her personal assistant to keep him close by, but in their hurry and confusion, they had not come up with any kind of backstory. He had not planned to be speaking at all. A major slip.

He stammered, "T-twenty."

General Wagner nodded, and his smile widened. "Ah, one of our Reich's youths. And no doubt you attended one of Adolf Hitler Youth Schools? Which one?"

On this point, Hagen had no answer.

Roesia broke in. "He studied in Frankfurt. I'm sorry, you never introduced us to this other gentleman?" She nodded to the silent man at Becke's back.

Wagner turned to her, opening his eyes wider upon realizing she was inquiring of the fourth man with him. He wiped his slender nose for a second. "Oh."

He gestured to a stocky man, who was bald and had a short crooked nose with a jagged scar that ran over the side of his face. Hagen recognized him as the man he had seen through binoculars the day before. He had led the attack at Earl Groscz Castle.

Wagner said, "This is Senior Leader Georg Martz. Gifted with sure, confident hands. Made it to Berlin Olympics boxing. Not a gabber. Speaks only as much as necessary."

Martz had pronounced creases on both sides of his face; the ends of his mouth were curved down, and he exuded a deep sense of suspicion and displeasure.

Wagner turned his attention back to Hagen, his eyes forming back to slits. "But let me ask, who is in your entourage, Dr. Lawerenze?"

Hagen straightened and spoke without thinking, "SS Trooper Ivan Messer, sir." The name of his brother had just slipped off his tongue.

Roesia offered, "I chose him as my personal assistant, General. High performance marks at his school. I insisted he drive us here."

"Messer," Wagner said in a contemplative tone. His cheek dimpled as he appeared to bite inside. He brought his attention back to Hagen, the corners of his mouth curling down. "Have we met? Your name is familiar."

"No, sir. I-I don't think so."

"Where are you from?"

Hagen lied. "Close to Munich. Starnberg. My father was a glassmaker. We traveled to a few towns nearby. Perhaps you have traveled around there?"

Wagner frowned, his skinny fingers resting on his chin and his index finger tapping. He finally shook his head. "No. Your German is southern, but...where were your parents from?"

"Outside Nuremberg, Erlangen; my mother was from the same place."

"Where did you complete your training?"

Sgt. Collins gave out a guttural groan from behind Hagen. Wagner's eyes shifted to stare past Hagen's. Hagen stepped back, relieved, and regarded Lt. David and Liam. Their faces were purplish-red, and they slouched down as they held Sgt. Collins between them. Both men looked as if their knees were about to give out at any moment.

"Oh," Roesia said in a haughty tone. "You're still here. General Wagner, please forgive me. Colonel Brose here became ill en route and has been rancorous during my entire journey. I could not enjoy a single detail. I gather he needs rest or to have a doctor or something." She did not wait for an answer, but shooed Rolph with one hand.

"Please see to him and have my assistant help with the luggage. I would like to speak to General Wagner and Dr. Mengele alone and in detail about their project without further interruptions."

Someone touched Hagen's arm and he turned. Rolph pointed down to the luggage and Otto spoke quickly to Rolph. "Take them to the suites we used two weeks ago. Hurry. We have much work to do."

Hagen hefted some of the luggage and followed Rolph up the winding staircase. Up close, Hagen noticed the banister had intricate designs that appeared to be men at various phases of turning into beasts. Lt. David and Liam struggled to stay close as they towed the sergeant between them. Hagen looked back once toward Roesia. She was speaking to Dr. Mengele. Wagner's stare, however, was fixed on him. Hagen snapped his gaze forward, stumbled, and bumped into the railing. He regained his balance and continued upstairs.

They came to the third floor and headed down a long hallway with elliptical crystal bulbs suspended from the ceiling. A crimson rug with patterns on either side sprawled in front of them. A heavy, musty smell hung in the air. They passed several paintings, but Hagen stopped to stare at one in particular. It was not a wolf, but a werewolf that stood on its hind legs, dawn showing in the background, the sun glowing brilliant red. Flesh dangled from the creature's mouth while two clawed hands dripped with blood.

Another oil painting showed a smooth-faced young man dressed in medieval garb who held the hand of a beautiful woman. Their faces displayed shock as they witnessed three people being burned at the stake.

Rolph explained, "These are said to be the original Wehr Wolff parents, Hans and Adelene Wehr Wolff."

The next painting reminded him of Justine. It showed an Asian woman wearing Persian garb, drawing a bow while two swords were fastened to her hips, curved blades visible. A man with a blond beard stood behind her, a broadsword held in the air.

"More descendants of the Wehr Wolff family," Rolph said.

Hagen passed a statue of a warrior dressed in knight's armor as Rolph stopped at a door, opened it, and set their luggage down inside the room.

Hagen stepped inside and contemplated the space. It had a living area and an adjacent room; they connected by an arched doorway leading into the bedroom, which had one oversized bed and a daybed pushed up against the wall. The living room had a sofa with a patterned fabric. Assorted tables and hutches were positioned around the room with framed pictures and knickknacks scattered among them.

Rolph stood by as Lt. David and Liam settled the sergeant on the bed. Sgt. Collins grunted, swinging an arm that slapped Liam's chin. Liam jerked his head back, his hat falling off, and his red-brown hair showing plainly.

"*Blo—*" Liam started to blurt. His entire body tensed, then froze. Grimacing, he reached for his hat, putting it back on. He kept his back to Hagen and Rolph as he put a pillow under Sgt. Collins's head.

Rolph stared at Liam without blinking. Hagen's palms were sweating, and he wished he had his gun. He turned to Lt. David, who stood at the foot of the bed, but the lieutenant either was pretending not to notice or was engrossed in pulling the sergeant's shoes off.

Did Rolph catch Liam's accent? Did his red hair raise suspicions? Rolph's expression appeared passive, though, and Hagen could not discern any concern or distrust in his stance. Rolph turned to Hagen, and Hagen glanced at the large suitcase where they had stored a couple of rifles, but he did not see how he could reach any gun in time.

Rolph took no notice, though, and pointed to a door across the hall. He spoke, his voice quiet and docile. "You can stay in that room." Then he indicated a second door next to Hagen's. "And I will get the professor to stay there."

Hagen creased his brow. What did 'get' the professor to stay there mean?

"Thank you," Hagen said. "That is kind."

Rolph gave a short bow and stepped into the shadows of the hall, where he stopped and turned. Hagen had his hand on the doorknob, about to close it, but paused as he searched Rolph's face, questioningly. Rolph's motivation appeared to be shrouded by darkness.

Rolph broke the silence. "SS are never polite." Hagen's stomach dropped. The young man stepped backward and disappeared into the shadows.

Hagen shut the door and leaned his back against it, as he closed his eyes. *He knows. We have to get Roesia and run.* The memory returned of him being a child and having his brother at his back, telling him to breathe. *Breathe.*

Liam and Lt. David were in front of him. The sergeant's snores were clear in the next room. Hagen wiped the beads of sweat dotting his hairline.

Lt. David gave Liam a reproving stare, and said in a hushed voice, "That was too close."

"W-what is it, Hagen?" Liam asked shakily, ignoring Lt. David. "You look like things just went arse over tits."

Hagen wet his lips, not sure what to say.

Lt. David asked, "What's wrong? What did that servant say?"

Hagen met Lt. David's gaze, making an effort to switch back to English. "He just told me SS are not polite."

"*In me hole!*" Liam exclaimed and glanced over at the lieutenant. "Fuck's sake, it's me fault. I'm sorry, Lt. David, but they know. We need to clear off."

Lt. David raised his hand for quiet, then leaned forward, his jaw set. "Is he going to report us?"

Hagen swallowed. "How could I know?"

Lt. David did not break eye contact. "You know the culture, language. Did he say it as a threat?"

Hagen inhaled, closed his eyes briefly, then opened them and shook his head. "No, I don't think so."

Liam asked Hagen, "Chap, you don't *think* so?"

Hagen's face turned red. "I-I just don't think he—"

Liam didn't wait for Hagen to finish but turned to Lt. David. "We're in the loo, Lieutenant. We need to sod off and vanish."

Lt. David rubbed his chin, thoughtfully, his eyes vacant. "Quiet, O'Malley. Let me think a moment. Messer did tell us that Ford said something about a spy. Could it be him? Or could he be a servant who feels no loyalties to the Nazis? Why would he offer that observation if he was going to inform on us?"

Sgt. Collins's hoarse voice called from the adjacent bedroom, "*Irishman,* don't get your knickers in a twist. I'm sure Kraut can pick up a threat in German. After all, bloody First Admiral Churchill and Commander Ford selected our ace for his blimey tracking skills. *Kraut...*"

Hagen looked through the archway into the bedroom, viewing Sgt. Collins on the bed. The man had lifted his head from the pillow. His face was sallow, and a bilious odor drifted from him.

"Just don't be a complete poof and bosh everything."

Hagen flinched, surprised the sergeant was now awake and coherent, then nodded.

Lt. David spoke with a crisp voice. "We wait. Liam, get the explosives and weapons ready. Hagen, you bring your bag of stuff?"

Hagen gave one quick perceptive nod. "It's here in Roesia's luggage."

"Right, well, we are going to have to move quick, with or without Roesia. We'll give her another hour, and if we don't hear from her, we'll make a move."

Twelve: Fancy

LT. DAVID AND Liam were seated on chairs by the bed, appearing on edge. Liam sat on his hands and nervously rocked back and forth. Hagen had been over to his suite for a couple of minutes. He'd ruffled the bed and put some clothes in drawers to make it look like he was staying there but then returned to Lt. David's room where all of them waited for Roesia.

A knock sounded on the door and Hagen flinched. He looked over to Liam and Lt. David, who were now out of their chairs. Lt. David stepped to the wall, out of sight, and took out his pistol. Liam moved behind Lt. David, Hagen's revolver in his hand.

Hagen opened the door to find Roesia standing in the hall, with Rolph behind her.

She whipped around to Rolph and said in an impatient tone, "Thank you, boy."

He bowed and departed. She came inside the room, shut the door, and then sat down hard on a cushioned seat, breathing hard.

She massaged her temples and stared ahead with empty eyes. Lt. David and Liam sat and waited for her speak.

She wrung her hands, then spoke with a chilled tone. "Major Becke excused himself after you left. The rest of us went downstairs to what must have been the dungeon long ago. We went down several flights, then a horrific smell hit me."

"What did it smell like?" Lt. David asked.

"Like dog shit, lots of it. I found something else out. They were building a dock for freight to come across the lake. They have too many weremutants now—not hundreds, but thousands—and they want to ship them across the lake to a train depot. They just finished construction of the dock yesterday."

Roesia stared ahead. Lt. David squatted down, then reached out and touched her hand. She startled and stared down at him. He removed his hand.

"What happened?" he asked.

She swallowed and spoke, her voice monotone. "Mengele pressured Wagner to have me sent here, not because he needs my help. He wants to gloat." The corner of her mouth curled up, not in light amusement, but a painful muse. "Apparently, my intel did not pick this up. But he had a crush on me, Dr. Lawerenze, when I was in grade school. Luckily the real Dr. Lawrence moved to Austria with her parents a year later and they never knew each other. Thought I looked good then. Thankfully, Dr. Lawerenze kept away from him during her formal school years and through medical college, and then lived in Austria." She paused, then looked up at Hagen and everyone else, confusion on her face. "What was I saying?"

"What did Mengele tell you?"

"Oh," Roesia said. "Right. He showed me his lab, asked me questions about this and that. I did my best to answer. He talked about how he had come to make mutants. The same thing that attacked us back at Earl Groscz Castle. He infects prisoners with werevenom. Wagner was in the room with us, fiddling around with microscopes, but I felt his eyes undressing me. That ruffian, Martz, just stood in the doorway, his eyes daggers. Then..."

Her chin began trembling. Hagen could almost envision the repulsive memory reeling through her mind. "Horrible screams. Human. The noises came from down the hall. Growling and ripping noises, too. Mengele picked up the phone, and they all left."

"What was it?" Liam asked.

Roesia shuddered. "I think Dr. Mengele is conducting his new *exciting* experiments, and something went awry and someone needed to be murdered, the SS troopers were called in."

"Do you think they suspect anything, Roesia?" Lt. David asked.

She shook her head. "I don't think so. We'd all be arrested by now and our suites would be downstairs in a nice dungeon cell rather than this plush room. Mengele has no suspicion, and I am pretty certain Wagner is the same. Only that Martz gives me a bad feeling."

Lt. David leaned in and asked, "They left you alone when they responded to this alarm?"

She nodded and wiped a tear from the corner of her eye.

Hagen asked, "What happened after they left?"

"I heard gunfire, and then it was quiet. Only Wagner and Mengele returned. And then that vile man asked me to stay in his suite tonight, next to his lab, in the dungeon."

"That smarmy Wagner?" Liam asked.

"No." Roesia shook her head. "The spindly wicked man, Mengele. He was panting, and his eyes were just...*wrong*. Like whatever happened had gotten him aroused. Like he wanted to release that sexual tension on me."

She clenched and unclenched her hands, then wiped them on her pants as if they had touched a pile of steaming shit. She stood up and went to a shelf, staring at the photos displayed.

"I think," Roesia said, in a distant tone, "Wagner doesn't want me to stay in the dungeon with Mengele. He thinks it improper for a woman, even for the wonderful geneticist I am. Can't recall ever taking a genetics course in my life." She turned to them, one finger nervously twirling her hair, and said with a laugh, "And Wagner and Mengele are having dinner with us soon. Isn't that lovely?"

She glanced over at Liam and Lt. David, then closed her eyes. "You can't come for the obvious reason; you don't speak German. We've been lucky so far, but it's not going to last." She looked to Hagen, and her cheeks suddenly shone with wetness.

Hagen didn't know what to say, and his next words rushed out. "At least Wagner doesn't want you to stay down there."

Roesia attempted to smile. "Wagner wants me to stay near his room tonight, after Dr. Mengele gives me the full tour. I'm sure I know why. The servant boy, Rolph, came in at that moment and said he set me up in a room near you. Wagner looked at Rolph, and I'm sure if looks could murder, Rolph would now be dead. But he gave in."

She sighed. "My God, they'll soon find out there was supposed to be a storm trooper unit with us, if something else doesn't happen first. I'm not sure how long we can stall. But there's something else."

Hagen and the others listened carefully, not wanting to miss what she was about to say.

"Whatever end goal Mengele was trying to accomplish, it is going to be done in the next two weeks. E-even in the best of circumstances, the British would not be able to send a new team in that short a time."

Her lips quivered, fresh tears tracking down her cheeks. "I'm sorry, I made a horrible mistake. I don't see how we're going to do this."

Liam stepped up closer. "Oh, lass, it's fine."

She leaned into his shoulder and cried. Liam rubbed her back, quietly humming a song. Hagen didn't know what to do. Lt. David stayed at the low table he was sitting on, his eyes shining with wetness.

Roesia leaned back, smiled at Liam, and kissed his cheek. "Thank you." She looked at Hagen and Lt. David. "I'm sorry. I don't know why I did that."

Lt. David offered a thin smile and suggested, "Could be because we're in a castle with the worst people known, Nazis. The SS, at that. Who are apparently conducting odious experiments." He took a deep breath and continued, "We're here. Let's make this count for the books. After all, history is written by the victors, not losers."

A small smile formed on Roesia's face. Liam stood up and held out his hand. She gripped it and pulled herself to her feet.

Liam grinned. "I must say, I want to stay. I ne'er seen me a weremutant. Except once, I did take a lass home with me after I had pissed down a half-dozen Guinness. I'm not absolutely certain, but I think she might have been one."

Everyone chuckled at this jest. Roesia touched Liam's chin and whispered, "Thank you." She wiped the remaining wetness from her face, reached inside of her jacket, and brought out a sheaf of papers. She handed the papers to Lt. David.

"We could make this work. Destroy the lab, at least. I don't know. I took this when they were gone. It was lying on a bookshelf and looked like it'd been long forgotten." She dusted off the first page and flakes of dust fell to the floor.

Lt. David flipped through the papers, and spoke in an awed voice, "It's a schematic map of the lower part of the castle." He unfolded one large paper and set it on the floor. As he examined it, his eyes widened.

"Look." He pointed down. "It shows the different entrances into the dungeon, and..." He tapped the map with his index finger. "This looks like a tunnel that goes to that airport runway."

Hagen asked, "You think we can steal an airplane?"

Lt. David was touching the map, and said, "They're getting it ready for the bloody Führer. I'm sure they have a few tin cans down there."

Liam smiled broadly at Roesia. "I must say, not sure if it's proper, but well done, Ace."

Roesia gave a small smile. "I believe the sergeant had a whiskey flask. I think a drink of courage is needed for what's coming next."

Lt. David sat back on his haunches. "I think we all will take one. Messer, tell her what that servant boy said."

Hagen told Roesia about Rolph's earlier remark—that SS were never polite.

She contemplated this new information. "I agree with Graham. He may be a spy or just a servant. Either way, if he was informing against us, we'd know. You don't offer that kind of statement if you want to sneak up on someone."

Lt. David nodded. "Agreed."

There was a knock on the door, and they exchanged nervous glances. Liam whispered in Hagen's ear, "You think they've been listening?"

Hagen shook his head; he did not know how, but he would have known.

Lt. David and Liam scrambled to the bedroom with the papers as Roesia fixed herself up then nodded to Hagen she was ready. Hagen opened the door, and Rolph stood in the doorway, folded clothes over one arm.

He did not meet Hagen's eyes, but bowed his head and said, "Dinner will be at seven o'clock." He held out the clothes. "These are for you and the other gentlemen. If they don't fit, I have more downstairs." Hagen took the clothes, which consisted of black jackets and pants. A shirt dropped to the floor; Rolph picked it up and once again handed it over. Hagen took the shirt, noticing Rolph's left hand for the first time and his missing index finger.

Roesia edged past Hagen, shaking her head. "Why I must be assigned to *such imbeciles*." She met Rolph's eyes. "These, these useless men...who were my escorts, are now all ill. They shall not be attending dinner. It will just be me and my assistant here."

Rolph gave a slight bow of his head and said, "We have asked for a doctor. He will be up soon."

Roesia grimaced, waved a hand in dismissal, and moved across the hall to her room, saying over a shoulder with an impetuous tone, "No doctor is needed for these brutes. I'm a doctor, after all. Let them sleep this ailment off; they'll be fine."

"As you wish," Rolph said.

Roesia was at her door, and said, "I just want to start my work. I will be ready shortly."

Rolph stepped backward and averted his eyes from Hagen's, then vanished down the hall.

Hagen went to his room where a couple pans of water had been placed in a spacious bathroom. Embroidered washcloths lay near them. He removed his chauffeur's jacket and shirt, then stared at his reflection in a full-length mirror. His thick blond hair was combed to one side, but a few strands had fallen over his forehead. He brushed them back with his fingers. The bruises he sustained not too long ago were purple and blue, and one spread on the right side, over his lean abs. Lying between his pectorals was the gold medallion. He closed a hand over it and hoped it'd bring back that dark surge.

But nothing.

Disappointed, he let it go, then fully undressed and spot-cleaned himself using a washcloth. The dress jacket and pants Rolph had brought fit perfectly, and he admired himself in the mirror for a moment. Liam came to his mind as he fussed with his collar. He imagined his sea-green eyes staring back at him.

Striking.

He walked back to Lt. David and Liam's room. The sergeant was sleeping, still dressed in his Nazi uniform, his chest rising and falling steadily, snores sawing from his mouth.

Liam sat on the daybed. He was alert, his arms crossed over his chest as he bit his lower lip. He had the look of someone who was about to walk the plank of a pirate ship, or have the hangman's noose drooped around his neck.

Lt. David knelt on the floor, scanning the assorted maps.

Liam got up abruptly, strode to the window, and then stood, staring out.

Hagen came to his side, and Liam startled but made room for him. "I can't stand the waiting."

Hagen didn't say anything but stared out the window. A green lustrous forest covered the side of the mountain as far as one could see, with a blue lake stretching off to one side. The sun was setting, glowing red-orange, and about to disappear behind a mountain range.

"Aoibhneas," Hagen said.

A smile lit Liam's face and his green eyes sparkled. He turned to Hagen and swiped at his face, removing any hint of wetness that had been there.

"What?" Hagen asked in a hushed tone.

Liam shook his head and turned away to glance behind them. Hagen looked as well. No one was paying them any attention.

Liam spoke in a hushed tone. "I thought I was fine with popping me clogs."

"What?" Hagen asked, not understanding.

"*Dying,*" Liam said with a sigh. "I-I guess seeing Hodges go, it's more real now. I just miss my ma. Even me worthless brothers. I'm probably never going to see them again."

A rush of emotion hit Hagen as he placed his hand on Liam's shoulder. Images flitted through Hagen's mind of friends he left long ago in Germany and those he'd left in America. His father. Younger brother.

"I know," Hagen croaked, a lump in his throat.

Liam turned to him, looking uncertain. "I want to ask you something."

Hagen gave him his full attention. "What?"

Liam appeared to be mortified for posing his next question.

"What is it, Liam?"

Liam swallowed. "D-do you, uh..." He turned to the window and stood, tapping his forehead on the window. "Bloody hell, what's wrong with me?"

"What, Liam?" Hagen asked.

Liam turned toward Hagen. "Do you fancy me?"

Hagen shook his head in confusion. "*Fancy you?*"

Liam glanced over Hagen's shoulder, and Hagen turned; Lt. David was focused on his maps.

Hagen glanced back to Liam, and asked, "What do you mean, fancy? *Ohhh.*" Hagen's face became hot.

"Never mind," Liam's said. His face turned a bright shade and he faced the window, his back to Hagen.

Hagen thought about it for a moment, and said, "I-I don't know. I never been asked that. Do you fancy *me?*"

Liam gave Hagen a quick peek, then peered back through the window and gave one perceptible nod.

Hagen said in a hushed voice, "But you said you have been with girls?"

Liam shrugged but made no reply to this observation.

A double knock came on their door, and Hagen flinched. Liam startled, too. They both turned to face the door to the hallway and waited. A second later, a triple knock sounded. Roesia. They had agreed upon a specific rap.

Liam's fingers brushed Hagen's. "Hagen."

Hagen met Liam's eyes. Tears had welled in them. They both glanced to Lt. David, who glanced at the door and then back over to them.

Liam eased his hand away and whispered, "Don't get caught. I've heard stories about what these people do."

"Lads, you ready?" Lt. David asked.

Hagen looked to the lieutenant, who had stood. He lightly touched Liam's arm, then turned and went to the door, where he took a deep breath and opened it. Roesia stepped inside and looked over at Lt. David and Liam. She wore a striking green corset that was snug over her breasts and a polka-dot dress that flowed down to the floor. A light gray jacket with round gold toggles completed the ensemble. In one hand, she gripped a black handbag.

"Crikey." A smile crossed Lt. David's face. "The sergeant may just rise from his beauty rest. You look smashing. If only I wasn't married."

Roesia looked down and touched her jacket. "Thank you, Graham. I must say, Dr. Lawerenze did have good taste, and it's fortunate we're the same size." She tugged on her corset a little. "Mostly." She waved a hand at them. "Enough pleasantries. We have some time before we need to be downstairs. Where are the maps?"

The lieutenant indicated the bedroom, and once there, she bent glancing at the maps, choose one, then turned to Liam. "Get that one and set it over here."

Liam picked it up and settled it on the side of the bed.

Roesia studied it. "The lower section is several floors rather than just one large basement. Mengele took me to his lab, which was not far below. The focus of your attack needs to be on the laboratory and where they are storing the research archives." She paused, thoughtful, and then tapped one location. "Mengele's lab is here. The floor and area where I heard screams was here, I think."

Lt. David pointed to a place on the map. "What's *Hundehütte* mean?"

"Kennels," Hagen said.

"Right," Roesia said, "This is where they are keeping...keeping God knows what. The weremutants they've created so far and are training. It's a vast area."

She leaned over and scrutinized the map. "Here." She tapped the map and Lt. David bent down. "This has to be it." Three bold typeset words were near the end of her finger. Versuchslabor. *Laboratory*. Versuchs. *Experimental*. And Forschungsbibliothek. *Research Library*. It represented a large area.

"Won't it be guarded as tight as a nun's knickers?" Liam asked.

Lt. David gave a chuckle. "O'Malley, you do come up with some old crafty ones and turn them to your own good."

Roesia leafed through the materials on the floor, not answering right away. She picked up a large, tattered roll and set it on top of the bed. It was an architectural blueprint. She kept focused as one finger slid over outlines of different structures.

Lt. David asked, "How many explosives do we have?"

Roesia raised an eyebrow, thoughtfully calculating. "I'm not a demolition expert, but enough to get the job done. Liam's right—that floor will be heavily guarded. You're going down below it, to this floor. This looks like it's the boiler area. Plant them here. This blows, and it'll collapse."

"The whole castle will fall, too?" Hagen asked.

Roesia straightened. "I don't know about that. But their research will be lost. It'll set them back." She looked up and caught everyone's eye. "Dr. Mengele should be killed." She swallowed.

"I'll do it," Hagen said quickly, interrupting her.

She met his gaze and said, "I was going to say I will do it. If I don't make it, then get out of here, report our mission to Churchill."

Hagen shook his head. "It'll be too late by then."

Lt. David glanced at Hagen and Roesia, frowning. "Is killing him necessary? We could actually make this work and all of us get out of here."

Roesia touched Lt. David's hand. "I don't know their end goal. But my source made it clear that they were creating something that could turn the tide in the Nazis' favor. Without Mengele, it'll be very hard. If I can't, I won't do it. I don't have a death wish. And Hagen, I want you to get out. You're a tracker, and everyone needs your help, okay?"

Hagen nodded. "Okay."

He wanted to touch his breast pocket. He had not forgotten that cloth. He wanted to feel that power, but now that he was here in the castle, survival had become his primary goal.

Roesia said, "Hagen, you can carry my briefcase. You have that gun Justine gave you inside?"

Hagen replied with a sharp nod.

"Good," she said. "Put the entire satchel in there, dynamite and all. And if things go—What is it you say, Liam?"

Liam questioned, "What?"

Roesia smiled. "Go arse over tits, then just make a run for it. You have the best chance of getting everyone out." She looked to Lt. David. "The weapons we have—do you have something I can carry in here?" She held up her handbag.

The lieutenant nodded. "Right, I think I've got the perfect thing." He moved to one side of the room where they kept a bag that was tucked between the wall and the bed. He riffled through it and came back, holding a miniature semiautomatic pistol. He pulled the lever back and cocked it, then handed it over. "It's ready. Safety is on." He touched the switch.

She turned it over in her hand. "It's perfect." She placed it in her bag.

Lt. David held out his other hand, asking, "Will these fit, too?" He was holding a grenade and a small leather case that was opened. Inside was a syringe, containing fluid, with a cap on the tip.

She pointed to the grenade. "I know what that is, but this?" She tapped the syringe.

"Found it on Commander Ford. Had a skull and crossbones over it. A couple of the syringes were broken. But, my guess, good ol'-fashioned poison."

She placed the syringe case in her purse and then reached out to take the grenade, looking down at it.

Lt. David pointed to the pin. "Pull that, should have three seconds. Got it off Commander Ford, too. Heard him talk to his men about it. They'd brought several, but I have only a few with me. Anyway, it's a modified grenade for British commandos. Packs more of a punch than the average grenade. They said it could take out a good-sized area, not sure how large. My guess is, you want to be far away."

She placed it in her bag and zipped it, then nodded. "It fits. That'll have to do."

Liam asked everyone, "What about him?" His gaze directed at the sergeant on the bed.

Lt. David said, "I'm going to take the explosives down. Liam, you're going to try to get the sergeant awake when it's time. You'll meet Hagen in the tunnel near a place they call the meat plant; it should be closed at night or have only a few people. I'll show you on the map where to go. Don't venture out of the tunnel—you'll get lost, get killed, or be captured."

Liam shook his head. "Are you off your nut, Lieutenant? I'm going with you—"

The lieutenant held his hand up, his voice sharp. "Liam, it's an order, and watch your tongue. I'm still your superior officer."

Liam was tight-lipped, his face red. Lt. David took a breath and pressed on. "If you can't rouse Sergeant Collins, then you're going to take the tunnel out of here." He placed a syringe on the bed similar to the one he had just given Roesia. Lt. David reached and brought up a map, placed it on the surface of the bed, then pointed to three places, saying, "These go all the way down through the dungeon and enter into a tunnel that burrows underground." His finger traced a tunnel to the area near the lake. "This is the airport area."

"*Foostering* our time, to find any airport," Liam said, his tone piqued. "Hagen and I can't fly worth a piss. And what the bloody hell am I to do with that syringe?"

Lt. David's eyes flared with irritation, and a strained smile formed. "I know you can't fly. But you will have to cut up through this valley. You'll need to try to cross back into Switzerland. And Liam, you know what the syringe is for. If Sergeant Collins doesn't get up, you can't let him fall into their hands alive."

Liam looked away, his lips pressed together.

Roesia offered, "Hagen, Liam, someone needs to report what happened here." She sighed. "Look, I think we all know this may not end well for any of us."

No one spoke for several moments. Hagen stared through the window, remembering the question Liam had asked earlier. He did not want to leave Liam alone. The sun had fallen, and shadows lengthened, obscuring any of the finer details of the surrounding landscape. But the moon had risen, and it was close to being full. Whatever youthful innocence Hagen had possessed, he felt it was being driven away with each second, and he was becoming an adult.

Lt. David broke the somber silence; he probably wanted to sound hopeful, but his tone fell short. "Our mission is to try to make it out alive. So we need to coordinate times."

They spoke for a few more moments, discussing the time Liam and Roesia would need to excuse themselves.

The eerie sound of a howl echoed out into the night.

Thirteen: Suspicion

IT WAS LESS than a half hour later, after key maps had been reviewed and timelines established, that Roesia decided she and Hagen should head downstairs to dine with their hosts. This way, they could impede anyone from coming up to Lt. David's door, and prevent the enemy from seeing something that raised suspicions or sent up alarms.

Hagen shook Lt. David's hand, and the lieutenant said, "Okay, boyo, I bet you had no idea you were going deep into Nazi territory last week, did you? Good luck, son."

Hagen nodded, let his hand go, and then stepped to Liam. Hagen's gaze fixed on those jade-colored eyes, barely hearing the farewell conversation between Roesia and Lt. David. He did manage to catch Roesia calling the lieutenant Graham again.

Hagen stared at Liam. No words were spoken, but a faint smile surfaced on Liam's face. Hagen returned it, then slugged Liam's arm, asking, "Is Ireland as much fun as you say?"

Liam beamed, eyes sparkling. "Abso-bloody-lutely."

"Then you'll have to give me a tour when we get back."

Liam nodded, strong emotions obvious in his expression. He reached up and wiped the corner of his eye. Hagen turned away, choking.

Roesia stepped to Liam, and spoke with a fond voice. The kiss Roesia planted on Liam's cheek gave off a clear smacking noise. "Be careful, Liam," she whispered.

Hagen placed his hand on the doorknob; Roesia was behind him, saying, "Okay, let's go."

Hagen opened the door, but Liam cried out from behind them, "Hagen, wait!"

Hagen turned as Liam rushed up, put his arms around his neck, and hugged him hard. When Liam pulled away, Hagen's hand stayed on his hip; he didn't want to remove it.

Liam spoke again, his voice cracking. "Don't be a complete muppet and get yourself shot."

Hagen smiled and nodded, then stepped back. His hands fell from Liam's sides as he turned to the hall and took the lead, Roesia following. The door clicked shut behind them. Hagen straightened the lapels of his jacket and willed his heart to slow as he tried to breathe.

Otto entered the hall and bowed. "Ah, excellent. They are downstairs. Please follow me."

Roesia went ahead of Hagen, asking Otto a few questions and keeping up her pretentious attitude. Hagen observed her stature as he kept a couple of paces behind. Her chin was held high as she stepped down each step with a poise that brought images to Hagen of what royalty must look like when they walked. Near the bottom steps in the large foyer, there were a few SS storm troopers speaking to Major Becke. The troopers performed the *Heil Hitler* salute, which Becke returned, and then the men exited through the front door.

Becke turned, and his eyes widened at seeing Roesia. He extended both of his arms. "*Du siehst wunder.*" Hagen's mind went blank for a moment until the translation came to him. *You look wonderful.* Becke apologized for his informality and took Roesia's hand as she came to the bottom of the stairs, and there he planted a kiss on her knuckles. He stepped back, offered her a winsome grin, and held his arm out for her to take. He did not even acknowledge Hagen.

Roesia hooked her arm over his, and they started forward. Becke's entire focus was on her, complimenting her attire. Hagen followed, fiddling with his sleeve, then froze, almost slapping his forehead. He had forgotten the briefcase. He turned and started back up the stairs.

"Where do you think you're going?" Roesia asked, sounding peeved.

"I forgot your suitcase, Doctor."

She waved her hand in dismissal. He hurried up the stairs, down the hall, and then to the room, where he gave only one quick knock before entering. Lt. David and Liam were in the adjacent bedroom next to the bed, and both jolted to their feet at the abrupt entrance.

Hagen scanned the room, saying, "Briefcase."

Lt. David scoured the bedroom area, then snapped his fingers and said, "It's by the shelf in that room you're in."

Hagen went to get it, and after grabbing the case, he starting back to the door. Liam came out of the bedroom doorway and quickly glanced back before he strode to Hagen. No one could see them. There was a wall between them and the bedroom.

Liam came up fast, wrapped his arms firmly around Hagen, and before Hagen knew what was happening, Liam tilted his head and placed his lips on Hagen's. Hagen did not pull away, but his eyes widened, and then after a moment, they closed and he returned the kiss. Hagen's free hand went to Liam's back, his fingertips touching the top of a firm buttock.

Liam pulled away. Hagen opened his eyes, feeling dizzy.

Liam winked and whispered, "Wanted to give yea an Irish good-luck kiss."

Hagen breathed out. "Thanks." He stepped to the doorway, his mind in the clouds.

Lt. David called from the bedroom, "Godspeed, lad."

Hagen waved and said, "Thank you." He glanced once more at Liam, who gave a small wave, which Hagen returned. Liam closed the door.

Hagen stood in the hallway, took a quivering breath, and whispered to himself. "I do fancy you, Liam O'Malley. I think I fancy you a lot."

With that, he hurried down the hall to the stairs and stopped at the bottom. The front door was cracked open, and there was a ruckus outside. Hagen hesitated but stepped toward the door; he poked his head through to see what was happening. The vehicles they had driven had been moved, but there was a small caravan of jeeps that sat in the driveway with three covered transportation trucks behind them, their engines running. Shouting commands from the officers came from different trucks. They were shouting for people to unload.

Hagen moved away from the front door and into the driveway.

Several soldiers were gathered at the back of the last carrier. People wearing plain clothing leaped down to the ground. A few stumbled, falling to their knees. They were mostly men with grizzled beards, but there were also women and some smooth-faced teenage boys and girls. Their faces were dirty, their hair messed, their clothes frayed and soiled.

Two men wearing white cotton lab coats and carrying clipboards were making notes. One was a small-framed man, and the other had a streak of white through his hair. The man with white streaks glanced at Hagen and then back to his work, making comments to the guards.

A couple of lead soldiers came around, jabbing their fingers at the disorderly prisoners. Low-ranking SS soldiers hurried up, barking orders for them to fall into line. The group did so, each holding their head down.

"Thank you," Hagen said in a choked voice.

Martz did not break his gaze, and asked, "How did you become Dr. Lawerenze's personal assistant?"

Hagen blew out smoke; the tears would not stop running. He said in a hoarse voice, "She selected me."

"Why?" Martz asked, and the man took in a long draw.

A second fit of coughing came over Hagen, and he held a fist to his mouth and caught his breath. "Dr. Lawerenze chose me herself. She never said why."

"Never met an SS man who didn't smoke."

Hagen put the cigarette in his mouth, and his mind whirled. *He knows.*

Martz asked, "You know these other men that came with you?"

Hagen shook his head.

"What about that younger man? You caught his eyes a couple of times when we met. You both seem chummy."

"Oh, w-we went to training together."

"You just said you didn't know anyone."

Hagen spoke with the cigarette in his mouth. "Oh, I forgot, we knew each other."

"Where did you meet Dr. Lawerenze? How did she come to select you to be her personal assistant?"

Hagen opened his mouth, but there was yelling and he turned. Soldiers were ordering prisoners to their knees—three elder men and one young man.

Martz snarled. "Must be new guards." He yelled, *"Hold your fire!"*

The three soldiers were far down the driveway and did not hear Martz. They pushed the men down on their knees and raised their rifles.

Martz yelled again, "Hold your fire!"

Three of them fired at point-blank range; three prisoners toppled over. The fourth soldier, who aimed his rifle at the young man, had not fired and looked up at Martz. His prisoner jumped up and sprinted away, glancing over his shoulder. A couple of soldiers raised their weapons. One fired, and the round zipped past Hagen.

Martz stepped forward and shouted, "Hold your fire, idiots!"

The guards lowered their weapons.

The young man was looking backward, making a fast sprint even for someone with a lame leg. He approached Martz and Hagen at a dead run. Martz strode toward the prisoner. The boy jolted to a stop. Martz erased the distance between them and threw two uppercuts and a hook in a blur. The young man fell on his ass, skidded over the ground, then lay huddled on his side, holding his stomach.

Hagen was frozen. Up close, the young man looked to be barely sixteen.

The boy scrambled up to his feet. Martz didn't move. The boy threw a punch. Martz bobbed his head out of the way, snapped a fist out into his nose, and the young man fell onto his back, his nose bloody.

Martz reached for his pistol, then kicked the boy in the stomach. The boy curled up on himself, grunting and whining. The soldiers who had shot the prisoners spread around Martz and Hagen.

Martz shouted to one soldier who Hagen presumed was the leader. "Imbeciles. Why are you killing them?"

"S-sorry, sir," an SS soldier said. "Three useless old men, and this rebel here who's tried to escape multiple times."

Martz snarled, "We don't kill them—they go to the feed plant. This one is perfect for the detained wolves. We just need to make sure he can't run again."

Martz pointed his gun down and fired. The young man cried out in pain and thrashed on the ground; the round had hit his knee. The three SS soldiers watching the spectacle chuckled. One joked that the boy sounded like a cow giving birth.

Martz ordered the men, "Hold him down." They moved and pushed down on his shoulders, and Martz turned to Hagen and held his gun out. "The other knee."

Hagen had forgotten the cigarette in his mouth, and stared at the gun in Martz's hand. He couldn't move. The mission was forgotten. Liam, Lt. David, and Roesia were a faint memory. Everything was blank. The only memory was of deer's eyes, and his brother's words. Martz narrowed his eyes at Hagen and pushed his heel into the boy's knee wound, at which the young man shrieked and pleaded for him to stop.

A voice from long ago whispered in Hagen's ear. *"Put it out of its misery."* Hagen acted without thinking; he reached up and took the gun. In one motion, he pointed it to the boy's head and pulled the trigger. Right before the flash of fire, the boy's eyes met Hagen's; then there was a resonating, concussive crack, and Hagen jumped, staring down. A bullet hole was in the middle of the boy's forehead. The realization of what he had just done came to him. He stepped back, facing Martz, the gun held to his side. He lifted his gaze to Martz and squared off.

Martz's face reddened, a fury beyond reckoning quivering over his face. "You disobeyed a direct order." Martz's eyes narrowed at the gun in Hagen's hand. Hagen felt a tsunami of conflict between fight or flight. The three soldiers were staring at the corpse but glanced to Martz and then to Hagen, bewildered by what had just happened.

The man with a cleft in his bottom lip came behind the soldiers and hissed, "*What is this?*" The hole at his mouth had been made not so long ago. Hagen started to raise the pistol but was startled at a voice behind him, nearly causing him to yank on the trigger and shoot into the ground.

"Excuse me, Herr Martz. But Dr. Lawerenze is asking for her suitcase."

Hagen turned and stared at Rolph. The servant came down from the front porch and to Hagen, speaking with an urgent tone. "Please, she is waiting."

Hagen became aware of his vise grip on Martz's gun. Martz's dagger-glare seared into him.

"My gun," Martz snarled as he held his open hand toward Hagen.

Rolph stepped up, touched Hagen's wrist, and whispered, "Let it go."

Hagen released it, his fingers brushing over the metal as Rolph collected it.

Rolph stared down it, took out the clip, and choked out the round. "A Luger P08," he marveled. "You modified the magazine spring. Marvelous." Rolph glanced over to Hagen, his eyes slits, and ordered in a hushed voice. "*Go.*"

Hagen moved quick, made it to the porch, and glanced back. Rolph stood close to Martz. The SS man's fists were clenched to his sides, and his face had turned several shades of purple. Rolph slipped the magazine back inside, the heel of his hand snapping it in place, and he lifted the weapon's butt up to Martz. "A most excellent weapon. My master had one that was very similar."

Martz snatched it away without warning, and his fist holding the gun sped forward too fast to see. He slammed the handgrip into Rolph's face. The servant dropped to his knees, and Martz hit him again and again. Rolph fell to his side and cradled his head.

Martz kicked him in the stomach. "I don't care why the general keeps you around; you're under arrest. It'll be my pleasure to show you what happens to meddlesome fools."

Hagen stepped out of the doorway and into the foyer, his hands shaking. Someone touched Hagen's shoulder. "Sir?"

Hagen wheeled around to see Otto. The butler's face was tense, and swallowing, he held his hand out to an elegant room beyond the foyer. "They are this way."

Hagen nodded. He picked up the briefcase he had set down near the door and wiped his free hand on his pants. He trembled—his mind was in an uncontrolled spiral. His bowels roiled and he had stomach pains. He'd just put everyone at risk. Liam's face was in his thoughts—he needed to warn them.

"Sir?" Otto said, holding his hand out.

Hagen became aware he had frozen in place; he managed to step forward. A door was in front of him, a multitude of voices on the other side. "I-I need—"

The door whipped open, and the dining room was visible with its elegant long table and a crystal chandelier hanging high from the ceiling.

The handsome blond-haired Becke was at the door, and he eyed Hagen. "We wondered where you went. We saved you a seat."

Hagen nodded and passed through the entry; Becke asked Otto for a particular wine.

Wagner, Mengele, and a few SS officers he didn't recognize were sitting at the table, all in a fit of laughter. Roesia held a glass of wine in her relaxed hand; she was sitting between Wagner and Mengele, laughing heartily. Becke returned and sat down directly across from Roesia. He glanced up to Hagen, suspiciously looked at the briefcase in Hagen's hand, and patted the empty seat next to him. Hagen came and sat down, setting the briefcase between his feet.

Roesia's grin turned to a sneer. "You brought my research?"

Hagen's mouth opened. He had no idea what she was speaking of.

"The briefcase, you daft boy," Roesia said.

"Yes, Doctor. It's here," Hagen replied, looking down at his dinnerware and fiddling with a fork, sliding it away from his plate. He brought his hands down under the table where he clasped them together to stop himself from fidgeting.

Hagen glanced back up to find that Wagner was only half listening to Roesia, his gaze focused on Hagen. Wagner touched the tip of his slender nose and took his scrutiny off Hagen.

The general held his wineglass up and spoke with a playful smirk on his face, his thin lips peeled back into a haunted grin. "A toast. To beautiful doctors." This was greeted by laughs and cheers. "And to a victorious fatherland. Heil Hitler."

Everyone around the table shouted cheerfully, *"Heil Hitler."*

Hagen hastily reached out for his wineglass and spilled a little over the rim; he took a swig and put it back down. His face was hot, and his clothes were sticking to him. He stared around at them. Everyone was giddy. He turned and caught Wagner watching him yet again. The man's eyes were cold—he wasn't smiling anymore. A waiter asked Wagner a question; his attention was off Hagen once again.

Hagen let out his breath, not realizing he had been holding it in. He looked across the table toward Roesia, wanting to catch her attention, but she was turned from him, speaking to an enchanted Dr. Mengele. His foot touched the briefcase, reminding him he had the revolver inside.

Rolph was lying. Roesia didn't ask for the suitcase.

How long until they figured out what had just happened? Would Martz interrupt their party because he'd disobeyed an order or because he suspected Hagen was not who he said he was?

Sweat trickled down Hagen's back. The panic that had seized him earlier had receded a little, but it was about to turn back into complete inundation. The floodgates were about to let loose. He didn't know what he might do, but running sounded good.

One thought repeated in his head over and over.

They know something.

Fourteen: A Tour of Mengele's Depravity

THE CHEF, A large man with loose jowls, came to their table to tell them what their palates were about to indulge in: a roasted pig, complemented by lightly seasoned potato puree, fried asparagus in herb cream, and red cabbage cooked with sweet and sour flavors. And for dessert, German chocolate cake. A few SS officers clapped their hands in eager anticipation. Hagen's stomach turned.

The chef finished and apologized. His piggy eyes shifted nervously to Wagner and said that there was, however, going to be a twenty-minute delay. The chef bowed to Wagner, his cheeks jiggling. Wagner merely nodded and waved his hand in dismissal.

"Dr. Lawerenze, would you like a tour of the facility?" Dr. Mengele asked.

Wagner grinned and slapped the table. "A wonderful idea."

Roesia touched a hand to her chest, "Oh, that would be lovely." She displayed an encouraging smile. Hagen guessed it had taken a great deal of effort to force the expression.

Dr. Mengele fervently rubbed his hands together. Wagner placed his SS officer's hat on his head, then turned to the guards, giving orders. Roesia grabbed her wineglass, glanced at Hagen for a moment, and then gulped her drink down. He tried to keep her attention, maybe get her alone by herself, but she turned and was speaking to an SS officer who had his enamored gaze fixed on her. Hagen got up, looked down at the suitcase that had been sitting near his feet, and wiped his sweaty palms on his pants.

Why haven't they arrested any of them yet? I made a mess of my answers with Martz.

Hagen regarded the enemies around him. Wagner was speaking to the guards, and Dr. Mengele had grabbed Roesia's hands as he told her what to expect. Roesia offered a limp smile, but her face had blanched. Becke was pouring himself a new glass of the wine that had been brought in by Otto. They obviously didn't have Martz's report yet, but when they did... Hagen's stomach hitched.

Dr. Mengele announced, "It's time."

Hagen picked up the suitcase and followed everyone, holding the case in front of him. It kept his now-visibly shaking hands under control.

A couple of minutes later, Hagen was near the rear of their group. A couple of SS guards were at the tail end. The impassioned Dr. Mengele was in the lead. Behind the Nazi doctor were Roesia and Wagner. Becke, as well as a couple of the SS officers, came along—they had all brought their wineglasses with them. Everyone, in fact, held a ruby glass of wine except for Hagen and Roesia.

Dr. Mengele came to a set of dark wooden doors. Two SS guards were on either side of the doorway, holding rifles and empty stares. Another SS guard sat at a desk, a red phone close at hand.

One guard pivoted to the door. He used a key to unlock it, then grabbed the metal ring doorknob and yanked hard. A loud creak, which seemed never-ending, sounded.

Stone stairs were leading down into pure hellish blackness. Torches spaced on the wall lit up and provided a gloomy luminance. Spine-tingling yelps and howls greeted them.

Dr. Mengele turned, saying, "There will be that noise until we get into the experimental laboratory section." He waved his hand for them to follow.

Wagner laughed—it looked like he was joking with Roesia. The superb Nazi posturing she'd been pulling off had vanished. In its place was a palpable terror. Her eyes were wide, staring into the void beyond, her face even whiter than it had been before. Her arms were crossed over her chest. Wagner placed his arm around her midsection, and she startled, looking to him. One side of her mouth curved up in what Hagen assumed was her best effort at a thankful smile. The two went down, and the rest followed.

Hagen and the group wound down flights of stairs and came to a wide passageway. Overhead were lamps, providing feeble light. Spaced out every twenty feet at one side the stone corridor were spiraling staircases. Hagen stepped out of line and took a few steps down one and peered over the railing. Another passageway was in view. The stairs looked as if they coiled deeper to more floors below. Numerous yelps drifted from below.

Justine had told him she'd seen thousands enter this castle and never come back out. *How deep does it go?*

No doubt, very deep.

A shrill shriek echoed. Hagen backed up the stairs and hurried down the corridor, catching up to the group.

An officer with a wineglass and amused grin stopped talking to his comrade and asked, "Ah, where'd you go?"

Hagen thumbed over his shoulder. "Had to pee."

The man laughed and continued talking to his friend.

Up ahead a large metal door was opened for their group. They moved through the entry. Growls and deep bass barks grew louder and echoed off the plain stone walls, which were lit with torches. The noise grew to a crescendo. Hagen placed a hand over an ear, his other hand occupied with holding the suitcase.

They moved through a wide stone archway and were then on an elevated walkway, a gritty wall on one side and a wooden banister to the other. Torches posted on the wall lit the path before them and what was below. A rancid stench assaulted Hagen's nose. *Dog shit.*

Becke stared down, took a sip of his wine. "Impressive!" The SS officers in front of Hagen pointed down, and one claimed something had eaten its mate.

Hagen stepped toward the banister but did not dare lean up against it. From there, he stared at the nightmare below. It was a thirty-foot drop to the ground where rows and rows of fenced-off kennels were located with a walkway between them for someone to move freely. Large lamps had been set around to give some illumination. But indeed, it was what was inside each kennel that engrossed and terrified Hagen.

Oversized wolves, many with large patches of hair missing. Not wolves. Mutated wolves.

Hagen saw where the SS officers were pointing and observed the grisly carcass of what must have been a weremutant.

Dr. Mengele pointed out from the front, shouting so that everyone could hear over the animalistic roars. "We have been experimenting with the werevenom and have gotten varied success." He waved his hand to the animals below.

Hagen peered closer. All the animals below had some type of a deformity. A great number had patches with no hair, and many had human fingers for feet, rather than paws. One had a human shoulder sticking awkwardly outward. Another had a human ear appendage next to its wolf ears. One even had a human face on one side of its hairy head. Dr. Mengele referred to them as weremutants.

A weremutant squatted, straining. It appeared to be defecating. Three beasts leaped from across the cage, tackled their prey, and started tearing and ripping at its neck. The attackers had two hands rather than paws, and gripped their prey with their fingers, tearing ruthlessly with their jaws.

"We think," Dr. Mengele said, his attention locked on the bloodbath of a spectacle below, "the weremutants who are passive and docile are targeted."

The weremutants down in the kennel flipped over the ground, yelping, and one rose. The vanquishing killers stood over the corpse; one held its prey with human hands, opened its mouth wide, and bit into a shoulder. The creatures all took their bites and sat back on their haunches, each chewing on a chunk of grisly flesh. One of them looked up at Hagen and the others, with tendrils of glistening flesh dangling from its snout. The creature lifted its hand, pushing the gory meat into its mouth with its fingers, its tongue licking each finger one by one.

Dr. Mengele held both of his hands together up in front of his face, in a position of prayer, his mouth ajar; he appeared to be awestruck.

Wagner saluted the murdering creature with his wineglass. *"Prost!"* *Cheers.* He laughed out loud and remarked, *"Das Herrenvolk!"*

The group moved forward, and Hagen followed along sluggishly, realizing what Wagner had just said. *Master Race.*

An SS officer gripped both of Hagen's shoulders, and Hagen turned to face a man who had jovial cheeks, a pointy nose, and a mole on the corner of his upper lip.

The officer grinned and said cheerfully. "See, they were once Jews and other inferior scum, and now they understand the importance of a master race."

Hagen forced a chuckle, saying, "Yes, so it seems." He turned back around and rubbed his forehead with one hand—a headache was coming on—and then he stepped through a double-set of doors. They were in a new corridor that had torches set close to each other, high on the wall. The worn-out stone floor had turned to marble. The area had been renovated. High-powered lights set in the ceiling replaced the torches. They turned a couple of corners, and the disturbing howling noises diminished and then were gone.

They came to a more compact room with a small squad of SS troopers. A vaulted door was to one side. The troopers stood at attention while one rotated the dial on a combination lock and twisted on a circular metallic wheel that served as a door handle, then yanked. There was a quick release of air, and the vaulted door swung open.

Dr. Mengele's expression was animated, reminding Hagen of a child who was about to enter a candy store.

The Nazi doctor scanned everyone in the room and finally rested his gaze on Roesia. "Here is where the real work is being done."

They were ushered through the door. Hagen felt faint—the air reeked of chemicals, ammonia being dominant. He was still on an elevated walkway, but in this location, it was less than ten feet down to the floor. The ceiling was over fifty feet above. A vast laboratory spread out before them, which was comprised of numerous cubicles, divided by thin walls and stopping at a solid wall farther back. Between the walkway where Hagen stood and the vast laboratory was an open space that had a charcoal-coarse surface; on it were several bleached white metallic pods, about fifteen feet in height and length. The pods were spread apart, and all of them were interconnected by narrow metal meshed walkways. A few guards, rifles held across their chests, were bent down, staring through holes at the tops of the pods.

Flush to the laboratory cubicles was a raised platform that was around forty feet in length. A man stood at a control center, which had multiple levers, along with hydraulic hoses attached to a console. Behind this station for personnel was the largest pod in the room, abutting the lab wall—it dwarfed the other pods in height, width, and length.

A squeal caught Hagen's attention, and he turned toward the far end of the room.

Two soldiers dragged a naked one-armed man over the walkway to a pod at the end, and yelled, *"Pod Ten!"*

Hagen directed his attention back to the person at the main console. The man pulled down a lever. Hagen snapped his focus back to the one-armed prisoner; a hatch popped open at the top of what must have been pod ten. The guards pushed the person into the hole, and the lid closed with a loud clank. A scream ensued from inside the pod, and then dead silence. The SS officers around Hagen laughed and clinked their wineglasses.

An officer with a thin face and a gross cleft in his bottom lip screamed, *"Beweg dich!" Move!*

Hagen's heart hammered, and he took one step back.

The group continued forward, heading down the driveway alongside the castle. No doubt they were being taken to entrance at the castle's side, the one he'd spotted on the schematics they had been reviewing earlier. A teenager, who was wearing a tweed hat and had an appreciable limp, turned his head toward Hagen. He was too far away to make out the boy's face, but Hagen could somehow smell his fear.

A guard shouted, *"Gesicht nach vorn!"* Hagen had yet to become lucid, the words were foreign to him at first, but they came to him. *Face forward.* The teen snapped his head around, trudging along. Hagen stepped backward and bumped into someone. He turned and found himself facing the bald man. Georg Martz. Up close, that jagged scar on his face was raised, wide, and red. It was recent.

"Herr Messer," Martz said.

Hagen spoke quickly. "M-my apologies. I just heard the noise." He started to step around Martz and head toward the front door, a mere ten feet away, but Martz blocked his path. Hagen stopped and held Martz's gaze for a moment. A solid lump formed in Hagen's throat at the expression he saw there, causing him to take a step back.

"D-did Dr. C— I mean, Dr. Lawerenze go to dinn—"

"Smoke?" Martz asked, offering his box of cigarettes to him. Martz's reptilian eyes never blinked.

Hagen started to shake his head, but not wanting to offend the man, he took one instead. When he reached up to the lid of the box, his entire body felt as if it was shaking, but his hand looked steady enough. He placed the cigarette in his mouth, and Martz handed Hagen a matchbox. Hagen removed a match and struck it against the box, but it snapped. He took out a second one, and it too broke in half.

Martz snatched the matchbox, and then removed a match with deliberate slowness. His wrist snapped, and there was a grating noise and a sizzle. He brought the match up, and Hagen cupped a hand over his mouth to block the wind and light the cigarette.

Martz inhaled and kept his attention locked on Hagen. Hagen drew in smoke and fell into a bout of coughing, a hand flying up to his mouth. His throat was tight, his eyes watered, and he was choking. After a few seconds, he felt he'd caught his breath and placed the cigarette back in his mouth, but barely drew on it.

Dr. Mengele was oblivious to the show at the end of the room, but stepped down the narrow staircase and across the floor with all of its pods. Everyone followed. A few personnel wearing white cotton coats carried clipboards and monitored the various pods; they peered through small windows on the pods and jotted down some notes.

Hagen stared back at the pods. *What are in those?*

Dr. Mengele stepped up to the platform and came to the console where the personnel monitored various gauges.

Dr. Mengele extended his arm, and said, "In these pods are the original creatures we captured inside Wehr Forest. We had more, but many have died, unfortunately—not for lack of being fed, either. We tried to train a few, but they are incorrigible, ignorant beasts. But too precious to be put down."

Hagen stepped over to the largest pod on the platform, close to the console, and leaned over to look inside a small, thick-plated glass window. Hagen gasped at the beast inside. Memories returned with a thunderbolt, of him kneeling down beside his brother. Hagen willed the old memory to vanish. He touched his forehead and stepped back, bumping into someone. He turned around. It was Roesia. She had her hands clasped in front of her. Hagen again peered inside the pod. The wolf was colossal in size and tried its best to pace back and forth in its limited space. It appeared agitated as it snapped its fierce amber gaze toward Hagen. It had no hint of mutations and reminded him of the wolves he had seen earlier in the day. The creature's nose flared, its eyes burned bright, and it bared its teeth. The wolf brought its head back and howled. Even outside the container, everyone in the room cringed and covered their ears.

Hagen staggered back; Roesia grabbed his shoulder and drew him close. The sound stopped, and she reached down, lightly touching his fingers, and stepped away a second later.

Wagner brought his hands away from his ears, frowning. "That beast should be muzzled."

"He was," Dr. Mengele said, his tone reverent, his eyes fixed on the pod. "But he takes them off, and three workers have lost their arms to this creature in the last two weeks. We keep him completely isolated in this particular pod that is specially reinforced."

Becke rubbed his chin, peeked inside the window. "Is this the one they call Riesig?"

Dr. Mengele frowned. "It is. But, Major, as you know, it is forbidden to ever name our subjects."

Hagen considered the name, though. It did fit. The German translation was *giant*.

Dr. Mengele said, "Now, if you would, follow me."

Hagen followed Roesia into the first laboratory; the rational side of his mind was trying to discern the purpose of the experiments conducted in this space. He distractedly set his briefcase by a table, not paying attention to anyone, his worries of being found out temporarily forgotten. Instead, he stared enraptured and horrified by the numerous decapitated weremutant heads on the counter. The mouths were pried open, their fangs on display, and vials were fastened in place underneath fangs to either side of the jaws. Liquid dripped from the tip of one fang into a vial.

Dr. Mengele waved his hand to a set of vials inside a rack, saying, "We gather their venom and conduct numerous experiments here, from trying to find vaccines to enhancing its power."

Dr. Mengele leaned closer to Roesia, and whispered, "Soon, we will create a serum that will make a formidable new species, and this creation will make the Fatherland victorious. Unfortunately, the subject we used to make the serum has grown too weak to be of any more use. His blood samples are now...spoiled." Dr. Mengele glared at Wagner.

Wagner's narrow face turned a hue of red, and he explained to Roesia, "We had a subject who could turn from beast to man at will—"

"General," Becke said, awed. "An actual werewolf! You said you had no such specimen currently!"

Hagen brushed a shaky hand over his breast pocket.

Wagner held his hands up in defense. "We *did*, though, but we accidentally caused the subject's ability to go inert. We cured him of being a werewolf, and I'm not even sure how we did it." Wagner rubbed the back of his neck with his hand. "I thought the subject was refusing to transform—"

"And he had Martz torture him to such a degree he's of no use to anyone," Dr. Mengele interrupted. "Not to mention, his blood is now unproductive." Dr. Mengele touched Roesia's arm; it wasn't much for anyone to notice, but Hagen observed her minute recoil.

"We are close, though, and have enough blood from this subject to make headway," Dr. Mengele assured her.

An SS officer asked, "Where do you get your specimens, Doctor?"

"We are supplied regular subjects from concentration camps. We take healthy specimens and anyone too young, too old, or who have ailments or show rebellious behavior; we feed them to these wolves. Or they go to the meat plant factory. And we do train the weremutants to obey our commands, when it's time."

They came into a new lab. A deformed man was hunched down inside a cage. He had patches of hair over his body, large nostrils, and long pointed ears. He sniffed the air and cowered away as far as he could. The man had probes inserted into his head, attached to wires that snaked to a machine where two lab-coated people watched dials. The man looked pathetically more human than animalistic.

A second SS officer came up, sipped his wine, and asked, "This is fascinating. What is your end goal, Doctor?"

Dr. Mengele glanced to Wagner, then addressed everyone. His tone took on a scholarly timbre. "We're trying to find ways to control werewolf changes. Use the ability to make a better foot soldier whose sheer keen senses will give him the edge, and who'll be able to take wounds without dying."

Hagen took a moment and wandered to a window that overlooked a large holding area. Prisoners wearing gray pajamas shuffled around the center of the room. Guards stood close by and yelled orders at them. Hagen leaned up against the window. A teenage boy with a large forehead was grabbed by two guards and pulled toward a door. There were multiple cages that hung from the ceiling, which contained occupants. A woman scientist came over to his side, and he straightened.

"We keep it very orderly," the woman said. "We tag each prisoner and account for age, sex, race, weight, and height, and take complete health histories. All these variables are essential when conducting an experiment. We will further divide this group and put them in the correct areas. That young subject there," she said, pointing to the teen with the look of a physical handicap being taken away. "I can assure you, he won't serve to be any good to us. He is retarded and serves better as a nutriment."

"Nutriment?" Hagen asked.

"Food, for the indigenous wolves."

"Oh," Hagen said. "That's excellent." He swallowed the bile that had risen in his throat.

Hagen pointed to the cages above the prisoners, asking, "What about them?"

"These are subjects that have been infected with a variation of the werewolf venom and are awaiting transfer to their proper unit to be observed. Once infected with a werevenom, no one changes in the same manner. We have some rooms where subjects have been diagnosed with cancer, but when infected with werevenom, beat it back."

Hagen nodded. The woman grabbed a couple of vials and left.

He stared at one cage, squinting at a face poked between the bars, then stepped back from the window.

Hagen turned, and Dr. Mengele was saying, "Dr. Lawerenze's research helped us with our humble beginnings. Dr. Lawerenze, would you like to share your research?"

Roesia was looking down at a man inside the cage and nodding her head. "I-I most certainly would."

An SS officer shouted. "They're going to be fed!"

The SS officers and Becke were the first out of the room. Wagner smiled at Roesia and held his hand to the door, saying, "Well, let's see, shall we?"

Dr. Mengele followed reluctantly. Hagen figured he probably wanted to talk more about the science being explored here.

They returned to the room with the pods where three SS guards were walking toward them; they came up the platform and dragged the mentally handicapped youth he'd seen moments ago. Up close now, it was easier to see his other handicaps. One of boy's leg was twisted to the side and his eyes were not even. The kid had a muzzle placed over his face, likely to muffle his noises, but the snivels and pleas were clear.

Two SS guards dragged the boy to a larger cylinder plate on the floor that was next to Riesig's pod. Hagen recognized one of the SS men from earlier; he had a cleft in his bottom lip, and Hagen noticed from up close that he could see a portion of the man's bottom teeth.

Wagner crossed his arms and addressed the cleft-lip man. "Dexer. I understand a few prisoners in our containment have tried to escape. Be sure to make them an example."

Dexer nodded and waved to the man at the console, who pulled a lever down, and then there were noises of wheels rotating. The flat cylinder that Dexer, the second guard, and the teenage prisoner stood upon rose in the air, alongside the pod. The kid's squealing was grossly clear.

The cylinder jerked to a stop, and Dexer yelled down. "*Open!*"

A large glass hatch popped open atop Riesig's pod. Dexer ripped off the boy's muzzle, shoved the screaming kid inside, and sealed the lid shut. The kid's face was pressed against the oval window, and he pounded on the thick glass. Hagen understood the boy was now in an enclosure that was hermetic to the creature below him.

Dexer looked down; the corner of his mouth curled up, and he shouted, "*Release!*"

The personnel depressed a button. There was a hiss, and the boy disappeared. This was followed by a thump as the boy hit the bottom of Riesig's cage. The shrieks increased in volume and the container shook. Blood splattered on the small bottom window that Hagen had looked through earlier, and it grew eerily silent.

Two SS officers snickered and clinked glasses with Becke, then quaffed down the remainder of their wine. Roesia's hand covered her mouth as tears pooled in the corners of her eyes. Hagen tapped her elbow. She whipped her hand down. Hagen touched his face, close to his eye. She wiped at her wet eyes with her thumb.

Wagner rubbed his hands. "Well, that was amazing, and I must say, I'm starving." He placed his arm around the crook of Roesia's elbow and pulled her along.

Dr. Mengele smiled. "Yes, dinner would be wonderful now." He talked to Roesia's back as she stepped across the floor to the far walkway. "Dr. Lawerenze, I'll show you the training area tomorrow, where we train our weremutants. We teach them to obey our every command. Martz has been instrumental in developing an effective program."

Becke had walked up to Riesig's pod and stared through the window, mesmerized by watching the wolf eat. "God, but it's wolfing him down."

Dr. Mengele stepped to his side, and told him, "When we first captured the indigenous beasts, they refused to eat humans. This one here was the last to give in."

Becke chuckled. "When you're hungry, I guess you'll eat anything. Even skinny Jews." Becke pivoted, stepped away, and headed toward the group. Dr. Mengele spoke to the man at the console. Hagen eased up to the window, not wanting to peer inside, but feeling he should. He peeked in to find Riesig lying on the ground, his paws over a grisly carcass as he gorged. Hagen stepped away, sickened.

A man with a lab coat came up to Hagen. "Every day, we make the beasts in these pods go to one end and close it off so we can clean inside. Dr. Mengele does not want these animals to get any diseases."

Hagen nodded, took a breath so his voice would not crack, and spoke in a quiet tone. "Very efficient." Hagen left the area, wanting to get out of this place as quickly as possible. He made it only a few feet before he stopped, turned around, and hurried back to the first laboratory room. Once there, he picked up the suitcase near the base of the table where he had left it. He looked around, but no one was in the area. He went to the next lab room, and stepped over to the window where he peered at the grouped prisoners in the center of the room. He glanced up at one cage suspended from the ceiling and regarded the prisoner inside.

Corporal Kirby.

Corporal Kirby had to have been infected by a weremutant when he fled. Hagen turned and hurried after the group; his stomach cramped, and he felt nauseated and uncertain if he could continue this charade any longer.

The memory of Liam embracing him was vivid, and their lips touching brought something—*motivation.*

He made haste, catching up to Roesia. He took the handkerchief from his shirt pocket, crumpling it in his hand. He had no memories from Euan of turning into a werewolf, so there was no surge of power. But it still comforted him.

Fifteen: Dinner is Served

EACH SECOND THAT Hagen sat at the dining hall table was excruciating. Crystal glasses clinked together and he cringed, a couple of officers guffawed and he flinched, and back in the kitchen, a pot clanked hard on the floor and he almost ducked under the table. He stilled himself by sitting on top of his hands. He leaned toward Becke, pretending to listen to the conversation Becke was having with a fellow Nazi officer. When Hagen glanced across the table, Roesia seemed to be in high spirits, appearing enraptured by Wagner, her wineglass held with one hand. The general's head was tilted back in laughter, his slender nose huge from Hagen's angle.

Dr. Mengele, meanwhile, leaned sideways from his chair, his chin close to Roesia's shoulder. He too was attentive to Wagner's discussion as well as the nape of Roesia's neck.

A large stainless-steel platter was set in the center of the table and the lid lifted off. A roasted pig with an apple in its mouth stared at him. Hagen's stomach lurched and a hand flew up to his mouth. He had to look away for a moment and take in a deep breath.

A waiter sliced off chunks of meat and placed them onto each of their plates. The memory of killing the teenager replayed in his head, over and over. He pushed it from his mind, and it was replaced with the SS guard, Dexer, throwing the teen with a limp into the pod. The boy had pounded on the pod window until he'd dropped to the bottom to be eaten by a colossal wolf named Riesig. Bile backed up in Hagen's throat, his stomach somersaulting. Hagen picked up his fork and knife, and cut off a sliver of meat. He placed it in his mouth and started to chew. It took enormous effort to swallow.

Roesia was speaking to Wagner, and the general's hand inched near hers, hardly a space between them. Dr. Mengele was engaged in a discussion with the man next to him. He said he planned to create weremutants who were immune to silver.

Hagen caught Dr. Mengele's conspiratorial whisper. "I'm close."

Hagen searched the dining hall for a clock. Eight thirty was the time they had decided. Around the table were a handful of SS guards standing close to the wall, pistols holstered in shoulder harnesses. A grandfather clock in the corner said it was eight. Hagen cut off another piece of his meat and placed it in his mouth, a physical revolt happening inside his digestive system that he tried to ignore.

Wagner spoke loudly from across the table. "We have heard there have been spies who have infiltrated the Nazi regime. We have been told that several of them are our own countrymen."

Roesia feigned shock. "Dear me." Roesia, at least, had found renewed strength to keep up her masquerade. She asked, "Do you think this place is at risk?"

Wagner took a drink of his wine and offered a somber nod. "I'm afraid it is. We had a base at a dam in Konstanz, which was recently sabotaged. We had to move everything to this location. Himmler has called for a thorough cleansing of all our forces."

Roesia shook her head, placing her hand on top of his. "The utter nerve."

Wagner smiled. "Sometimes, these people are the ones closest to you. Sadly, no one can be trusted. But I assure you, Dr. Lawerenze, I will root them out."

Hagen looked over Wagner's shoulder and did a double take. Martz was peeking from a doorway. Hagen averted his eyes, barely glancing back up. The man marched up to the table, his eyes on Hagen, then bent over and whispered into Wagner's ear.

Hagen tensed. *He's going to inform on me.*

Hagen caught the name, "Rolph," and the last part, "I was looking for you."

Wagner said, "I was downstairs." He bit his lip, stood up, and placed his napkin on his chair. Roesia turned to him and he bowed to her, saying, "Excuse me. I have some business to attend. I shall leave you in good hands, though." Wagner followed Martz out of the room.

Becke asked Hagen, "Dr. Lawerenze says the other two officers are now sick?"

Hagen laid his fork down harder than he'd intended; it made a sharp clink on his plate. "They all had a fever."

Becke nodded and swirled his wine in the glass before taking a swig. "And Herr Messer, you say your father was some kind of glassmaker? What kind of glass?"

The whirlwind that blew in Hagen's mind had transformed into a hurricane, and thought was becoming difficult.

Are they toying with us? Or are they just taking their time? Hagen swallowed. *Or they only suspect me.* And once Martz was consulted, and it was learned an SS soldier had disobeyed a direct order, then more questions would come. Hagen, unable to think of a creditable lie, answered Major Becke in truth.

"My father perfected his own design of binoculars, and then invented new telescopes. He worked with the government..." He was talking without a pause, and then realized where his words were leading. His father had proposed a prototype binocular for the German Navy, which was then brought to the attention of an American contractor on vacation, who had offered him a job in the USA. His father's life pursuit—to take his children to America.

"To what?" Becke asked.

Hagen heard himself answer, but his voice did not seem like his own. "To develop binocular lenses for the Navy."

"Ah, that's marvelous! What company does he work with?"

Hagen wiped his mouth with his napkin. "I'm sorry, Major Becke. I must use the restroom."

Becke regarded Hagen as he sipped his wine. He opened his mouth, but closed it as someone tapped his shoulder. He then turned to the SS officer adjacent to him.

Hagen placed his napkin to his mouth and breathed in and out hard. Across from him, Roesia was doing her best to appear cheerful. Dr. Mengele was staring at her with awe.

Hagen rose from his chair, picked up his suitcase, hurried through a nearby door—and almost ran into Otto. The butler was speaking with a young waiter and giving him orders. The servant nodded and headed toward a close hall.

Otto noticed Hagen. His attention moved to the suitcase and back up to Hagen, one of his eyebrows arched. "Everything okay, sir?"

"Restroom?" Hagen asked.

Otto pointed to the hall where he'd seen the waiter depart. "On your right," Otto said.

Hagen stepped into the hall and noticed the adjoining elegant living area.

A voice shouted from behind him in the dining hall. *"Fire."* He paused, crooked his neck, and focused. He didn't smell any smoke. Someone shouted, *"Upstairs!"*

Hagen came to a dark wooden door and stepped in. He locked the door, hurried to the toilet, kneeled on both knees, and vomited everything he had just eaten. He sat back on his heels, his arms resting on the toilet seat. Time ticked by, and someone knocked on the door, then a muffled voice came through.

Liam. What about Liam?

Hagen flushed the toilet, stood up, placed the suitcase on its side, and considered his options. Lt. David would see to it that Liam got inside the passageway. He would be fine. Liam would live. He had to.

Hagen wiped the sweat from his brow and resolved to do what he must. He opened the briefcase, stuck his hand inside the leather satchel, and removed the revolver, double-checking it was loaded. He flicked his wrist, and the momentum made the gun's cylinder snap shut. More knocks, harder this time and more intense. Hagen inserted his weapon into a pocket. He poured several bullets into another pocket, closed the briefcase, and stood facing the door. His was short of breath and felt light-headed.

This was it. He wasn't going to make it. None of them would. He opened the door and recognized the SS officer with the flabby cheeks, pointy nose, and the mole near his lip. The large man grasped Hagen by his shoulders, shook him, and grinned, then went into the bathroom. Hagen again wiped away a thin layer of sweat that had gathered on his forehead.

No particular plan had come to him, but he found himself walking into the living area. The secret passage he was supposed to use was back near the staircase, and he could detour through the living room.

A sharp whisper came from the far side of the living area. *"Pssst!"*

Hagen peered across the room with its posh furniture. Liam's head popped into view from the side of a hutch and then vanished.

An SS guard came into the living room and Hagen nodded to him, sat down on the sofa, and asked the man in a casual tone, "Is there a fire?"

The SS guard regarded him with narrow eyes, and answered, "Upstairs. But it's being contained." The guard moved off toward the dining room.

Hagen got up, hurried toward the hutch, and disappeared around it to where Liam was hunched. Liam appeared spooked. In his hands was the small-barreled assault rifle. He smelled of smoke.

How did he make it here without being spotted? The staircase was at least two hundred feet away.

Hagen glanced over his shoulder; the murmurs and laughs from the dinner guests floated toward them from the dining hall. He pushed Liam back inside a nearby dark room and against the wall so that Hagen had the vantage point of the living room.

He leaned in and whispered, "Liam, what're you doing?"

"S-sarge," Liam said in a hushed voice.

Hagen covered Liam's mouth and leaned up against him. Two guards walked past their door; they had small rifles held across their chests. Hagen waited a couple of moments.

"Hagen," Liam said from between Hagen's fingers.

Hagen brought his hand away from Liam's mouth and repeated his earlier question, "What are you doing? We're supposed to meet at the meat plant."

"Got bloody lost. And Sarge went arseways. Could not believe me eyes. He got off the bed, and bloody hell, the next second, he crawled over the floor." Liam's back scooted down the wall, and he sat hard in a crouch.

"Liam, is Lt. David planting the bombs?"

Liam shook his head. "Bleeding hell. I don't know."

Hagen clenched his fists, terror gaining hold. "Liam, they're going to notice I'm gone. We should go—"

"Hagen, Sarge went mad."

"Look, I think they know about me."

"Jerries busted in, throwing a wobbler," Liam said, speaking as if Hagen had not spoken. "I made out yea name." He stopped, glancing at Hagen. "Did you get separated from Roesia?"

"I got sidetracked."

"Sidetracked?"

"Outside with Martz," Hagen started to say, but then he grabbed the front of Liam's shirt. "*Liam.* When did this all happen?"

Liam looked up to Hagen. "Not very long ago."

Hagen realized Wagner might have sent guards after him when he didn't come in with Roesia. Once he'd entered, though, Wagner had probably decided to wait.

Liam started talking again. "Sarge crouched down like he was on the loo and, and someone fired. Lt. David fell over; a lantern hit the ground. A-a fire broke out—"

"Liam, where is Lt. David?"

"Sarge, h—he ripped off one's lug hole with his teeth, Hagen."

"Lug hole?" Hagen asked.

Liam tugged on his ear with one hand, then rolled his eyes as if Hagen had no brain, and continued his tale. "Sarge cast one across the room with one hand, he did. Lieutenant David pulled me out of the room, took me to the secret passage. He ordered me to get out and head across into Switzerland." Hagen touched Liam's mouth to quiet him and stuck his neck out. It was still clear.

Liam licked his lips. "I lost me way, thought I heard Roesia's voice. Happened to come out a door into a hall, then wandered around. Happened to see yea coming out of that hallway."

"There's a door close by? In the hallway?"

Liam nodded.

Loud voices caught Hagen's attention and he straightened. He stepped to the doorway and peered across the living area, toward the hall where he had gone to the restroom. His breath stopped. Martz was speaking to the SS guard who had seen him earlier. The guard held his hands up in doubt and jabbed his finger toward a couch. Martz turned his head in that direction, then up and their eyes locked.

Martz straightened and yelled, "Seize him!"

Liam pulled on Hagen's shoulder. They ran through the darkened room, knocking over a table. Glass shattered.

Liam yanked open a French door, then turned down a hallway, huffing over his shoulder. "Hagen, the door's this way."

Hagen followed Liam, digging the pistol out from inside his jacket. They turned a corner, and two SS soldiers ran toward them; they froze, then raised their guns. Liam fired his weapon from his side, and the rounds smacked into the wall close to the soldiers. A few hit one SS man. Pieces of shredded oil paintings and wall plaster spewed over the floor. One soldier's rifle fired from his hip, and the ceiling above Hagen exploded, debris falling on his head. Hagen had already aimed his revolver at the second soldier, fired two shots at center mass, and was rewarded by the man staggering backward and falling to the floor. Liam's rifle made a *click-click-click* noise.

Hagen pulled on Liam's arm. "They're dead, Liam. Come on."

Liam let up on his trigger, removed the empty cartridge clip from his gun, and dug into the small satchel over his shoulder. They came to the end of the hall where they could turn right or left.

"Which way, Liam? The passageway?"

"Left," Liam answered, sliding in his new ammunition clip, and then he cocked his gun. Hagen felt they were going in a circle, doubling back.

They came to the bathroom that Hagen recognized as the one he had just used earlier, and froze. "No, Liam, wrong way."

Liam said, "This way." He pushed on the wall opposite the door; there was a click, and the wall swung open into a dark corridor. Liam was partially into the doorway when the bathroom door opened behind Hagen. Hagen turned quickly. The pointy-nosed SS officer who had a mole near his mouth was facing him.

His eyes lit at recognizing Hagen. "*Feuerwerks!*" Hagen's numb mind registered the meaning. *Fireworks.*

The SS officer's smile faded at seeing the pistol in Hagen's hand as he registered Liam standing halfway inside the secret passageway, holding a rifle across his chest.

Hagen raised his pistol. He did not hesitate.

Sixteen: Secrets Inside Darkened Tunnels

HAGEN PUSHED UP against Liam's back, his teeth chattering. The darkness engulfed both of them. Ten minutes had passed since he and Liam escaped into the concealed door, and ten minutes since he had killed for a third time. Hagen could hear shouts and footfalls outside the wall, but it was obvious that no one knew they were in a secret passage. Progress was at a tortoise's pace, given the lack of visibility, but sped up when light shone through cracks in the wall.

Liam turned a corner and blackness surrounded them. Liam tripped, but Hagen had his finger looped into his belt and yanked. Liam fell back against Hagen and into his arms. Their cheeks touched.

"Bloody fucking hell," Liam whispered. *"Stairs."* Liam wiggled forward out of Hagen's hands and shuffled quietly down the stairs. Hagen squatted and reached until he felt the edge of a step.

"Hagen?" Liam spoke in a hushed voice.

"Yeah, behind you." Hagen tucked his gun into his coat pocket, gripped his briefcase with one hand, and slid the other over the wall as they crept down the stairs. He reached the bottom, and though he didn't think it was possible, it was even darker.

"Liam," Hagen whispered as he groped in front of him. Liam struck a match, and Hagen could see he was leaning against the wall.

Liam uttered, "Bloody dark as feck." He turned in a circle, the flame illuminating the small area. Stone stairs were behind them, a narrow arched corridor with a high ceiling in front of them. The fire dimmed and went dark. Liam fumbled with his matchbox.

Hagen caught a scent and grabbed a handful of Liam's shirt at his stomach. "Keep them for later. This way."

Hagen had one hand out, his other clutching Liam's clothes. He stepped through a cobweb and pushed it from his face as he dragged his fingers along the gritty wall. He focused his senses, letting them guide him.

"Bleeding hell," Liam whispered as he tugged on Hagen to quit walking.

"What?" Hagen asked, alarmed.

"Me leg is cramping," Liam answered as he bent down. Hagen leaned against the wall, his hand laying low on Liam's back.

A soft rustle sounded, and Hagen asked, "What are you doing?"

"Massaging it out." Liam groaned and sat down on the floor.

Hagen sat down close to him, his hand on Liam's leg.

Liam kneaded his calf for awhile before finally slowing. "Oy, I think it's better now."

Liam struck a new match, which illuminated his handsome face. He leaned forward and spoke in a soft, helpless voice. "I-if I don't get to say it later, it's been me pleasure to know you, Hagen Messer."

Hagen leaned his head against Liam's. "I wish we could go back to that first day we met."

It happened quick. Liam's mouth was on his, the kiss deep and passionate. Hagen came up onto his knees, pressed his body against Liam's, and rubbed his hands over Liam's back. Liam pushed his hands to the back of Hagen's shirt and scraped his fingernails over his shoulders and lower back. A hungry groan escaped Liam. Hagen groped Liam's arse. He then moved one hand under the front of Liam's shirt; he outlined the vee of his abdomen with his fingertips, then dipped into the front of his pants, touching Liam's pubic hair.

Liam broke the kiss, took off his shirt, and pushed Hagen's up over his head. Liam fumbled with the front of Hagen's pants, then unbuttoned them and shoved them down. Hagen skipped Liam's buttons—he clutched Liam's waistband and wiggled it down over Liam's hips until there was no resistance. Liam leaned forward, his mouth clinging on Hagen's.

Hagen shifted his body as he lay his back down on the gritty and grungy rock surface. Liam was on top of him, continuing to kiss him hard. He grinded his hips up against Hagen's pelvis, his cock squeezed against Hagen's, sliding against it. Hagen's breathing hitched as he raised his hips off the ground, over and over. He embraced Liam, clawing at his bare asse. Hagen came as he pushed his mouth into the nape of Liam's neck, letting out short whimpering cries as his body convulsed and he groaned in ecstasy.

Liam thrust, shoving his dick farther inside Hagen. He placed his lips against Hagen's cheek and moaned, *"Oh, bloody fecking hell."* Warm liquid spurted onto Hagen's stomach. The convulsions lasted for several more moments, but it was a blissful eternity. Adrenaline pumped through his body, as if his head soared in the heavens, and he had no words to speak.

Liam stopped moving, though he still lay on top of Hagen. His sweaty cheek pressed against Hagen's. His raspy breaths quieted, and he rolled off, his hand sliding over Hagen's bare abdomen.

Gradually, Hagen sat up and patted the ground around him. Feeling fabric, he grabbed his shirt and wiped himself off, then put it back on. There was grit stuck to his back so he fanned his shirt until it fell off. He rose to his feet and pulled up his pants, then leaned his forearm against the wall, put his head in the crook of his elbow, and caught his breath.

After a few moments, Liam whispered, "Can't find me bloody fags."

"Fags?"

"Oh, here they are," Liam said. A sizzling sound erupted and a bright tiny match glowed as Hagen discerned the cigarette that dangled from Liam's mouth. He brought his hand up to light his cigarette, and the flame flickered.

"Wait," Hagen said and grabbed Liam's wrist, pushing it down.

The fire died. The small breeze was perceptible and clear now. Hagen grabbed Liam's sleeve and pushed forward. Hagen took a breath, his mind focused. He came to a corner and rounded it. Pinholes of light shone on one side of the wall, and Hagen let Liam to and step forward cautiously.

Voices drifted from an adjacent room. Hagen felt a sense of dread as he recognized the person speaking. Wagner. Hagen peered through a miniature hole. Liam came up to his side and stared through another peephole.

Wagner stood in the middle of a room that held a meager amount of furniture. Two SS guards were just inside an open door, and other guards were outside the room. Rolph was bare-chested, his wrists bound above his head with a rope secured to a hook on the ceiling. One side of his face was reddened and blood dripped from an ear. There was an SS trooper in front of him. Hagen could see it was the same one who had a hole in his bottom lip; the same one who had fed the limping boy to Riesig. *Dexer.*

"You never answered my first question," Wagner said, crossing his arms over his chest. "My patience grows thin." He wiped a thick layer of dust off the surface of a desk, then sat on its edge and fixed his officer's hat on his head.

"Martz has ways to make you speak that don't involve all this hitting and are much more efficient. Where were you last night?"

"I was here, General Wagner," Rolph answered. "Up in the west tower, making sure your men had ammunition for antiaircraft."

"And the *rest* of the night?"

"I have a girlfriend. She's two kilometers from here. I'm sorry. I should not have left."

"Is that the truth?"

"Yes, General."

"*Dexer*, not the face, please," Wagner said in a bored voice. Dexer strode up and delivered a round of upper cuts into Rolph's abdomen. The blows from the impacts punctuated the air. Rolph's body jolted and his arm muscles flexed. When Dexer stepped back, Rolph's chin touched his chest and spittle dribbled from the corner of his mouth.

Wagner stood up and jabbed his finger at Rolph. "Do you know about my missing silver ammunition?" Wagner removed his semiautomatic and waved it in the air. "This is one of the few weapons we have that fires silver bullets. Everything else has disappeared."

Rolph shook his head, and mumbled, "No, no."

"You see how this looks, don't you?" Wagner asked. "My silver ammunition stash has gone missing. Last night, you were absent. Today, you interfere with Martz. I'm very vexed."

Rolph did not speak but spit blood from his mouth.

Wagner said, "I spared you when we took over this castle. You said you would help me. You did give me blueprints, showed me secret corridors and the passage to the lake where we built an airfield and now a dock. But your impetuous behavior is not bearable."

A line of phlegm dribbled from Rolph's bottom lip. He spat again, and it was gone.

Wagner hissed, "Are you working with the allies? You a spy?"

Rolph shook his head. "No. I belong to the Nazi party."

"You are collaborating with this Ivan Messer?"

Hagen breathed heavier. Wagner did suspect him.

Rolph emphatically shook his head. "No, no, sir. Never."

"Why did you interrupt Herr Martz outside? You told Messer to go back inside."

"I didn't know. I thought Messer shot the prisoner as ordered. I swear, General Wagner."

Wagner touched his hat's bill and paced across the room. "Do you know this Messer? His last name is one we have been tracking."

"Herr Wagner?" Rolph asked, half raising his head.

Wagner flicked his fingers, and Dexer threw three consecutive uppercuts into a kidney. Rolph groaned out miserably, choking and coughing.

Martz came to the door, out of breath, and said, "Sir."

Wagner whirled around and stood in a regal position with his chin up. "What is it? Did you arrest Messer quietly like I asked? I don't want to alarm Dr. Lawerenze yet."

Martz shook his head. "No, sir. He's fled. Guards have been killed. It's certain. He's a spy."

"Where is he?" Wagner hissed.

"We lost him. He's somewhere in the castle. We think he's inside some secret tunnel." Martz stepped inside. "That's not all, sir. You said he probably poisoned the officer, then the other two men that came with him. They're all dead now. He must have torched the room, set a timer when he went back up. We're putting the blaze out now. We have a unit of soldiers missing as well. He somehow killed them and stowed a machine gun downstairs."

Wagner scratched his slender nose, placed his hands on his hips, and drew in a breath. "Get him. I want you to question him and make him talk."

"What about Dr. Lawerenze?" Martz asked.

"What about her?"

"Should we at least question her?"

Wagner sighed and shook his head. "No, she's innocent of this matter. Clearly, Messer wiggled his way into becoming her personal assistant. You need to question him to see how far this goes. Find out how he managed to get on as her assistant. Find out how he poisoned those officers and killed them. Who trained him? Polish resistance? British? Russians?"

"What about those Brits we pursued last night at Earl Groscz Castle? Could be related."

Wagner shook his head. "No. That unit was going to parachute in until their plane crashed. We were lucky they didn't get any closer."

"I received the intelligence records for this Ivan Messer," Martz said. "Says he died in 1930. This kid, if he is a spy like I'm sure he is, probably just picked out some local person's name."

"Did your intelligence report say anything else?"

"Yes. Ivan has brothers in America. We are tracking family history. We should be receiving intel on them any time now. But why would Ivan's brother be here and then use his brother's name?"

Wagner shook his head. "How should I know? Maybe he doesn't even know his name has actual importance. Or thought we had no idea. I'm sure those British spies were going to parachute in and then coordinate with Messer. We do have a banquet in two nights, prominent guests coming—including the Führer. They probably wanted to assassinate the Führer. No doubt steal our secrets. No. Dr. Lawerenze is innocent. And besides, Martz, you know women don't parachute." Wagner turned toward Hagen, his narrow face pink. Hagen almost stepped back but kept still. *He can't see me here.*

Wagner spun to Martz. "That reminds me. You still have units in Wehr Forest looking for those escapees? I doubt they made it from the crash; you said it was completely demolished."

Martz answered, "No word yet. But we have search teams who did disappear last night."

"Disappeared?"

"Yes, sir. Even the hounds are gone. Maybe more rogue wehrwolves in the woods?"

"It's possible; I'm sure we didn't catch all of them."

Hagen glanced over to Liam, who was staring through the peephole. He caught Hagen's eyes and Liam's lower lip trembled. Something indeed had been out there that night.

"But why would those wolves come out of hiding now?" Martz asked.

"They're stupid beasts with no brains," Wagner said, flapping his hand. "Dr. Mengele gives them too much credit. We'll round up any of these wolf survivors very soon. Any useful information from the prisoners you caught from the Groscz Castle?"

"One prisoner had been infected with the werevenom, has a fever, and is useless. The other, I think, is a British commando. He was unconscious, as you know, but I was just told he's awake. We put him upstairs, close to the library. Has some memory lapses, but believe me, I'll find out what he knows."

The two stopped speaking, and Hagen looked back through the peephole.

A man who wore small thick-rimmed glasses had come to the door. His hair was greasy and combed back. He was dressed in a regular German uniform.

He held out a sheaf of papers and glanced to Martz, looking uncertain as to who to address. He finally turned to Wagner. "Sir, these are the documents Martz asked for on Ivan Messer."

Wagner set the documents on the desk and flipped through the pages. Martz came to his side.

Martz commented, "It's the intel from America. His family history."

Hagen held his breath and tensed.

Martz picked up a photograph and breathed, "H-he's one you've been searching for."

"*God*," Wagner said, taking his hat off and pushing his fingers through his thin hair. "It is true. He's one of them." His thin lips formed into a smile, his face nothing but glinting white teeth. "How wonderful, indeed."

Wagner straightened, his eyes narrowed, and he told Martz, "The mission has changed. Our spy is not an Ivan Messer who died in 1930 but Hagen Messer, and essential to Nazi Germany."

Martz picked a photograph from the table and nodded his head. "Yes, sir." Even though it was a distance away from Hagen, he could see it was a black-and-white photo of a young man in paratrooper gear. It was a picture of him.

"Any man," Wagner said, "who harms Hagen Messer will pay a dire price. He must not die. Make this order crystal clear."

Martz placed his hat on his head, stopped at the doorway, and asked, "Did SS headquarters in Stuttgart send those reinforcements?"

Wagner furrowed his brow. "Dr. Lawerenze told me the force with her was rerouted along the way and sent with an advance team to the front in France. Since our phone lines are down, I've sent a messenger to Samerberg for new reinforcements."

Martz nodded and then he was gone.

Wagner told the clerk that he was dismissed and focused his attention back on Rolph. Wagner cocked the pistol he had been holding. "I'd hate to waste a silver bullet, but I think it's time to put you out of your misery. Frankly, I think it would put me in a much better mood."

Rolph stared straight at Wagner, and his eyes flickered. Wagner touched his head as if a headache had come on, and lowered his gun.

Did Rolph just do something to Wagner?

Rolph spoke fast. "I can help you."

Wagner brought his hand down and lowered the gun to his side. He chuckled with an amused tone. "Oh?"

Rolph's eyes were bright, and he stared straight at Wagner, but he looked as if he was seeing nothing ahead of him.

What is he doing? Is he considering his options? Stalling?

Rolph's eyes focused, and he spoke with a subdued tone. "For one, I can help you capture Hagen Messer."

Wagner raised both eyebrows, and the corners of his mouth faltered but raised a second later. "Ah, is that so? Please indulge me, where is he?"

"He's watching us," Rolph said, and he turned his head and met Hagen's eyes.

Hagen shrunk away; his back collided with the wall and he fell down on his ass. Wagner was yelling orders in the other room, and Liam was at his side, his hand under his arm, lifting him up to his feet.

Liam pulled him forward, and they were back in pitch-blackness. Hagen tripped over Liam's feet, and they both fell to the ground; Liam broke his fall, though. Hagen was up first, pulling on Liam, his mind in full panic.

Hagen pleaded, "Liam, get up, get up!"

Then Liam was up. Hagen ran blindly into the darkness, his senses telling him where to go. They wound down a staircase, heading far into the bowels of the castle, then came to the bottom and headed down a new corridor.

Dim light shone ahead. Hagen reached the illuminated section and looked up. There was a grate overhead, and the lights from the room above him provided visibility. A couple of soldiers were walking on the metal meshed surface, both of them speaking in casual voices. Liam took the lead, and they sprinted under the floor and more unsuspecting guards.

Growls and barking came from ahead, inside the tunnel, and Liam slowed. Hagen stumbled into him and stared down the dim corridor. A familiar scent permeated the air.

Weremutants.

Beams of light flashed ahead. A couple of soldiers were being pulled forward by a grotesquely deformed weremutant who had a muzzle over its mouth.

The soldiers were pointing at him, and shouting, "*We found him!*"

Voices came from behind them. "*We're coming! Keep him there!*" Scrapes of clawed feet rang through the tunnel—those of the weremutants trying to gain purchase on the stone ground.

Liam brought his rifle up. "Shite, Hagen, luck is just not on our side."

Hagen stared in front of him, behind him, and then up. Hagen pushed Liam's gun barrel down and said, "Lift me up."

Liam looked up, slung his rifle over his shoulder, and laced his fingers together. Hagen stepped into his hand, and Liam hoisted him up.

Hagen gritted his teeth and pushed up hard on the metal meshed floor grate. A squawk sounded, and it was free. He pushed it aside, then gripped the ledge and crawled up over the edge. He put his briefcase to the side and reached down into the hole. Liam gripped his hand, and Hagen, jaw clenched, hauled him up. Liam seized the edge of the opening, but the harness on his rifle caught on the ledge. As he wiggled to free the harness, it snapped and the rifle fell clattering to the stone floor below.

They both scrambled up to their feet, then Liam stared down at his rifle. "Shite!"

A soldier shouted, "*He's escaping!*"

Shots were fired. Rounds ricocheted off the ledge near Liam's foot. Sparks spewed up, as he stepped away. The muzzled weremutants were barking angrily now from both ends of the passageway.

Someone below yelled, "*No shooting! No shooting! Take him alive!*"

Hagen pulled Liam into the corridor that lay in front of them, yelling, "*Move, move!*" Liam quickly dug into his satchel and brought out Captain Ford's semiautomatic pistol. He removed spare clips, dropped the bag upon the ground, and stuffed the extra ammunition into his pocket.

Hagen's heart pounded; he had but one thought and that was to escape. He opened the briefcase at a run, removed the satchel inside, and placed its strap over a shoulder, then let the case fall to the ground. He dug the revolver from his pocket and opened the cylinder. He glanced down at the cartridges, trying to figure out which ones had been spent, and then slowed, finally stopping at a set of double doors with a circular vault lock on it. Hagen pulled out the spent cartridges, placed in new silver rounds, and closed the cylinder.

Liam had grabbed the wheel of the vault and wrenched on it, his face reddening with the strain. At first, it didn't budge, then squealed as it started to rotate. The door came open an inch, as a heavy fog drifting out, cold and wet.

Hagen looked behind them. The shouting of the guards drew closer. Hagen met Liam's eyes. They both nodded at the same time, and Liam pushed the door open, ready to meet whatever was going to be on the other side.

Seventeen: Through the Meat Factory

HAGEN WAS THROUGH the vault door; he stepped into a heavy fog as cold air blasted over him. Ice packs were stacked to the side and frost coated the walls. A freezer room. The ground was slippery, but Hagen kept his fast pace and looked over his shoulder.

Liam pointed in front of Hagen, and shouted, "Watch out—"

Hagen slammed into something, then slipped and fell. The air was knocked out of him as he slid over the damp floor. His pistol was knocked from his hand, and as he pushed both hands out to stop himself, they were engulfed in a thin layer of icy water. His feet hit a wide stone pillar, and he spun on his arse, staring at the macabre picture above him.

Human corpses hung from meat hooks—men and women with frost formed over their hair and eyebrows. Each carcass had been bled out, a slit across the throat. Their glassy eyes were open. The pointy ends of hooks were impaled through shoulders or chests. The corpse Hagen had struck rocked sideways.

"*Hagen! They're coming!*" Liam yelled as he came around the side of a corpse.

Shouts came from the other side of the door. Their pursuers would be within spitting distance any second.

Hagen scanned the room in a panic, searching for his gun. "*Go, Liam. Hide!*"

Hagen frantically searched the floor. There! His revolver lay on top of chunks of ice several feet from him. Liam saw it and moved, going to his knees and sliding; he grabbed the pistol and tossed it. Hagen caught it one-handed just as the thick door was flung open and a weremutant with a muzzle stuck its head inside. Hagen sat up, aimed, and pulled the trigger; the gun bucked in his hand and his ears rung. The hairy beast's head jerked to the side, and it fell. The soldiers cursed and shouted in alarm.

A motor charged to life and machinery whined around him. The human corpses bucked in the air and started moving in a zigzag fashion. It reminded Hagen of seeing into a fancy tailor store in Philadelphia.

The two SS soldiers who had come inside were disoriented, jumping out of the way of corpses that were in motion. Hagen had one sighted; he fired and the soldier held his ribs. Hagen fired at the fallen soldier two times, and the SS man rolled onto his back, not moving. The second soldier whirled his rifle toward Hagen, apparently forgetting Hagen was to be taken alive.

A series of gunshots blasted out next to Hagen, and the soldier's expression turned from surprise to pain. Liam was firing, both hands on his pistol. The soldier stumbled backward—rounds smacked into him and his blood misted the nearby corpses. The soldier fell to his knees, holding the rifle with one hand, the barrel pointed up as his weapon discharged. Holes appeared in the carcasses around the guard. One split from a meat hook, abdomen and legs spilled to the floor. Liam continued to squeeze his trigger, making a steady pace forward. His shots now going wide.

Hagen breathed, sighted on the SS man's chest, and fired once; the gun jerked hard, the report deafening. The soldier tumbled onto his back, his rifle skating away. Liam's pistol made a dry click-click-click, and Liam looked down at it bewildered.

Hagen got up onto his feet, grabbed Liam's sleeve, pulled at him, and scolded, "God damn, Liam. You don't have to use every single fucking bullet!"

"*I'm a fecking Airman,* Hagen, not a blimey Infantry man."

"Not anymore," Hagen said, and pulled him to the opposite side. There was a slanted wide chute that headed down into a darkened spacious room. Hagen peered over the ledge. The lower floor was barely lit, making it difficult to discern what was ahead. Hagen recalled that this area was named the meat factory. The human carcasses had to be pushed down these chutes to be processed into ground food by machinery below. Hagen's stomach lurched at the thought.

Liam slammed home a new clip and cocked his gun. Hagen climbed on top of the chute, stared down, then glanced over to Liam. "Liam, come on. Put your feet on the side so you don't slip down."

Liam peered down and swallowed. Hagen tipped the empty shells from his revolver. He fumbled inside his satchel and loaded new rounds;

a few fell from his fingertips and rolled down the shaft. The growl of a weremutant became audible over the machinery in the room behind them. Hagen closed his cylinder and got on top of the chute; he opened his legs wide, his shoes touching the ledge, and scooted downward at a slow pace. He looked behind to discover Liam doing the same, taking it easy and slow. Squeaks from their shoes on the metal were loud, but the machinery above them continued its drone, and Hagen assumed it drowned out their clambering.

They were halfway down the chute when they heard from above them the sound of excited voices—SS soldiers. A weremutant howled; Hagen's skin crawled.

The machinery went silent, and Hagen said in a hushed voice, "*Liam.*" Liam froze and looked down at him.

"Put your head down," Hagen said.

Liam put his head flat to the chute. Hagen raised his revolver, took a breath, squinted, and aimed up at the edge, waiting. The head of an SS soldier popped into view above them, scanning the area. Hagen adjusted his aim and pulled the trigger. Part of the man's ear vanished. The soldier yanked his head back out of sight and howled in pain.

"Oh shit," Hagen said.

"*What?*"

"Missed."

Hagen began to move at a quicker pace, when Liam cursed. His incline turned abruptly into a plateau. Hagen came to a halt and stared around. Liam stopped behind him. They were on a conveyer belt. Far down the line, it led to a large opening with jigsaw teeth whirling in circles, which no doubt would turn him into pulp. The floor was ten feet below them, and Hagen jumped down. Liam rolled to the edge, ready to follow when a shot was fired from high above them and a series of ricocheting zings echoed out.

A soldier yelled from above them. "Idiot, the general wants him alive!"

A second voice whined, "He shot me! And there's two of them!"

Liam fell off the side, landed on his feet, then tumbled to the floor. His gun slid from his hand, but Hagen picked it up and handed it back.

"You okay?"

Liam shook his head but took his gun and stood up. He grimaced and limped forward. "Cocked up my ankle."

Hagen grabbed Liam under the arm, pulling him. They hid under a large piece of equipment as Hagen frantically searched for a door.

Liam pointed. "Them stairs, I see a door up there."

Hagen pulled him along as Liam limped hard on his ankle, following as best he could. They went up the stairs. Hagen reached a walkway and went around a corner, then came to the door. He yanked on the knob, but it didn't budge. It was a thick wooden door with two bolt locks. Hagen stood to the side and aimed his gun at the bolt, ready to shoot. Liam grabbed his shoulder and pointed in the direction they had come.

He spoke in a hushed voice. "They're coming."

Someone came around the corner. Hagen quickly shoved Liam's arm aside as he raised his rifle and fired. The stray bullet made several *zings* as it bounced off various pieces of equipment in the room below.

Liam lowered his gun to his side and said in disbelief, "*Lieutenant David.*"

Lt. David came forward, his face pale and his jaw clenched. Hagen recognized that the satchel over his shoulder held the plastic explosives.

Lt. David waved for them to follow him. "I was waiting for you both to show. Guess you made it, albeit not through the tunnel. This way. Move it."

They followed him around the corner, the growls of the weremutants resonating through the tunnel.

Lt. David pointed his finger to the bottom of the wall. "Go."

A square panel was missing in the wall flush to the walkway. "Liam, move your arse," Lt. David said, and coughed. Liam hesitated, but Hagen waved his hand impatiently, and Liam crawled through the opening.

Lt. David looked at Hagen's satchel, reached out, and asked, "Still have the old woman's dynamite?"

Hagen nodded, then grabbed a handful of silver bullets from inside his bag, stuffed them in his pocket, and handed it over. The lieutenant waited, cocking his ear as the growling became clearly discernible. It came from between two large green tanks, which had several wheelbarrows around them. Lt. David heaved the bag; it flipped through the air and landed on the ground, sliding a few feet closer to one tank. The snout of the weremutant came into view close to the bag, sniffing at it. The grotesque head snapped up; one eye glowed tawny, a muzzle fastened over its face. Its human fingers grasped the edge of the wheelbarrow. The soldiers with it pointed their guns upward, shouting in surprise at seeing the lieutenant.

Lt. David growled, *"Get down."* Hagen went down as the lieutenant opened fire at the satchel of dynamite, and a concussive explosion followed. Lt. David fell backward onto his ass as Hagen reached out, grabbed Lt. David's hand, and pulled him inside the crawlspace to safety. A second explosion thundered, and the walkway crumpled away.

Lt. David tried to catch his breath as he lay inside the crawlspace, Hagen and Liam close by. "You okay, lieutenant?"

"Keep silent," Lt. David ordered. "They might hear us."

Several minutes later, they quietly exited the cramped space and made it to a dark, narrow corridor that had a small rivulet of water running down the middle. There was light from farther into the tunnel, which gave some illumination. Hagen and Liam shivered from the cold as they rested against the wall and told the lieutenant everything, from the tour of the laboratories with Roesia to all they had heard when they had stared through the peepholes.

"That could work in our favor," Lt. David grumbled. "They put Ness upstairs? Near the library?"

Hagen nodded.

"There may be a way to get back there after we plant the explosives." He rubbed his neck and asked, "They think Hagen is the main culprit?"

"Yes," Hagen answered.

Lt. David chuckled. "Because you used your last name? Had you been a no one, they would have never known. Did you know you were part of the Wehr Wolff family lineage?"

Hagen shook his head.

Lt. David leaned against the wall and grimaced. "Smells bad," he muttered.

"What smells bad?" Liam asked.

Lt. David wiped the profuse sweat that had formed on his brow. "It seems like too many coincidences, doesn't it? Roesia was going to impersonate Lawerenze, but that mission fell through, only to align up perfectly here. Now, all of a sudden, I'm standing before Hagen Messer, a member of the Wehr Wolff family, and who, by the way, the Nazis would love to experiment on."

Liam scratched his head. "Bloody hell, you're right. You think the Nazis set this up?"

Lt. David shook his head. "Now, that would be bloody impossible. I don't know. It just smells wrong." He glanced to Liam and Hagen. "Okay, so they don't yet suspect Roesia. And they think we're all dead."

"Did you plant any explosives?" Liam asked.

Lt. David shook his head. "No, everything happened too fast. I got lost and, well, found the meat plant and decided to wait for you guys." He shifted and grimaced again, gritting his teeth.

"What's wrong?" Hagen asked, his voice rising in concern.

Lt. David sighed and looked up at him. "Shot."

Liam and Hagen said at the same time. *"You're shot!"*

"Quiet, lads," Lt. David said, putting a finger over his mouth. He looked both ways along the corridor. "Had some medicine, but it's wearing off." He fumbled in his bag and pulled out one of the large folded maps he'd had earlier. He unfolded and laid it on a dry spot on the stone floor. He removed a cigarette from his tin container and patted his front pockets and grumbled, "Where's good ol' Kirby when I need a light?"

A sudden image of Kirby was ripe in Hagen's mind, and he shivered. He had yet to mention to anyone that he had seen him.

He turned to Lt. David, gloom eating at his hopes now that Lt. David was shot.

"Here, sir," Liam said, pulling out a frayed box of matches.

Lt. David took the matchbox from Liam. He asked lightheartedly, "Nothing like a good smoke to relax?"

Liam admitted, "Aye, smoke me ciggies since I was ten. Calms me nerves."

"Hmm," Lt. David said, lighting his cigarette and scrutinizing the map.

Liam whispered, "Did you see Sergeant Collins again?"

Lt. David did not reply at first, but stared down at his map in concentration, dropping the burnt match, then lighting a new one.

He finally looked up and shook his head. "I don't think we'll see him again." He rubbed his face and looked back down at the map. "Don't speak German. But I recognize the, uh, feed plant—I guess that's what they call it, and we're here." Lt. David touched the map. "I know where we need to go." He dropped the match, then folded the paper and tucked it in the front pocket of his jacket before taking a couple of breaths.

"H-how bad is it?" Hagen asked.

"Can't say," Lt. David said. "Haven't had much time to get a full medical exam." He chuckled. "We'll go in a moment. Just give this old man a second to catch his breath."

"You used to build castles, Lieutenant?" Hagen asked. "I see those blueprints, and I see gibberish."

Lt. David chuckled. "No, never built any castles, or houses for that matter." His eyes focused. "But always loved planes. Always loved flying. Father was a mechanic and did planes, fascinated him. I helped him as a boy, flew some he fixed up when I was barely sixteen. Guess I was lucky the whole time and never knew it. Flying things then would make your knees weak with dread."

He blew out smoke and reflected for a second. "World War I came. I was the same age as you lads. The officer in charge asked if anyone knew how to fly, and I raised my hand, rattled off my very small resume. I was assigned to the *Armstrong Whitworth*, an open two-seater cockpit. A rackety thing that carried a meager number of bombs."

Hagen knelt by the lieutenant, whose voice was soothing. Liam had squatted close by; he too appeared relaxed by the lieutenant's tale.

"Once, I was flying solo in a single-seater. A Vickers F.B.5. A rickety thing. Crashed a couple times and lived. And I got this." He pointed to the scar on the side of his face. "Lass put out a paltry one hundred horsepower. Compare that to the twelve hundred horsepower of the Night Angel." He gave a short laugh, grimaced, and drew on his cigarette; the end turned to red embers and he blew out the smoke.

"Well, where was I?"

"Solo?" Hagen replied.

"Right, we had flown into Germany, had brutal engagement. Gun was hit and didn't work. Well, I got separated from everyone. Flying on fumes and gun was broken. I thought, sooner than later, I'd bought it. It happened at that moment, I was flying over some mountain ranges, and I stared out into the horizon; the sun was setting and, well, it was—"

"Aoibhneas," both Liam and Hagen finished.

Lt. David raised his eyebrows. "What's that mean?"

Hagen answered. "Breathtaking."

Lt. David grinned and raised his cigarette. "Bravo, that's it."

"What happened next?" Liam asked.

Lt. David raised his chin and shrugged. "Well, I crash-landed, of course. No gas means you can't go any farther. Turned out I'd gotten really turned around and was over the Alps of France. We have only a smidgeon of control of our destiny; the rest is God and luck. I had one thing I could control." He held his index finger up. "Do you know what that was?"

Hagen and Liam exchanged glances, then looked back to the lieutenant and shook their heads at the same time.

He smiled. "I could remember the love I had for a woman I would later marry. That's all that mattered then. I returned to England. I had a full grown beard by the time I got back. I married that lass, too." Lt. David drew on his cigarette. "I got off course there. But after flying over and over, you get good at reading the ground below. I can see minute details that look the same to you, but not to me." He patted the pocket holding the map. "All that's to say, reading this here map is much easier than looking at terrain some thousand meters below."

Animated growls reached them. Hagen stood, staring in the direction they were coming from. Beams of light flashed far away upon the tunnel's wall. German words echoed.

"What are they saying?" Liam asked.

"To take me alive," Hagen answered in a subdued tone.

Hagen looked between Liam and Lt. David's faces. "The only ones who saw you with me were those SS guards chasing us, and they're dead. The others right now think you were Nazis, who I killed, and that your bodies were burned upstairs. I should surrender. You could complete the mission then."

Liam's mouth dropped open, and he shook his head vigorously back and forth. *"Bugger all, no, Hagen."*

Lt. David rose, gritted his teeth, gripped the back of Hagen's neck, and leaned in. "Now, that was brilliantly said and does make me proud." He flicked his cigarette into a narrow flow of water, saying, "The Night Angel crew may have no plane, but we're still a crew. Besides, my quick smoke break probably didn't help matters either; gave them a good scent. In retrospect, a bad idea, but can't go backward, just forward. Now, let's go."

Lt. David stepped forward, and Hagen and Liam followed.

Eighteen: The Irish Tale of the Werewolf

HAGEN REMAINED CLOSE to Lt. David. When he stopped abruptly, Hagen came up on his toes and tried not to fall headfirst into him. Hagen looked over the lieutenant's shoulder and saw that they had hit a dead end. Pins of light came from different fissures in the stone ceiling. The growls grew in intensity at their backs. But it was another distinctive noise that caught Hagen's attention. A loud continuous roar that made the walls and floor vibrate.

A river? It sounds like a white-water river.

Liam pointed his pistol down the corridor. His hand trembled. "They're getting close."

Lt. David lit a match from Liam's matchbox, brought the burning flame up, and moved it along the wall. His eyes lit up, and he blew out the tiny fire. He glided his hand over a ledge on the wall, then pushed and pulled, though nothing happened. He continued to creep his fingers over the wall, and as he shoved his palms, it moved an inch inward. Lt. David dug his finger into a groove and pulled. A series of clacks followed, and a stone door pushed inward.

Lt. David looked down, saying, "Brilliant. Watch your step and close it behind you."

Hagen tugged on Liam's collar, pushing him through the opening. Hagen stepped down, then turned and shoved the door closed until there was a loud click. Hagen followed steps that wound down a narrow staircase; both of his hands extended to either side to help keep his balance. He placed his hand on the wall and snatched it quickly away, pulling at the cobweb stuck to his fingers as he reached the bottom where Lt. David and Liam waited. Lt. David touched a doorknob, then met their eyes, his lips pursed together. He twisted and the door opened outward, and he went through it. Liam entered next.

Hagen stepped through the door and shut it, admiring how the door was camouflaged by the pebbly stone wall. This area was far under the castle, in yet another corridor, but had a vaulted ceiling with vertical wooden pillars spaced every few feet. Torches burned high on the wall.

"Come on," Lt. David said, and stepped through an archway that led to a bridge that sprawled across a thundering waterway, only a few feet below. He had started over the causeway when two SS guards stepped from a doorway on the opposite side, one with a smoke in his mouth, as they casually conversed. One did a double take, gawking over at them.

Lt. David lifted his rifle stock against his shoulder and fired one short burst. One guard jerked to his left and toppled over the stone railing, his rifle flying as the man splashed into the rushing water. Lt. David had already shifted his aim to the second guard as the SS man brought his own rifle up, when Lt. David's weapon hacked out a staccato measure of sharp cracks. The second guard staggered back, hitting the doorway's edge, and slid down. His head hanging down—he did not move.

Lt. David trotted to the dead guard, poked his head into the doorway, and said over his shoulder, "Toss him over."

Hagen knelt by the corpse's feet, grabbed the ankles, and pulled. The body came away from the wall. Liam grabbed under the guard's armpits, and they both heaved the body over the side, into the tumultuous water.

Liam picked up the German rifle, admiring it. It was a shiny, short-barreled weapon, and had a foot-long clip that stuck out from the top.

He met Hagen's eyes and lifted it up. "Dogs bollox, but she's sound."

Hagen tapped the clip that stuck out from the top. "May have enough bullets for you, too."

Liam grinned.

Lt. David moved ahead, Hagen and Liam followed him into a vast room with large bags stacked to one side. In the center of the room were a myriad of pipes that branched in every direction, the noise of water rushing through them. The lieutenant crouched next to a pile of bags and stared over them, looking around.

Hagen peered out into the dark room, whispering, "Looks clear."

The lieutenant pulled his leather bag off his shoulder. "I'm going to set these up. If Rolph is indeed helping, they will be coming." He pointed across the bridge they'd just crossed and handed Hagen his rifle. "Guard the bridge."

Lt. David disappeared inside the room, and Hagen knelt next to the stone archway, resting the stock of his rifle on his shoulder.

Liam went to the opposite side of the entrance, about ten feet from Hagen, and half raised his weapon, then glanced over to Hagen and asked in a hushed tone, "You think the sergeant turned into one of those things?"

Hagen glanced over at him, then back across the bridge. "You saw him, not me."

Liam faced forward and spoke in a neutral tone. "Me gormless brother would tell me scary tales at bedtime. Gave him a stiffy, I s'ppose, to see me wake up in a scream. A real twat, my eldest brother. One seems to be a wee relevant. A small Irish hamlet was once plagued by a wolf that killed its livestock. There was a boy named Colm who was known to prattle on, the youngest of five brothers. He not only swore he saw a wolf out in the field that had one eye and smelled of loganberry, but accused a local farmer who lived alone and happened to have a patch over his eye. Colm's family thought he was a wee touched, paid him neah attention. The next full moon, Colm's eldest brother vanished."

Something metal fell to the floor in the dark room at Hagen's back, and he turned his head.

He observed the lieutenant in the far corner of the room, then returned his attention to the bridge. "Well, what happened? Might make some haste."

"Right," Liam said. "Well, the pattern continued; every full moon, a brother disappeared and everyone ignored Colm, who swore the farmer was taking them. Well, it came to him and his last brother. Colm snuck to the farmer's house on the same day the full moon would be out and, not knowing what else to do, tiptoed up to the napping one-eyed farmer. He pulled out his slingshot. Aimed and fired, hitting the farmer's other eye, and scurried off, but not before seeing he had completely blinded the man."

Liam didn't speak but shifted his position, and Hagen asked, "And then what happened?"

Liam glanced up at him, confused, and smiled. "Oh, right. Colm went to bed that night in peace, but awakened when he smelled loganberries and heard a growl at his door. Colm sat up, and across the room, he saw a one-eyed wolf, carrying his only surviving brother's severed head. The wolf dropped the head, licked its chops, and strolled to Colm. Colm's last thought before he was eaten was of running across a loganberry farm near the farmer's house. A feeble bad-tempered woman he'd known for years had been working her garden and she screeched for him to get off the property. She, too, had had an eye patch."

Hagen shook his head. "Your brother was an asshole."

"Aye, he was," Liam said. "I don't know why I told that story, just seemed right."

Hagen told Liam, "When I went on a tour with Roesia, I saw Corporal Kirby."

Liam snapped his head toward him. "*In me hole!*"

"He was changing into a mutant wolf, I think. The Nazis are creating a new type of army."

Silence ensued.

"Hagen, promise me something?"

Hagen turned to him.

"If I become of one those things—kill me."

Hagen shook his head. "That won't happen, Liam."

"Just promise me."

Hagen turned to him. "How could I ever do that? I-I..." He looked away. He didn't know the name of the feelings he held for Liam, but they were deep. He took a breath, and said, "I would if I thought there was no hope." Liam nodded and met Hagen's eyes, then looked back across the bridge.

After a spell, Liam asked, "You think Roesia will get out?"

"Liam, I don't know if *we're* going to make it out."

Just then, beams of light flashed on the wall on the far side of the bridge. Loud, low barks were heard over the roaring river.

Liam tensed and Hagen told him, "Wait for them to be out in the open." Hagen then yelled over his shoulder, *"They're coming, Lieutenant!"*

A muzzled weremutant's snout was visible on the other side of the bridge. Hagen' dusted the trigger with his finger. An SS guard was in view, then a second one. Liam opened fire. Fragments of stone sprayed up in the air, divots appeared in the bridge railing, and the two guards went down, leaving the two weremutants loose and charging. Liam's rounds tore at the beasts but did not cripple them.

Hagen stepped back, dropping his rifle, and tugged at the revolver in his pocket. The beasts approached fast, and Liam stumbled backward, tripped, and fell on his ass, then slid past Hagen. Hagen stood with his feet apart and aimed.

A human nose hung from the beast's throat. Hagen squeezed the trigger, and its head jolted to the side, then it fell on the ground and slid to an abrupt stop. The second weremutant was through the opening. Hagen readjusted his sight and took one second before firing at the body. The creature yelped, fell onto its side, and started to get back up. Hagen brought the muzzle point-blank range to its head and fired.

Hagen peered around the ledge of the archway and saw that several SS guards were crouched low on the bridge, pointing at him. He stepped to the side, out of sight, and looked at Liam. He guessed they had not seen Liam, and still thought Hagen was acting alone.

Hagen pushed on Liam's chest, saying, "Hide."

"What? No," Liam said, his voice rising.

Lt. David came around some equipment and ordered them in a hushed voice. *"This way."*

They weaved around the pipes in the room until the back entrance to the bridge was no longer visible.

Liam spoke in a quiet, hurried voice. "Lieutenant, I thought there was only one entrance."

Lt. David didn't answer but came to a far stone wall, feeling along it. "It's here somewhere. I just saw it." He grasped inside a vertical line with his fingers, and yanked, causing a panel to fall to the ground, revealing a meshed gate on the wall, which went into a wire cage enclosure. Lt. David clutched a handle, slid it open, and stepped inside the small-wired pen. Hagen stood outside the wired cage and glanced at Liam, who was staring wide-eyed into the confined space.

Lt. David rolled his eyes, grabbed Hagen's arm, and pulled him inside. "Liam, move it."

Liam obeyed by stepping inside. Lt. David slid the gate closed. He studied the side of one wall, which had a couple of levers, and slammed one up. The cage they were in ascended upward at a rapid rate. They were cloaked in blackness for a moment before light passed over them, and then more blackness. The pattern continued. Hagen's stomach flipped, and he felt a sense of vertigo and tottered backward into the corner, his back hitting a hard surface.

Hagen braced his hands on either side of him, his body completely tense, and Lt. David leaned against the wall, his hand on the control. Liam sat down in the far corner, his wide eyes looking around him in fright.

Lt. David offered a small smile. "It's okay, boyos. Got to give it to the builders of this place. A hydraulic lift. Probably included long ago when the idea of lifts was not even a glimmer in most people's heads."

Lt. David pushed the lever down halfway, and the elevator slowed. He appeared to be reading words that were scribbled on the wall. They were in German, and Hagen assumed he had memorized the map well enough to know what floor he wanted. Then he shoved the lever all the way down, stopping the movement of the cage. A wall was in front of them with light seeping through cracks. There was a word written in front of them that said *Bibliothek*.

Library.

Lt. David pushed on its center; there were crackles and grates, then the panel fell outward. A foyer opened in front of them with a knight's armor on one side and a few oil paintings hung along the wall. A couple of lamps provided illumination. Lt. David slid the meshed gate open, and they climbed out.

Lt. David stepped to the window and stared out at the stars and moon in the sky, then looked around them, appearing to be getting his bearings, and mumbled, barely intelligible, "Looks like the right place. We're going to see if we can get Ness."

Lt. David grimaced, then touched his lower back and waved for them to follow. Hagen noticed for the first time that the lower part of Lt. David's shirt was blood-soaked. The lieutenant froze in place, and Liam and Hagen leaned into the wall behind him. The sound of men speaking was clear and coming from an opposite door. Lt. David looked behind them, bit his lip, and faced the door, raising his rifle. Hagen understood—there was no time to flee.

The door opened, and the backside of an SS officer was visible. He was speaking to someone in the next room. Liam removed his revolver and brought it up.

The officer continued to speak to whoever was in the room. "SS Oberführer, Martz will be here shortly. Get me when he comes, and we'll get this scum to talk." He turned and startled when he was faced with Hagen.

The rifle in Lt. David's hands cracked out firepower and the SS man threw his hands in the air, reeling back through the doorway. The lieutenant did not hesitate, but moved inside, Hagen one step behind. An SS guard had been sitting on the edge of a desk and, at the ruckus, had instantly risen to his feet. Another man in a white coat with blotches of blood on it had been hunched over a table with horrific sharp instruments on it. He too had wheeled around. In the middle of the room was Ness, sitting in a chair, his wrists pulled behind his back and bound. Lt. David fired at the guard next to the desk as Hagen and Liam picked out the last target and killed him.

The firing ceased, and Hagen stared down at the dead men, then over to Ness. Lt. David removed a long thin blade with a smooth handle, took it from a table, and cut Ness's hands loose. Ness had burn marks on his face. He brought his hands to his lap; the missing tip of one finger had been cauterized.

I think they just started.

Liam and Hagen caught Ness as he fell forward out of his chair, then helped him kneel down on one knee.

Ness placed a hand on his knee, stood, and eyed the lieutenant's blood-soaked midsection. "Plant the bombs?"

"I did," Lt. David answered. Then he dug in his pocket and brought up a stopwatch. "We have twenty minutes."

"What about Roesia?" Hagen asked.

The lieutenant shook his head. "She's on her own now, Hagen."

Ness looked down at Liam's hand. "Is that Captain Ford's?"

Liam looked down at Captain's Ford pistol and met Ness's forlorn stare. "Aye, it is. He saved us, but never made it."

Ness nodded and scanned the area, ordering, "Messer, isn't it? Hand me the pistol on that dead man. And grab me a rifle." Hagen bent down over the corpse lying halfway into the door, removed the pistol, and handed it over, then retrieved an automatic rifle.

Shouts came from down the hall, and Ness ordered, "Go."

Lt. David looked toward the elevator then down a separate corridor. He touched the pocket that held the map. "There's a secret passage close by; it's connected to the one Liam and I took earlier. We could all make it."

Ness shook his head. "Go."

Lt. David didn't argue but grabbed Liam's arm. "Hagen, stay on my heels," he said forcefully.

Hagen glanced over his shoulder as Ness took position by the corner of the wall and braced the butt of the rifle on his shoulder.

The voices grew louder, and Hagen caught a few words. *"Prisoner's free!"* Gunfire drowned out the next voices.

Ness fired short controlled bursts, expended shells bouncing off the stone floor at his feet. Rounds smacked into the area around Ness, and pieces of wooden debris spewed up in the air.

Hagen, Lt. David, and Liam went around a corner while the firefight continued to roar behind them. The harsh crack of a pistol spurred Hagen to push everyone forward.

German voices were screaming, *"Kill him! Kill him!"*

They reached the end of the hallway that split into a T. Lt. David hurried to the wall, splayed his hand over it, and pushed along.

"It's here somewhere."

Shadows danced on both sides of the corridor.

Hagen said, "They're coming." He looked around them, stepped to a door, and surveyed the room. It was empty except for a few pieces of furniture and a king-size bed by the window. He turned and grabbed Lt. David's shoulder. "There's no time."

The lieutenant frowned and relented, then followed Hagen inside the room. Hagen stepped over to a bi-fold closet door, yanked on a handle, and the door folded open.

He grabbed Lt. David's sleeve, pulling him inside. *"Go!"*

Wagner's voice shrieked from down the hall. *"Hagen Messer!* It's over! You're surrounded. Surrender and you'll come to no harm!"

Hagen shoved Liam into the closet next to Lt. David and started to shut the door, but Liam blocked it from being shut.

His eyes pleaded, he clutched Hagen's shirt, and he shook his head and whined, *"Don't, Hagen. Please, don't."*

Hagen put his hand over his mouth, reached up to his necklace, and pulled the medallion over his head.

He tugged Liam's hand off of him and placed the medallion in his palm whispering. "For luck."

Liam glanced down at it, then back up to Hagen, his widened eyes terrified and pleading. Hagen closed the door shut until it clicked. He placed his forehead on the wooden surface and took in a deep breath.

He whispered through the horizontal vents on the closet door, "Lieutenant, just get Liam out of here. *Please.*"

He stepped out into the hallway, a numb buzz in his head as his feet moved him forward. He held his revolver up; it hung upside down from its trigger guard over his index finger.

An SS guard's head poked around the edge of a hallway and turned back to whoever was on his side. "He's surrendering."

Three SS troopers came into view, their submachine guns at their sides. "Put it down," one shouted. Hagen tossed the gun, and it clattered to the floor as he held his hands up. He glanced over his shoulder and observed other SS troopers sneaking up from behind him.

The dry voice of Wagner made him face forward. "That, Hagen Messer, was an impressive run."

Wagner weaved between the guards. His eyes were slits and his hands were laced in front of him. Someone was a few feet from his back and keeping pace. Hagen recognized the black-bearded young man, Rolph. His face was bruised, and he had a fat lip.

An SS trooper fastened handcuffs on his wrists, which lay flush against his waist. Time had slowed, and Hagen had the strange feeling that this was not happening.

Wagner came up, rubbing his chin. "Clever with the elevator. Not even Rolph knew of it. And, oh, we found your bombs. Rolph located them for us. He has a good nose. Very clever, where you put them. Would never have guessed. I'm afraid Nazi Germany will reign on."

Hagen's heart sank—his hopes were crushed. His gaze fell to the floor.

"Foolish to use your real last name," Wagner said. "Then, using your dead brother's name was just stupid. I'm not sure what kind of spy you are—lazy or just an imbecile. We have many questions for you. Oh yes, many questions. Martz, unfortunately, will not have as much latitude with you as he gets with most prisoners. Do you know why? Do you know why you are so precious to Nazi Germany?"

Hagen's thoughts reeled, and he remembered sitting in the *Night Angel* with Liam, back in England, looking out on an airfield. He remembered Liam taking him to the Irish pub by the airbase. He had never wanted that time to end.

"Look at me," Wagner ordered.

Hagen's head did not budge. A tear dropped from one eye. Wagner repeated his command, his tone quiet, but the menacing presence behind it was clear.

He pronounced each word carefully. *"Look at me."*

Hagen slowly brought his head up and met Wagner's hard gaze. The corner of Wagner's mouth curved upward. "Dr. Mengele and Dr.

Lawerenze will have their work cut out for them." He tapped Hagen's chest. "You, scum, are a descendant of the Wehr Wolff family. That makes you a top experiment priority."

Hagen turned his head away, breaking the stare, and found he was staring at the wall Lt. David had touched earlier. He noted bloodied handprints on the wall where Lt. David had put his hands. He snapped his attention away, meeting Wagner's now triumphant leer.

"I-I will not tell you anything," Hagen said, and bit down on his lip, angry with himself for his voice breaking.

A frown formed on Wagner's narrow face, but in the next second, it transformed back into a grotesque grin. "Many have made that claim; none, though, have kept their word. And besides, we really just need your blood." He gestured his hand to the guards to lead him away. Hagen glanced back over his shoulder. Wagner's attention went to the wall for a second, where incriminating bloodied handprints were located. Hagen stared down at his hands that had no blood of them. *Would he notice?*

Wagner's concentration was interrupted by a guard who informed him that their prisoner, Ness, was indeed dead.

Wagner grunted and ordered his men to clean the area as best they could, or block it off if necessary, since they were soon expecting guests. Wagner led Hagen and his escorts down the corridor. He did not look back at the wall with its incriminating evidence. Hagen faced forward, his chin on his chest.

At least Liam will escape.

Nineteen: Xylander and Houk

May 12, 1940
Wehr Wolff Castle, Nazi Germany

THE TRIP TO Hagen's new home below the castle was a mixture of sheer terror, stupefaction, and blurred moments.

His guards took him inside a small room with bookshelves on the far wall, a long table at one end, and a diagram of the castle hanging on the wall. Martz and the cleft-lipped Dexer waited for him a few feet from the doorway. Martz murmured to have Hagen's handcuffs removed, and one of the guards quickly complied.

His guards squeezed his arms. Dexer stepped up, his bottom teeth gleaming through his hole. That wound was still raw and hideous. Dexer stared at Hagen and, without warning, punched him in the stomach. Hagen collapsed to his knees, coughing and rasping. Hagen could envision the handkerchief in his pocket and, with it, the dark power.

I want that power. Now. Please.

Someone pulled on his hair, and Hagen looked up at Martz, the man's hard gaze piercing into him.

Martz spoke, his voice steady and calm. "I taught Dexer that. Effective, isn't he? If it was me, you'd not able to breathe again." He patted Hagen's cheek with stinging slaps. "You and I in a ring, I'd turn you to mincemeat. But that would not do; I will break you but keep you very much alive. Why did you give your brother's name? Why did you say your name at all? What was your mission?"

The guards pulled Hagen back to his feet. Martz took Hagen's right hand and twisted his finger. Hagen bit down on his lip but didn't make an utterance. He was losing his ability to think clearly, though, and soon everything would tumble out of his mouth.

Martz kept hold of Hagen's finger and asked in a calm, collected manner, "You think you can keep your tongue still? That's a great fantasy. Who was your contact? Who's helping you?" Martz rotated his wrist, and Hagen's finger snapped.

Hagen shrieked out in pain, but his guards kept him in place.

Martz stared down at the broken finger, and asked, "Dexer, what did the general say?"

"Broken, but alive."

"Right," Martz said, and grinned. "I have a soft spot in me, though, Messer. Let me fix that." Martz grabbed Hagen's finger, yanked, and it crackled.

Hagen cried out in pain, streams of tears falling from his eyes.

"What finger is next?"

Hagen muttered, "S-stop. I didn't know."

Martz frowned, leaned closer, and asked, "Didn't know what?"

"I didn't know the Nazis wanted me."

Martz straightened. "No idea you had family lineage to the Wehr Wolffs?"

Hagen met Martz's eyes and shook his head. The truth he felt was so much easier to speak than keeping up any lies. Hagen looked back down. He was fatigued, hungry, and demoralized. His hopes had been crushed, and the only thing that kept his mouth completely sealed was not any loyalty to governments, but Liam. The image of Liam kissing him was vivid. *I have to protect him as long as I can.*

Martz asked, "Who are your contacts?"

Hagen's head bobbed, and he met Martz's hard gaze for one second. "N-no one. I swear. I was not supposed to meet anyone here." Again the truth.

Martz placed his hand over Hagen's pinky finger. "What about the British team? What do you know about them?"

Hagen took a second to think on the question and whispered, "W-who?"

Martz twisted his finger, and there was a crack. Hagen screamed and squirmed helplessly against his captors.

He groaned, tried his best to bend over with the guards holding him, and managed to say, "I-I swear."

Martz did not let his broken finger go, but growled in his ear. "I don't believe you, Hagen Messer." Martz snapped his small finger back in place, and Hagen howled in pain, beads of sweat pouring down his face. "You have many fingers. Many toes. I'll do this all night."

A guard came into the room. "Sir."

Martz turned around. The guard said, "We have an incident, sir. Someone has spotted a weremutant loose in the castle."

Martz grumbled and told the guards, "Take him to the security lab. Hand him over to Xylander."

Hagen cradled his hand. His mind was numb, but he could not help feel the terror that he would soon speak.

The guards shoved him forward until Martz said, "Stop."

His guards jerked on Hagen's shoulder and turned him.

Martz stepped up, and Hagen flinched and averted his eyes away. Martz didn't speak for a moment, and Hagen kept his eyes lowered.

Martz leaned forward and said, "Feel lucky you get a break. Take that time to think real hard about what comes next. Play the brave game for long, and I'll be irked, and I will seek my own revenge. I know you had contacts here. One, maybe two, or three. I can't torture you to a slow, painful death, but if I find your contacts, I'll do whatever I want with them. Maybe you won't care about the first I find, but sooner or later, I will find someone you do care for. And you know what?"

Hagen's gaze barely moved up, catching Martz's placid face.

Martz whispered into Hagen's ear, "I will torture them until you give me answers, and if I so much as think you don't answer fast enough or have calculated a half-truth with a lie, I'll keep torturing. Just because I can." Then Martz was gone and his guards shoved him, guiding him down a winding staircase. That same scent of dog shit filled the area, and he knew the weremutant kennels were close.

They took him down a winding staircase into a wide concrete corridor with an arched ceiling. After a hundred feet, they halted in front of a thick iron door. One of the guards opened the entry while the second one guided him through. He stepped onto a raised platform. It extended to a wall on one side while on the opposite end, railing overlooked an area with white walls and long narrow aisles with cell doors on either side. Across the platform was a modern laboratory that had glossy metal tables and chairs with restraints spread around the room. The area stank of a mixture of chemicals, and once again, as in the laboratory, ammonia predominated here.

A shelf up on the wall held assorted beakers with different colored chemicals in them. Hagen surveyed the cells below. Down the aisle a nude prisoner lay in the middle of a tiled floor; both of his arms were thick, muscled, and had hair that sprouted all over. His body and legs were freakishly emaciated.

A prisoner with no shirt was shoved out of a cell to a guard standing by a large cube-shaped container with a long metal handle on the side. The guard picked up the handle of a poker that lay inside—the end glowed red. The prisoner was made to kneel. The red-hot end was pressed against the bare skin of the man's shoulder, and the man let out a horrific shriek; the swastika brand was clearly visible when the poker was removed.

Hagen was taken over an elevated walkway and down stairs. He observed one man shackled in a chair close to the laboratory section: his head hung down and IVs stuck in his arm, fluid running through them. They came to an aisle that was ten feet across, metallic doors spaced out on either side. A man dressed in a lab coat came down the aisle, stepped to a cell door, and opened a sliding section in the door at eye level; he stared into the small window, then slammed it shut. Hagen recognized the man from earlier, when he'd been outside and witnessed the prisoners being unloaded. The man had streaks of white in his black hair. He glanced up at Hagen for a cursory second before moving to another door.

As a couple of naked prisoners were escorted into cells, Hagen noticed their deformities. One prisoner had hair growth heavily on only one side of his body, and his hands had slender elongated claws extending out of their tips. The second prisoner had thick tuffs of hair on his face, shoulders, back, and legs. His shoulders were broad, but his legs were spindly.

Two SS guards approached Hagen. One towered over him; he had shifty, beady eyes and a belly that drooped generously over his belt. The other man was short and had a squished chin and a small mustache that resembled the one Hagen had seen in newspaper pictures of Hitler.

The SS guard who had escorted him downstairs handed papers over to the obese man, and addressed him as Xylander. "This scum is a spy and top priority to Dr. Mengele's experimentation. General Wagner ordered him to be broken, but not killed. He's very special."

Xylander whistled. "My pleasure. Very well, leave us." The SS guard left the room. Xylander walked around Hagen, poking his back, his shoulders. Hagen kept his head down. Xylander gripped his upper arm and felt over his biceps. He crouched down, placed a hand on his quad, and kneaded his knuckles into his muscle.

Xylander stood back up, cupped Hagen's chin, and lifted hard so Hagen was looking at him.

He pushed Hagen's lip away from his teeth, peered at his gums, and spoke with admiration. "Impressive. Houk, let's show this prisoner his accommodations, shall we?"

The squished-chin man smiled, which made it seem as though his chin completely vanished. Hagen was taken to a nearby steel door. Xylander opened it and pushed Hagen inside. The room was bare except for a small-frame bed fastened to the wall on the far side and a metal toilet in the corner.

Xylander did not let his arm go, and whispered in his ear. "Kneel."

Hagen got down onto his knees and glanced back after a moment. Both men held metal rods, Xylander slapping one into his palm. The man grimaced and brought the weapon back over his head. Hagen cringed and closed his eyes. Sharp pain exploded in his shoulders and he fell to his side. The hard metal slammed into his side, his stomach, and back. He covered his head, but they were not trying to hit him there. The men cursed him and called him a traitor and a coward. Hagen held the handkerchief tightly in one hand.

When the pummeling was done, Xylander grabbed Hagen's wrist, pulled him to one side of the room, and secured a handcuff over his wrist; it was connected to a chain soldered to the wall. Hagen wheezed, his vision fuzzy with wetness.

Xylander squatted down, out of breath after his exercise, and rested a hand on Hagen's thigh. "We expect strict obedience here, or you'll get much worse." The fat man's fingers inched up Hagen's thigh and his foul breath reached his nose. "Wagner said broken, and by tomorrow night, you will be. By next week, you will know the scum you are." Xylander inched his hand up higher, his fingertips close to Hagen's crotch; his breathing became hitched and his tongue slipped out of his mouth, gliding over his lips. "Houk, close the door and help me haul him over to the cot."

A loud clanging noise erupted outside the doorway, and both Xylander and Houk jumped.

Xylander pulled his hand back from Hagen and looked over his shoulder, asking, "What the fuck is that?" There was shouting, and then a cry of surprise and a shriek of pain outside.

Houk looked out the door and grew tense. "*Room five*. Specimen thirty-one is out! I'm getting reinforcements." Houk departed.

Xylander grumbled and stood, then looked down at Hagen and left. The door closed behind Xylander, the room becoming pitch black. The shouting continued, and several pairs of feet came by his door. There were cracks of gunfire.

It grew quiet after a while, and his eyes adjusted to the dark until he could observe his room. It was a padded cell with only a small window in the door, which could only be opened from the outside. A vent was above him in the ceiling. He stared over at the far toilet and bed. How he was supposed to use either one was beyond him. The chain would not allow him that much movement. Hagen let his head hang down, and he cried like he never had before, not even when his mother had died. Despair filled his heart, and he realized this was where he was going to die. A prisoner of the Nazis, used for experimentation and only God knew what torture before he was finally allowed to die. He wiped the tears off his face. The interrogation would happen soon, and he had absolute doubt regarding his resolve.

One anguished thought repeated in his mind. *I'm not going to make it. I'm going to break.* It was true. He barely had any fight left in him.

Sleep came and went in brief spells. Nightmares filled his mind during each fleeting rest. He pointed the pistol down at the boy and fired. He closed the closet door, telling Liam and Lt. David to run, but this time, Wagner caught Liam. Dexer held Liam down, asking Hagen questions, and Hagen sang and sang and told him everything. Martz stepped up, sweat gleaming on his bald head, as he waved a hot poker in front of Hagen's face. He did not speak with his normal calmness, but with a hiss, a forked tongue slipping from between his lips.

"I do it, because I like it." He lowered the poker toward Liam, and his friend whined, and Martz thrust the red end into Liam's eye.

Hagen screamed himself awake.

Hagen's body ached, his throat was dry, and his stomach growled. They had given him water but, to this point, no food. During the night, he'd waddled on both knees as far as his chain allowed, shoved his pants down, and urinated, some of the liquid running back toward him. The remaining liquid drained to the middle of the room that dipped down to a small grate. Two hours later, he'd had a bowel movement, and once again, he'd tried to stretch his chain as far as he could. With a pungent stench assaulting his senses, he pulled his pants back on and crawled into the corner again.

Time passed painfully slowly. High-pitched shrieks spilled out into the night, followed sometimes by laughter. Sometimes it was mere silence, which, to his mind, was worse because he waited and waited for something to happen but nothing came. He dozed for a short period and awakened with a start.

The noise of laughter was at his door. He recognized the three men. Two were the wards who had beaten him last night. There was the debased Xylander, who Hagen was convinced had more in mind for his body than any of the others. And then there was Houk, and the other was Dexer.

He picked out the words spoken by Dexer. "The general does not know how he made it so far last night, and all alone. Had explosives, too. We're not sure where he got those. He took out several guards. Martz thinks he had to have had help. General Wagner says it was a fluke and now calls him Herr Fluke. Martz will get answers. And they're doing an extensive search..."

Hagen lost track of the conversation; beads of sweat dotted his forehead, and his heart raced.

What are they going to do to me? What is Xylander going to do to me?

The door opened, and the men came inside. Dexer came in first and leaned against the wall, the other two men remaining near the door. Houk grimaced, waved a hand over his nose, and smiled, his tiny chin a nub.

He chortled. "Smells."

Dexer asked, "You have a good-night shit, Herr Fluke?"

Hagen did not answer but stared at his bed.

Dexer said, "You gave a good show last night. Shooting that halfwit in the head. Almost convinced everyone. You have to be the dumbest spy I've ever seen, though, using your own name. And a name wanted by the Nazis." Dexer laughed.

Xylander chuckled, came forward, and bent down, the only one who did not appear to be repulsed by Hagen's stench. "I'm just surprised this nitwit could kill so many. He looks like a stupid lamb." Xylander patted Hagen's cheek, his fingers not moving from his skin, and asked, "Why did you kill those men you were with? Then burn them? Were they on to you?"

Houk slapped the wall playfully, releasing a sharp hee-haw laugh. Xylander slapped Hagen's face hard, and his face stung.

Xylander leaned in. "You've been lucky? Your luck seems to have ended."

"What time is it?" Dexer asked.

Houk took out his pocket watch. "Eleven hundred."

Dexer grinned and said, "General Wagner ordered 'broken but not killed' so we need to make sure he doesn't die of dehydration." He turned to the two men, saying, "Shall we give him a drink?"

Xylander stood up, grabbed his large belly, and chuckled. Hagen scooted back to the wall. They unbuttoned their pants, then pulled them down to their thighs. Warm liquid sprayed onto Hagen's neck, ear, and shirt, then soaked into his clothes. Hagen gritted his teeth and stared down at his lap. One of the men farted, and there was boisterous laughter, followed by more flatulence.

Hagen rolled to his side, and someone sighed over him, zipped up their pants, and Xylander said, "You're welcome, Herr Fluke." The men laughed and moved away to the door.

Hagen placed an arm over his eyes; a hard cry wanted to come, but he pushed it back.

Houk asked, "Should we take him to the coop?"

Xylander said, "We better wash him up."

"I'm going to have a smoke," Dexer said. "One of you have a light? Ah, thanks."

Urine and tears dripped off of Hagen's nose.

One of the guards saying *rampant weremutant* caught his attention. He remained on his side while he quietly listened to the conversation.

Dexer was speaking. "Five guards were ripped to shreds last night. The men were all disemboweled, left to die a slow agonizing death. A couple of soldiers said they saw a weremutant."

"Ah, killing for sport? That sounds like a true SS," Xylander said, and laughed.

Houk asked, "Where is it now?"

Dexer answered, "No idea. But you'd think it'd be easy to spot. Hairy, walks on all fours, has claws and fangs."

Houk said, "Someone on the watchtower said at zero-one-hundred, they'd seen something careening across the parapet bridge and thought at first it was some SS officer, but it was crawling over the ground."

"Was anyone bitten downstairs?" Xylander asked.

Dexer answered, "Dr. Mengele doesn't think so. Records don't indicate any SS guards leaving their posts without permission. Anyone bitten is quickly quarantined. You know the routine."

"I tell you what happened," Xylander said. "One of those guards doing guard duty in the kennel got bitten and didn't tell anyone. If one of those new mutants we've been training bites someone, I'm told the changes happen in less than twenty-four hours. Their venom works much quicker than those things they call wehrwolves."

"Maybe," Dexer said, sounding reflective.

Hagen lifted his head an inch, his mind reeling. Martz had been interrupted last night by a weremutant in the castle. No doubt, this was the same one.

Sgt. Collins?

"General Wagner and Dr. Mengele," Dexer said in a shocked voice. "I thought you were meeting us at the coop. The prisoner reeks."

Wagner came into the room with a hand cupped over his nose and mouth. He spoke, his voice slightly muffled. "I am too eager. Hello, Herr Fluke." He brought his hand down as a smile curved across his face. "Today, I hope, you will give us answers. Comrades, step out so Dr. Mengele can get what he needs, then hose him down; his stench offends me. Afterward, bring him to me." Wagner departed, and everyone but Dexer stepped out of the cell.

The stench of ammonia pervaded his nostrils. Dr. Mengele came inside, and though his entire area stank of that particular chemical, Hagen was convinced the doctor had to embalm himself in it on a daily basis. The two personal assistants who followed him inside were the ones he had seen outside with clipboards the night before. The small-framed man with a goatee removed vials from a leather bag.

Dr. Mengele came close, not seeming to mind Hagen's stench; he held his palm out to his assistant. "Meyers."

The goateed man, Meyers, looked around and tried to find a dry area to place the rack of vials that he had removed from his bag; he finally chose a spot to set them down and duly handed a vial to Dr. Mengele.

Dr. Mengele readied a syringe as he said over his shoulder, "Take his cuff off." Dexer came forward to comply and, in a short time, removed them.

Dr. Mengele told Hagen, "Put your arms out."

Hagen hugged his arms to his chest. Xylander came and slapped his face. Hagen's ear rung from the strike.

Xylander bent down and pulled hard on Hagen's ear and whispered, "Keep this up and I promise I'll let every guard on this floor do you at night. As many times as they like. Understand?" Xylander straightened and lorded over Hagen.

A tear rolled down Hagen's cheek, and his lips trembled, but he straightened his arms out. Dr. Mengele grabbed a wrist and turned it so his forearm was pointed upward.

Dr. Mengele pressed his finger along Hagen's veins and ordered, "Ball your fist." Hagen gritted his teeth and did as he was commanded. "*Yessss*," Dr. Mengele said, "That's it."

There was a pinch as a needle was pushed into his arm. Hagen grimaced and felt light-headed, so he turned his head away. Dr. Mengele continued to remove vial after vial of Hagen's blood, handing them to his assistant. Hagen's dizziness increased, and he felt squeamish that so much blood was being removed. His heel tapped on the ground over and over as he strained to hold still, but he couldn't help but fidget. Dr. Mengele finally removed the needle and stood, a satisfied smirk on his face. The man with white streaks in his pitch-black hair came and took away the case of vials.

Dr. Mengele told Xylander, "Be sure to feed him today. Three meals." Then he and his personal assistants departed.

Feet shuffled closer, but Hagen didn't move.

Xylander kicked him hard in his hamstrings. "I'll feed you. Just wait. Get up. Houk, get the hose."

Xylander came and grabbed Hagen's arm.

Dexer said from behind him, "Don't keep the general waiting long."

Houk returned with a hose in his hands.

Xylander took it, saying, "Get a uniform."

Houk looked back at Hagen and then to Xylander, reluctant to leave, but he obeyed and left.

Xylander shouted, "Strip!"

Hagen jumped at the volume, got to his feet, and brought his unsteady hand up to a button on his shirt.

Xylander screamed, "Faster!"

Hagen flinched and moved quicker, pulling off his shirt. He glanced up at Xylander and looked away. Those eyes—they were glazed with a ferocious hunger.

Hagen stared at the floor, his body shook, and a complete numbness filled him. He unbuttoned his pants and pushed them down to his ankles, leaving nothing on but his soiled drawers. A dirtied light blue cloth lay on floor. Euan's handkerchief. He hooked his fingers into the band of his drawers, and they fell to his ankles. He stepped out of them and hugged his chest. Nothing happened for a moment, and then he glanced at Xylander, who appeared transfixed.

Xylander said in a hoarse voice. "Put your arms up." Houk returned with clothes in his arms, and looked over at Hagen, scrutinizing his nakedness. "Turn it on, Houk."

Houk went outside. Water trickled out of the nozzle one second, and in the next, it came in an ice-cold jet stream. A steady torrent slammed into him; Hagen slipped and came down hard on his side. He reached out quickly, grabbed the wet cloth before it went into the drain, and wadded it in his fist. He curled up into the fetal position, wishing nothing more than for this nightmare to be over. Xylander barked for him to stand up. He got up to his knees, then to his feet, and Xylander shouted for him to face the wall and spread his legs. The water thrust against his back, his buttocks, and stung his legs.

"Turn around!" Xylander barked.

Hagen turned, covered his face, and bent down when the jet stream punched him in his testicles. The water ceased, and he stood, crossing his arms over his chest and shivering. Xylander came up to him. The man bent partially down and stared hard at Hagen's face. Xylander raised his hand in slow motion. He brushed his fingers against Hagen's cheek, slid them toward the back of his neck, and then over his shoulder. Hagen flinched, a whine escaping his mouth. Hagen saw that Houk was transfixed on him.

Xylander glided his fingertips over Hagen's wet skin, down his spine, to his lower back. Hagen squeezed his arms over his torso. He tapped his fingers on his upper buttock and rubbed his crack with a light playfulness, then firm and hard. Xylander's breathing changed, and he fully groped a buttock. Foul breath brushed against Hagen's face, the smell of onion assaulting his nose.

Xylander said in choked voice, "Houk, close the door. We have plenty of time for this. Plenty of time." Someone shouted in the aisle and suddenly the hand was off of him. *"What the fuck is it now?"*

Houk peeked out the door. "Someone is here."

Xylander shoved a towel in Hagen's arms and spoke with a thick voice. *"Dry off."* Xylander stepped back, watching him intently.

After a few moments, Hagen was dry. His mind numb, he sluggishly put on the frayed gray clothing Houk had brought. He looked down and saw the soiled handkerchief on the floor. Xylander and Houk were turned away, so he reached down, moving in slow motion, and picked up the soaked cloth, then stuffed it inside his waistband. His body trembled violently, and he seemed unable to focus as he held his arms close to his chest, seeking their protection from any further molestations. The manacles were placed back on his wrists and ankles.

Xylander came close; his mouth an inch from Hagen's head, his breath blew against his inner ear. Xylander spoke with deliberation, making sure Hagen understood each word.

"Remember, Herr Fluke, you're my ward. When you're not being interrogated or with Dr. Mengele, you belong to me. Speak against anything now or in the future, you'll regret it. They just want your blood and only care that you're alive. I have clever ways of making pain that don't cause permanent damage."

I can't do this. I can't.

Hagen could feel a sense of panic creeping up his spine as each second ticked by. If he was about to be interrogated, he knew he wouldn't be able to withstand what he supposed waited for him. He shuddered at the thought of what would happen should he fail to protect Liam or Lt. David or Roesia for that matter. He tried to focus on the here and the now and leave Xylander's threats, equally as frightening, for later.

Xylander grabbed his arm and pulled him through the doorway, out into the laboratory aisle. A figure moved in the corner of Hagen's eye, and he flinched, glancing furtively at the person who stood close to the door. Hagen and the two SS guards froze in their places.

Rolph was standing front and center and met Hagen's eyes for one second, then moved to Xylander. "General Wagner is asking for the prisoner."

Twenty: Splat

XYLANDER AND HOUK led Hagen from Dr. Mengele's laboratory and down a narrow passage that had slick walls and large lamps overhead. He was taken to a vaulted door, which was opened by a guard, and pushed inside. The room was immense and cylindrical.

He stared up at the walls surrounding him. He was reminded of an abandoned farm that he'd visited before he had shipped out. The place had a silo where they once stored crops; he had gone inside the barren place, looking up at the spherical structure that stretched high into the air. Bright sunlight had poured through an opening at the top. This building, though, was much vaster, but similar. Unique to it were the wide elevated walkways, high on the wall.

The most bizarre and morbid sight was that of nude prisoners suspended high above his head. They had ropes secured to the prisoners' ankles and more cords wrapped around their waists. The thick cables fastened to pulleys on horizontal beams far above him; and each pulley could be operated by personnel on sky walkways. Many prisoners had muzzles over their faces, and some thrashed on their ropes while others were curled up and trembled. Hagen tried to count the number of hanging prisoners, but there were too many to count in quick order. He was shoved forward and lost his balance. He put both hands out in front of him to break his fall, then remained on his knees, his head hanging.

A pair of boots were suddenly in front of Hagen. Dexer spoke above him, addressing Xylander. "The general will be here any second. Never good to keep him waiting."

Xylander's voice was surprised. "I thought he was waiting."

"What?" Dexer asked.

"Never mind," Xylander said. "He doesn't stink any longer."

Dexer grabbed a handful of Hagen's hair and pulled. Hagen gritted his teeth and grabbed the hand that clutched his hair, then met Dexer's eyes.

Drool seeped out of the hole in his lip, and he wiped it away. "Time for questions and answers."

Martz stepped next to Dexer, his expression neutral. "General has come to call him Herr Fluke."

"Fitting," Dexer said, and released Hagen's hair.

"Look at me, maggot," Martz growled.

Hagen met Martz's ferocious but somehow blank gaze. "General Wagner will be here, special for your interrogation. I'm sure you haven't forgotten our conversation last night. Remember this. There will be a point when Wagner won't need you. So if you lie, I swear, you *will* regret it." Martz shouted, "Show him!"

An SS guard wheeled out a dolly with a naked emaciated man strapped to it. Hagen attempted to understand what he was staring at. It was a man, not one of those weremutants, but he appeared to have weremutant limbs that had been transplanted to different parts of his body. The man's eyes twitched from side to side, his mouth was open in the silent scream of someone who had suffered unbearable pain but no longer had a voice able to share his nightmare. Dexer came up to the man, scanned him up and down, and patted one furry forearm that was complete with a clawed hand, which had been attached to the elbow.

"This," Martz said, "is the ingenious idea of Dr. Karl Gebhart, who shall be coming for our Grande banquet. Tomorrow, yes?"

"Yes, sir," Dexer replied.

"Dr. Gebhart has been conducting many transplant experiments and wants to learn a way to transplant appendages to amputee soldiers on the frontline. We have modified it here and are seeing what we can do with different species." Martz waved his hand at the SS guard, who pivoted the dolly and wheeled the disfigured man away. "We have many special experiments we are running, and are too happy to make you a subject in them. Or, if I find someone you care about, I will make them an example, because I can. *Just remember that.*" Martz shifted his gaze over Hagen's shoulder, then straightened. "The prisoner is ready, General Wagner."

"Turn, *Herr Fluke*," Wagner said.

Dexer grasped Hagen's bicep. The grip was like a vise, and Hagen held back a cry as the man whipped him around hard. Hagen faced Wagner and his entourage, including Major Becke and, close to him, Roesia. He tried to meet her eyes for a second, but she did not look at him, staring over his head instead.

Wagner smirked and looked back at Roesia. "Dr. Lawerenze, your personal assistant."

Her eyes met Hagen's then, and her face changed in one instant. Her brow knitted into a forlorn frown, her jaw set, and her arms crossed over chest.

She shook her head and whispered, "*Y-you lying scum.*"

Wagner tittered and flicked lint off his sleeve. "Don't worry, Dr. Lawerenze. He will be dealt with properly. And, I assure you, kept alive so you and Dr. Mengele will be able to carry out your experiments. And now, Dr. Lawerenze, I'm told Dr. Mengele is in the laboratory, running analysis on his blood; I will have a guard escort you."

Roesia lifted her chin indignantly. "I want to hear everything this traitor has to say."

Hagen was escorted toward a circle area that was sunken, a dome-shape set of bars over top of it. Outside the barred area were several chairs ready for an audience. Xylander tugged on his arm, guiding him through the strange cage's entry, a steel-barred door stood opened and looked as if it could be secured close with several bolts.

Behind Hagen, Wagner spoke casually as if addressing a lecture hall. "Sometimes we have live experiments conducted here, or sometimes interrogations that must be carried out more in the open. Above us is a moon roof where we can let in moonlight and make proper observations here inside the coop."

Reaching a wooden chair with several straps connected to it, Xylander shoved on Hagen's shoulder, making him sit down hard. Houk stood near, studying Hagen, and he scratched his nub of a chin, came over, and knelt down to unlock Hagen's shackles. They clattered to the floor. Hagen rubbed a wrist and peered up. Wagner and Becke were conversing outside the barred cage. Roesia had sat down in a chair, and her eyes met his for the briefest of moments before she glanced away. Her face had been placid, but Hagen couldn't help but notice she was wringing her hands. She had a small purse slung over her shoulder.

Martz stepped through the coop's door and to a nearby table with shiny metallic devices, ranging from pliers to sharp scalpels.

Hagen's handkerchief lay near his feet. After glancing quickly around, he stooped over and picked it up, then tucked it inside his shirt. It was strange—it held no luck he could see, but it was his talisman; a doorway to a power that gave him insight to what it felt like to have no vulnerabilities.

The same small-framed man with a goatee, Meyers, came over and grabbed one of Hagen's hands, placing it on top of the chair's arm. He hooked a leather strap around his wrist and pulled it tight. The assistant did not meet Hagen's eyes. The second assistant with white streaked through his wavy black hair placed sharp instruments on a table. Hagen tried to distract himself from what was coming and to remember the assistant's name—the one who was middle aged and had those distinguished streaks of white in his hair. He could not remember. This second assistant departed. Meyers laced each single finger down so that it was extended out and could not be moved. Hagen's ankles were secured to the chair frame.

Xylander and Houk left the enclosure, but not before Xylander glanced back at Hagen. The man's eyes were filled with something of lust and dark desire. Hagen's stomach became queasy, and he gawked down at his feet, trying not to think of the horrid sexual fantasies no doubt seething in Xylander's mind, of what he wanted to do to Hagen when no prying eyes were near.

Wagner fussed with his uniform before placing his hat on his head and entering the metal cage. He clucked his tongue, started to pace in front of Hagen, and spoke in a calm manner.

"Here, Herr Fluke, is question-and-answer time. I will not normally be here. I rarely come to this place. But you are very unique, and tomorrow is a rare banquet. We need answers quickly. Cooperation means less pain; no cooperation means, well, you understand, right?"

Wagner stopped his pacing. "Dr. Mengele assures us he needs only your blood. Does not find the remaining parts of you…uh, useful. As long as you live, and have no infections, we are fine. So limbs, ears, eyes, are not essential to his study. Understand, Herr Fluke?" Wagner smiled. "I have some simple questions today, very easy to answer." He pointed in the air.

Hagen did not need to bring his gaze up. He remembered well what he had seen.

"Up there," Wagner said, "is our new experiment of will. If they let their bodies extend, a second pulley tightens over their balls. I'm told it's an experiment on willpower and endurance. I find it useful for prisoners who we want alive but need to break."

Wagner pointed outside the cage, and Hagen followed his finger's trajectory. There was a metal flatbed that had a naked prisoner with rope tied in knots over his hands and ankles so tightly the prisoner was suspended in the air. The man's arms were disfigured, as if pulled out of their sockets, and his legs rotated in a grotesque manner. The man appeared to be dead.

"And of course, how could you not recognize the medieval rack. German engineering. Martz also has many other tools at his disposal."

Wagner sauntered up close to Hagen. "Who do you spy for? The Russians? Americans? British? French? Poles?"

Hagen stared forward and bit down on the inside of his cheek. His training of what to do in an interrogation was minimal, but he remembered his instructor's drilling to remain quiet, and if one had to, keep the answers short and vague. But it was what Hagen had overheard that now rolled around in his mind. The instructor had said, sooner or later everyone breaks.

"Where were you born?" Wagner hissed. "What's your first language? Who was your contact here? How many more of you are there? What do you know about my units in Wehr Forest that have vanished?"

The questions continue to roll off Wagner's tongue. "You have Commando training, I surmise. Killed several of my guards...or did you have inside help?" Wagner asked, tapping one of the prison bars with his index finger. "So many questions we have and so many methods of gathering intelligence, Herr Fluke."

Becke came to the door of the enclosure, where he leaned with arms crossed.

Wagner offered Hagen a patient smile and said, "These, Herr Fluke, are questions that are really easy to answer. Where did you train? What was the purpose of your mission? Were you sent to just destroy the facility, or assassinate Doctors Mengele and Lawerenze, too? Or did you come for others?"

Wagner moved his finger back and forth, saying, "At some point, today, you will sing." He sighed. "Xylander. Get a rope ready upstairs. I think we're going to need it. When you cinch up his jewels, do it looser than the others; we don't want his ball sack to fall off—it has for so many. We may need that part of him." A lecherous smile formed on Xylander's face as he waddled across the room.

Wagner nodded to Martz.

Hagen tensed as the assistant, Meyers, came and laid a round stick over the end of his fingers to secure them to the surface even more than they had been already. Martz stepped closer, rolling a pin between his fingers to gain Hagen's attention. He then set the tip of the pin just under the edge of Hagen's fingernail and pushed, slowly. Hagen resolved to stay still, gritting his teeth from the pain. Martz gazed at Hagen as he slid the pin deeper. Once the pain registered, Hagen screamed in agony.

Martz brought out a second pin, then a third, and finally a fourth; each time the procedure was the same. However, by the fourth pin, Hagen was dripping with sweat, blood fell from his fingertips, and his throat was raw from his screams.

Roesia's high-pitched shout rang in Hagen's ears, but he could not decipher her words until she repeated herself. *"Answer him, you traitor!"*

Hagen's head swam, sweat ran down his back, and he dry-heaved. Roesia stood at the door next to Becke, pointing a scolding finger at him. Martz turned, glowering at her for being interrupted during his work. Wagner raised an eyebrow and turned, too, a displeased frown on his face.

Wagner raised his hands to placate Roesia. "Dr. Lawerenze, I assure you, we will—"

She stepped forward, not looking at Wagner but with her attention fixed on Hagen, tears falling from her cheeks.

"You don't understand. I trusted him. I trusted him." She jabbed her finger at Hagen. *"Answer him, traitor!"* She wiped tears from her cheeks, saying, "Did you know about the banquet tomorrow? Did you know the Führer was attending? Eichmann? Himmler? Dr. Goebbels? Hermann Goering? Were they your targets, too? Were you going to take everyone out?"

Roesia's jaw quivered; her hand was stuck inside her purse as she stared down at him. Was she asking him a question in code? Was she asking if she should take them all out right now? She was. He knew it. He would not hold out.

Hagen bit his lip and started to nod his head when someone outside the cage shouted, followed by more strident yells of surprise.

Hagen glanced outside the cage. Several SS guards were pointing upward. Hagen looked up to see a shadow falling straight at him. He tried to duck, but since he was restrained to his chair and couldn't move, he cringed instead. A loud thudding sound smacked into the top of the cage, followed by a wet, splattering noise. Hagen glanced about.

Meyers's face and jacket were covered with large splotches of dark red fluid and what appeared to be chunks of flesh. The small man flicked pieces of fibrous material from his goatee. Roesia had spongy pieces of debris in her hair, which she picked out, staring at them with incomprehension. Wagner had a coil of slimy yellow flesh on his face. He peeled it off, disgusted. Hagen brought his eyes up to the bloodied body that had slammed onto the top of the cage. Entrails that had not already plopped out dangled from the corpse's abdomen. A thick rope of tissue fell to the ground, coiling and making a hissing noise.

Hagen stared up again and squinted at the bloodied disfigured face that was meshed into to the bar. *A prisoner?*

Becke spoke in a hollow voice. "*Xylander*?"

It was indeed the same man.

Wagner flicked blood off his fingers. "Dexer, Houk, get this prisoner to his cell." Dexer stepped forward as beckoned, pushing the shocked Meyers out of his way.

Wagner jabbed his finger, commanding, "Guards, bring me this trai—"

Two definitive thuds interrupted Wagner. Hagen flinched, and everyone around him jumped, as well. Hagen looked around him, bewildered by the peculiar noise. He met Roesia's befuddled expression as she wheeled in a circle, trying to find the source of sound.

"Good God," Becke uttered.

Hagen followed his gaze and then stared in surprise. Meyers and Houk had been skewered to the floor by two long slender metal spears. One rod penetrated the back of the assistant's head and went out through his mouth. Blood dribbled from the man's mouth, his body convulsing. Dexer had fallen onto his arse and stared with wide eyes.

A metal spear was impaled Houk's back. His mouth producing sickened mewls. His fingers nimbly touched the stake near the exit wound at his right pectoral, his fingertips dipping into the blood that oozed down the slender pole.

Hagen looked up. Silver streaked through the air, went between the bars on top, and flashed before Hagen's eyes. There was a loud twanging noise as a javelin-like weapon vibrated where it thumped into the floor close to Wagner. Wagner grabbed his ear, then brought his hand to his face. Hagen observed red fluid dripping from a wound there. The general moved then, apparently forgetting all reason.

A ping came from the top of the cage as a metal spear flipped in the air, clanging down on the floor outside the barred enclosure. It had to have hit a bar. Another silver streak flittered in front of Hagen, closing in on Dexer, who'd gotten back up. The man moved fast and leaped backward. The slender pole thudded into the ground. Dexer grimaced with pain as he toppled over, then groped his way to the door where he stood and lumbered away, dragging an injured foot and a trail of blood behind him. It must have grazed him.

Becke and Martz scampered out of the cage. An SS guard came to the coop door, and stared in at Hagen and Roesia.

Roesia hesitated and glanced back at Hagen with helpless eyes. The SS guard beckoned her. "Move it."

Hagen stared up into the air. A suspended prisoner, who had been tethered up, was falling. The body made a wet splat as it hit the floor some distance away. Another prisoner was dropping rapidly, the man screaming all the way until he hit the ground with a wet thud. The entire room really came to life then. It was raining prisoners who'd been suspended overhead. A series of splats came one after another. The SS guard at the doorway locked the cage door and ran toward the far wall.

Roesia stepped forward, turning in different directions and seemed to be analyzing the beehive of confusion as SS guards ran in different directions while bellowing out orders. She regarded Houk, who gritted his teeth, both of his hands gripping the rod impaled in his body. She glanced to Hagen and back to Houk. She took the cap off her syringe and glanced around them, then stuck the needle into Houk's neck and pushed on the plunger, the same syringe that Lt. David had given her. She placed the syringe back in her purse and zipped it up. Houk groaned loudly, seized, and then his head fell forward motionless. He looked very dead. Roesia reached out and poked the man's head.

She came to stand in front of Hagen while scanning the area around them. Several guards were scrambling about. No one was paying them any attention. She gingerly removed the pins from the ends of his injured fingers.

A tear dripped down her face as she whispered, "Hagen, I'm so sorry."

Roesia stood back, then came next to him.

While she observed their surroundings, she spoke in a hushed tone. "This will keep them busy for a while. I don't think they will interrogate you anymore today."

Hagen spoke, looking straight ahead, trying to make it so his lips barely moved. "I heard someone is killing guards in the castle."

She put a hand to her mouth, feigning shock at the scene around them for any observers. There were none. A troop of guards rushed by and did not even glance over.

She said, "The killings have alarmed Martz. He pled for Wagner to cancel the banquet, but Wagner does not want to show any sign of problems. They are going to bolster security. Is it Sergeant Collins, you think? I mean, he was bitten, and they don't know that."

"I don't know," Hagen answered. "I assume no one found out about the original SS soldiers we ambushed?"

"No. I fed them lies. And I think they are so smitten with me and excited to capture you, the lines have thankfully been down; they have forgotten. Hagen, Dr. Mengele thinks he can improve the serum in one day; he's so confident he has killed the prisoners he was using and started anew. He thinks he'll have a new serum by tonight, using your blood."

Hagen didn't speak, feeling crushed.

"What happened to everyone else?" Roesia asked.

"I don't know. I hope they escaped."

"Wagner wants to show you off to Hitler tomorrow. I can detonate a grenade then, if you can hold on. W-we'll take as many of them as we can, including Mengele. Let's hope our charade can last one more night. What do you want to do, Hagen?"

"Yes, kill them all," Hagen answered.

"Tomorrow, Wagner has told me he wants to take a photograph of you, and wants to include prominent leaders in the picture—Mengele and Hitler, too. I will do it then. W-we won't get to say goodb—" She swallowed and said, "Thank you, Hagen."

She moved to the other side of the barred enclosure, where she sat on the floor and waited for someone to let her out.

Twenty-One: The Stranger in the Dungeon

MUCH LATER, AFTER the suspended prisoners had showered down from the ceiling, their bodies rupturing onto the ground, the silo was returned, relatively, back to normal.

Three SS guards hurried to Hagen's cage and unlocked the door. Roesia stood up when the guards arrived; she crossed her arms and impatiently tapped her foot, waiting for the door to open.

She strutted out, her chin up, effused with an imperious air, and said over a shoulder, "To think you made me sit in such abominable conditions!" The SS guard said he would escort her back. She swatted his hand away, telling him. "I think not!" She strolled across the floor and was gone.

Now that his original wardens, the gropey Xylander and the chinless Houk, were thankfully deceased, he had three new SS guards assigned to him. They took him out of his chair, placing manacles over his wrists, but did not bother with placing any restraints around his ankles. Hagen sensed the men were terrified by the recent events. A guard circled around. Hagen presumed him to be the unit leader; he disappeared for a moment, to return a couple of minutes later.

"He goes to the dungeon."

The dungeon? Not Mengele's lab?

Hagen's journey to the dungeon consisted of traversing several narrow staircases, vaulted Gothic corridors, with air that turned to bitter cold. Hagen stepped into an area that had a handful of guards sitting at a table, playing cards under a dim light. Their rifles leaned against the wall close to a large stone archway. Cash and valuables were spread over the surface. Hagen would have bet that the men were gambling with confiscated monies and jewelry from prisoners. The men stood; one man wobbled on his feet, his eyes bloodshot. The unit leader stated that Hagen was to be placed in a cell overnight.

Someone pushed Hagen's shoulder, and he stumbled forward, moving into a corridor that had a straw-and-dirt floor with cells on either side made of rusty vertical iron bars, which appeared to have been constructed hundreds of years earlier.

His SS escort gripped the indented handle of his cell and pulled. A noisy creak followed as the rusty door came open, then Hagen was pushed inside. His manacles were removed. A lumpy straw mattress was in the corner, and a hole in the ground would serve as his commode. The iron door was slammed shut, then locked.

Hagen thanked his good luck that they had not fastened him to the wall, and he was even more thankful they had not taken him back to the hermetic laboratory chamber where the air had been thin and sterile. Here, it was not good, being moldy with an acerbic bitterness, but it beat Dr. Mengele's hellish laboratory. Either these guards were giving him a break or simply did not know that the order was to keep him in Dr. Mengele's laboratory. Most likely, it was the latter. The men had forgotten to give him a meal, but he had no plans to complain.

Several moments later, Hagen sat on his bed against the far wall; he stared vacantly across his cell and out through the bars. He wondered if Liam had made it out. The thought that maybe he hadn't caused his eyes to water, and he gave a shuddering sigh.

Dirt shifted outside his cell and he tensed and straightened. The shadows shifted, and a hunched figure creeped to the front of his cell. A snout was visible, pointed in the air as it sniffed. Two hairy clawed fists moved between the bars, a shredded sleeve cuff visible over thick shaggy forearms. The clawed hands opened and something plopped to the ground, and then the hairy fists were gone. The thing outside his cell moved, and white fangs glinted from its mouth.

A weremutant? Is it smiling?

The creature fumbled at its chest with its paws. Hagen leaned forward, terrified to swallow. In the feeble light, he saw that it wore a frayed and soiled Nazi shirt. The creature flung an object between the bars. It skidded over the ground and stopped in front of Hagen's foot. Hagen picked it up but kept his gaze on the creature. The snout receded into the shadows, and a guttural growl was audible.

The word was clear. "Kraut."

"Sergeant Collins?" Hagen croaked.

Hagen came up his feet and quickly strode forward to grip the bars, peering through the gloom, searching for the sergeant.

"Don't leave me," he whispered with quiet desperation.

The shadows were quiet, though. Hagen opened his hand to stare down at a small rectangular object. A swastika on both sides. Hagen's mouth curved upward. A lighter. He bent down and peered at slimy flesh. He had hunted enough wild game to know he was seeing a pair of kidneys and a liver. He presumed the wild game in Wehr Wolff Castle were Nazis? A tin canteen leaned against the bars.

Hagen's smile turned into a grin. "And give us a Fuck You, Hitler." He peered through the bars into deep shadow, and said in hushed voice, "Sergeant, bring a key next time."

He picked up the tin canteen, unscrewed the top, sniffed, and took a deep drink of cool water. He lowered the canteen and closed his eyes. Water had never tasted so good. He scuttled to one side of the room and scooped up a handful of straw that he mixed with unidentified material from the raggedy mattress, then laid it on the ground. The lighter flipped open and the flame lit the debris that fizzled and burned quickly. This was not going to be a well-done meal. After several trials and errors, it was good enough. An image popped in his head of his father and brothers around the table when Ivan had been alive. They all had their heads bent in prayer. Hagen gave a quick prayer, then sank his teeth into the meat. His mouth watered and tears of gratitude poured down his cheeks. It was the best thing he had ever eaten. He was soon licking his fingers and looking around for more, but it was all gone.

He lay down on his bed, his stomach full, then sat up, as a thought popped into his head.

When was the last time I prayed? Was it right after Ivan died?

He got out of bed, knelt, and closed his eyes, saying, "To all that have died, I hope you have found your home. Thank you, Sergeant Collins. And God, please help Liam, Lieutenant David, make sure they are safe." His lip quivered. "Please watch over L-Liam and let no harm come to him." A tear trickled down his face. "I'm sorry, Kirby." He licked his lips, and for all the time that had passed, he spoke his brother's name. "And Ivan, I miss you so much. I hope you found peace wherever it is you go once you die." He lay back down, wiping his face.

A feather of a voice spoke, and Hagen tensed. Was God finally speaking to him? The whispery voice came from the wall closest to his head; he scampered onto his hands and knees until his ear was to a crumbling crevice in the stone wall.

The words he heard were clear. "Are you real?"

Hagen sat back on his haunches, then placed his mouth close to the fissure. "Hello?"

No one spoke. Hagen was about to return to his bed, convinced he was hearing things, when a male voice asked, "What's the date?"

Hagen hesitated and reflected; the day when he'd first met Liam up through this one had blended together. "I think it's May twelfth or thirteenth. Nineteen forty."

The person did not respond to this statement, but Hagen thought he heard a soft cry.

"What's your name?" Hagen asked.

It was several moments, but the person responded. "Euan."

Hagen placed both of his palms on the wall, and asked, "Euan Hartley? The businessman?" He already knew it was. He sensed the man on the other side, and something wafted from him. Death.

A raspy *yes* was uttered back. "Who are you?" Euan asked.

"We were sent to save you."

A soft chuckle met this.

Hagen squinted and stared through the crack but could not see anything. Suddenly, a bright amber eye popped into view, and Hagen flinched.

Euan laughed, his voice hoarse. "And who shall save you?"

Hagen rested his forehead on the wall and had no answer for that. He spoke close to the fissure. "They say I'm from the Wehr Wolff lineage, and are using my blood."

"I'm sorry to hear that," Euan said, then asked, "What's your name?"

"Hagen. Hagen Messer."

"*Hagen,*" Euan whispered. "Why did they send you down here, not to the lab with the other rats?"

Hagen sat down. "A mistake, I think. Why don't they keep you up in Dr. Mengele's lab?" Hagen sat up, staring at the worn iron bars as a thought came to him. His tone was excited as he said, "We can break out. Can't you turn into a werewolf at will?"

"No," Euan said. "Not anymore. I could, though. The only miserable thing I managed to keep are these bloody yellow eyes." Euan tittered. "Good for a circus. Not to break out of prison, though."

"Did they keep you in the lab...before?"

"When I could turn into a werewolf. They kept me inside that coop; silver has the ability to weaken your senses, energy, everything. Regardless, I got away twice. Martz broke my leg, but I still got away, and then Martz amputated my feet while I was awake." Euan paused for a time before continuing. "Those haven't grown back, but I must marvel, in the form of a werewolf, you can fight any infection and overcome any injury. Now that ability is gone, and my time is near."

Hagen was stung by the cruelty, but he was not the least bit shocked given all he had witnessed of the horror that thrived within these walls. "You said you used to be able to change?"

"In banking, you would say they voided my abilities," Euan huffed, and then he laughed in a merry, psychotic laugh. "But not on purpose, rest assured. You should have seen Wagner and Martz. They created an antidote by accidentally using my blood. Dr. Mengele thought he had created a serum that would boost my genetics and make my blood type more volatile, help him create his own version of Nazi werewolf soldiers. I think he was very close." Euan gave a hoarse chuckle. "But instead, he created an antidote. When I would not transform from human form to werewolf again, Wagner thought I was disobeying and had Martz punish me in ways I'd rather not talk about now. That bloody loon, Mengele, took my blood over and over, but said it was spoiled, and in Wagner's fury, they sent me down here to rot."

Hagen leaned his head on the wall. "They have an antidote?"

"I've seen it work, too," Euan said. "Administered it to weremutants and they returned back to humans in a matter of seconds. No deformities at all."

Hagen took this information in.

Euan whispered, "Hagen?"

Hagen cocked his head to the side. "Yes?"

"I have had the strangest dreams these last couple of nights."

"What?"

"My wife, three Christmases ago, I think, gave me a silly gift. She made out it was really fancy. Turned out to be nothing but a handkerchief. I never thought much of it. Put it in my sock drawer until she passed away a year ago. Cancer. I-I've been having this dream over and over that she is giving me a small wrapped box, that teasing look in her eyes. She tells me to open it. I dream this over and over. I don't know why I'm telling you this. It's just weird, something so small, could be so important. I just want to touch that fabric before I die."

Hagen reached into his shirt and touched the soiled handkerchief. The hole in the wall had barely enough room to jam the cloth through if he wished to. These dungeons were ancient and in complete disrepair. His fist tightened over the cloth, though. This was his only connection to that dark power. He would not give it up.

It's my talisman. His hand lowered from his pocket.

Hagen licked his lips. "What's it like? When you turn?"

Euan spoke, his voice quiet. "When you *Become* a werewolf, you know a new darkness. It's intoxicating, and you never want to turn back to a human. When you are human, though, you find you have new powers. Mine was seeing through the eyes of others... past, present, and future."

Hagen crossed his arms over his chest, brought his knees up, and felt the overwhelming weight of fate struggling against him. He whispered to himself, "I would like to *Become.*"

Hagen jumped at Euan's voice. "How I have dreamed to have that energy pour through me again. God, but I would rip all those Nazi demons to scraps and make them pay. If you do, embrace it, but loathe it, too. I think it could be a wondrous curse."

Euan didn't speak for a while, and when his voice returned, he spoke as if he had not taken a long pause. "I saw something once. Viewed a scene through someone's eyes. The person who I was inside, he was hanging onto a ledge, about to fall. In my sight was the smooth face of a young man, who held his hand out, and told me to grab his hand. The person, who I was, said, 'Remember, Hagen, you're a Wehr Wolff.'"

"Who was the person?" Hagen asked. "Did he have red hair?"

"I could not see his face clearly," Euan uttered.

Hagen settled back, Euan did not speak again. Hagen opened his mouth on several occasions to speak but thought better of it and remained quiet.

Later, he licked his lips and said, "Euan?" He repeated his name, but no answer came.

Hagen's eyelids grew heavy, and he woke himself a couple of times with his own snores. He had been dreaming. Dreaming of his brother, Ivan. He turned on his side, crossed his arms over his chest, curled up, and tried to get warm. Ivan's painful groans from a long time ago were almost audible. Hagen fell asleep, those memories he had forgotten from so long ago returning.

He and Ivan had been in Earl Groscz Castle, and the floor had given way. The holes to that sketchy memory filled back in, and he remembered, what now seemed a lifetime ago.

A word drifted from his lips. "Breathe."

Twenty-Two: Breathe

1930
Hagen's Dream

TEN-YEAR-OLD Hagen stared down at Ivan. His brother dangled in the air from the edge of the hole by one hand. His knuckles were white. He gritted his teeth and stared up at Hagen with a helpless expression. Hagen knelt on the ground close to the hole; a grating sound came from below his knee. He stared past Ivan into the room below. A faint light emitting from a far window showed a dusty floor several feet below.

"Hagen, the floor is giving way!" Ivan rasped.

Ivan attempted to pull himself up, but several sharp cracks erupted. The floor gave, and Hagen was free-falling, and then there was blackness.

How much time passed until Hagen awoke, he would never know, but his eyes popped open, and the groaning of his brother was close. Hagen sat up, the debris of the stone floor surrounding him and the jagged hole above him. A small divan not far from him was tipped over, and he wondered if it had broken his fall.

Metal gleamed in the corner. The rifle he had been carrying. His brother's weapon was not in sight, probably buried under the rubble. A moan to his left made him turn; Ivan was lying on his back, his teeth bared as he attempted to sit up and shove a stone boulder away from his ankle. His face had cuts, and his lips were bloodied. Hagen crawled to his brother and pushed on the boulder. It was too heavy, and he could not budge it.

A fierce growl came from above them, and Hagen snapped his attention to a shadow that crept close to the hole's edge in the ceiling. The hackles on his neck rose. The wolf was huge, too big; he felt he was in a dream. The beast snarled, and sharp teeth shone as it crouched, looking to and fro, searching for a place to land in the room Hagen and Ivan had tumbled into.

Ivan spoke in a hoarse voice. "*Hagen, run.*"

Hagen backed toward the corner of the room, keeping his eyes on the wolf. He shouted, "*Be gone!*"

The wolf cringed; its ears flattened against its head, a continuous snarl escaping its mouth. Hagen dropped to a knee, and he reached with a shaky hand until he touched a gun barrel. His hand gripped the midsection of his rifle. He whipped the weapon up, not taking any time to aim, and fired. The crack from the rifle caused the wolf to flinch and it moved back two steps and lowered in an even tighter crouch, about to leap.

"*Breathe, Hagen!*" Ivan screamed.

In one second, Hagen bolted in a new round while he took in a short breath. His mind cleared, he fired. He was rewarded with a wolf yelp, and then it disappeared from sight. Hagen raced across the room to a closed door that went to the staircase. He locked it with a deadbolt. A moment later, a heavy object pounded on the other side of the thick door and the entire doorframe shook.

He hurried back to his brother, uncertain what to do. Ivan was up on his elbows, staring back at the door where the wolf was trying to break in. He scanned the room, then pointed to a far paneled door.

"*Hagen, there, go.*"

Hagen didn't listen but set his rifle down, placed his hands against the boulder, and leaned forward. He clenched his teeth, took a breath, and thrust his arms out with everything he had. The boulder budged for a moment. Ivan whimpered and scooted back on his elbows. The boulder rolled, and the momentum shoved Hagen back; he slid to the floor.

Ivan whined and moaned and wormed his way to a chair. He grasped the chair from his horizontal position and hauled himself up, every movement followed by a pitiful groan. He sat up in the chair, panting.

Ivan shook his head, asking, "Hagen! Why won't you listen? *Go! Find Father.*"

Hagen picked up the rifle, came to Ivan, and put his hand out. "No."

Ivan sighed, gripped his hand, and Hagen helped him up to his one good leg. Ivan placed an arm around his shoulder, and they moved to the far side of the room. Hagen's brother leaned heavily against him. Hagen tossed his rifle to the ground to keep his balance. He then reached out, grabbed the knob, and opened the door.

A man's baritone voice came through the barred door. "And where shall you run to, Hagen?"

He and Ivan froze; a chill ran up Hagen's spine. There were whispers on the other side of the door. Ivan's face turned even paler, and he clutched Hagen with the arm draped over his shoulder.

"The Devil is behind that door—move, brother."

They were through the doorway into a darkened room filled with cobwebs. A loud thwack sounded in the adjacent room, and wood cracked and creaked. The room had giant-sized wheels and pulleys, and they moved around the equipment. The sound of wood splintering echoed; this was followed by a loud crash. Hagen and Ivan reached the far side where there was a stone railing and ropes dangling in front of Hagen that vanished into a black hole. Hagen had heard that some people came to abandoned castles for thrills; for many it was rappelling.

Hagen got up on top of the short wall's ledge and stretched his hand out across the dark abyss. His fingers dusted a rope, and then he fell forward. His heart was in his throat, but his brother grabbed hold the back of his pants and kept him from plummeting down into the darkness.

The noise of sharp nails hitting stone drew close. Hagen reached with more brazenness, gripped the rope. He pulled it back and handed it to his brother.

Ivan sat on the ledge, swung his good leg over, and cried out in pain. "Hold my neck, Hagen."

Hagen hugged Ivan's neck, and Ivan started to push off. A wolf jumped up, its forepaws planted against the railing, blood dribbling from its raw eye socket where Hagen had shot it. Its mouth, full of sharp teeth, snapped out over the ledge. Those fangs meant to snatch Hagen off Ivan's back even as he clutched Ivan, who parried the bite with his forearm at the last second. The wolf's jaw closed tight over Ivan's arm, and Ivan cried out in pain. Hagen lashed his fist forward, his knuckles punching into the slimy, sticky eye socket. The wolf was gone, and Ivan was free.

Ivan pushed off and gripped the rope with both hands.

"Hold on, Hagen," Ivan said as he descended. They moved fast, and Hagen stared up above them, but he saw only blackness. Then the taut rope became slack, and they were plunging down.

Ivan hit the ground first with a loud snap and Hagen fell on top of him, the breath knocked out of him. He rolled across a slick floor, hitting a stone column with his knees. He was dizzy and felt he was going to pass out, but he didn't. Hagen stared around him in a panic. He was inside a vast crypt that had stone pillars around it. Engraved inside the pillars was the signet of Groscz. Crossed axes.

His brother's moans had changed in volume and intensity. Hagen crawled over to him, staring down at the lower half of his brother's leg. It was bent awkwardly. Ivan's eyes were wild, and he thrashed his head back and forth in agony.

The gravelly voice spoke behind him in disgust. "He already has the smell of death." Hagen spun and faced a young man with a black beard and dark eyes, who wore a thick robe. "But you. You have the smell of freshness."

Hagen stepped backward, forgetting his brother was at his heel and tumbling over him. Ivan gave out a high-pitched cry and coughed.

The man smiled and stepped up. He stopped and sniffed the air. "Oh my, this is interesting and unexpected. You both have the smell of the Wehr Wolffs. One of us, are you? Such a coincidence, isn't it? Not many Wehr Wolffs left, in fact. Died or murdered... many by me. I had no idea you existed." The bearded man chortled and turned to Hagen. "And you have a unique scent, too."

Hagen opened his mouth, but only a small squeak came.

The man chuckled. "Oh, my apologies, we have not made proper introductions. Adolf Tabor Wehr Wolff."

Adolf tapped his chin and said, "Ah, you don't even know your own history? Don't worry. Our leaders, all of them, are noble, pompous asses. All believe humans are sacred. Frankly, I just don't think they have ever taken a bite of real meat—there's nothing better than human flesh. And why should the humans rule, when we are clearly the strongest?"

Shadows moved behind Adolf and two large wolves came into view. One was the creature he had shot, with the gored eye socket. The second wolf had dull brown and white fur.

Adolf gestured at the two wolves flanking him on either side, saying, "And the Wehr Wolffs demand allegiance of these creatures of Wehr Forest who have lost the secret knowledge to turn at will. I will not limit these wehrwolves' breeding. I will encourage them to feast on human flesh. And why limit their gift? In fact, and not let them infect all of humanity, and turn all of humanity into beasts with one ruler?" He touched his chest.

Adolf leaned against a pillar. "I'm sure your nanny told you tales of us at night, to keep you inside? I'm sure you don't need any history lessons on the basic werewolf." He grinned, and his teeth had changed; they were fangs. "I would like my own history lesson, though. So many questions I asked my tutors, and they never gave me a straight answer. Why does silver cause us such problems? Put it on, and the skin itches and crawls. Put a lead bullet through my chest, I'll be alive. Even if you shoot me in the head, I bet I'll live for a long time. But one damn silver bullet, one vital organ, and I'm done for. Then there's the damnable moon. Change any time, but have the moon become full and my powers increase tenfold and I'm ravenous. Maybe I should have done the research like my tutors advised." He shrugged. "Oh well, I was always told I was a disappointment to the family. Dark magic has recently become my forte."

The one-eyed wolf next to Adolf snarled and glowered at Hagen. Adolf smiled, saying. "Of course, he's yours." He shrugged, telling Hagen in a playful tone, "Seems that she's a bit peeved you shot her eye."

Adolf cocked his head and sniffed the air, then leered. "Oh, how exciting. Your father comes. He's close, and has several men with him...and a boy. Your younger brother?" Adolf gave a sharp laugh, his pointy white teeth flashing. He shrugged his shoulders, and the robe covering him fell to the ground. He was completed naked. "I will wait for them, and that'll be a great feast. I think I might like to keep the boy; I will be his tutor, how about that?" He looked down at his nude body, back up to Hagen, and laughed hard. His body transformed in a matter of seconds, his hands and feet changing to claws, thick hair sprouting over his entire body, a snout forming on his face. The laughter turned into a guttural growl.

The two creatures flanking Adolf ambled forward, the hair on their spines raised, drool dripping from pointy fangs. Hagen covered his brother's head and cried. Something moved close by him, and his gaze came up. A silhouette stepped out from behind a pillar, a rifle raised and pointed at Adolf, and the person whispered. It was a woman's voice.

"Tabor, you traitor."

The one-eyed werewolf flinched and wheeled toward the intruder, then roared and charged. The riflewoman redirected her sight to the storming beast, and the muzzle flared. A loud crack erupted, and the round nailed the creature's head. Fleshy, grisly debris erupted from the back of its skull, and the now no-eyed creature dove to the ground.

The brown-and-white beast lunged, gliding through the air, its gnarly claws raised, and its jaw agape. A sharp report blasted in the air, a wave of fluid sprayed, and the beast landed unstable on its hind legs and swung long steely nails at the shooter. The riflewoman was quick and sidestepped the hit, then cocked her gun and fired point-blank into the beast's flank. The werewolf staggered sideways, opened its mouth, and wheezed; a mist blew from its nostrils, and its eyes rolled back as it collapsed.

Adolf had already charged, covering significant distance. He roared, his neck extended in preparation to rip into the shooter's shoulder with his long fangs. The shooter did not hesitate. With no time to reload her rifle, she swung the stock into the creature's mouth; a dull sound following the hit. Adolf's massive body bumped the riflewoman and she was off her feet. The rifle flipped through the air, then hit the ground and disappeared behind a pillar. Adolf, seeing he had the advantage, rushed the fallen riflewoman, who had rolled to her feet and into a kneeling position. Hagen's defender reached over her shoulder, grabbed a sword hilt, and pulled, revealing a bright silver sword.

The swordswoman slipped sideways and the blade streaked through the air, hitting the wolf's side. Adolf gave a hideous, angry, deep-throated roar. Dark fluid sprayed over a nearby gray pillar. The wolf bellowed in anger again, standing up on its hind legs, towering over the swordfighter before it struck with its unbelievably lengthy claws. The sword sped in two arcs. The beast yowled in pain, and half an ear was severed and more flesh twirled in the air to land close to Hagen's foot. Adolf staggered back a couple of paces, his forepaws back on the ground.

Hagen stared down at the pieces of long, raggedy nails. One lengthy nail was attached to a grisly toe and transformed before his eyes to a severed finger. He looked back up.

Adolf circled his assailant. His head was lowered, lips pulled back, and his long razor-edged fangs were visible. Blood dribbled from Adolf's wounds to the floor, and his injured front paw oozed with it. A distant shouting came from one end of the room. Hagen heard his father's voice calling his name. Adolf glanced from the swordsman to Hagen, and then he turned and vanished into the shadows.

Hagen's defender kept a defensive position for another second, then rotated the sword once in her palm. The the next second, it was back in the sheath over her shoulder. The swordswoman stepped closer and squatted in front of him. Before he fainted, he saw his hero's face. He did not know her name in 1930, but he would in 1940.

Justine. The Keeper of Wehr Forest.

Hagen had awakened in a strange bed several hours later, and heard his father's tormented voice through the door. Hagen had cracked the door open, peeking out. His father was speaking to an elder man who was dressed in a robe and had a black beard with the tip braided.

His father's voice was tiny. "Your wife saved my son, but you can do nothing for him?"

"No," the man answered. "These are mortal wounds, Herr Messer. The broken leg is beyond repair, but most pressing, he has internal bleeding. He is in a coma and will not awaken. You must let him go."

Hagen's father pulled out something from his pocket and shoved it in the man's hand, then snarled, "Take this cursed relic. I don't want anything to do with it. It was his mother's, and she was his favorite. Let it be buried with him. I never want anything to do with the Wehr Wolffs again. I shall take my sons away from this place." His father came toward Hagen's door.

The object that his father had placed in the man's palm was a medallion.

SOMEONE KICKED HAGEN in the stomach, and he grunted. Hagen opened his eyes and sat up straight. An SS guard hovered over him and barked, "Get up!"

Where am I?

Recent memories came to him—he was a crewman of the Night Angel, crash-landed in Nazi Germany, and they had pretended to be Nazis....

I killed an innocent kid.

The memory of his time with Liam and Lt. David before he'd been captured was vivid, but even more clear were the few moments he'd had alone with Liam.

The molestation in the shower intruded, and the torture, and then being brought here.

The SS guard who stood next to him placed his foot on Hagen's shoulder and pressed down hard. "Get up, scum. The Führer wants to see his prize tonight." He looked up at a slant-nosed guard, the same one who had escorted him down the night before.

The memory of the dream came again, and he recalled his father learning of his brother suffering mortal wounds. *Adolf.* He had forgotten about him that night.

There was a scuffle of feet close to Euan Hartley's cell, and he saw two men carry out a rail-thin body that had no feet. Hagen stared at the emaciated body with all its deformities, and he looked down by his mattress where there was a light blue cloth. The handkerchief was partially covered by straw. Euan had asked for it the previous night.

Shame reverberated through Hagen. For Euan, it was priceless. For Hagen, it was a key to pure, dark power. He did not want to become like that Adolf, who had killed Hagen's brother.

Bent Nose pulled Hagen to his feet.

The guards placed manacles over his wrists and ankles, and another guard stuttered, "Dr. Mengele was furious. He wanted to know why this prisoner was placed down here."

Bent Nose gripped Hagen's arm and shoved him out into the darkened corridor. The guard briefly touched his head in discomfort. "That miserable servant said so. The one who is always with Wagner. Just don't say anything." He stopped, touched his forehead again, and groaned in pain.

Rolph told them to take me to a dungeon?

A second guard growled, "Why would he tell you to do that?"

Hagen focused on Bent Nose, who merely shook his head.

"What's fucking wrong with you?" the other guard asked.

"No, it's nothing. My head has just been in pain since yesterday."

Hagen remembered peering through the eyehole at Rolph telling Wagner he could help him. His eyes had flickered, and he'd looked as if he had some kind of mind-persuasion power.

Did Rolph do that? Does he have some special power? Like Euan had spoken of?

Hagen was led through the dungeon to the staircase. As he climbed, he replayed the dream he'd had overnight and sought out any people Hagen might potentially know within the dream.

Justine had cut part of an ear and a finger off of Adolf. Rolph was missing a finger, but that could simply be the rough life in Germany. Or from being in war. It did not mean anything—or did it?

If Rolph was Adolf, then he had not aged much, though it had been only a handful of years. Did he have strange powers like Euan? Instead of seeing through people's eyes, perhaps he did not age?

One question Hagen wanted answered.

Is Rolph on my side or not?

Twenty-Three: Hagen's Worst Fears Realized

May 13, 1940
Wehr Wolff Castle, Nazi, Germany

HAGEN'S ESCORTS BROUGHT him up a winding staircase where the bright sun shone through a small window that illuminated the dusty landing. Hagen glanced out the window and down below where there was a great blue lake. But it was the craft in the sky that got his attention.

His escorts stopped, and the unit leader said, "Look at that."

There was a gigantic balloon that glided high above them, a fuselage attached to the bottom with several windows along its side. *A Nazi airship.*

Several fighters flew around it and slanted down toward the lake where they must have planned to land. Hagen was pushed, and he continued up the stairs.

He was eventually taken to a tiled room with a floor drain, told to undress, and was then again sprayed down with a hose. The water was bitterly cold, but these guards merely taunted and shoved him. None molested him. He was given new clothes, then led down a corridor. Several SS soldiers marched past him. Hagen observed that a few of the rooms he passed were filled with SS men. It appeared that the new SS storm troopers had finally arrived.

His escorts returned him to Dr. Mengele's laboratory. A guard gripped his shoulder, and asked the SS guards present, "What's the order? Secure him in the chair?"

The SS guards exchanged confused looks. Hagen's gaze meanwhile roved the area. A number of SS guards wheeled gurneys out of the rooms from the same area where he had been held. Pale corpses lay on top of each one.

What happened to them?

Dr. Mengele drifted down the aisle between the prisoners' cells, his face pale as he stared back and forth at the dead bodies being carted from rooms on either side of him. The doctor mumbled under his breath.

One of Hagen's escorts announced, "Dr. Mengele, your prisoner."

Dr. Mengele brought his attention up to Hagen, goggled at him for a second, then gazed around him with a dumbstruck expression. The doctor licked his lips, pushed his greasy hair back, and came to Hagen, fixing his alarmed gaze on him.

He spoke in a barely audible voice, but Hagen caught the words. "I almost lost my most precious subject."

Wagner's voice rang in the room, demanding "What happened last night?" Wagner came into Hagen's view. His injured ear had been bandaged. The entourage behind the general was as usual—Major Becke, Roesia, a couple of SS guards, and, trailing far behind them, Rolph.

Dr. Mengele did not appear to hear the general speaking, but wrung his hands and watched as the dead subjects were carted away.

"Dr. Mengele!" Becke shouted.

The doctor flinched and turned to Becke, then to Wagner, and said, "Last night, a-after the incident at the coop, someone activated the lethal gas I had devised as a failsafe, and it went through the vent of every subject's room. T-the subjects were all terminated." Dr. Mengele pointed to Hagen. "It was just luck that this prisoner was not inside his room, or he'd be d-dead like the others. He was detained in the dungeon."

Wagner balled his hands into fists. "Arrest everyone who was in this laboratory last night. *Everyone.*"

Dr. Mengele's eyes twitched. "They have. Martz is questioning them." His eyes narrowed on Wagner. "It's best if he not harm my last personal assistant, Uli. It took me a long time to train him, and Meyers is dead now."

Wagner cocked his head in irritation. "Martz knows what he's doing." He clucked his tongue, stared upward, and asked without meeting anyone's eyes, "And who escorted this prisoner to the dungeon?"

No one spoke. Hagen kept his gaze averted. Wagner stared at his escorts and finally placed his hands on his hips.

The leader stuttered, "W-we did, sir."

"Who ordered you to take him to the dungeon?"

The unit leader, who had decided to take Hagen down, swallowed as his expression went vacant. He pointed over Wagner's shoulder. "He told me to, sir."

Hagen followed the trajectory of the man's finger to Wagner, but the general half turned, stepped aside, and revealed Rolph.

Wagner wheeled back to the SS unit leader. Wagner's face turned several shades of red. He called to the guards, who were carting a dead body out, and had them halt.

He ordered them, "Detain this servant, and don't let him out of your sight."

The men moved, taking out pistols and pointing them at Rolph.

Wagner scratched his chin and regarded the SS unit leader with suspicion. "And why did you take orders from a servant?"

The unit leader's tongue slipped out of his mouth, wetting his top lip. The man's expression reflected he knew he had made a huge blunder. Wagner's hands patted his belt, undid the thin leather strap over his semiautomatic pistol, took out the gun, and cocked it, then held it to the SS leader's head before lowering it and firing into the man's foot.

The man crumpled where he stood and cried out in pain.

Wagner ordered, "Take him to Martz. Find out what he knows."

Wagner turned his attention toward Rolph, the gun now pointed at his head.

"*Speak!*" Wagner shouted.

Rolph glanced up to Wagner, and something flickered in Rolph's eyes as he said, "You can't shoot me yet."

Wagner lowered his pistol, touched his head, and grimaced. Hagen looked around, but nobody had noticed the exchange. Hagen had seen him do this once before. He turned his attention back to Rolph, but Rolph turned his face away.

"Forgive me, General Wagner," Rolph said. "He asked where you kept the prisoner. I said I was just a servant, but then I did say 'the dungeon.' I thought that's where you wanted him."

Wagner continued to rub his forehead as if a headache had appeared out of the blue. He smiled and cracked out a high-pitched laugh. "You are truly stupid." A tiny trickle of blood came out of Wagner's nose, which he wiped away in the next moment, never looking at his hand as he dried it on his pants.

Rolph nodded his head. Wagner ordered the remaining guards, "Secure him to that table. And someone get me Martz."

The men motioned their gun muzzles for Rolph to advance toward a nearby table. The man complied, not offering any resistance.

Becke looked around them and asked, "Can't we just get new subjects?"

Dr. Mengele licked his lips. "I had perfected the serum and infected the new subjects. They would have been the perfect specimens."

Becke's face wrinkled in confusion. "For what? For these new prototype soldiers?"

"Yes. Super-soldiers," Dr. Mengele answered, and sighed. "Major, you just came from Berlin this week, and I have yet to discuss this in detail. I derived a new serum from a subject with Wehr Wolff traits. Interestingly enough, a British man named Euan Hartley."

"A serum to do what?" Becke asked.

"To create a super-soldier in the field who has extraordinary hearing, sight, smell, and strength. And who is not easily killed. I was growing extra limbs with the new formula. We had been making quite good progress until—" He extended his hands out, turning in a circle. "—this."

"And we can't do it again?" Becke asked, his brow furrowed, still clearly confused.

Dr. Mengele replied, "We gathered several vials of blood from the subject, Euan, after we had him change into werewolf form, which served as the most promising option. But it makes it harder because he can kill us. I got what I needed. I was using this new subject to merely improve the formula." Dr. Mengele nodded his head at Hagen. "But someone stole all of the base formula, as well as all of my research papers." He opened his palm, a vial of purplish fluid displayed for their sight. "This is the only new serum I have, the one I was testing." He placed the vial in a leather case and set it delicately in the front pocket of his shirt. His face was ashen. "I'll have to begin anew with Messer. This is a major setback."

Dr. Mengele came to Hagen and raised his hand to Hagen's face. It looked as if he was about to pet him. "I will have to infect this subject with werevenom so I can finish my research. I hope I can control him better than Euan."

"And what's so special about the Wehr Wolff family?" Becke asked.

Dr. Mengele turned toward Becke. "Strangely, members of the Wehr Wolff lineage are bred to be the most powerful werewolf anyone has seen, and each has his own special powers." Everyone's gaze pivoted to Hagen. Hagen looked away and noticed that Rolph had been restrained on the table. He was staring up at the ceiling with a blank expression.

Becke jabbed his thumb at Hagen. "You're saying this prisoner is a werewolf?"

"No," answered Dr. Mengele, irritated. "He has to be infected first. I've tested his blood and now know he has the trait. I won't know how strong it is until I infect him."

"And we haven't done that yet, right?" Becke asked, appearing tense with unease as he considered Hagen.

"Not yet," Wagner said. "But you can see why it's important to house him here and not have any deviations in detainment protocol. And with someone loose in the castle, killing, and with the incident yesterday, we need to make certain everything is under control."

"Is this Messer the last member of the bloodline you know of?" Roesia asked.

Martz came into the room, and Dexer followed him with an appreciable limp. Martz considered Rolph, restrained to the table, and answered Roesia. "The few there were of the Wehr Wolff clan have fled. The only one we found is that miserable servant on the table."

Martz stepped to Wagner's side and looked at Hagen. "But this Herr Fluke has a father and a younger brother in America. If we captured them, this would be adding wondrous specimens to our regime." The corners of Martz's mouth twitched. "What do you think, Herr Fluke?"

Hagen avoided the man's gaze. His entire body had become tense, and his mind reeled with a new terror.

Martz said, "Tonight, I'll be talking to a few foreign military officers employed in the intelligence operations we have overseas. Going to discuss a plan to capture your family."

Hagen didn't meet his gaze. Droplets of sweat ran down his spine.

"Anyone see anything useful last night?" Wagner asked Martz. Hagen assumed he was referring to the interrogation of the medical staff and guards.

Martz shook his head. "One, sir. Dr. Mengele's personal assistant thought he saw someone."

Wagner frowned and stared at Rolph. "Get this witness."

Martz flicked his hand at Dexer, and the man pursed his lips, then wheeled around and limped down the stairs.

An SS guard hurried into the area and made his way directly to General Wagner, then whispered into his ear. The general gave one perceptible nod. He spoke quietly, and the guard quickly left the room.

Wagner stood to the side of Rolph's table, and said over his shoulder, "Major, our guests are here. We have a ferry coming across the lake, as well. Would you please make sure they are well cared for, and let them know I will be up momentarily?"

Confusion showed on Becke's face at being dismissed, but he put on his hat and said, "Yes, sir."

Hagen's palms were damp, and he shifted on his feet. A new energy was buzzing in the air that he didn't like. He stared at Rolph's face. Then the servant turned his head, meeting Hagen's eyes.

"Dr. Lawerenze," Wagner said. Hagen caught a strange edge in his normal flat voice. "I am told you were once a surgeon at Hirschfield Hospital before taking on your research in genetics?"

Roesia startled. "I'm sorry, General, what?"

"You trained under Dr. Arnold Bastion, yes?" Wagner asked.

"Oh, you have met my former mentors?" Roesia asked, her confidence fading, her purse hugged close to her chest.

Dr. Mengele gave Wagner a quizzical stare. "General, Dr. Lawerenze and I have important work to do—"

"I'm sure you do," Wagner interrupted, gesturing to Rolph. "It would be a waste to kill this servant. He is not guilty of anything but stupidity and not knowing his place. But at the same time, had he not said the word *dungeon*, then our most precious prisoner would be dead. So, I shall let him live but teach him a lesson in obedience. I think it would be wonderful if Dr. Lawerenze would perform an amputation. You can pick the limb. I don't care."

Roesia's face flushed, and she appeared dumbfounded by the suggestion. It was a strange time for a memory, but a scene from old times returned to Hagen, of fishing on the lake, his father throwing the caught fish into their boat, their mouths gasping for air. Roesia had the same look.

She swallowed. "Of course."

She locked eyes with Hagen, and he merely nodded, completely dazed by the pace of events unfolding in front of him. He hoped his gesture signaled what he meant.

The game is up. Take out the grenade.

She turned to Dr. Mengele, "I will need the proper tools, Doctor."

Dr. Mengele said, "Of course," and turned, yelling to lab workers.

Roesia dug inside her purse, removed the grenade, and yanked out the pin. The grenade rolled from her fingers, and clinked to the floor, coming close to Wagner's feet. She had the pistol in her hand next. Her purse dropped to her feet, and she aimed the pistol at Dr. Mengele's head, ready to shoot him for good measure. The doctor stared in absolute bafflement at the end of the muzzle. She pulled on the trigger, but the weapon made a dry click.

Wagner nudged the grenade away with his foot, and mused, "I think this charade is over."

Hagen's captors squeezed his arms. They, too, were surprised by the new development.

Wagner turned, raised his pistol toward Roesia, then lowered it and strode forward. He punched Roesia in the stomach with the hand holding the gun. She bent over from the blow, and he brought up a knee that connected with her face. She fell back into the wall, then onto her side, clutching her face.

Wagner waved to Martz. "Make sure she has no other weapons." Martz bent down and patted at her body. Wagner sneered, "We don't know your real name, so 'whore' will do for now. This morning, we took the privilege to exchange your grenade with a fake and empty your gun. A spy, you may be—we'll find out—but a novice. A real operative would have noticed the weight change."

Dr. Mengele sputtered out, "W-what is happening?" He had slumped against the wall, his hand on his chest, disbelief radiated from his face.

Wagner glanced at Dr. Mengele, then back down to Roesia. His pistol trained on her. "I will tell you, Dr. Mengele. I am not a man who admits errors well, but I have made a big one. It all seemed quite too convenient at first—our Herr Fluke, operating alone. But things unraveled slowly, then moved faster. Herr Fluke giving us his real last name did not spell a rookie as much it did pure ignorance. Then his race through the castle alone and without help seemed amazing."

Wagner waggled his gun. "Then our men found buried parachutes last night at the base of a cliff near Earl Groscz Castle, and reported it to Martz. Another team found the burned remains of transportation trucks at the bottom of a ravine with bullet-riddled bodies. In this rubble, we found a silver prosthetic leg with swastikas." Wagner raised his eyebrow. "That fat man you brought with you. You said he was Colonel Brose, yes? No matter, you will tell me soon enough. The Colonel Brose we have learned was with Doctor Lawerenze lost his leg in the invasion of Poland, and apparently was at the bottom of this ravine. Our phones worked this morning, and Martz found out that Stuttgart sent out a storm trooper unit that was never re-routed. Not to mention that Dr. Lawerenze was mentored under Friedrich-Paul von Groszheim at the Wilheim Medical Institute, not any bastion. That was enough, but I revisited the area where we captured our Herr Fluke." Wagner's hard gaze moved to Hagen. "Saw those handprints on the wall. Our prisoner never had blood on his hands. He was not acting alone. If there were more with him, then it probably means the people he traveled with, and it means Doctor Lawerenze is not who she says she is."

Steps could be heard coming over the elevated walkway, and Hagen looked up.

Wagner snapped his head up at the sound, taking in the incoming guards. He chuckled and snapped his fingers as if he had left out the most important detail.

"Perfect timing. With Rolph's help, my men raided an area of the castle this morning. Seems I misunderstood the order of events. Our intruders are all truly just happenstance. What a coincidence and good luck for the Führer!"

Two SS guards were dragging a prisoner between them. The detainee's head hung to his chest, and the men pulled the detainee down the steps. The prisoner wore a torn and raggedy Nazi uniform that had splotches of blood on it. The prisoner had dirty reddish-brown hair, and light stubble over his face.

Hagen began shaking, and he whispered to himself, *"No, no, no... Please, God, no."*

Liam brought his head up, and all of the air left Hagen's lungs. His legs gave way until he was completely held upright by the SS men. Liam's face was thinner and had smudges of blood under his nose and cheeks; the areas under his eyes were sunken from a lack of sleep.

One of Liam's escorts said, "The other one was already dead. His body is at the coop, awaiting your inspection."

His body? Hagen shuddered. *Lt. David?*

The smile on Wagner's face grew into a beaming grin.

Martz asked, "What about that overweight man dressed as the colonel? You find him?"

The SS guard shook his head. "No, but we are still searching."

Wagner nodded, one hand continuing to massage his temple. "Likely, that man was injured on their way in. His act did look very real. I think it's safe to presume he died somewhere in the castle. Ohhh, I think we found the culprits who have been going around our castle, maiming and disemboweling my men." He looked at Liam, waggling his finger, and said, "You all started a rumor of a weremutant running rampant. You will wish we disemboweled you after I'm done."

Dexer limped into the area from the other side of the room, accompanied by Dr. Mengele's personal assistant. Hagen recognized the lean middle-aged man with thick black hair, streaked with white. Hagen peered at him closely. He had a shaven face, black eyebrows, and a cleft chin. His name escaped him.

Dr. Mengele stepped closer. "Uli, you saw someone last night?"

Wagner's expression grew merrier. "Ah, and is this the witness?"

Dexer nodded and leaned against the wall to take pressure off of his wounded foot. "He said he saw someone leaving the area last night and didn't report it."

Uli's youthful face quivered, and he wrung his hands in front of him. "I-I'm sorry, sir. I did."

Wagner asked, "Uli is your name?"

"Y-yes."

"Ah, very good, very good. I assure you, you will not be harmed. But tell us, who is it you saw?"

The man glanced at the blood on the floor from the SS unit leader whom Wagner had shot earlier. Uli swallowed and did a cursory glance of everyone in the room, then did a double take when he saw Rolph. He started to bring his hand up and froze. Hagen turned toward Rolph; the servant had a hard stare focused on Uli. His eyes were doing a strange dance. Uli's hand went to his head as his eyes squinted shut.

"Uli?" Dr. Mengele asked. "W-was it Rolph?"

Uli's eyes appeared vacant, and he licked his lips, "What?" Uli shook his head, then wheeled around and pointed. "H-her, sir. I saw her leaving."

Roesia stared in disbelief.

"As I expected," Wagner said. He gestured to Liam and Roesia. "Prepare these prisoners for interrogation."

Dr. Mengele held his hand up. "We have to find out where all of my vials of new serum went."

Wagner nodded. "We will, Doctor. We will."

Wagner put on his hat, about to leave, but stopped midstep, snapping his fingers. "Almost forgot." He looked around, and his eyes lit up. He went to the area where they branded prisoners with swastikas and picked up the handle of the branding iron. The end glowed red.

He strolled over to Rolph and looked down at the man, saying, "I wasn't joking earlier. I don't want you to die—you are quite valuable. You don't need to lose a limb, though; just your eye."

Rolph appeared fatigued, his forehead sweaty as he simply stared upward.

Wagner thrust the hot iron into Rolph's eye; the man arched and gave out an ear-splitting scream. Amidst the horror, Hagen observed a trickle of blood coming from Wagner's nostril. It dribbled to the brim of the man's top lip.

The smell of burnt flesh besieged Hagen. Guards dragged Liam into a laboratory room and pulled out batons as they stepped inside. Dull thuds echoed from in the room, and short cries from his friend echoed out.

Hagen fainted.

Twenty-Four: Martz's New Prisoners

May 13, 1940
Dr. Mengele's Top Secret Laboratory

HAGEN HEARD HIMSELF scream out loud and awoke with a start on a metal-framed bed. His feet smacked down onto the ice-cold floor. He was inside his white padded laboratory room and thankfully wore no manacles over his wrists or his ankles. The large vents in the ceiling loomed over him.

The nightmare he'd just had was fresh in his mind. Liam was being held down by Dexer and a second SS guard. Liam had his eye burnt out. But this was just a nightmare, and not true...yet. There were new bruises in the crook of his arm. They had taken more blood while he was out. He pulled on his thin shoes and paced back and forth in his chamber. Tears built as he tried to finger his hair back into place.

Harrowing images of Liam being branded and tortured reeled through his mind. He whispered, "Oh please, God, please don't hurt him." He whined, "You promised." He pounded a fist into the wall, "*You promised!*" He knew, though, that no one, including God, had ever made him any such promises.

He was in Nazi Germany, and whatever was going to happen was beyond his control. *We have only a smidgeon of control of our destiny; the rest is God and luck.* Those had been Lt. David's words to him.

He leaned his forehead against the wall, tears dripping to the floor. He slid to his knees, crying and hiccuped from his bawling.

The memory of Roesia clutching her stomach was vivid; he breathed in short gulps. *What are they doing to her? Will they hurt Liam to get her to talk? Yes, of course they will.*

Hagen stared at his nails, which had turned purple and black underneath. He was their most precious prisoner, and they had just started torturing him yesterday before being interrupted. What would they do to someone who was not their most precious prisoner?

He envisioned limbs being amputated and men like Xylander doing God knew what— removing teeth, transplanting limbs for experimental purposes. Hagen batted his head against the wall.

Ivan's voice whispered in his ear. "Breathe, Hagen."

He looked up at the ceiling, swallowing the lump of bile in his throat. He wiped his face with his shirt and noticed they had left a rag by his toilet; he blew his nose into it. He splashed water from the toilet on his face and then sat on the floor in the middle of his room, near the grate, and closed his eyes.

He inhaled deeply then exhaled, and his mind cleared to some degree; the ghastly images slowed and he took another deep breath.

He uttered to himself, "I have a touch of control over my destiny; the rest is God and luck." He focused his breathing and lost track of time.

The locks to his door jiggled, and he rose to his feet, facing his fate.

An SS guard at the door, barked, "Move it."

Hagen stepped through the door into the corridor. Four SS prison guards were waiting and surrounded him. He was moved down to the end of the aisle toward the main lab. He glanced back at Liam's door— the window on the outside was closed.

His escorts stopped, and the guard asked, "Where's the dolly?"

There was an argument, and two departed. Hagen's guard ordered him to sit down in a chair set close to a raised platform. He did as commanded. The guard turned and spoke to his comrade. Heavy footsteps approached from behind Hagen. There was a thump and he turned.

Rolph knelt a few feet away, his head down, manacles fastened over his wrists. An SS guard barked orders to an assistant close to him. Rolph brought his head up. Hagen couldn't look away from the appalling face that now had a grisly red burnt eye socket.

Hagen's fury grew and he growled, "*Youuuuu.*"

Rolph's nearby guard was not paying him any attention, instead yelling loudly to a man in a white lab coat.

Hagen leaned forward and hissed, "You betrayed me. I know you killed those last subjects. I know who you are. I'd gladly take out your other eye."

Rolph whispered something. It sounded like he had said, "It wasn't me." He mumbled more.

"*What?* What did you say to me?" Hagen demanded.

"We all die in the end," Rolph said hoarsely. "We must choose who, or what, we live for."

Hagen rose out of his chair, knocking it over, and yelled, *"Don't you understand?* They're going to torture them! And they're going to hurt him to get her to talk because they think she killed them! To get to me! They'll do it because they can!"

The SS guards in the laboratory were on alert now and came forward, but a couple of leaders held them at bay. They were enjoying the show and chortled at the spectacle in front of them. Martz came into the room, looking amused by the confrontation.

Rolph licked his cracked lips, and croaked, *"Then save them."*

Hagen bellowed, drew both of his manacled hands back over his head, and slammed them down on Rolph's face. The cuffs' metal sliced the side of Rolph's face, and Hagen brought them down again. Rolph fell to his side. Hagen kicked him as hard as he could, over and over, screaming and cursing unintelligibly. The SS men around him roared with laughter.

Someone grabbed Hagen's shoulder, and he turned and punched out with both fists at Martz, one after the other. Martz dipped fast under the hits, and his fist barreled into Hagen's stomach. Hagen fell to his knees, the breath knocked out of him, and he wheezed.

Martz bellowed, "Bring him!"

Hagen pressed a hand to his stomach as he tried to catch his breath. He saw someone being wheeled forward, who was fastened to a dolly. Hagen looked away from the spectacle coming toward him.

No, please no.

"Herr Fluke, see the creation we made of your friend," Martz said.

"No, no, no," Hagen croaked, squeezing his eyes close. Martz clutched his hair and turned him so he was facing the dolly.

Martz spoke with a hushed tone, close to his ear. "We only had the last few hours, not much time. But we did what we could. The limb transplant experimentation seems like a dead-end to me, but what do I know? I'm just an SS man who does as his Führer bids." The man tittered, and Hagen closed his eyes tight—he never wanted to open them again.

The squeak of turning wheels drew closer. Martz said, "As for this creation, though, I don't think it serves as an advancement to any science. No, I think we did this *because we can.* Look, Herr Fluke."

Hagen kept his eyes squeezed shut and shook his head.

"*Open them,*" Martz ordered.

Something in his voice made Hagen obey. He gulped and opened his eyes. Dexer was in front of him, his mouth curled in a grin, the hole in his bottom lip showing off a couple of molars. Hagen expelled a sigh of relief. A two-wheel dolly sat upright next to Dexer and on it was someone who was clearly not Liam.

A weremutant was secured to the surface. Multiple leather restraints were fastened over wrists, chest, midsection, and two tightened around the ankles. The thing—*No, it's man*—on the equipment stared up at the ceiling. He had varied human limbs sewn onto its body. On parts, there were patches of hair, but in other places, there was human skin. The snout had been removed from the face, a human nose replacing it. His mouth was open wide, a pathetic groan drifting out. This thing, this person, was in pure agony. Something about that face deformed by plastic surgery did look familiar, but he couldn't place it.

Martz let Hagen's hair go, and said, "Ah, you recognize your friend, Corporal Kirby?"

Hagen was in shock. *Corporal Kirby?* He had never liked the man, but no one deserved to become this utter horror. Tears ran down his face.

Martz gestured to Kirby and ordered a guard. "Take this *thing* off and put it in a room. Two hours before the banquet—secure our Herr Fluke to the dolly." He squatted close to Hagen. "We have guests who want to meet you, Herr Fluke. Very much so."

The weremutant was unstrapped and pulled off, a low-grade mewl coming from its mouth. The creature fell to the floor and tried to move, but it only cried in pitiful torment.

Rolph was pulled to his feet and taken out the door into the hallway. Martz held a gold medallion in front of Hagen's face. "Found this on Liam. Swears he doesn't know anything about it. I thought I might ask him again."

Hagen's eyes widened.

Dr. Mengele came forward and spoke in an awed voice. "Give that to me." He took the necklace from Martz and held it in his hands. "A Wehr Wolff relic. It will go well with my other pieces."

Martz glanced to Dexer and back to Dr. Mengele. "You collect Wehr Wolff heirlooms?"

Dr. Mengele barely nodded. "I planned to don that silver revolver tonight. This, though, is priceless."

Martz waved his hand to Hagen's guards, and Hagen was shoved forward. Dexer limped over and held a muzzle in one hand that Hagen recognized as one of the devices placed on weremutants' snouts.

Dexer leaned up and spoke in his ear. "That whore of yours was fun last night. A few of us took turns. Maybe we'll let you watch next time. After the party?" Drool seeped out of the slit in his lip, and he wiped it away. He brought the muzzle up and said, "You'll wear this tonight. Makes it more dramatic." He handed it to a guard, and Hagen was shoved back into his room.

The guards slid food under Hagen's door an hour later. He tried to eat but couldn't. It was a few hours later when he was retrieved. A guard pushed the upright dolly into the middle of his cell. His back was pushed up against the surface, and he stood in place as the guards fastened the leather restraints over his chest and midsection. Both of his arms were pushed to his side and leather strips wrapped over each wrist, and then the same done to his ankles. The final touch—securing the muzzle over his face. The mask obscured his sight, giving him narrow tunnel vision, but at least he could turn his head if he wanted to. Someone tilted the dolly backward, and he was staring at the white ceiling where the vent was located.

They rolled him out into the hallway. How was one to know when they went completely insane? Did it just happen and you never knew any better? He wanted insanity, or better yet, to live in a world of fantasy rather than what he thought he would be forced to live through for his remaining few weeks or months.

They stopped at the coop, and he was wheeled close to the silver enclosure where he had been placed for his torture the day before. A couple of weremutants were inside the enclosure, pacing back and forth. Dr. Mengele wore a gray tweed suit. He pulled the leather pouch from the inside of his jacket, looked at it with endearment, and stuck it back inside, then yelled orders.

Close to the coop was a cart that had a body on it with bloodstained clothes. Lt. David's glassy eyes stared upward.

Martz looked down at the lieutenant. "Don't worry. I'll make sure that Irishman lives a much longer time." He pointed to one side of the room where Hagen remembered the racking machine was located.

They pushed Hagen forward, and along the wall was the German-engineered rack designed of metal—on it was his friend, Liam. He was stripped naked except for his shorts. His arms were fastened above his head, and his ankles bound by ropes that were tight and kept him suspended over the surface of the table. Liam bared his teeth.

Martz turned to Hagen. "He's been like that for a while. A demonstration tonight. A traitor and spy is a perfect example."

Hagen averted his eyes and found he was staring at the coop with the weremutants inside.

"Oh," Martz said, following his gaze. "They want to see what happens with these things when the moon is out. It's almost a full blue moon." He pointed up in the air. Hagen tried to look up, but could not with his head attached so firmly to the dolly.

"Allow me," Martz chirped, as he stepped behind his dolly and tipped it backward. Hagen stared up at the ceiling. There were a few prisoners suspended in the air, their ropes wound around beams that were horizontal over them, then to pulleys on the walkway. Over the beams was an observatory hatch that had been opened, white puffy clouds floated by. Rolph was being taken up a walkway, and ropes were being attached to him. He was to be suspended as well. Wagner must have felt that Rolph had not learned his lesson yet.

Martz brought him upright and, before his guards wheeled him away, noted, "Under the moon, full or almost full, these things go crazy. Our leaders will get a Roman gladiator fight to remember after we stick a few prisoners inside."

Twenty-Five: The Nazi Ball

Evening of May 13, 1940
Wehr Wolff Castle Ballroom

DROPLETS OF SWEAT slid down Hagen's spine. He made fists and tried to glance around him, but the restraints that fastened him to the dolly made it difficult for him to maneuver. The dolly was tilted just a few degrees, so he could observed what was happening in front of him. He was in a darkened corridor with several SS soldiers around him, a short line of figures in front of him. He had been in this position for a long period of time—he was uncertain how long. His hands had gone numb from the leather straps taut over his wrists.

Lining the hallway in front of him were the *exhibits*, all of them waiting to be paraded through the ballroom. A couple of hospital beds held patients who he presumed had undergone some type of transformation or had the experimental limb transplants. Some cages held full-grown weremutants. A few SS soldiers had reins fastened to trained weremutants who wore muzzles like his own. They were all a show for the guests.

Hagen picked up the sound of announcements in the gallery, and then the door at the end opened; a crowd stood close on the other side, and they jeered with animation. The line in front of him advanced out through the entry. Someone tipped his dolly backward and he was rolled forward. After several moments, the line thinned and they were close to the door. When it was opened fully, someone announced:

"A spy captured by General Wagner. Vital to the success of the Führer. This specimen's blood will ensure victory for the Führer." A thunderous round of applause erupted.

His handler pushed his dolly through the doorway. Hagen's stomach seemed to pitch back and forth. Bright light hit his eyes; he closed them for a second, then reopened. He was in a large ballroom filled with men in suits, clapping their hands. Glittery balls hung from the high ceiling, rotating on their suspensions and sparkling like jewels. The room, at a glance, appeared to be dominated by men, but there were a few women scattered about, many of whom had champagne glasses in their hands. He observed weremutants in various forms, locked in their cages that had been wheeled to the side, close to the wall and stationed behind a red velvet rope.

He was rolled in a large circle in the midst of the spectators. Most peered at him, interested at first, but they soon grew bored. A middle-aged man who had an aristocratic countenance and was dressed in a tuxedo with a pink bow tie, beamed with excitement at seeing Hagen.

A raised stadium occupied the space near the stage, full of people who wore either a Nazi officers' uniforms or tuxedos. The stage and stadium was veiled with bright red cloth that had black swastikas on it. Several Nazi banners were draped overhead.

Wagner stood onstage behind a large microphone, making introductions. He held a wadded-up cloth in one hand and dabbed his nose every so often. A trickle of blood was coming from his nose. The man standing behind Wagner and being introduced looked familiar. He had a small mustache on his top lip, short-cut black hair, and a tailored jade jacket with the swastika on its sleeve. He stared down at Hagen, scrutinized him with arctic eyes, and watched him as he passed. That was Adolf Hitler.

A brown-haired woman with a black mole on her cheek, wearing a gaudy red dress, hurried over. The woman asked Hagen's handler, "May I?"

"Of course, Duchess," his handler said.

The duchess peered closely at Hagen. Her face was whitened with powder; she had on dark lipstick, and her eyelashes were black, fluttering up and down as she scrutinized him. She poked his chest with a finger tipped with deep purple nails, then slid her fingertips from his sternum to his stomach. She appeared fascinated. She dropped her hand down to his waist, and approached his loins with her fingers. Hagen tried to push his hands forward, but was fastened tightly to the flat surface of the dolly and could not move.

The butler, Otto, came to the duchess and held out a tray with two wineglasses on it, saying, "Your 1929 Corton Clos De Bressandes, Lady Mitford." Otto looked around, searching for someone, and Major

General Becke weaved out of the crowd. Otto bowed his head. "Ah, the 1921 Hallgartener Mehrho¨elzchen Auslese you ordered, sir."

Major Becke glanced over Hagen's shoulder, waving his hand in dismissal to his chaperone, gesturing that he should move Hagen away.

Becke nodded to the duchess and said with a charming voice, "Quintin Becke, Major of the SS. And everyone knows you. You're Lady Ivonne Mitford. It's a pleasure."

She gave a curtsy. Hagen felt a sense of vertigo as someone tipped his dolly and began to push him forward.

Duchess Mitford said, "French wine is wonderful. After you conquer them, I hope you are able to leave the vineyards intact..."

Their voices trailed off as the crowd parted around him, many taking long ogles at him, inspecting him from head to foot.

Wagner's voice continued to waft from the speakers around the room.

The aristocrat with the long nose and pink bow tie came up and brought the back of his hand to his forehead, as he muttered, "Ah, I knew it, a true Wehr Wolff in flesh and blood."

There was loud applause.

A new man started to speak and the crowd hushed. Adolf Hitler now stood at the podium.

Hagen was taken to the sealed off area that had burgundy velvet rope with gold hooks clasped to chrome stanchion posts. This decoration separated the assorted live displays from the guests. Behind the rope were SS soldiers with their weremutants on leashes. The strange-looking beasts were sitting on their haunches and looked around them through golden eyes. Multiple SS soldiers stood close at hand, all of them holding automatic rifles. Hagen was turned so that he faced the crowd and could see part of the stage—including the masterful orator. Everyone in the crowd was attuned to Hitler, whose oration was growing in crescendo and tempo as the man smoothed back the bangs that had fallen over his forehead.

Dr. Mengele stood near the rope, and at his waist was the revolver Justine had given Hagen. The doctor appeared enraptured by the speech. His assistant, Uli, stood not far away, swirling a glass of champagne. He glanced back at Hagen, then turned away just as quickly.

A man in overalls passed him, opened the top of one weremutant's cage, and poured in pieces of raw meat. The weremutant sniffed the meat and started picking up the reddish goulash with a human hand that had claws extending from its fingertips. It shoved pieces into its mouth, then picked up what appeared to be a finger to gnaw on it.

The crowd erupted. "*Heil Hitler, Heil Hitler, Heil Hitler.*" They all straightened and thrust their right arms, saluting the orator. Hitler pushed his bangs back, then thrust his fist up in the air, asserting that they would be victorious in France and soon the British would be defeated. He spoke on about the destiny of the German people and how the bane of their existence would be dealt with decisively—Jews, homosexuals, blacks, Gypsies, and the list went on.

The people around Hagen shouted madly and saluted at certain times, thrusting out their hands over and over again, screaming out "*Heil Hitler.*" The speech ended, and the crowd lit up with a renewed merry energy; glasses chinked and toasts were made.

Martz sauntered up in a tuxedo, rubbed his chin, and appeared amused to see Hagen in this state. He opened his mouth as if to speak, but an SS guard ran up, sweat on his brow.

He leaned forward and spoke in a hushed voice. "S-sir, we have an emergency."

"What now?" Martz said in a stern voice.

"T-the servant."

Martz furrowed his brow. "Rolph?"

"H-he turned."

"Turned into what?" Martz looked at the man with a shocked face.

The guard gulped and said, "A-a beast."

Martz squealed, "He turned?"

The soldier nodded his head. "A-and he escaped. He's somewhere in the castle."

Rolph changed? Hagen pressed his wrists up against the restraints. *He's coming for me.*

Martz asked the soldier, "Where's General Wagner?"

The soldier pointed toward the end of the room. "In the study with Eichmann and Himmler." Martz barked orders to a few nearby guards and hurried away with the soldiers at his heels.

Dr. Mengele was a few feet away but had not caught any of the conversation. He had been telling a bored-looking gentleman he knew how to make weremutants immune to silver. A small-statured man stepped up to the doctor, and Hagen recognized him as one of the people who'd been sitting on the stage earlier.

Dr. Mengele gripped the man's hand. "Doctor Kramer, I've heard much of your work."

Dr. Kramer smirked. "Eichmann and I are coordinating the construction of concentration camps. You'll be furnished with an endless supply of subjects for your research. We're setting up plans to liquidate several ghettos including Warsaw, and as we increase our territory, our prisoner supply will only grow."

Dr. Kramer removed champagne glasses from a tray for himself and Dr. Mengele. "And, oh, I've met your brother, Josef Mengele. He's an up and coming officer in the SS medics. I'm sure he'll be of your stature any time."

Dr. Mengele gave a smug smile and dismissed the comment with his hand.

Dr. Kramer pointed to the gun at his waist, and Dr. Mengele unholstered it, saying, "This is an original weapon used by the Wehr Wolffs. I've collected an assortment of their weapons and keep them in my new chalet a few miles from Berlin." He holstered the pistol and brought out the medallion that had been Hagen's. "This relic is priceless, though; dates back to the Ancient Egyptians and is said to hold special powers inside that the Wehr Wolff covet."

Dr. Kramer clasped Dr. Mengele's arm and pushed him forward toward the stage. "Let me introduce you to Dr. Oskar Dirlewanger. He runs an SS penal unit and wants to bring his operations here." They weaved between the people toward the other side of the room.

The aristocratic-looking man with the pink bow tie approached Hagen, carrying a champagne glass in one hand. The smell of lavender assaulted Hagen's nose. A lascivious smile spread over the man's face, and he felt the leather muzzle that was fastened over Hagen's face. He then slid his hand along Hagen's cheek, and tugged gently on Hagen's hair and outlined his ear with his fingers.

"Oh my, how I would like to put you in my collection. C-can you hear me?"

Hagen swallowed and gave a nod.

The man smiled and licked his top lip. "I-I'm Duke Waldo Jank. I work closely with Himmler. I-I'm his occultist consultant, you could say." He leaned closer. "I'm going to make a case to Himmler for you to be spared and given to me. Isn't that wonderful? I have a castle close to Czechoslovakia where you will reside. It would be a horrible shame to kill a descendant of the Wehr Wolffs. I am not sure if General Wagner has the foresight, but you should produce heirs to your legend. I could give you concubines; we could accomplish so much together. There's so much more, too, we can do..." He sighed, and quaffed down his drink.

A dumpy man with a full mustache tapped Duke Jank's shoulder, and said, "Duke Waldo Jank?"

Duke Jank turned, smiled, and said happily, "Ah, Baron Reil, you see..." Duke Jank extended his hand toward Hagen, saying, "It's true. The Wehr Wolff legend in flesh. Wehr Wolff descendants may turn themselves into werewolves at will and have lorded for centuries over second-class wolves in their kingdom. We can rest the debate."

Baron Reil chortled, pulled his coat over his protruding belly, and sipped from his glass. "Nonsense, Duke. First, I have yet to see anyone change from man to beast and back to man. I can concede they found mutant wolves in Wehr Forest that are some rare interbreed of wolves and our geneticists are making what progress they can with our rudimentary technology in breaking their gene code. But they are not a true werewolf." Baron Reil peered closely at Hagen. "Tell me there, boy. If you can change into a werewolf, why do you just stand there?"

Duke Jank said in a frustrated tone, "He can't change until they infect him with true werewolf venom. His genetic trait makes him the most formidable werewolf you could imagine, though."

"Hmmm," Baron Reil said. "Well, I do give it to the Wehr Wolff clan. They changed their names long ago and remained hidden. What'd they call this castle? Volker Castle? Whatever it was, it did not fool the Wehrmacht. They still found them. I'm surprised you haven't convinced Himmler to find this Wehr Wolff insurgent—what was his name?"

"Tabor Wehr Wolff," Duke Jank answered. "I've heard that he likes to call himself Adolf now. And I have tried to have the Nazi leadership help me find him. But he's vanished. He disappeared long ago, in 1930 after he and his followers warred against the Wehr Wolff family and lost. The Wehr Wolff mythology says he has been taught dark witchcraft."

"So goes the legend?" Baron Reil suggested, and raised his glass, taking a gulp. "I'm an occultist enthusiast like you, but a true dark witch?"

"Not any kind of witchcraft," Duke Jank said. "But a satanic witchcraft that goes back eons."

"Now that," Baron Reil mused, "is interesting. Whatever he is, he does sound like he'd be a champion of Nazism and us aristocrats. Let's find him, shall we?"

Duke Jank frowned and took a swig of his drink. "I agree. I have done much research on him. It is said he has learned the power to change the way he looks. And can camouflage himself from other Wehr Wolff members. Not to mention, he has learned the art of controlling his age."

"He's immortal?"

"No, he just ages very slowly. And I have an idea of why he's stayed in hiding."

"Oh," Baron Reil said, amused. "Please tell?"

"He was waiting for this one," Duke Jank said, pointed to Hagen. "I've come across some recent research. The werewolf goes back to the Ancient Egyptians. The myth is that, on the night of a blue moon, a full werewolf can drink the blood from another Wehr Wolff." He pointed his thumb to Hagen again, saying, "Thus becoming a dark lord of magic who would be immune to silver bullets and, well, much more formidable."

"Ah," Baron Reil said. "Sounds like a true fable. When does that happen? Maybe we can trap him?"

Duke Jank balked. "I don't know. That's a grand idea, though. So easy. How have I not thought of it? We need to figure out the day of the next blue moon. Isn't it soon?"

A new male voice spoke from their backs. "Actually, there's a missing detail in there."

Duke Jank and Baron Reil turned, and Hagen was looking over their shoulders, as well. He recognized Dr. Mengele's personal assistant, Uli. The two aristocratic men glanced at each other and then back to the middle-aged man with a rift in his chin and bright streaks of white in his greased-back hair.

Uli stepped between them. "It's not just every blue moon," he said with a chuckle. "But when the planets of this solar system align with planets of another universe, known as Khonsu."

Duke Jank said, "I'm sorry, what is your name?"

"Uli Deist. I'm Dr. Mengele's assistant." Uli shook both of the men's hands and smiled politely at Duke Jank. "I've heard you have very extensive labs at your castle?"

Duke Jank smirked. "Some of the finest. I've had a recent investor visit who wants to push my research forward."

Baron Reil furrowed his brow. "I never heard of this other, uh, galaxy? Is it maybe called the Andromeda galaxy, discovered by—what was his name?"

Duke Jank answered, his attention focused on Uli. "Edwin Hubble."

Uli shook his head. "No, no. It's another universe. No scientist has the ability to see it. It is light-years away."

Duke Jank laughed hard. "What're you saying? Light-years?"

"Yes," Uli said. "It would take millions of years to travel to. But beings from the universe once happened by our world and helped create our Ancient Egyptian empire. It is from them that the Wehr Wolffs have their origins."

Baron Reil brought up a monocle, stared through it, and eyed Uli. "That's an astounding concept. Another entire universe with beings. Like aliens?"

Duke Jank breathed out. "Where did you read this?"

Uli smiled and said, "It comes from texts of the Ancient Egyptians, lost long ago. And blue moons occur every two years. But these alignments happen once every five hundred years with a blue moon. Tomorrow night, in fact."

Baron Reil asked, amusement in his voice. "So, this Tabor Wehr Wolff—"

"Adolf Wehr Wolff," Uli said, and offered a piqued smile. "That is what he calls himself now."

"Right," Baron Reil said. "This Adolf wants power to do what?"

Uli smiled, sipped his drink, and said, "What else? Dominate the world, of course. Turn humans into creatures he controls. Keep enough for slaves and his own experiments."

"Astounding that you know so much," Duke Jank said.

A couple of women barreled through their grouping. Two SS officers were with the women, their arms around their waists, and looked very inebriated. Baron Reil bumped into Uli and spilled his champagne over Uli's white shirt. Uli looked down at his clothes in disgust, narrowing his eyes at the woman, a flicker of something raw and furious behind the look. He stormed off.

A brunette woman with a sequined red dress put her full face in front of Hagen's and said, "Oh, look, it's that traitor. Is he really a werewolf?" She touched her nose to his muzzle, her eyes a few inches from his. She smiled. "Oh, hello." She stepped back, touched her chest with one hand, and said over her shoulder, "Oh my, he's a very handsome spy."

The SS officer pecked her cheek and glanced to Hagen. "Yes, I had dinner with him. I told General Wagner I didn't trust him. It was because of me that we caught him."

"Oh my," the brunette woman exclaimed. She touched Hagen's thin prison uniform on his chest and slid her palm down to his stomach.

The second woman, with blonde hair tied into a double bun on top of her head, came up. She was much bolder as she placed her hand on his waist, then allowed her fingers to scratch down the side of his arse.

Her admirer, another officer, said, "Yes, I was at the same dinner. I helped with the search and found him after he had shot an officer straight through the head."

The blonde-haired woman giggled. "You both are *so brave*. I could not imagine going against such a ruffian."

Both of the men were enamored, staring at the women and kissing their cheeks and neck.

One man stopped kissing long enough to say, "You want to see where he and the other these intruders stayed? It's nothing but burnt shambles now. But should be interesting, no?"

The woman kissed the man's mouth and placed her open hand on Hagen's arse. The man paid no attention to Hagen, and she shuddered as the man kissed her ear.

She exclaimed with a husky, breathless voice, "Oh yes, that would be spectacular." She removed her hand and turned fully to the man, placed both hands on his cheeks, and kissed him. They moved away, but the brunette woman glanced back.

Her eyes widened as she pointed down at Hagen's feet. "Oh, my. Isn't that darling? What is it?"

Hagen looked down, but his vantage point made it difficult to see. He leaned forward as far as his restraints allowed, and his eyes widened upon seeing the squat, massive creature dressed in a Nazi uniform. It had a long snout and sat on its haunches, close to a knight model with armor. Another cart was on the other side, which blocked its view from anyone in the main ballroom. Its ears were pressed back against its head, and it munched happily on grisly red meat held with both clawed paws, one of which looked partially human. Its golden eyes were fixed on its meal. But what made this beast stand out was the tattered Nazi uniform it wore. The sleeves had been ripped open and showed off muscled forearms that were covered with long, thick hair. Where the shoes should have been were nothing but clawed feet, and the pants' cuffs were shredded, showing off hairy thick calves.

Hagen muttered, "Oh my God, it's you."

The beast quit eating. Its lips peeled back and a row of long sharp teeth were evident.

The blonde woman placed a hand over her mouth and giggled with a nervous edge. "Oh my, I think he's smiling at me." Her eyes widened. "T-those are long teeth."

Her man, who had been conversing with a man in a tuxedo, turned around and wobbled. The woman held him up.

He squinted at the creature and waved his hand in dismissal. "Don't see anything but one of Wagner's Great Danes." He put his arm around her lower back and whispered in her ear. She bent her head back and laughed hard, and then they were gone.

Hagen shifted on his dolly. His entire body sweated. Something solid was placed inside of his waistband. He pushed his hip against the surface—whatever it was, it had a sharp edge. He winced from the pinch. Hagen glanced down at the creature, which was busy again, eating its grisly meal.

He whispered, "Sergeant Collins?"

The creature glanced up for one second, gristle dangling from the corner of its mouth. Hagen stared around him. The two occultists were still nearby and had gone from arguing about the existence of a universe no scientist could see with a telescope back to whether the dissenter Adolf Tabor Wehr Wolff was still alive and whether beings not from this planet had created the Ancient Egyptian empire, let alone borne earlier ancestors of the Wehr Wolffs.

Duchess Mitford approached Hagen. She had her arm laced into the crook of Major Becke's elbow.

Hagen caught the last part of the conversation from Becke. "It's a marvelous mansion in Berlin, once belonged to a banker. Not the largest home I own, but very impressive. I would be flattered for you to visit."

Duchess Mitford smiled at Becke. "Oh, I would be delighted." She leaned her head against his arm and glanced down. Her eyes widened in delight. She grinned and pointed toward Hagen's feet. She reminded Hagen of when his father had taken his younger brother to a traveling zoo in Munich long ago and his brother had pointed at every single creature.

She asked with an amused tone, "Oh, my. How peculiar. What is that? I never saw *him* put on display like the others?" She touched her mouth, a childlike grin forming under her fingers as she giggled. "Oh, that's so darling, how did you get clothes on him? *How adorable!*"

Becke glanced over at Hagen, his eyes slits, then looked down and jerked in surprise. "I-I don't know. It is quite curious, isn't it?"

Hagen looked around them. The weremutants the SS soldiers had on reins were agitated. The men were giving them commands, but none were listening. They were looking toward Sgt. Collins. The men pivoted their beasts around, and several soldiers followed them from the area—likely trying to act before there was any incident. Before one weremutant left, it turned toward Hagen, snarling, but its owner barked out an order and it was gone, too. The area around Hagen was completely empty of soldier personnel except for two guards with rifles.

Hagen's dolly tipped back, and someone pulled it back a couple of feet. There was commotion behind him. They were moving a cart with a cage on top that was supposed to contain a weremutant. The handler was excited and asked what had happened to his beast.

He shouted, but no one was listening to him. "It's dead! Something killed it!" The handler yelled at the nearby soldiers, demanding answers, and stomped out of the roped area, his hands held out in front of him, blood covering them. The last two SS guards followed him.

Duchess Mitford did not pay any mind to the frantic handler, but hopped up and down and demanded, "I want a photograph of him. All of us."

"Y-yes, of course," Becke said, but the rest of his words were drowned out by Duke Jank and Baron Reil, who were having a rancorous argument over how a parallel universe could exist.

"What?" Duchess Mitford asked.

"I was saying," Becke said, "I don't understand why it isn't under restraints. This is irregular."

"Oh, silly," Duchess Mitford said. She slapped his arm and made pouty lips, then spoke in a tiny voice, "I don't care about that. I want a picture."

Becke squatted down, leaned closer, and stuck his finger out at the domesticated-looking beast, and then he stared up at the duchess. "A-and that's an officer uniform."

Sgt. Collins quit chewing its meal, looked up at Becke, and brought its clawed fists down, one hand clinging on to its meat. He continued to chew but leaned forward, sniffing the tip of Becke's finger.

"You see that," Becke asked in a disbelieving tone. "H-how... Why... Do you see the SS storm trooper Captain?" Becke looked around him in a frantic manner, his index finger continuing to point toward Sgt. Collins.

The woman giggled. "Oh, I doubt I would know an SS storm trooper leader if he bit me—"

Duchess Mitford's mouth froze when Sgt. Collins snapped out and took off Becke's hand at the wrist as if it was made of butter rather than skin and bone. Becke fell back on his ass and brought his ragged bloody stump up, his mouth a humongous hangar of shock. Blood spurted onto his face. Duchess Mitford placed both of her hands over her mouth; a shrill scream commenced and the few people close by startled, and then stumbled backward over each other. A band had started playing on the stage and drowned out her screams. The reality of his condition hit Becke and he roared in pain and fear.

The two occultist gentlemen, Duke Jank and Baron Reil, dropped their glasses and scampered off with several other witnesses. Yet, the crowd in the ballroom did not seem to be disturbed. Nearby, people were looking over and trying to figure out what was going on. But the surreal noise of champagne glasses clinking together and guffaws of laughter drifted from all directions of the room. The band played a merry tune.

Someone cheerily shouted, *"Heil Hitler."*

Hagen stared down at Sgt. Collins. Becke's severed fingers stuck out of his lips, and then Sgt. Collins swallowed them whole. The creature looked at Hagen, made a series of growling noises, and then without hesitation, he turned and leaped on top of the shrilling duchess and ripped her throat out with his teeth. Blood spurted onto Sgt. Collins's face and onto the floor. A man who seemed frozen in place had his white suit pants plastered with glistening red. More people shouted out alarms.

The crowd in the room still had yet to disperse. Becke got to his knees and pulled out his pistol, then pointed it at the hackled back of Sgt. Collins, who still feasted upon Duchess Mitford's opened neck.

Hagen shouted, *"Sergeant Collins!"*

Sgt. Collins whirled around in a split second and swatted the gun out Becke's hand, his sharp claws severing another couple of Becke's fingers. His other clawed hand streaked across Becke's belly, and Becke fell back, then slid into the base of Hagen's dolly.

Sgt. Collins vaulted up high and soared through the air, causing shouts of surprise. He was weaving through the crowd, causing havoc. Shocked hollers and screams came, and more people stampeded out of the hall to the outdoors. The band faltered on the stage.

Becke staggered to his feet, his eyes huge, blood seeping over his bottom lip. His bloodied stump was stupidly held out in front of him, and his one good hand held back the intestines bursting out of his abdomen. He stumbled into the velvet burgundy rope that closed off the area and a chrome pole toppled over, making a distinctive clonk as it hit the marble floor.

Sgt. Collins's shadowy figure leaped in the air again in the middle of the room. The ballroom was alive with terrified screams as he made his way toward the area where the prominent guests were seated. Ear-splitting machine-gun fire thundered and a crystal ball suspended from the ceiling blew apart, causing fragments to pour down onto the guests. The crowd disbanded in every direction, clawing and falling over each other in complete hysteria.

Uli came running from the dining room area and looked around, his hair disheveled.

He pointed to Hagen, saying, "Get him out of here!"

Someone grabbed his dolly and pivoted him so that Hagen faced a doorway.

Dr. Mengele flanked him and shouted, *"Go, go, go!"*

A loud clamor of chaos was at his back as he was wheeled toward a side door. A group of SS soldiers piled out of the doorway, several splitting off, but many surrounded him.

Dr. Mengele grabbed Otto by his lapels and ordered him to show them the quickest route down. "Your miserable life depends on it. Get this prisoner down into the laboratory!"

They went through the doorway and approached Wagner, who was backed against the wall. He held the raggedy cloth to his nose, and the white material had turned red.

Wagner shouted orders to soldiers with automatic rifles, who surrounded a small hunched figure in between them. Adolf Hitler.

Wagner shouted, "Get the Führer out the back! Move it! *I'll get Himmler! Dexer, with me!*"

Wagner grabbed Dr. Mengele's jacket and jabbed his finger at Hagen. "Get him downstairs and lock him up tight."

Dr. Mengele's wetted his top lip with his tongue and gave on slow nod.

Hagen's dolly pivoted, and Wagner, Hitler, and the others were out of his sight. His handler rolled him down the corridor at a rapid pace, then took a sharp turn at the end. He was being rushed along a dim hall with a mix of soldiers and servants darting in different directions. Dr. Mengele came up to his side, calling out for people to get out of the way. A few of the guests were with them, trying to slip through on one side of Hagen. One woman in a beautifully woven dress tried to push in front of Dr. Mengele, who shoved her back.

A door opened in front of Hagen, and bright light spilled out into the hallway. An SS officer stepped in front of Hagen's path while pulling up his pants. The officer's eyes widened upon seeing Hagen careening straight at him. He put his hands up in defense.

A girl poked her out the door, asking, "Where are you going, baby—" She screamed upon seeing Hagen.

Dr. Mengele fell back, ramming into the far wall. Someone jerked Hagen to a sudden stop, and he instinctively threw his hands forward causing his right arm to come free. Stunned, he wiggled first his fingers and then carefully, his wrist. No, he wasn't dreaming; his hand was free. Around him were shouts for the man to get out of the way, but no one paid Hagen any attention.

Light from the room flooded into the hallway and allowed him to see that the restraint over his right wrist had been severed.

Why did that give so easily?

Sgt. Collins. He had been sitting near his side before anyone noticed… but for how long?

Enough time to gnaw or slash through my restraints.

Hagen peered down at his ankles. His restraints over one leg had been partially severed. The restraints over his left arm and chest remained tightly secured, though.

And this pressure against my waist?

Hagen slid his right hand over his waist and his fingertips glided over the hilt of a knife.

That'll be helpful.

As Hagen sped forward, he replayed that guttural growl Sgt. Collins had made. They'd not been randomly animalistic snarls—they'd been words.

He had said, "Get fighting, or get dying."

Twenty-Six: Get Fighting, or Get Dying

HAGEN KEPT HIS right arm pressed against the surface of the dolly and pretended he was unable to move. The last hour had been one blur of humiliation at being on display, seeing Sgt. Collins, and the pandemonium that followed. Now, he had a chance to escape. It was difficult to keep his arm down as the dolly was jostled and bucked, but he succeeded.

Otto shouted for everyone to turn left at a corridor ahead. As Hagen's dolly careened around the corner, it teetered on one wheel. Hagen kept his right arm firmly planted against the surface, praying he was not about to crash. Both wheels landed back on the floor, and he was whisked forward, hurtling straight ahead. Dr. Mengele came alongside him, panting, keeping pace with him, the most precious prize. The group of SS soldiers in front of Hagen were about to hit a dead end.

The passageway made a T, and the lead soldier looked over his shoulder, yelling, "Which way?"

A formidable shape slipped through the shadows from one hallway, snatched the lead SS man off his feet, and disappeared back into the darkness. A horrific scream filled the hallway. Three SS soldiers charged ahead and opened fire on whatever was there.

Dr. Mengele shouted for them to retreat. Hagen's dolly coasted in the other direction. More shrieks arose from behind. They came to a staircase, and his handler pushed him, lost his grip, and Hagen's dolly fell on its back and skipped down the steps. There was shouting above him as his dolly jerked to a stop, and Dr. Mengele bent near him. Hagen was pushed down the few remaining stairs. A few SS soldiers clambered ahead.

Dr. Mengele's voice shouted close to his ear. "Take that door, right there."

They shoved him through the doorway. It was a large room with a smattering of furniture and a faint light. Hagen was rolled to the far back wall and swiveled around, then his handler asked which door in the back to take. No one answered him, and the handler sprinted away. He had the vantage point of the entire room in front of him but squinted in the dim light. SS soldiers moved around, falling over furniture. Dr. Mengele was close at hand and commanded the guards to secure the door to the main hallway. An SS soldier raced forward and tripped over an ottoman.

"Where's the fucking light?" Dr. Mengele screamed.

People continued to stream through the open door...and Hagen recognized some as guests but one in particular—Baron Reil.

Hagen took the knife from his belt, clenched his jaw, and sawed hard across the restraint over his left wrist. The leather snapped in two. Lights flashed on. He dropped the knife—it slid under a table.

Hagen groaned, "Shit." He laid both arms on the surface of the dolly, hoping the broken leather went unnoticed. He glanced down at his ankle restraints. One had broken completely. The other one held by a strand. The door slammed shut, and Dr. Mengele bolted it, then leaned against the barrier. Dr. Mengele turned, surveying the area.

Hagen pressed his ankle against the restraint, trying to break it. But it held. He glanced around. There were SS soldiers in the room who were armed with automatic rifles.

Seeing Otto hiding under a nearby table, Dr. Mengele unholstered his revolver and cocked it against Otto's temple. "No one is taking this prize from me, you understand? I want him in my lab."

Otto vigorously assented. "Y-yes, yes." He pointed to a dark nearby corridor.

Dr. Mengele lowered the weapon and ordered SS guards, "Grab the prisoner. We're moving."

There was a knock on the door then. Dr. Mengele and every soldier in the room froze midstep and raised their weapons toward the door.

A man's voice drifted through the door crack. "It's clear. It fled upstairs. We have a new route for you." It was Uli's voice.

Dr. Mengele said, "Open it, hurry." The door swung open, and Uli staggered through the doorway and slammed it shut behind him. Uli had a thick blanket over his body.

He sat down on his haunches and shook.

Dr. Mengele asked, "Uli, why are you wearing that? And what's going on out there? You said that thing went upstairs? Are you sure?"

Hagen's eyes were fixed on Uli's head. His hair was pushed behind one ear, although only half of the ear was there. Uli straightened, met Hagen's eyes, and the corner of his mouth curled.

Uli glanced around at everyone and sighed. "This has been very inconvenient for me. I made sure the guards found your friends, *Hagen.* You were well secured and would not move. Your friends would have suffered if you tried to escape. I even killed all those pathetic prisoners and planned to pin it all on that servant. But this had to happen and now things have changed." He touched his forehead. "And t-that servant, he did something to me."

Uli faced Hagen, and his eyes glowed a sinister tawny color. "We just had to wait one more night. Just had to *wait* for all the guests to leave and I would have terminated the important ones—all in a stealthy decisive manner. It would have been quite simple. I'm vexed, Hagen Messer. Very vexed."

Hagen shouted through his mask. *"It's pure luck you found me!* I'll end my life before you take me! You'll never get your wish!"

Uli brought his head back and laughed hard. *"Luck?"* he brought his gaze down and fixed it on Hagen. A clownish grin reached from ear to ear, the tips of his teeth changing. "You think you being assigned to a mission to fly into Germany was luck? Or being given a handkerchief connected to Euan that lured you here? Or you being re-routed and your plane crashing close to Earl Groscz Castle where we first met? You believe all of that was just chance?"

Dr. Mengele frowned, looking between Hagen and Uli. "W-what? What are you talking about, Uli?"

Uli glanced to Dr. Mengele, barely seeming to notice him, and turned back to Hagen. "That, my dear pathetic Hagen, is what you call black magic."

"Uli!" Dr. Mengele shouted, trying to get his attention.

Uli rolled his eyes and muttered, "My name is not Uli." He let the blanket drop off his shoulders and revealed his complete nakedness. The couple of women in the room screamed at the indecency, as if this incident compared to all the others that had happened was too over the top. Baron Reil mumbled unintelligibly.

Hagen stared down at one of Uli's hands, still held to his side. He had four fingers.

Hagen pressed his ankle against the restraint, gritting his teeth, knowing these women were about to see much more than a peep show. And Baron Reil was about to witness firsthand a human changing into a werewolf.

For there stood Adolf Tabor Wehr Wolff.

Dr. Mengele stammered, *"Y-you're mad."*

Adolf, aka Uli, let out a sharp laugh. "That means a lot coming for you, Doctor."

Dr. Mengele brought the revolver to Adolf's head. It shook visibly in his hand.

Adolf sniffed the gun, then grimaced and remarked dryly, "That scent offends me, Doctor Mengele. Silver." Adolf dipped his head, away from the barrel, then gripped both of Dr. Mengele's biceps and pulled.The doctor shrieked in pain as Adolf yanked outward. The fabric of Dr. Mengele's dress coat ripped, and blood spurted in all directions as Adolf wrenched the man's arms from their sockets. The armless Dr. Mengele stumbled and fell where he yowled and thrashed in pain, the floor thick with blood.

Adolf dropped the doctor's arms and transformed with eye-blinking speed. Hair grew at a rapid rate on his body, long slender teeth extended over his lips, and large muscles bulged over his entire form. He had been huge when he was a boy, and now he was colossal. Adolf grabbed a nearby SS guard; the man soared across the room and hit headfirst into the far wall. Other SS soldiers fired. Adolf leaped from one place to the next, easily ripping them in half. Their torsos and legs slapped against the walls with squelching sounds.

On the other side of the room, Baron Riel backed away until his thighs bumped into the side of a couch. Adolf turned to him and attacked without warning, biting off the baron's shoulder and snapping his neck as well. Two soldiers and one woman ran to the door, screaming, and got tangled in the doorway; Adolf vaulted through the air and swiped his long claws across their backs. Large volumes of blood spilled to the floor. Adolf turned and attacked another soldier, who scurried across the room.

Hagen ripped the muzzle off his face and yanked hard against the restraint over his ankle. It did not budge.

Adolf swiveled toward Hagen, a toothy grin spread over his snout. Bloodied intestines dangled from his mouth. The beast sauntered to Hagen and crouched low to the ground.

Two SS soldiers came to the entrance, carrying machine guns. They stood in shock as they surveyed the room for a brief moment before scurrying away. The room was devoid of any movement other than Hagen and Adolf.

Martz peeked in the door, a pistol in his hand. He stared at the large wolf that had its back to him, then glanced to Dr. Mengele's mutilated body a few feet away. Martz crept through the gore at the entrance to Dr. Mengele's corpse, his eyes never leaving the werewolf.

Growls mewled out of Adolf's mouth, and somehow Hagen understood what he was saying. "Come freely or by force."

Sgt. Collins's words came strongly to mind. *Get fighting or get dying.*

Martz quickly sifted through Dr. Mengele's pockets. He grasped the leather pouch that held the serum then turned to hurry to the door. Adolf whirled and roared at the intrusion. Martz flinched and slipped on the slick, bloody floor. He brought his gun up and fired several shots without aiming. The shots were wide, and two smacked into the wall close to Hagen's head. Martz quickly scurried through the carcasses at the entry, but his gun tumbled from his hand. Adolf charged. Martz made it to his feet and sprinted away.

Hagen unfastened the restraints over his chest. The shredded strap was still secure over his ankle. Grimacing, he jerked his leg forward, a slight tug, and it was free. He leaped off the dolly, stumbled, and gathered his balance before making a sprint to the nearby corridor. He glanced back to discover Adolf had changed course and was on Hagen's heels; he knocked into Hagen's back. Hagen staggered, slammed into the glass of a hutch, and hit the floor hard.

Darkness engulfed Hagen.

HE WOKE TO find Adolf standing over him. Hagen screamed in pain as Adolf bit down on his leg, then dragged him as Hagen's hands flailed, his nails scraping against the surface of the floor. He stared toward the darkened corridor. Something, monstrous in size, was shrouded in the darkness. An amber orb glowed.

Hagen reached out as he was dragged, and pleaded, "Sergeant Collins, help…"

A snout eased out of the shadows, then a head, followed by a massive body. A gigantic wolf stood, snarling, its hackles raised. This was a much, much larger wolf than Sgt. Collins. It opened its mouth, showing off its fangs as it roared; spittle flew through the air. Hagen flinched from the thunderous bellow and covered his ears. His leg was released from its painful vise as the newcomer sprang forward, soared over Hagen's prostrate body, and slammed headfirst into Adolf.

The beasts twisted and bit, overturning as they crashed into furniture. They slammed into a far wall, and it exploded from the momentum. Large billows of dust and debris blew through the air. There were snarls and growls, and the tearing of flesh emanating from the next room.

Hagen got to his feet and surveyed the massacred bodies on the floor. Otto was cowering by a china cabinet.

Hagen limped to the man. *"Get up."*

The man cried, tightly closing his eyes. A roar came from the adjacent room, with more ripping of skin. Otto moaned.

Hagen squatted, and said, "You're taking me out of here."

The man whimpered and nodded. Hagen grabbed the man's shirt and lifted him to his feet as he glanced toward the tumultuous battle between beasts in the far room. A desk was crushed as the werewolves landed on it.

Hagen yanked on Otto's collar and towed him. He stepped through Dr. Mengele's blood to his severed arm, which still held his revolver. He wrenched the gun from the rigid fingers and stared at the doctor's corpse. Then he grabbed the sniveling butler again and yanked him to the carcass.

Otto urged him, saying, "Sir, we must hurry. They'll come for us."

Hagen ignored Otto and bent over the dead body; he took off the gun belt when he noticed silver bullets were fitted in the leather loops. He surveyed the gory body until he found the medallion had partially come off of Dr. Mengele's neck. He reached down, took the necklace from the dead man, and gripped the piece tightly in his hand.

He nodded to Otto. "Let's go."

Otto started to lead Hagen out of the main doorway, but Hagen said, "No, Martz went that way. Another way."

Otto did an about-face and led him to the darkened corridor where the mysterious wolf had first appeared. They went upstairs and into a hallway. Otto turned toward the direction of the ballroom, but Hagen grabbed Otto's collar and jerked him to a stop.

The man fell back against the wall. Hagen shook his head, saying, "No. All the way down."

Otto's eyes widened even farther. "D-downstairs? You'll n-never make it. Surely, General Wagner knows what happened, and he's waiting for you. A-and they reinforced the area with more troops this morning, more than I could count; you'll die."

Hagen clutched Otto's coat with both hands, shook him, and spoke through his teeth. "*I am not leaving here without my friends.*" Hagen brought the revolver up, cocked the hammer back, and put it inside Otto's mouth. "You want to help or not?"

Otto moved his lips; the words he spoke were jumbled with the barrel in his mouth.

Hagen removed the barrel and leaned close.

Otto pleaded, "P-please don't. I-I'll help."

"Which way?"

Otto pointed, his arm shaking. "T-there's a lift this way. N-not the same one you and your friends took. A-another one. I-it's not on any of the maps."

"Lead the way."

Otto led Hagen down the hall, past the stairway that went to the area where the two beasts fought a fight to the death. Something tugged at Hagen's mind, but he pushed it away. It returned, though.

The wolf that had attacked Adolf—it had only one eye.

Twenty-Seven: Reunion

THE ELEVATOR STARTED its descent into the bowels of the castle. Hagen leaned against the wall, keeping his gaze on Otto in the corner. Hagen ripped a piece of cloth from his shirt, made it into a bandage, and wrapped it over his thigh, which now had puncture wounds and had bloodied his pants. He straightened to find Otto staring at his chest where the medallion lay outside his shirt.

Hagen reached up and gripped the gold piece in one hand. "You know what this is?"

Otto startled and met his eyes, his lips quivering; his face was flushed, and Hagen guessed he had the same general look of someone about to have a heart attack. The exertions were probably taking their toll on his old body. Hagen touched the butt of the pistol held in his holster. The intimidation worked, and Otto licked his lips and held his palms up to Hagen.

"Long ago," Otto said, "before I ever became a butler at Wehr Wolff Castle, I was a mason and helped with repairs on the castle. My mother had worked as a housekeeper when I was a child—took me along with her, which is how I know so much about the place." The cage they were in slowed. Otto looked around them, jostled the lever, and the elevator rattled and continued to descend at a slower pace.

Otto wiped sweat from his forehead and continued the tale. "A woman came in from Wehr Forest, carried some kind of lever-action rifle and had a sword sheathed over her shoulder. I heard later that she was called the Keeper of Wehr Forest. I'd seen her a few times before; someone told me she was a peacekeeper of sorts, making sure no one wandered into Wehr Forest who shouldn't, or wandered *out* who shouldn't. The wehrwolves of the forest followed her and considered her some type of godmother. People also said she had some kind of sixth sense; others said she was a witch of sorts."

"The medallion?" Hagen asked.

Otto nodded. "Yes, I was hauling quarry the day she came to the castle. She came up from the road and asked for my help, saying her horse had gone lame, and she took me to where she'd left her wagon. She had some boy with her. He was laid out on a makeshift bed of sticks. His face was thin, battered, and bruised, and his destroyed leg was in some kind of cast she had designed herself. She said she was taking him to Wehr Wolff Castle. He looked to be on the doorstep of death. I-I didn't ask questions, but we carried him the rest of the way in my carriage."

Hagen leaned forward, his fists clenched and his mind daring to hope, and asked, "*Who was the boy?*"

He shook his head. "I-I don't know. The family moved me away to another residence soon after. They gave me more pay and never gave me any reason. I didn't mind. I had been asking for a raise. I didn't return here until someone informed Wagner about me and suggested I come here to help him. Wagner made me convert to Nazism and used me. When I came, there were three servants, and the number grew of course. Rolph was one of the original servants. A lad, really, barely in his early twenties."

Hagen looked at the lever that would take them back up, and stammered this time. "D-did anyone ever call him Ivan?"

"Ivan? No, sir. Just Rolph."

Hagen rubbed the back of his neck, biting his lip. *It couldn't be. How could it be?* This man had informed against him and had helped Wagner catch him.

"What about this medallion?" Hagen asked.

"The woman, before I left, she took it off her neck and placed it on his chest, saying it was a talisman. Had belonged to a powerful woman from long ago, and she swore it would keep him safe. I was told later that the boy died of his wounds, and the day before I left for my job, I buried the casket close to the family grave."

Hagen did not remove his attention from Otto. The butler licked his lips. "I swear, sir, that's all I know."

"You look inside?" Hagen asked.

"Sir?"

"The casket! Did you *look inside it* before burying it?"

Otto shook his head. "That'd be most improper, sir."

Hagen asked, "What did she look like?"

Otto's face showed more confusion.

"This woman. The Keeper of Wehr Forest."

"O-oh," Otto stammered. "She was Oriental, but German mixed."

The elevator came to rest, and Hagen grabbed the clasp and yanked the door open with a loud squeak. He stepped out of the elevator, then looked back at Otto, who was hunched in the corner. Hagen brought his hand up, beckoning him to come.

"S-sir?" Otto whined.

"Until I retrieve my friends, you're my guide."

Otto's expression turned from terrified to petrified, understanding the bargain he had to fulfill in order to live.

"You see," Hagen said, "I learned this from the Nazis. If I put your best interest first in helping me, then you'll find the easiest route with the least resistance."

Otto nodded. "O-ok, sir. My mom never took me into the bowels. This was said to be haunted. But I know one route."

"Where would they have taken Lieutenant David's body? Would it be near the heavily defended location?"

Otto reflected. "If they haven't burned it or disposed of it out the hatch, it would be in the mortuary. That's still a good distance to the coop, which is where the others are being held."

"Go," Hagen ordered, and then he followed. They wound through several narrow vaulted passages; Hagen kept the revolver raised in front of him. There were shouts that echoed off the walls. SS storm troopers were being marched in coordinated units in different directions. Hagen's leg throbbed, the pain having grown in intensity.

He grabbed Otto's arm and had him stop so he could rest. "How much farther?"

Otto pointed diagonally across the hall to several feet away, where the wall jutted out and there was a large archway. "It's just there, sir."

Hagen stepped in front of Otto, hesitated, and looked at the man. If any Nazis were inside, he needed to take them by surprise.

He leaned close to Otto and whispered, "Stay right here. I'm going in first. Are you going to run? If you do, I'll kill you."

Otto swallowed and shook his head. Hagen brought his weapon up, drew the hammer back, put his back to the knotty wood of the doorway, and listened. He glanced to Otto, who had shrunk against the wall, hidden by shadows. Hagen gritted his teeth, swing around the corner with his pistol up, and dashed inside. A sharp pain flashed through his leg at being forced to move quickly.

He looked around, lowering his gun. There were several pale corpses on top of stone slabs. Some of them had clothes, others didn't, and a few were shriveled, deformed prisoners. A few had SS uniforms. There was an open back door next to a vast gate; a breeze blew through.

Hagen started to call out for Otto to come into the room but froze. His gaze fell on Lt. David's body. His face was discolored, and he was still dressed in his tattered Nazi clothes.

Forgetting Otto in the hallway, Hagen stepped over and patted Lt. David's chest where there was a pocket, mumbling, "Where are those maps, Lieutenant? Come on, *please.*"

Hagen didn't find anything in the man's pockets. He had no solid plan that would enable him to rescue Liam and Roesia. If he was not careful, he was about walk into Wagner's open arms. No doubt, Wagner would gladly take him back. Hagen would kill himself before that happened, but not until he euthanized his friends.

A scent he'd caught before coming into the mortuary lingered in his senses, and he looked around.

Blood. Lots of it.

A thick pool had seeped around a morgue slab platform. He stepped closer to investigate, then stopped and stared at the heap of freshly killed bodies on one side of the slab. Nazi guards. A few had been dismembered, and others had deep slashes over their torsos.

Hagen caught Rolph's scent and the soft padding of feet from one side of the room. Hagen wheeled around, his gun aimed at Rolph, who weaved between the mortuary slabs. Rolph had a shabby blanket drawn over his shoulders; it covered his entire body. One side of his face had a deep laceration—blood oozed from it, dripping onto the blanket. Rolph froze and leaned against a slab, staring at him with his one eye, the other socket a vile dark-red rawness.

"Thought you would come down here," Rolph said, and held up a handful of maps.

Hagen's hands shook as he gripped the raised pistol with both hands. He didn't trust his voice, but he spoke anyway. "W-who are you?"

The corner of Rolph's mouth curved up. "You have her eyes. We were both so young when she died, but her eyes... they were gripping, like yours."

A tear ran down Hagen's cheek, the gun wobbled, and his voice cracked. "T-tell me, who are you?"

"What does your heart say, Hagen?"

"I-Ivan?" Hagen croaked, and the gun lowered an inch.

A small smile spread over Rolph's face.

"I-Ivan?" Hagen repeated, his pitch rising.

Rolph straightened and squared his shoulders, then nodded.

Hagen lowered his gun, his mouth working as he stuttered, his words all but nonsensical. "B-but it can't be. They said y-you had mortal wounds and d-died."

"As a human, yes," Ivan said. "They didn't know how to tell our father I would transform. He was suspicious of the Wehr Wolffs, though for Mother's sake, he was friendly. But when you *Become*, your body completely heals." He held his hands out, and his smile grew. "It is good to finally see you again, brother."

Hagen's sweaty palms gripped the gun harder, and he raised it once again. "But you informed against me."

"I did that for a reason. But I'm also the one who killed that repulsive man, Xylander. And I'm the one who left the maps for Roesia to find. I'm the one who sent the wolves of Wehr Forest to help."

"Why didn't you come yourself?"

Ivan grimaced. "I can see things. I saw you would be safe with the wolves. And I felt Justine was wounded and needed my help. I found her and took her away so she could heal. It was a great risk to leave the castle."

"You gave Commander Ford the medallion?" Hagen's fist clenched and unclenched on his gun. *Is this really Ivan? My brother?*

Ivan shook his head. "I'd hidden the medallion in the castle when the Nazis came, but Adolf found it. He went to Commander Ford in the form of Uli and gave it to him. Ironically, he showed Ford a true vision of what would happen if Adolf took control. A world filled with creatures ruled by Adolf; he convinced him that you could stop him. Except, Commander Ford did not know he was talking to Adolf."

Hagen shook his head in confusion, tears shone in his eyes. "What do you mean he showed him?"

"We all have our powers. Adolf has many. One is that he can show images of future events to humans. That, combined with a bewitching spell on Ford, was enough to keep the man from asking lots of questions."

"T-the medallion," Hagen said, "had a power, too. I felt what it would be like to become a werewolf. It was like the handkerchief I was using to track a prisoner, but much more powerful."

"Adolf no doubt bewitched the medallion so it would connect to you whenever you made contact with it, and used it to lure you here." Ivan held his hands out. "The feeling—nothing like it, is there?"

Hagen looked away for a second, then met his brother's stare and whispered, "No."

"You are going to *Become* now, Hagen. You must be cautious of its powers."

Hagen stared out of the opening at the back of the mortuary and changed the subject. "You never answered me. Why did you inform against me? I saw you use your power. You can make people do things. You did it with Wagner at least once. He lowered the gun. Then with Uli... you made them believe it was Roesia who killed those subjects! Why didn't you use it to help me?"

Ivan leaned back against a slab. "When I use that ability, it can cause side effects that can, well, cause lots of other problems. I used it on Adolf, not knowing it was him. Because he's Adolf Tabor Wehr Wolff, he would have soon figured out it was me, and then he'd have known I was a Wehr Wolff. It was a mere last-ditch effort to keep myself from dying. I have tried to be as quiet as a mouse while here. I've been waiting for Adolf to reveal himself." Ivan stepped closer, wincing as he walked.

"I informed against you, Hagen," Ivan said, "to keep you close to me. As you know, Adolf summoned you here with his black magic. Nothing was a coincidence. He was not about to let you walk away. And I assure you, Adolf is not dead. I'm sure he's gone back to Wagner to tell him whatever he needs to say to catch you. He cares nothing about Nazism, finds it repugnant. He is the one who exterminated Mengele's subjects. He wanted me out of the picture, thinking I was a spy put here by the Wehr Wolff family. He just didn't know I was a Wehr Wolff." Ivan chuckled. "But why did he really kill those subjects? As insane as he is, he finds the idea of the Nazis using Wehr Wolff blood to create super-soldiers detestable. Funny if you consider the idea that, if it was up to him, he would turn all of humanity into a regime of creatures who would follow him."

"Can't you smell him? Or sense him?" Hagen asked, annoyance in his tone. Liam was still imprisoned, and God knew what torture they had inflicted upon him. Or were inflicting now.

Ivan moved closer, touching Hagen's shoulder. "Adolf changed his appearance and his smell using his learned sorcery. He hid well. I had to wait for him to reveal himself. Justine helped me make my scent undetectable."

Hagen sighed and replaced the gun in his holster. A couple of tears overflowed and ran down his cheeks. He whispered, "I cried night after night when I thought you were dead."

Ivan's mouth drew down, his eyes moist, and he looked sorrowful. "I'm so sorry, Hagen. I'm sorry for Father, too, but I'm truly sorry for you. I could never tell anyone." He lifted his gaze to Hagen.

"As the eldest brother and the sole Wehr Wolff steward, I implore you to leave." He pointed to the open gate that was at the back of the morgue. "You can go through there. This is my mission, not yours, Hagen, and besides, you're wounded. I will get them."

Hagen shook his head. "You said I am about to *Become*. This will heal—you just said."

"It will. All your senses will heighten. They already have. Hearing and sight. And then you will go into a hibernation period for several hours, and you'll be vulnerable and useless. I have no idea when this will happen."

Hagen straightened and crossed his arms over his chest. "I'm staying here."

Ivan sighed, and asked, "Tell me, this Liam, you love him?"

Hagen whispered, "I-I do. How do you know that?"

Ivan grunted. "I can smell it on you." He kept his focus on Hagen and took his hand. "Hagen, I promise to get Liam and this Roesia. You have my word."

Hagen shook his head. "I'm not leaving without them. They come out with me, or I die here."

Ivan grinned and bowed his head. "Just like the day you saved me, brother. You have our father's build—his hands, legs, his face—but our mother's resolution. *Die or live, living for the heart, that truly matters.* Maybe not her words, but ones she often repeated. We do it together, then."

The tears ran down Hagen's face, and he embraced his brother. Ivan held onto the blanket with one hand, wrapped his other arm around Hagen's neck, and squeezed. They stood for several moments, just hugging each other. Hagen stepped back and wiped his face with his arm, then surveyed his brother more closely. He peered at his brother's raw eye socket. He had received that because of Hagen.

"H-how bad does it hurt?"

"Painful, yes. But I'll survive." Ivan nodded to the archway. "Otto! I can smell you. Come inside."

The butler stepped inside and looked nervously around. Ivan stepped closer and said, "I thank you for bringing my brother to me."

Otto opened his mouth and glanced from Hagen to Ivan in bewilderment, then muttered, "*Brothers?*"

"Why did you convert to Nazism, Otto? Don't lie—I'll know," Ivan asked.

Otto licked his lips and shook his head. "I was never really. You understand? We all have to."

"Ah, true," Ivan said. "But I understand you conspired with General Wagner before he attacked the castle. You gave him information that helped him kill many people here; he almost captured a couple of Wehr Wolff young."

Hagen came to Ivan's side. "He said he was brought on later, after they had raided the castle."

Ivan raised an eyebrow. "A lie. Is that your story now, Otto?"

Otto didn't speak but appeared to shrivel before Ivan. Hagen had the feeling he wanted to flee the room, but some power from Ivan held him in place as if by trance.

"You're ashamed of conspiring with Wagner?"

Otto gave one sharp nod.

Hagen looked to Ivan. "But Justine brought you here after you were injured."

Ivan nodded and said, "Yes, she did." Ivan met Otto's eyes, and sighed. "I cannot kill a member of the Wehr Wolff family." The small man relaxed. "But, I can't have you roaming the castle as we lead an attack, either. You might want to warn Wagner, and I can't have that, as my brother would be at risk."

Otto's mouth opened to speak, but Ivan spoke first, his eyes flickering back and forth. "You will leave Wehr Wolff Castle and never return. You will go to the lake, and if anyone asks, you will tell them General Wagner ordered you on a private mission to the base being built on the other side of the lake. Yes?"

Otto touched his forehead and nodded. "Y-yes." He turned, stumbled, then got his balance and moved toward the opening at the back of the morgue. A moment later, he disappeared through the hole.

Ivan turned to Hagen, and said, "He'll make it out alive, or that'll cause him to go crazy. Come, brother. We have little time."

Twenty-Eight: The Wehr Wolff Legend Lies Within

HAGEN FOLLOWED IVAN through secret passageways and, after a short time, found himself in a plain, moderately sized crypt that had arched stone ceilings. Wide columns were spread along the room with designs of warriors dressed in old military garb.

Hagen wheeled around and a sharp pain spiked in his leg—he winced and asked, "What is this, Ivan?"

"Once it was a war room where swords, spears, and shields were made." Ivan stepped to a wall that was built of bricks and pushed it until it swiveled open. Hagen stepped inside and stared around him at the weapons in the vault. There were swords, bows and arrows, and spears, all made of silver.

Ivan grabbed a silver spear and moved toward the end of the room. Hagen asked, "Doesn't it hurt, to touch it?"

Ivan set his spear down, knelt before a safe, and rotated the dial. "It does, but you train your body and mind. After a while, you can overcome the fatal allergen."

"That day you attacked from high above—how did you have so many spears?"

Ivan opened a safe and sifted through materials. "I figured the coop room was the ideal location for Adolf to make his sacrifice. At the time, he had worked on Euan until he was of no use. Then Adolf summoned you through his sorcery. I planned to attack him the night he tried to make the sacrifice. There's a corridor behind the wall where I set up spears. Adolf almost caught me that day, and I'm sure he's destroyed that room now."

Hagen peered over Ivan's shoulder as he rummaged inside the safe, and observed, "Your throws were deadly."

Ivan paused, then said over his shoulder, "I have to admit, except for Houk, I was aiming at Martz. A shame I could not have killed him. It spooked Adolf, though, and I risked much."

"You could have hit me."

"Come, brother. They were nowhere close to you." Ivan took a leather briefcase out and set it down.

"Why didn't you kill Wagner or Martz earlier?" Hagen asked.

Ivan glanced up. "I did not want to raise suspicion, and wanted to remain hidden from Adolf. I thought of hiding Wagner's ammunition, but it turned out that Adolf did that for me. That's what caused the place to be reinforced like it is now."

Ivan placed three black grenades inside the briefcase. Hagen recognized the weapons. "Lieutenant David was carrying those."

Ivan nodded. "Indeed. I stole them. Well designed, too, and from my assessment, designed to pack a better punch than any regular grenade I've seen." Ivan retrieved a leather pouch from inside the safe, which looked similar to the one Martz had taken from Dr. Mengele's corpse.

Hagen asked, "Does that have the serum to turn someone into a super-soldier?"

"No," Ivan answered. "It's something else. I'm giving it to Justine."

Ivan opened the leather pouch and checked inside. There were three vials fastened to one side and a syringe on the other. The vials had a turquoise liquid inside them.

Ivan went rigid and stuck his nose in the air. "Adolf. *He's here.*"

Hagen tensed, drew his gun, and crouched. He looked around and said in a hushed voice, "Where? I thought you couldn't smell him?"

Ivan pressed down on Hagen's revolver. "I don't mean he's here with us in the room. He's close, though." Ivan's eyes grew distant and then focused. "He's gone back to General Wagner in human form, like I suspected he would. He's preparing a trap to catch you. And Hagen, you should sense him too, now that he has revealed himself."

"Do you see what's going to happen?" Hagen asked. "You see the future?"

"I'd call it intuitive sight. I see blips of images and make sense of them in a few seconds, and it helps me plan a course. I am sometimes wrong. Come, brother. We need to hurry. I know where we can go."

Ivan shoved on a column, and there was a click and a small door flipped open. It did not look like a staircase or anything to crawl through. In fact, it looked like a disaster in waiting.

"Ivan?"

"Remember when we used to slide down the bank into Aachen Lake?"

Hagen squinted down into the hole. "But we could see the lake! I can't see anything."

Ivan said, "You want to save your friends?" He threw his spear into the orifice; there was a loud clonk and then a grating noise as the spear slid down. Ivan placed his satchel over a shoulder, sat on the edge, and vanished from sight. Hagen sighed and secured a leather strap of the holster to keep his revolver from falling out. Then he put his legs over the ledge and pushed. He whisked down a smooth surface, which wound in long curves—he gave a short cry at a sudden drop. Then he popped out of the opening onto a flat surface, came to an abrupt jarring stop, and stared up at his brother.

Ivan put out his hand. Hagen reached up until their fists clasped, then was up on his feet. Hagen looked around them to find he was in a drainage tunnel. Ivan had his spear in hand, pivoted, and moved forward. Hagen trotted to catch up with him.

Ivan asked, "Your leg still hurt?"

Hagen bent and touched his leg close the bandage. "It's fading. Probably all the moving around."

Ivan shook his head. "It's the werevenom. A new type of adrenaline will pump through your body. Painful wounds will be numbed. And your senses, they will not just double, but quadruple. But this is short-lived; it will then crash and you'll become feverish... and then you will *Become*."

Hagen asked, "Was Mother a werewolf?"

"I don't know, Hagen. I believe she kept her distance from the family because of Father. She kept us near the Wehr Wolffs at the same time. Persuaded Father to take us hunting in Wehr Forest. Father was suspicious of the rumors of the Wehr Wolffs, though. In those times, and now, being a werewolf is akin to being a devil."

The drainage duct curved—there were drips that grew in volume. A familiar scent came to Hagen. "Weremutants. Where are we?"

"We're under the kennel area." Ivan stopped in his tracks and cocked his head, looking around them.

"Ivan, what—"

Ivan put his hand up for silence and reached out to place his palm against Hagen's chest. "Quiet." Ivan leaned close to Hagen's ear and whispered, "Something is not right." He straightened and his eyes widened. "I made a mistake. The mission...*it's changed.*"

A tumultuous roar echoed in Hagen's ears, and the stench of foul water hit him. A deluge was barreling down the tunnel, coming their way.

It's coming right at us!

Wagner, he presumed, was flooding the drainage duct. Ivan grunted, dropping his spear and bag. He shrugged his robe off his shoulders; he was still naked underneath. Hagen had a second to take in the numerous deep lacerations that covered his back and arms, and that his skin was slimy with fresh blood.

He got all those from fighting Adolf?

Ivan pressed the leather satchel into Hagen's hands. "Put it over your shoulder." Hagen followed instructions, and without warning, Ivan stooped, pressed his shoulder against Hagen's abdomen, and heaved him over his shoulder.

"Ivan!" Ivan's hand grasped Hagen's thighs and bolted at an amazing pace down the tunnel. They were heading straight into the vociferous flood.

They raced around a bend. The flood was closing in. Hagen could almost taste the repugnant sewer water. Ivan stopped, bent his knees, and vaulted upward into the air. Hagen felt a sense of vertigo. Their ascent ended, and Hagen rose off of Ivan's shoulder and came back down, his groin crashing into Ivan. Hagen slipped down Ivan's front, and Ivan grabbed out, his hand catching the medallion necklace around Hagen's neck. Hagen jolted to a stop, suspended in air.

Ivan growled, "Hang on to me, Hagen!"

The necklace broke, but Hagen gripped his brother's midsection in time and made his way up his torso where he clung to Ivan's neck. Hagen looked down at the drainage duct floor. Ivan had managed to leap an impossible ten feet or more. They were swaying in the air. Torrential water passed under them. Hagen shifted his body and managed to look up. Ivan's fingers gripped a stone ledge. Above them was a large orifice closed off by a metal vent.

Ivan groaned. "Shoot the vent."

Hagen drew his revolver with one hand and fired at the vent. Sparks spewed into the air. He fired three more times. The vent finally fell, tumbling into the water below. Ivan gritted his teeth as he gripped the ledge with both hands, his knuckles on both hands having turned white. The necklace of the medallion was wound around the wrist of one of his hands.

"Go, Hagen!"

Hagen placed his gun back in the holster. He stretched up and gripped the vent's edge with his fingers, then clenched his jaw as he grasped it with one hand. He pushed off Ivan and grabbed the edge with both hands, then swayed in the air as he strained and tried to pull himself up. The lack of food and the blood they had taken from him had taken its toll. He was not in his best form. Ivan's hand pressed up hard against his arse. Hagen was propelled up, and with that, he easily pulled himself inside the duct.

The passage was narrow. He had to lean back to turn himself around, and then he poked his head out to look down to his brother. The haunting memory of when he'd been ten years old returned, his brother dangling in the air and staring up at him with pleading eyes. This time, Ivan's eyes were not pleading, though; instead, they were determined.

Ivan barely had a grip by his fingertips as he looked up at Hagen. Hagen reached down, and pleaded, "Ivan, grab my hand."

Ivan met Hagen's eyes, and said, "Remember, Hagen, you're a Wehr Wolff." Ivan let go and plummeted down, vanishing into the violent torrent.

Hagen yelled in a high-pitch voice, "*No!*" He stared down at the roaring flood, at the water hitting the sides of the duct, spraying up and wetting his face. He crawled away from the opening and sat with his eyes closed, breathing heavily. His hand touched the butt of his revolver as his breath slowly calmed, and then he placed the leather satchel over his shoulder. He reloaded his gun, turned, and crawled forward.

The memory of his brother saying *"You're a Wehr Wolff"* was front and center in his mind.

Twenty-Nine: The Rescue

HAGEN CRAWLED THROUGH the duct while the image of his brother falling into the torrent replayed in his head. The words he'd spoken before he fell resonated in his mind as his nose caught a familiar scent that was acrid and foul.

Ammonia.

He followed it, took one turn, and then another. After a few moments, he came to a slotted vent and peered through it. He viewed the large laboratory. The spacious warehouse region had several cubicles within it that had thin walls partitioning one lab area from another. A few people in lab coats bustled around. Right below the vent was the room that held decapitated heads and vials set under the fangs for gathering venom. He had toured this same room the first night in the castle.

Hagen narrowed his eyes as he focused on the front of the laboratory where a handful of SS storm troopers were spread out. But that was not what caught his attention. Near the area where the cubicles ended, close to a raised platform, were the pods. Inside them were the captured wehrwolves of Wehr Forest. The largest pod set up on a raised platform and was juxtaposed against the myriad of cubicles that filled the warehouse space.

What did they call the one inside the largest pod?

Riesig... Wehrwolves.

And who do the wehrwolves follow?

Hagen sat, facing the grate, and kicked out, twice, and again. There was a grinding noise, and after another kick, the metal shifted. He touched his leg; the pain had indeed receded. He kicked out one more time, and the vent tumbled to the floor. Shouting filled the room.

He did not hesitate but scooted to the ledge and stared down. He had little time. It was an eight-foot drop, and he pushed off. His feet hit the ground, and he rolled on the floor and came up to his knees. The place where Adolf had bitten him still pulsed with a fiery sting, but there was a surge of adrenaline rushing through his body now. He had waited a long time for this sensation to be one with him, and the corner of his mouth curled up. He rose to his feet and took out his revolver.

Two SS guards bolted through a door. They raised their rifles and opened fire. Beakers shattered around him. Hagen had already aimed at the doorway before they'd even entered the room, and he fired two shots with barely a pause between them. One SS guard's head jerked back; the man hit the doorway and slid down it. Blood streamed from the hole in the middle of his forehead. The second guard's eye was bloody gore, and his body was pitched over a countertop that had racks of vials on it. He and the glassware crashed to the floor.

Hagen crossed the room toward the dead SS guards. A third guard poked his head through a door on the other side of the room. Hagen did not stop walking but aimed midstep, barely taking in the target before he fired. Brain debris sprayed against the door, and the dead SS soldier slumped to the floor. There was panicked shouting on the other side of the room as a Nazi leader ordered the men in the adjacent room to charge.

His senses were at full force, and whatever venom the werewolf had given him with his bite, it had indeed intensified the entirety of his perceptions—smell, sight, hearing, and a sixth sense that was growing exponentially. Hagen placed his revolver in his holster and removed a grenade from his bag, then pulled the pin and tossed it across the room. It went through the door. He dipped down, snatched a dead soldier's machine gun from the floor, and sprinted through the doorway and across another small room. He picked up the sound of screaming—
"*Grenade!*"

Three SS guards came through a door he was sprinting toward, but Hagen had already smelled them and fallen to his knees in a slide. His rifle pulsated in his hand as he fired at them. Their bodies were riddled with holes, and two collapsed. The third man retreated in the direction he'd come. Hagen slid through the doorway. A thunderous explosion filled the entire area behind him, the adjacent walls obliterated, and the chemicals in the room sprayed over them, turning into a blazing fire.

The SS guard who had been retreating had run smack into a suspended weremutant that was in the middle of the room. It was skinned and had electric probes connected to its muscles. The soldier and weremutant toppled to the floor, the creature mewling out in agony.

The guard had dropped his rifle but rolled over and reached for his pistol. Hagen was already up, and his rifle barrel pressed against the man's forehead.

"Don't," Hagen ordered. The guard brought both hands up in surrender. "Why are you trying to kill me?"

The guard pleaded, "Please, don't kill me."

Hagen aimed at the man's knee and fired one shot. The SS man shrieked in agony. "Your orders were to take me in alive?" Hagen yelled. "Why are you trying to kill me now?"

The man whined. "P-please. General Wagner wants a man named Rolph. We were told to take you if we could, or kill you."

They wanted Ivan now.

"Who's helping General Wagner?"

The man moaned from his pain and pressed his hand against his knee, rocking back and forth. "I-I don't know him. He was the assistant to Dr. Mengele. But he says he was really placed here special by Himmler to keep an eye on things and root out the Wehr Wolff. Someone named Uli."

Hagen asked, "Uli said he's Himmler's spy? And Wagner just believed this?"

The guard nodded his head vigorously.

Hagen placed the barrel to the man's forehead, glanced away, and pulled the trigger. There was a definitive splatter onto the floor.

Hagen straightened. The only noises now were the mewling of the skinned weremutant, the fire at his back, and SS guard reinforcements getting ready to storm the room he now occupied.

General Wagner wanted someone who could turn from man to beast at will, and he had Ivan. Now Adolf had Ivan, too, and it was optimal for Adolf to get rid of Hagen.

Hagen stepped up to the pathetic weremutant, pulled out his revolver, and put it out of its misery. He opened the cylinder, and the spent shells fell to the ground. He put in new rounds, closed the cylinder, and reholstered his pistol.

Why did they flood the drain?

His senses picked up images. His brother could see the future, but Hagen could see things that had happened from the smells around him. It was as if those odors had their own imprints of memories in them. He had not known this until now; this was how he'd always had deft tracking skills, skills that he'd taken for granted.

Now, though—everything was enhanced.

Uli had given General Wagner ideas about how to catch Rolph. Hagen bent his head, and more images flitted through his mind. His brother had transformed when he fell into the torrent, but it made little difference, as the flood had taken him to a section where they had placed a silver net and caught him.

General Wagner did indeed now have his brother.

Hagen opened his eyes and stepped from the room into a new laboratory he'd never seen before. It had varied weremutants held inside cages. They all had silver chains wrapped over them—and while they were all in torment, some were in less agony than others. A couple had silver chains swaddled over them, but beside the discomfort of being unable to move, the silver was not causing them any pain. Several vials set on the counter held coarse herb pellets inside them, and the German word Immunität was scribbled over the front. *Immunity*. It looked as if Dr. Mengele had found a way to make the weremutants immune to silver.

Voices caught Hagen's attention. He smelled men on the other side of the wall. He raised his rifle and fired short bursts; holes battered the surface as he swept the weapon. Bodies dropped one after another, and when his it clicked empty, he dropped the machine gun.

He took out his pistol and went out the door onto a raised, latticed steel platform; he was in the area where the pods sat on the floor below. He glanced over at Riesig's enclosure, near the main console.

A wounded SS soldier got close to Hagen and raised his rifle, but Hagen shot immediately upon entering and the man flipped over the railing, onto the floor below.

He aimed his pistol toward the corner of Reisig's metal pod and fired just as a guard poked his head out from behind the pod. Part of his head vanished, and he collapsed to the ground. Hagen pivoted, keeping his arm straight; the revolver extended out and targeted the floor below, which had the several pods. A soldier appeared from the flat top of a pod, his rifle on his shoulder. Hagen pulled his trigger, a shot thundered out, and the SS man tipped over and plummeted to the other side. Three SS soldiers weaved between the forklifts, machinery, and pods. Hagen aimed, breathed, and his muzzle flashed; the gun roared, and his ears rung. He stared down at the motionless men now lying on the ground.

He opened his cylinder so that the empty shells spilled out and clinked on the surface close to his feet. He stopped at the top of the steps. He turned to Riesig's pod. Amber eyes stared at him from the window, the glass fogged from the beast's breathing. Hagen stepped back and looked across the room toward the doorway where he sensed the presence of several men.

He put his hands up, his gun held in one hand, the empty cylinder hanging open, and yelled, "Wagner! I know you're there. I surrender. Don't fire."

He sidestepped and came up behind the main console on the raised platform, then glanced back. The metal paddock that held Riesig was twenty feet behind him, flush to the wall. He sensed movement from the doorway across the room and faced forward, surveying the far raised walkway. Several SS soldiers moved out of the archway and hurried across the steel walkway, then down the stairs. They spread out in front of him, their guns trained on him.

Hagen stared at the archway. "Wagner, I know I'm not a priority anymore. But I still have use, yes? I give up. Just show me my friends. I know they're there with you."

Dexer came out; he held Roesia in front of him. She wore a ratty prison uniform; her face was bruised and her lip swollen. Martz came into view. Behind him, a soldier wheeled Liam out on a dolly like the one Hagen had been on. Martz held a machine gun with both hands. He came to the far stairs and stepped down them, his rifle trained on Hagen. The soldier stopped Liam's dolly at the top of the stairs.

Martz sidled over to have a better line of sight on Hagen. He squinted an eye shut, and said over his shoulder, "Give me the word, General. He'll never use his leg again for the rest of his miserable days." Martz's eyes narrowed at Hagen. "Though few they are. Whatever you or Ivan did to the general, Herr Fluke, you will regret it."

Hagen was genuinely befuddled. He ignored this remark, however, and yelled, "*Wagner!* Why won't you come out and talk?"

Martz looked over his shoulder, then back to Hagen, speaking through a smirk. "I had a fun time with your Irish friend. He wasn't so flexible as I had hoped. Remember our promise? You become useless to Wagner, I do what I like. You went against me and I said I would make sure you paid. You're a real idiot to surrender."

Hagen's keen sight observed Martz's finger brushing the trigger.

"You might miss, Martz," Hagen said and touched a lever that would open a wehrwolf pod. "And I might pull this. It says Pod Five. That'd be unfortunate, as you're standing in front of pod five."

Martz tensed and swallowed.

Hagen said, "Let me see Wagner, and promise me you'll let my friends live in the dungeon, and I'll go peacefully."

Martz gave one perceptible nod. A few SS soldiers came up the steps toward the main console where he stood.

"It's clear, General," Martz said.

General Wagner came out the door, and close behind him was Adolf. Adolf had found some clothes and was no longer wearing a lab coat but a Nazi officer uniform. The scent of the clothes was brand new, never worn. Adolf had to have kept those close at hand in case he needed them, in the event he wanted to carry out another untrue story, like being Himmler's secret agent. Adolf appeared amused as he stared at Hagen.

Hagen regarded the general. *What happened to him?* Wagner no longer wore the same assured air. He held a new rag to his long slender nose. His face was pale, and he had an unsteady gait. There was something else. A feverish sickness wafted from the man. In the next moment, he realized this was a side effect from Ivan. Ivan had said his powers could cause major side effects.

"You captured Ivan?" Hagen asked. He dropped his gun, his hands went behind his head, and he studied Liam for a second. His friend's face was bruised, one eye almost closed and the other staring at him in despair. Roesia was close to Liam, held by Dexer; she kept her head down.

General Wagner narrowed his eyes, and then he brought his hands down and laced them in front of him. "Ah, you know, then? A second Wehr Wolff under my nose the whole time. And your brother, at that."

"You sure you have all the Wehr Wolffs?" Hagen asked.

Wagner raised his eyebrows. "*What?*"

Hagen chuckled, and Wagner's eyes twitched, growing furious. Blood started to run out of a nostril, and the rag flew up to cover it. Wagner glanced back to Adolf, who shrugged.

Wagner turned to Hagen, and yelled across the room, "What's so funny, Herr Fluke? *I've got your friends, you fucking idiot!*"

"You're egotistical, and that's truly what makes you blind. Earlier, upstairs, I was on that dolly. Your men were shredded by a wolf. Martz looked through the door. What'd he say he saw?"

Wagner glanced to Martz.

Martz spoke through his teeth. "Your brother, scum."

"Ivan is who you think you saw? But how many eyes did it have?"

A light danced in Martz's eyes and realization dawned over his face. The creature he had seen had certainly had two eyes.

"Say, General," Hagen asked, "where is all your silver ammunition?"

Wagner glared at Hagen.

Hagen pointed to Adolf. "He hid it. *Why?*" Hagen hissed, "*You idiot!* You didn't just have one Wehr Wolff under your nose, nor two, but *three*. Your Uli there is Adolf Tabor Wehr Wolff. One of the most infamous ones ever known."

Wagner glanced back to Adolf, to Martz, and then toward Hagen.

Adolf mused, "He's quite the liar, sir. Thinks he can raise your doubt. A stupid folly."

Wagner's eyes were slits. "You, Herr Fluke, will be broken, but not killed—no, no, no, not before you and your brother fulfill the Führer's dream of creating a new army. You, Ivan, one way or the other—Nazi will get its Wehrmacht's Wehr Wolff Army."

SS soldiers approached him from both sides, their rifles raised. One SS man put his rifle strap over his shoulder and removed a pistol, glared at Hagen, then advanced at a quick pace.

"Fuck the Führer," Hagen said.

Wagner's face turned beet red, and his mouth worked, but no words came out.

"Herr Fluke," Martz snarled as he braced his rifle on his shoulder. "I will hear your squeals for nights and keep these friends of yours alive for my pleasure. This Irish one here will have a limb amputated each week. I'll let you pick. I'll keep him alive for months, just because I can."

Wagner came down the stairs to the main floor below, removed his pistol, and found his voice. He ordered the men near Hagen, "Take that fucking scum! Now!"

The SS man holding a pistol came up and swung his butt down to Hagen's temple. Hagen ducked the gun, and it slammed into his shoulder. Hagen's knees buckled, and he put his hands on the console.

The SS soldier pressed the end of his gun barrel against his head, and hissed, "On your knees, scum, or I'll make you squeal right here."

Hagen yanked down on several levers. The SS guard's mouth turned down in shock, and Hagen's elbow flashed across his body and hit the weapon away from his head so that it flipped through the air. He pulled down on more levers. The SS man punched Hagen in rage as Hagen pulled the last lever.

Around them, there were loud whooshing noises and sharp clangs. All metal pods on the floor containing the originally trapped wolves of Wehr Forest opened. Hagen shifted, glancing around the edges of the console. SS men shouted in panic. A huge gnarly snout slipped out from one opening, sniffing the air. Machine-gun fire erupted. Wagner stared around the room with large eyes, and his weapon pointed to and fro. Behind Hagen, a door clanked open, and the SS man next to him spun around, his eyes widened, and his mouth fell open. The colossal beast known as Riesig skulked forward. Its tawny eyes glowed as he tipped his head back and gave a penetrating bellow. The SS man fumbled for his dropped pistol, forgetting that Hagen existed, while other SS soldiers around him fled. One SS soldier ran backward in a panic and flipped over the railing close to Hagen.

Riesig stormed forward, his long fangs protruding from his jaws before they clenched down on the screaming SS man's shoulder. The creature wrenched its head back and forth, then let go. The man flew through the air, blood spurting out from the gory hole of his arm socket. In a matter of seconds, Riesig dispatched men closer to Hagen.

Riesig turned to Hagen, crouching, its eyes trained on him.

Hagen whispered, "Save my friends. Bring me Wagner. And be careful, Adolf is here."

Riesig blinked but kept its gaze on Hagen for one more moment before he vaulted over Hagen's head to the floor below, and tore into its feed, satisfying its long famished hunger.

Hagen leaned back against the console, hidden from any shooters. Stray rounds hit the wall and the steel paddock in front of him, ricocheted off, making a series of *tzings*. With no time to think, Hagen took a quick breath, picked up his dropped revolver, then reloaded it and holstered it. He grabbed a fallen machine gun and checked the ammo in the clip while registering the spasmodic machine-gun fire interspersed with incoherent cries and pleas.

He peeked around the console's ledge, trying to take in the bloodbath below. Less than thirty seconds had passed since he had opened the doors, but the place had since transformed into a macabre sight.

The sides clearly had been evened out.

The wehrwolves had decimated the entire force. Blood and gore lay on the floor below. Dismembered limbs and weapons were scattered. Though the wehrwolves had been hit by rounds, none had fallen or even seemed injured. Instead, they all had a vivacious appearance and exuded a cheerfulness at having been set free, and on top of that, a meal made of their tormentors and jailers. Hagen peered up at the elevated walkway where two wehrwolves had leaped to maim the soldiers who had stupidly remained there, attempting to make a stand. Hagen went down the stairs, his gunstock on his shoulder, but there was no enemy to fire at, so he lowered his weapon.

The dolly that Liam was restrained to had fallen down the stairs and was at the base. Roesia was close to it, hunkered down, hugging Liam's neck, her face pushed against his. She flinched at the howls, the guttural roars, and high-pitched shrieks that surrounded her, not bringing her head up to look. Hagen smelled her terror and sensed her resolve to remain with Liam. The wehrwolves didn't pay her or Liam any attention, though. They, in fact, had cleared the area around them.

Adolf was nowhere in sight. Neither was Martz. Dexer, however, had fallen off the walkway and was wounded and attempting to crawl away.

Hagen signaled to a wehrwolf, saying, "Bring him to me."

The wehrwolf obeyed.

An SS officer limped toward the stairs, the back of his shirt completely burgundy, the scent of his blood attracting Hagen's notice. It was General Wagner. The general's pistol with its silver rounds lay useless in the middle of the floor, his severed hand still gripping the gun.

The panicked man stumbled and fell down before he scrambled up the walkway. Instead of going right to where Martz and his men had once been and two wehrbeasts were now located, he went left to the opposite archway, which was clear and would take him to the weremutant kennels. Riesig charged, sprung from the floor, and glided in the air, heading straight for Wagner. He landed close to him, his massive weight throwing Wagner off his feet and into the wall.

Hagen yelled, *"Alive!"*

Riesig glanced toward Hagen, one vast paw on the middle of Wagner's back. He bent his head and, not being gentle, bit hard into Wagner's shoulder, then lifted the screaming man and bounded off the raised platform. The beast made a flawless landing on the sludgy floor. Riesig dropped the whining General Wagner at Hagen's feet.

Hagen inspected the chamber they were in. He signaled to three wehrwolves, "Check the labs behind me. Make sure that no others are lurking about." The two entrances on the walkway now had wehrwolves close to them, crouched down and acting as sentries while the other wehrwolves feasted.

For the moment, the room was secured. Hagen pointed to Wagner, met Riesig's eyes, and said, "Watch him."

Hagen trotted to Roesia and Liam.

Liam lay on the floor now, his restraints were removed and the muzzle gone from his face; his head was in Roesia's lap. His nose was crooked and bloodied, his face swollen, and one eyelid was unable to open. His chest and abdomen were bruised, he missed several fingernails, and some of his fingers were misshapen. He was breathing hard as Roesia petted his head, her arm wrapped around his chest. Obviously in shock, she met Hagen's eyes, her cheeks wet. Hagen knelt and gently reached out, but brought his hand back. There was nowhere safe to touch without causing pain.

Liam's one eye fixed on him, and the side of his mouth curved up.

Hagen wiped his eyes and nodded.

A shriek caused him to flinch, and he turned, knowing who was being brought to him. A wehrwolf had its jaw clamped over Dexer and dumped him close to Hagen. The man fell out of its jaws and rolled on the floor, his bloodied body covered with puncture wounds. Dexer crouched as he panted and moaned, then put his hand up to ward off Hagen.

"Dexer," Hagen said. "I need information—" But before he could speak further, Roesia grabbed Hagen's gun from his holster, pointed it at Dexer's upraised hand, and fired. The round blew off Dexer's finger and hit his lower jaw, rupturing the portion that was left. He fell back, writhing and shrieking with horrific noises.

"That was for Liam, you sick fuck." She squatted, aimed at his groin, and fired point-blank. Dexer squalled and thrashed in uncontrollable fits over the floor. "*And that,*" Roesia said, through gritted teeth, "*was for raping me.*"

Roesia straightened, her stare fixed on the agonized man. Hagen regarded Roesia, the memory of Xylander fresh in his mind. He waved to the wehrwolf standing over Dexer. It clamped its jaw over Dexer, dragging him away as two more joined it, tearing and ripping at the shrieking man. Roesia watched them gorge on Dexer. The screams faded quickly, and the man became an unrecognizable lump of shredded flesh; the wet smacking was the only audible sound that came from the wehrwolves as they devoured the remaining portions.

Roesia turned to Hagen and handed him his gun, which he placed back in his holster. She pointed to Wagner. "Ask him what you want."

Hagen nodded and stepped to stand over Wagner.

The menacing General Wagner had been transformed into a whiny shell of a man. He had gotten up to his knees and held his bloody stump to his chest with his head bent in capitulation, whimpering. A profuse amount of blood dribbled from one of his nostrils.

Riesig's snout was close to Wagner's face, and every time the beast breathed, the cowering man moaned.

"Where did you put my brother?" Hagen asked.

Riesig growled. Wagner flinched and gave a surprised squawk. "W-what?"

"My brother, where is he?"

Hagen flicked his fingers, and Riesig's jaw opened an inch, his growl growing in intensity.

"Is he in the coop?" Hagen didn't feel this was true. That area was close by, and he didn't sense him there.

Wagner almost brought his head up, but it remained bent down, and he finally spoke after another second. "N-no."

"Why not? It's made of silver," Hagen said.

"Someone blew it up."

Adolf had done that, Hagen surmised. He wanted to move everything upstairs. He wanted a confirmation, though.

"Then, where—" Hagen straightened, his eyes open wide, and he stared up at the elevated walkway, toward the wehrwolf sentries. One's hackles were raised, and it was growling.

Hagen yelled, "Run!"

Machine-gun fire exploded out from the nearby archway, rounds hitting the wehrwolf standing guard so that it backed up at a fast pace, flinching and yowling in pain before it toppled over the railing, landing on the floor motionless and dead. The wehrwolf at the other door retreated, leaped over the railing, and came down to them, then backed up to Hagen in defense, growling.

Liam cried out in pain as Hagen carried him at a dead run, heading toward the stairs while screaming to everyone, "Run! They have silver rounds!"

He glanced over his shoulder; Roesia was at his heels, but she stooped, grabbed Wagner's severed hand from the floor, and wrenched the pistol from the rigid fingers. A soldier's head popped from the archway as he tossed in a grenade. Another one flew in the air.

Adolf had to have shown the Nazis where the hidden ammunition depot of silver was.

Riesig had Wagner in his jaws and leaped in the air to get onto the platform. The two grenades exploded, and Riesig howled in pain as Hagen dove through the door, hitting the floor, and Liam rolled from his arms.

Roesia was knelt next to him, staring out the door. She yelled, "Hagen, let's go."

Hagen pivoted to the door, his hand stuck inside his satchel as he removed his own grenade. He stepped out the door and observed that Riesig had dropped Wagner and landed on the top platform close to his metal paddock, then rolled over on his side. Riesig got back to his feet. One wehrwolf closest to the stairs had been heavily peppered by the shrapnel, and it limped toward Hagen. Hagen smelled the silver.

SS soldiers flooded out of the doors, their guns raised, and opened fire. A wehrwolf charged them but was cut down by the soldiers.

Hagen pulled the pin and threw the grenade toward the walkway. "Move!"

He pivoted, shoving Roesia, and scooped Liam back up. "Liam, grab my neck if you can." Liam placed one arm around Hagen's neck, his faced pressed against Hagen's cheek. They squeezed through another doorway.

What is that scent? Fresh air.

Wehrwolves rammed through the thin walls, and Riesig took the lead in front of Hagen, barreling through each panel as Hagen shouted. "There's a back door where they bring in prisoners and supplies!" Two consecutive explosions thundered out behind them, and there were a series of crashes, the collapsing of structures.

They came to a warehouse area with a ceiling at least fifty feet above them and stacks of wooden boxes in several rows. They hurried between aisles of crates and came to a steel wall where the wehrwolves paced back and forth along the wall and howled. The shouts of SS soldiers were audible behind them. Riesig crouched close to Hagen, ready to make his last stand.

Hagen whirled around, searching for a device that would open the door. Liam moaned into his neck. Roesia darted to a cable that was suspended from the ceiling and depressed a button. There was a series of loud clanks, and a section of the wall in front of them lowered. Fresh air and rain whipped inside the area. Three wehrwolves leaped onto the steel door's edge as it came down, and vanished over the ledge. The door came down all the way—they hurried out. Hagen looked around him. There were some parked transportation trucks. The few SS guards close to the area were killed by the wehrwolves. One SS guard had been climbing into a fuel truck, and his eyes widened at seeing a seven-foot-tall wehrwolf standing over him. It swiped its claw out, and the man's severed head skidded over the gravel drive.

Hagen set Liam down close to a head-high concrete wall, and said, "I'll be right back."

Liam muttered, "Sure, boyo, I'll wait here."

Hagen glanced around, looking for Roesia, but she was rushing toward the fuel truck. Riesig glared at Hagen, and Hagen pointed to Liam. "Guard him."

He raced back to the steel door, toward the cable switch inside that dangled from the ceiling. The yells from SS soldiers were drawing closer. He depressed a switch, closing the steel door. He drew his revolver, pointed it at the device, and fired. Sparks spewed in the air, and there was a gaping hole in the panel. He wheeled around; an SS guard had come out of a far door and was turning toward Hagen. Hagen fired, and the man's head snapped back, his helmet flew off, and a hole in his forehead could be seen before his body disappeared back through the door.

Hagen spun, re-holstered, and sped toward the rising door. He gritted his teeth and jumped, his fingers gripping the ledge as he pulled himself up and scooted over the top, then fell to the other side as the door clanked closed. He hit the ground, and Riesig came to his side. Bright beams of light hit Hagen, and he shielded his face; the fuel truck skidded to a stop in front of him, dust billowing up in the air. Roesia jumped out of the driver's side. Hagen climbed to his feet, then pointed to Liam who was still leaning against the wall.

"Drive. I'll get Liam."

There were loud shouts from the other side of the wall. Hagen picked Liam up with no time to be gentle. Liam whined in pain. He ran to the truck, placed him in the passenger seat, then scooted him into the middle. Liam groaned at being moved. Roesia depressed the clutch; there was a squeal, and she pushed back on the gear again until the vehicle moved backward. She slammed the gear shift again and the back tires spun; gravel flew and pelted the steel door, and they roared forward.

Hagen looked behind them; the stone facade of the castle was in full view. No one was pursuing them at the moment.

"Where do we go?" Roesia asked.

Hagen pointed out the window. "Follow him." Riesig was flanking them. His amber eyes glowed as he stared up at them. The wolf pulled ahead and took a turn toward the tall wall, going toward a gate manned by Nazi personnel. Two soldiers pointed their rifles their way. Roesia gripped the gear shift, a squelching noise followed, and she slammed the vehicle down into a lower gear. The engine revved, and Hagen bucked forward as their momentum slowed, his arm out across Liam to keep him from falling forward into the dashboard. Roesia's knuckles were white, gripping the steering wheel with one hand and the gear shift with the other.

"Wait," Hagen said.

The wehrwolf survivors Hagen had rescued from Wehr Wolff Castle charged the sentry force at the gate and slaughtered them.

The truck lurched forward and came to a full stop at the closed gate. Hagen stepped out and over a couple of dismembered bodies as he looked around. A few wehrwolves paced along the wall frantically. He came to the gatehouse and went inside to find a console and red phone. It started ringing, a light blinking on and off. He yanked down on a handle. A nearby reel spun and squealed, a sharp clang erupted, and a drawbridge lowered in front of their truck.

Hagen jumped back into the vehicle, and before them was a narrow suspension bridge that spanned over a small canyon to the mountainous terrain with a lush forest. The hair on the back of Hagen's neck rose; he sensed the shooter on the opposite side before the two sharp cracks came, a muzzle flashing each time. Hagen had drawn his pistol and aimed it, but just as quick, he lowered his weapon. A body fell in front of them and disappeared into the canyon. Another body streaked by. Heavy gunfire erupted from on top of the wall, followed by a crack of fire from the other side. The machine guns above them grew silent.

Riesig and the wehrwolves hurtled forward over the suspension bridge, and Roesia glanced at Hagen. He shrugged and holstered his pistol. Roesia pushed on the gas and the vehicle went forward. Halfway, Hagen leaned over, trying to see below the bridge, although nothing but fog was visible. He looked behind them, stared up at the wall through the misty rain, and saw nothing. The smell of death, though, on top of the parapet, was acute.

At the end of the overpass, their truck dipped down onto a dirt road that curved up to the summit of the mountain. Hagen leaned forward, staring through the windshield in search of the sharpshooter. The beams of light lit the worn dirt path and tall trees edging either side. A person dressed in a hooded robe stepped out in front of them, a silver hilt showed over a shoulder. A lever-action rifle was in the person's hands and a satchel slung over one shoulder.

Roesia slammed on the brakes, and Liam snapped forward. The vehicle shuddered because it was still in gear, the engine stalling. And Roesia placed her hand on Liam's leg, looking at him, and asked if he was okay. He only whimpered. Hagen stared intently at this mysterious person he had met not just a few days ago but long ago in his past. The person pushed the hood down, and Hagen took in the gray hair. *Justine.*

Large wehrwolves were on either side of her, and Hagen knew they were not the same ones that had escaped from Wehr Wolff Castle. Riesig walked up to her, and she put out her hand and touched the wolf's head. Riesig sidled away, and then Justine stepped forward with a severe limp. She came to the driver's side. Her face was bruised, he assumed from injuries sustained when she'd helped them escape from Earl Groscz Castle. She scanned everyone's faces, stopping on Liam, who leaned against Hagen, his eyes partially closed. She turned her attention back to Roesia and Hagen, then reached into her robe, brought out a white bag, and gave it to Roesia.

"Give the boy a shot; it's morphine." She leaned her rifle on the truck and stepped toward the bridge, went halfway, knelt down, and removed her satchel.

Roesia took a syringe out of the bag and handed it to Hagen. He poked the needle into Liam's arm and pushed down on the plunger.

When he glanced up again, he tensed. There was a movement under the bridge. "No," he said and placed his hands on the dashboard.

Two weremutants came from under the bridge, just a few feet from Justine. Standing, she unsheathed her sword and severed both heads in two quick swings. One beast's head bounced off the bridge. A third weremutant came from under the bridge and charged her from behind. Justine turned and flung her sword. It flipped through the air before striking the creature's head, stopping it dead in its tracks.

Justine did not hesitate, but knelt again and fiddled with something inside the bag; Hagen's sensitive nose picked up sulfur. She was lighting a match.

She stood, leaving the satchel, and hurried forward at a hobbled trot. She removed the impaled sword from the beast and returned to their vehicle. She retrieved her rifle, went to the passenger door, and stood up on the step, then placed the gun strap over a shoulder and waved her hand.

"Go."

Roesia turned the ignition and the engine rumbled to life; she pushed the clutch and shifted into first, the truck bucked and moved forward. The wheels hit potholes and Hagen's teeth jarred.

Hagen leaned over to look out of Roesia's rearview mirror. A thunderous explosion erupted behind them. Liam and Roesia startled. Fragments of the bridge plummeted down into the canyon, only a gaping hole left in the center. A grating noise drifted from the structure closest to Hagen, metal screeched as a portion collapsed and vanished from sight.

Roesia was staring at her sideview mirror too, barely pushing the gas, awed by the spectacle.

"Follow Riesig," Justine said.

"Why did you have morphine?" Hagen asked.

She answered, her voice flat, "I've been expecting you."

Riesig led them over the treacherous road. Other wehrwolves could be seen running in the forest on both sides of the jeep, the numbers increasing as they continued on. Riesig turned off the road abruptly, and Roesia wrenched on the wheel so that the tires dropped down onto a trail covered with weeds and shrubbery.

After a few minutes, Hagen's nose twitched and his stomach growled. The sweet smell of meat stew filled his senses as a cabin came into view. Hagen salivated. He had forgotten how famished he was.

Thirty: A Time to Heal, and a Time to Become

ROESIA PARKED THE fuel truck close to the front of the log cabin. Justine hopped down and headed into the house. Even though it was May, the mist had turned into an icy cold downpour mixed with sleet. Rivulets of water poured from Hagen's hair and face, droplets scuttling continuously onto his chest and back. Roesia, her arms over her chest and still wearing the thin prison uniform, was hunched over by the hood of the truck.

Hagen told her, "Go, I got him."

She didn't argue but turned to hurry through the cabin door. Hagen stepped up on the truck step and stared at Liam. The medication had made him calmer. Hagen placed an arm under Liam's thighs; the other went around his back, his fingers touching his rib cage.

Liam hollered, *"Bugger to shite."*

"Sorry," Hagen said, gently shifting his hand to pull Liam against his chest. Hagen made his way to the open cabin door with Liam in his arms, kicking it closed behind him. Warmth greeted him. Justine was lighting several kerosene lamps set around the cabin.

Roesia was at the fireplace; red embers in its hearth warmed her as she rubbed her hands above the heat. A cast-iron pot and kettle were suspended over hot coals. Thunder rumbled outside, the only noise beyond the mix of water and ice that pelted the windowpanes. *This is where Ivan must have brought Justine after she helped them escape and was wounded.* He regarded the lever-action rifle she had set on the kitchen counter, it being of a different design than the last one he had seen. He assumed she must have her own weapons and supplies stored somewhere nearby in case she ever had to come to this location.

Justine cleared off a long table near the fireplace, then placed a couple of thick blankets on top and waved for Hagen to place Liam on them. Hagen did as directed as she beelined into the kitchen, rummaged around in the cabinets, and placed the ingredients she found in a mug. In the light, Hagen could clearly see Liam's cruelly twisted fingers and the raw ends where his nails used to be.

Justine took the kettle off the fire and poured hot water into the clay mug she'd prepared, then blew on the steam. She looked to Roesia and Hagen. "You'll need to get out of your clothes. There are some here you can have. I am going to fix his fingers." She brought the mug over, and told Hagen, "Lift his head."

Hagen put his hands under Liam's shoulders and propped him up.

Liam turned to Justine and noticed the mug in her hand. He lifted an eyebrow and croaked, "Bloody tell me you found some Guinness?"

"Much better than that," Hagen said, not knowing what he was about to be given. "Drink up."

"It'll take the pain away," Justine said in thickly accented English. "And you'll sleep good. I have only a few vials of morphine, and you may need those later." She put her hand behind his head and pressed the cup to his mouth. He sipped, wincing.

Justine paused, then asked, "Hot?"

Liam whined, "Bloody tastes like piss."

Justine placed the lip of the cup to his mouth once again and tilted it until everything was gone. She brought the cup away and went to a hutch to pick up jumbo-size scissors. Stepping over to Liam's waist, she slipped one blade under his waistband and closed the teeth together. She continued this method to cut away material and reveal bruises over his thighs, quads, and calves. His shorts were soiled with dirt and grime. She pulled them off too, then settled a blanket over him and brought it up to his waist.

Hagen blanched at the deep-purplish bruises all over Liam's abdomen and chest. Roesia had a hand over her mouth as she stared down at him.

Justine said from their side, "Go, change. It will be some time before it takes full effect. Clothes are in the bedroom—take whatever fits."

Hagen turned away and started toward the bedroom. Seeing Liam so helpless reminded him that Ivan needed him. Hagen pushed this thought from his head and riffled through the closet, searching for clothes. Roesia found some items, and she sat on a stool, her back to Hagen, and changed.

The image returned of Ivan from years ago when he had been wounded and Hagen was at his side as he fainted, and never seen his brother again.

Soon. Soon, I will get him.

Hagen located some pants and a shirt, put them on, and returned to the kitchen. Roesia stood close to the fireplace. Justine stirred a pot of stew with a ladle, then glanced over her shoulder at him and nodded. She stepped away toward the table where Liam lay and picked up a cloth that she rolled up.

Justine put up to Liam's mouth. "Bite on it. To help with the pain."

Liam bit down, and she waved to Roesia and Hagen, telling them, "Hold him."

Roesia stepped closer and placed her hand on one shoulder, and Hagen did the same. Justine grabbed Liam's wrist and picked up his hand. Liam flinched. In a delicate manner, she placed his hand on her palm and scrutinized a finger.

Liam's body tensed, and Roesia pushed his short bangs back. "*Shhh.*"

Justine gave a forcible tug on a finger; an audible crackle followed, and Liam shrieked and thrashed. Hagen pushed down on his shoulder to keep him in place. Justine continued to methodically study each broken finger as she performed the same procedure for each, and then she set that hand down and moved to the next.

Beads of perspiration covered Liam's forehead, chest, and abdomen. He panted from the exertion. Sweat trickled down Hagen's spine from watching the painful procedure and from keeping his friend still. After a few moments, Justine was finished. She placed Liam's hands on two flat boards, then wrapped cloth around them. She soaked a sponge with warm water and dabbed it over Liam's face, chest, and stomach, then did the same to his lower region. She leaned her ear against his chest, then barely slid her fingers over it and his rib cage and on down his leg. He winced a few times. She waved for Hagen and asked him to roll him to his side.

He pushed him onto his side. His bare buttocks showed, and his bruised hamstrings were in full view. She put her ear to his back, asked him to breathe in, and slid her hand over his shoulder; she touched a spot on his rib cage and asked if it hurt.

"Bloody hell, it does!" Liam gasped.

Justine stood, and Hagen let Liam down gently. She pulled the blanket up to his neck. Liam panted, licking his lips.

She told Hagen, "He has broken ribs, strained ligaments and muscles in his legs and arms. One arm is broken. I'll set it after he takes another batch of painkiller. He can't move for a month, probably longer, and that might still not be possible. He may never walk again. I don't know if he has any ruptured organs inside. If he does, he'll probably die."

Hagen's entire body tensed at these words, and Justine touched his shoulder. "But for what it's worth, I feel he will live. He's not spitting up blood or bleeding from any orifice. I'll have to splint his fingers and put a poultice on the nail-bed wounds, but after you eat. I will feed him now; you need to eat." Justine propped up Liam's head and placed a rolled blanket under it, and then she picked up a bowl with stew and started to feed him. Hagen waited a second, then departed, his stomach roaring in pain.

An hour later, Hagen had sat down; his new dry long-sleeve shirt and thick fabric pants at least warmed him. His belly was full, and he was beyond sleepy. He had the chills, and his body ached one second and the next it was fine. Whatever adrenaline rush he'd had that had numbed his pain, it had receded. Roesia had lain down on a blanket on the hard wooden floor and said she was just going to close her eyes for a moment. Snores poured out of her mouth a second later. Hagen looked across the room to Liam—his chest rose and fell at a steady rate, his breathing heavy. Justine came by and set a cover on Roesia.

Justine came to him and squatted down, touching Hagen's forehead and his cheeks. "You have a fever. Let me see."

"What?" Hagen asked, willing his eyes to remain open and reminding himself his brother was trapped in a castle not far away. He started to get up. "M-my brother."

Justine stayed him and shook her head. "You're no good to your brother right now. You'll be an easy mark, and Adolf will capture you in your weakened state. Adolf bit you, yes?"

Hagen nodded. "How did you know?"

Justine gestured to a satchel close to the table Liam was on and right inside the lip a crystal was visible.

"You can see the future?"

"Future. Past. Present. Anything it wants to show me. It's how I knew you were coming from that bridge. Let me see the bite."

Hagen stood up and unbuttoned his pants, then let them drop, his face turning red. Justine scooted closer and touched close to the bite wounds. His rain-soaked clothes had cleaned away most of the excess blood. A deep purple color surrounded each particular bite mark.

Justine stood up and looked at him. "Soon."

"I will *Become* now?" Hagen asked as he pulled his pants back up. It was an effort to hide his excitement. He wanted to feel that adrenaline.

Justine regarded him and answered, "I can only say what normally happens. You change, stay in werewolf form maybe a night or a few days, then change back. You'll only have a few memories of what happened. Over time, you may gain control, or not." She wagged her finger in front of Hagen's face. "But your eyes tell me, Hagen Messer, that you have coveted this time?"

"W-what?" Hagen asked, and shook his head. "What do you mean?"

Justine sighed. "It is no matter now. It is your destiny. Tomorrow is the blue moon, and the planets align with Khonsu. A power of darkness will fill your veins, and you, Hagen, must push it back. You can turn partially, but do not let it take you. For if you do, your human mind will disconnect. If the power takes hold and you fall in love with it, you could be this for years, maybe for the rest of your life. Only a few things can make you turn back to human."

"What is that?" Hagen asked, and swallowed the lump in this throat.

Justine rattled off the possibilities, sticking a finger up at each option. "You are knocked unconscious. You are severely wounded and the power wanes from you for good. You have overeaten. And..."

The reality of what was coming hit him, and he spoke, his voice distant. "And what?"

Justine shrugged, though. "Willpower will bring you back. But it need be connected to something of worth in this world. Love is the best path."

Hagen stared across the room to a sleeping Liam; the flames from the fireplace at his back unfurled inside the hearth and crackled.

"When will I finally be ready to turn?"

Justine shrugged on her thin coat, picked up her lever-action rifle, and checked her ammunition loaded inside the breach. "Soon. You will feel it when it comes. You must resist the change, though, because once you do, you may not be able to return...for a long time. The torture you have been through and the blood fighting, it has darkened you, and your mind will readily embrace the werewolf form." She pointed close to

Roesia, where another thick blanket had been laid out, a makeshift pillow on top of it, and a cover close by. She said, "Sleep, Hagen."

Justine stepped to the kitchen, donned her thick robe, and picked up a leather bag.

Hagen asked, "Where are you going?"

"Tending to those you saved. Some have been wounded. I will mend what I can. And I'm going to re-park the fuel truck to the side of the cabin." Justine grabbed the doorknob but stopped as Hagen asked his next question.

"When we met before, why didn't you tell me all this?"

She opened the door. A cutting, cold wind blew through and slapped Hagen across the face. She turned to him and said, "You were not ready, Hagen Messer Wehr Wolff."

She was gone then, and when the door shut, a cozy warmth enveloped him again. He lay down so he could stare at the fire. He pulled a cover up to his waist and did not see how he could sleep—he was about to become something beyond human. A minute later, his mind drifted. He woke himself with a snore, and then his eyes closed again, and he was sleeping.

It was a deep slumber that wormed down into a cozy jet-black cavern that had no end.

THE HARSH WIND blew against the windowpanes, and a relentless rain assailed the outer cabin walls and glass. Hagen started awake, rose to his elbow, and looked around the room. The fire had burned down; gray ashes were piled up, and a few log fragments glowed red. The temperature in the room had dropped. The flame in the kerosene lamps had diminished, and shadows danced around him. He sat up and looked around. Roesia was not there—there was only a wadded-up blanket pushed against the wall. He stood and stared down at his body, surprised he was nude. He stepped across the room toward the table where Liam slept. But no Liam was on top, and neither were any covers. He stared down at the surface, the red embers from the fireplace giving some light, at the wetness glistening on the table's surface. He slid his fingers through the fluid, then brought them up, placing them under his nose. A repugnant ammonia scent filled his nostrils.

"Nooooo."

A voice snarled behind him. *"Heil Wehr Wolff."*

Hagen wheeled around to face a freakish creature who was close to seven feet tall. Its head almost touched the ceiling. The face was disfigured, but it had a resemblance to someone quite similar. The body was hairy; it wore no clothes and had slender muscled legs that bowed outward, ropey powerful arms, and a clawed hand clenching something that dripped blood onto the floor. The face was human, and fangs extended out of its mouth.

The oversized creature kicked something, and an egg-shaped object rolled toward him and bounced off his foot, then twirled in one full circle. He stared down at Liam's severed head. Liam's vacant eyes stared up at him, his mouth opened wide in terror. Hagen snapped his gaze up.

The beast leered, showing off its bloodied fangs. Hagen recognized the person.

Hagen bellowed out in pure rage from somewhere deep inside; the yell metamorphosed in one instant and came out as a booming howl that shattered the windows of the cabin and rattled all the floorboards.

He had been staring at himself.

SOMEONE SLAPPED HAGEN'S face hard, and he sat up, hearing himself still caught in the scream. Roesia knelt beside him; she was quite alive. Hagen stared around the room lit by a subdued daylight. A steady *tap-tap-tap* of rain hit the glass near him. He got to his knees and looked toward the table. Although Liam's chest did not appear to be rising under his cover, with crystal clearness he heard an intake of breath and then a release.

Roesia asked, "Hagen, are you okay?"

He ignored her. The smell of cooked food hit him, and it should have made his mouth water but didn't. Instead, another scent in Justine's kitchen caught his attention—it was red and bloody. Hagen glanced down, discovered he was bare naked, and grabbed his cover. He draped it over his shoulders and clenched it shut in front of him to shield his nudeness. The clothes he had been wearing were clumped next to his bed. He'd taken them off during the night. The room had a chill, but he felt hot.

Justine stepped out of the kitchen, stared at him, and the corner of her mouth curled up. "It has begun already. Alas, Hagen Messer, you have no need to fear, you are a true Wehr Wolff."

"How long was I out?" Hagen asked.

"It's afternoon now," Justine answered.

"Why didn't you wake me?" Hagen scolded.

Justine waved her hand in dismissal. "You weren't ready, but now..." She shook her head, not saying another word, and returned to the kitchen.

He turned to Roesia. She gasped, her hands over her mouth.

Roesia whispered between her fingers, *"Y-your eyes."*

Hagen got up and stepped into the adjacent room, which had a mirror. There he stopped, realizing he had no pain in his leg—none whatsoever. He opened his blanket and looked down; his leg no longer had purplish bruises or even puncture wounds, for that matter. He dropped the blanket and stepped slowly to the mirror to take in his nude reflection.

He had been fit, but he now had a defined eight-pack abdomen; his chest, arm, and leg muscles were defined and toned, and if he wasn't mistaken, there were more of them. But that wasn't the most striking feature.

His eyes had turned a mesmerizing mix of blue and gold.

Thirty-One: A Siege on Wehr Wolff Castle

May 14, 1940
Several Kilometers from Wehr Wolff Castle

HAGEN SAT ON the floor and leaned against the wall. With begrudging effort, he ate the meal Justine had made for them: cooked venison and greens. His stomach hungered for something different, though, and that desire was growing in intensity. The nightmare of seeing himself as a werewolf lingered in his mind, and an ominous dread swelled inside him.

Roesia was on the opposite side of the room, eating her meal with ferociousness. She glanced up a couple of times at Hagen, then looked away when Hagen met her eyes; she had become a bit skittish since seeing his new eye color.

Justine shook Liam's shoulder, and he started awake and looked around him, his gaze stopping on Hagen. Liam's face had more color, and his lips were pink rather than pale.

Liam croaked, "Oy, Hagen, but you shine. I'm sure I've the look of a regular mog."

Hagen made his way to Liam's side, a smirk spreading over his face. He raised his eyebrows, and he dusted his fingers over the top of Liam's. "Mog?"

Liam laughed, coughed, and groaned. "Yer such a bloody *Yankee*. *MOG.* Mistake of God."

Hagen smiled, pushed some of Liam's bangs back, and said, "You are not going to win any gentleman contest soon. How do you feel?"

Liam brought his hand up in front of his face and considered his hand. His fingers were now in their individual splints, each one wrapped with twine.

His voice rasped, "*Brilliant.* Jolly time I had in that castle. I'm now as useful as tits on a bull." Liam laughed again, then winced and his eyes closed as he bared his teeth in pain.

Hagen touched Liam's cheek with his finger. "Maybe you should not talk right now. Rest."

Liam opened those jade-colored eyes; they were focused and intense. "Hagen."

Hagen leaned forward.

Liam whispered, "You were in me dream last night. We were in a pool in the nip. We were, yea know, nogging, and it was brilliant. You had to go, though, and left, but you never came back."

Hagen put his hand close to Liam's hand. "I'm right here, Liam."

"Aye, but you're going back for yea brother?"

Hagen nodded. Liam stared up at the ceiling, and his eyes were watery. "Don't be a complete muppet, Hagen Messer, and die. You promise?" He looked up at Hagen, the usual humor in his eyes gone. "Don't yea be going and being a pain in me hole. You come back."

"I will," Hagen whispered, and rested his hand close to Liam's face. He wanted to stroke him, but not in the presence of the others.

Justine came up next to Liam with a cup of her special tea, and the scent of acridness drifted to Hagen. Last night, it had been savory—now, it was repulsive. He hungered for raw meat.... No, that was not quite it.

Bloody meat.

Justine tried to feed Liam, but he blocked her with his hand and looked up to Hagen. "Don't forget your promise. I'll just be here pulling me wire."

Hagen smiled and stepped away to the window as Justine cared for Liam. After Liam was fed, he lay awake for several minutes, struggling to keep his eyes open, but finally they stayed closed and he slept.

Justine turned to Hagen and handed him a gray cup, steam rising from the dark liquid surface. "Here."

Hagen grasped the cup with both hands, but a sharp burn scorched his hands in one instant and he dropped the cup; it clinked onto the floor and spilled its contents. He stared at his palms, which had reddish marks but returned to normal within a space of a few seconds. He looked up to Justine with a bewildered look.

She picked the cup up and nodded. "As I thought. You are ready." She held the cup up, and explained, "Silver. The liquid was just lukewarm. That sting is something you must learn to bear. Here."

She dropped a couple of coarse pebbles into the cup, and said over her shoulder, "It's called Silvium."

Roesia observed the dried herbs on the counter that had been placed in Hagen's cup. "I saw these. Mengele called it something similar." She picked up one, turning it in her fingers, and said, "He said it came from a plant in Ancient Egypt that's thought to be extinct. He had one whole section in his laboratory, testing it on those mutants. I think he was trying to find a way to make them immune to silver, his end goal to combine it into the serum he designed."

Justine nodded. "It does make one immune to silver. The herb is unlike any. Once harvested, it can stay potent for years." She held the cup up to Hagen's mouth, tipped it so he didn't have to touch it, and he drank a gulp. She gave him the drink and he quaffed it down.

It was instantaneous. Something new surged through Hagen. Justine held the cup out for him to take. He hesitated but grabbed the cup with one hand anyway and felt no pain. He marveled, tipping the cup to and fro in his hand.

Justine turned to Roesia. "An herb that makes one immune to the allergies caused by silver. I too thought it no longer existed except for what I grew. I thought I had the last." She shrugged and considered Roesia.

A flare of pain radiated over Hagen's fingertips, but he held the cup for a few more seconds; it became a blistery throb. He put the cup down and rubbed the end of his fingers.

"But it does not last long," Justine said dryly. She picked up the cup, tilted it, and steadied the remainder of the contents inside. "Your mother used to grow it, and it was said she always kept it with her, closest to her heart." She set the cup down and sighed. "If what you say is true, then this could spell doom if Mengele was successful in fusing it with a serum."

Hagen stared through the window, up at the cloudy sky, sunlight filtering through cracks in the clouds. It was going into late afternoon. After his night of rest, he did not just feel rested, but rejuvenated. A new blood now coursed through his veins.

"I'm leaving to get my brother," Hagen said.

Justine placed some dishes in the kitchen and nodded. "I know."

Roesia pulled a dark sweater over her head and the layers of clothes she wore, and asked, "You have a plan?"

Hagen shook his head.

"I'm going, too," she said.

Hagen whirled around to her and frowned deeply, then clenched his fists. "I'm going alone."

"No, you don't understand; I'm going to destroy the laboratories for good. Or try."

Hagen continued to shake his head. "Before, I encouraged everyone to go inside. But it was foolish. Many have died or worse. I will not have you dying for a mission you can't complete. You'll stay here with Liam, and both of you will get out when you can."

Roesia stared out the window. "Did I ever tell you I had family in Poland?"

"What?" Hagen asked. "No."

"An aunt and uncle and a cousin. When Germany invaded Poland not that long ago, I learned my uncle was killed during the invasion. My aunt was stripped of her home and sent to a ghetto, and I've lost contact with her. My cousin had a mental condition, and I was told he was shipped away to a concentration camp. But I later learned it was no concentration camp but something called an e-extermination camp." Her mouth quivering. "I found out through my source, they were killing the mentally ill, physically handicapped, anyone deemed incurable, killing them by gas. M-masses of innocent people. I couldn't believe it, but I heard tidbits here and there and understood the people in charge, these Nazi leaders, were truly depraved. I learned later, they were sending these same people to the Wehrmacht's Mutante Wolf Program. I became resolute and crossed into England to tell them about the secrets I'd gathered. I now have no doubt what the Nazis are capable of. I'm grateful beyond words to you, Hagen, but I plan to destroy that place, or die trying." Tears slipped from her eyes.

Hagen's shoulders relaxed, and he stared out the window. "Then do what you must. I don't know where you will get explosives, or how you will get inside, or if I can help."

Roesia came up to his back and hugged him and placed her head on his shoulder. "Get your brother, Hagen. This is my mission, my choice. They will not capture me alive—this, I promise."

Justine said from behind them, "There is a way for her to get inside. And I have explosives. Lots."

They both turned at the same time.

Justine said, "I have a cellar near here, stocked with weapons and explosives. I will go with you to the wall, but no farther. I'm afraid my wounds have yet to heal and I would slow you or put you at risk." She gestured toward Liam. "I will watch over the boy here, and if you don't return, I will take him to a place several kilometers away. A safe house. True friends of the Wehr Wolff. But we must make haste. The moon will come up soon, in hours, and Adolf will perform his ritual."

Hagen peered out through the window to the quiet woods. The scent of the wehrwolf was near, but nothing else.

Where are the Nazi search parties?

There was no scent of humans anywhere near. Why had the Nazis not sent out reinforcements to scour the area for him and the others? He rested his hands on the windowsill, and next to them was the leather pouch Ivan had given Hagen. He opened it and looked inside. There had been three vials on one side, but one had been smashed, and the second had a chip at the bottom and the contents had all leaked out.

He muttered to himself, "Only one is left." He held up the pouc. "What is this? Ivan said he was going to give this to you."

Justine stared at the case and placed her hand over his wrist. "Nothing that matters now."

Roesia took the leather pouch and carefully plucked the intact vial out; she brought it up to the window and squinted at it. "That vile man, Mengele, showed me a horrific lab. Demonstrated how he could cure a weremutant. The liquid had a color of turquoise."

Hagen more closely eyed the vial in Roesia's hand. The memory of Euan Hartley was fresh in his mind.

Justine nodded and frowned. "It is an antidote. It was derived from Euan Hartley. A member of the Wehr Wolff lineage who is now dead."

"I met him before he died in the dungeon," Hagen recalled, his voice faint. "He said they accidentally made him a permanent human and he could not change back. They punished him for that."

Justine nodded. "I collaborated with Ivan. They used Euan's blood to create an antidote to the werevenom. I asked Ivan to steal some and bring it to me."

"A true antidote?" Roesia asked, both of her hands cupping the vial carefully.

Hagen wheeled on her. "Then I can use it?" Any notion that he could take away the wondrously dark and powerful surge of energy he'd long coveted caused him nausea. *But I could hurt people I love. I could kill Liam.*

And the worst... I might never turn back.

"Yes," Justine nodded, her face somber. "But you will not live up to being a true Wehr Wolff."

"If Hagen took a bit, would he be better able to control himself?" Roesia pointed out.

Justine frowned. "I don't know. If you are too weakened, then Adolf will be able to defeat you and your brother will die."

Hagen clenched his fists, swallowed, and nodded. He had to rescue his brother.

Justine left them and came back a few minutes later with a hard metallic case. "Place it in here. It shall not break. Made of a metal the Wehr Wolffs used long ago to forge their swords."

Hagen opened the case and placed the vial inside.

Roesia asked Justine, "What was your plan?"

Justine turned, waving for them to follow.

Several moments later, they stood by an open cellar door. Several handheld weapons were inside, along with a stash of dynamite and modern plastic explosives.

"Where'd you get this?"

"The Wehr Wolff family," Justine answered.

Hagen picked up a modified metal bolt gun and rotated it in his hands with admiration. It had a cylinder barrel on the bottom, which appeared to contain a volume of arrows. He stepped out of the cellar, and Roesia and Justine's voices drifted up after him from below. He looked down at the gun and toggled a switch. An arrow tipped with a silver arrowhead locked in place. He aimed, observing that several wehrwolves were watching him from behind trees and did not growl or scurry from him— even though they were in his line of sight. Hagen pointed the crossbow away from them and fired; the bolt thwacked loudly into a tree twenty feet away. He looked down and nodded his approval at his new gun.

Justine came up next to him and put a crossbow in his hands with a different design than the one he'd been holding. This one had a reel on its side, and where the bolt should have been was a hook in its place. It was to be used as a rappel.

"My mother designed these," Justine said. "She was an inventor. Made that bolt gun you have in your hands."

Hagen looked down at the bolt-action gun, giving her silent praise for the precision of engineering.

Roesia came up the stairs from the cellar, a bag over her back, a lever-action rifle slung over a shoulder, and an ammunition belt filled with cartridges full of silver tips slung over her chest. She cocked the rifle, sighted it, lowered it, and glanced to Hagen and Justine.

"It's good enough, I suppose. Better for weremutants, though, than a storm of Nazis."

Justine shook her head. "Wehr Wolff Castle is no longer held by the Nazis."

Roesia furrowed her brow. "What do you mean?" She turned to Hagen for an answer. Hagen met Roesia's eyes and peered into the forest, the scent of dew and rain prevalent. He knew why he did not smell Nazi search parties.

"Adolf," Hagen answered. "He's taken over Wehr Wolff Castle. And his army is the weremutants—they answer to him."

Thirty-Two: War Against Adolf

HAGEN SPRINTED THROUGH the forest, leaped over a clump of fallen trees, and landed easily on both feet on the other side. His energy had not just been renewed, but rather invigorated. He felt capable of any mighty feat. He carried the bolt gun in both hands. A lever-action rifle was slung over one shoulder, tied down so it would not jostle. The revolver was in its holster, fastened at his waist. His belt loops were replenished with new cartridges with silver tips. One of Justine's swords was inside its sheath, fastened over his back, the hilt sticking out over a shoulder.

A clamorous stampede surrounded him—paws digging into the forest loam and advancing. Around him were the wehrwolves that had been held hostage in Wehr Wolff Castle, as well as the ones that had been guarding Justine's cabin. He glanced over his shoulder; trailing behind him and his army was Riesig. Roesia was on his back, gripping his fur with both hands, her face pushed up against his neck, holding on for dear life. A couple of wehrwolves carried satchels fastened over their backs, which contained the explosives for Roesia.

The sun was going down, and soon Hagen would be out of time. Ivan would be sacrificed, and he'd be too late. A new scent hit him, and he slowed, pointing his hand. The group turned diagonally, continuing on without him, and then they were out of sight.

Only one wehrwolf stayed with him, a rucksack over its back. He weaved between trees and came up to a canyon edge. Across the twenty-foot gap was a steep rock wall that he had to scale to get to the base of the castle, a hundred feet up.

A new darkness pumped through Hagen's veins; he felt a wholeness he had not known was possible. He was pushing back his urge to revel in it—the memory of Euan's handkerchief vivid in his mind. A guilt crept up, but Hagen focused. He needed to wait before he allowed himself that power and fully became a werewolf.

Hagen stared up at the parapet. His senses told him what he needed to know. No sentry was up on this part of the wall. He removed the crossbow from the rucksack on the wehrwolf's back. The creature spun and left him, heading off to join the larger group. Hagen placed the rappel gun's shoulder strap over his neck and stared across the canyon. He turned around, stepped several paces, and wheeled around, then sprinted forward until he reached the edge and sprung. He soared over the canyon and landed on the other side, finding purchase with his hands.

Hagen climbed upward with much less effort than he'd thought it was going to take, finding footholds with pure, uncanny deftness. He came close to the rocky cliff of the castle base. The rappel weapon's strap over his shoulder broke, and he darted one hand out to catch the weapon before it plummeted into the canyon below. He tossed it over his head onto the four-foot-wide ledge that was set at the castle's base. In a matter of seconds, he'd pulled himself up, knelt, aimed it upward, and pulled the trigger. The reel spun, the hook flew high into the air over the castle wall, and the wheel quit its spinning. He pulled back on the line until it became taut, then ascended the rope at a quick pace. After pulling himself over the protective wall, he sat back on his haunches and listened to the sounds around him. He peered inside the courtyard and toward the castle. A monumental force of weremutants was in the courtyard, milling around. *How many? Over a thousand.*

A Nazi dressed in a guard uniform stepped out of the castle onto a balcony that was several feet over the beasts' heads. Two other guards came up behind him, pulling a prisoner between them. Their captive was dressed in a Nazi uniform. Hagen sensed them now; Adolf had kept a large force of Nazis.

The man read the paper in his hand. "H-his excellency and the rightful Führer, Adolf Taber Wehr Wolff, declares any dereliction of duty is tantamount to treason. This man who was caught sleeping is sentenced to death by consumption." He waved to the men behind him, who flung the detainee off the balcony. Ropes had been tied over the traitor's ankles, and he jerked to a stop at the bottom. The creatures gathered close, and their screams grew in intensity.

The man who had read the paper looked straight ahead, staring in Hagen's direction, and announced, "We have shipments of prisoners en route. Adolf orders all young, weak, and elderly to be consumed. The rest are to be conscripted into the Wehr Wolff service."

In other words, the uneaten prisoners would be infected and allowed to turn into weremutants.

Hagen receded into the shadows. He rushed over the top wall, came around a corner, and pulled his trigger, knowing what to expect since his senses were too keen to let him down. Two bolts hit the unsuspecting guards square in their throats. Three weremutants rushed him, and his bolt gun made successive *sffft-sffft-sffft* noises, each silver arrowhead piercing an eyeball. One dead weremutant toppled off the ledge and started to fall to the courtyard below, but Hagen grabbed its hind leg in midair and gingerly tossed it back up onto the top. The body smacked onto the stone, reminding him of the sacks of potatoes he used to unload back home.

He sprinted forward, then slowed down and hid in the shadows that were growing longer and longer. Dusk was here. He concentrated. Justine had informed him of different entry points, saying which ones might have fewer guards. She had taken a small wehrwolf force and moved close to the front where she would put herself in plain sight and act as a decoy. The castle was alive with excitement and many were preparing to attack her group. He sniffed the air. There—he knew where to go. A place that was guarded, but several had been pulled off duty.

Hagen advanced over the parapet. The shadows moved in front of him. Bolts flitted through the air from his gun and slammed into weremutants' heads. He vaulted over the bodies without pause. In front of him was a nook in the wall where a large number of sentries guarded, made up mostly of weremutants, with just a few Nazi guards patrolling an old drawbridge of the castle.

He dropped off the wall, and several bolts streaked out from his weapon to find weremutant targets. A second later, he landed on a winch, high off the ground, and pulled the sword from his hilt. He slashed across the thick rope, severing it; the line coiled. Nazi soldiers started to fire from the ground, but he had already vaulted back into the air, his bolt gun held in one hand. He brought his sword back over his head with his other hand and dropped straight toward a rope fastened to a pulley. He swung again and severed it. He had a foothold high up on the wall, and looked over. The bridge fell down at a high speed as divots appeared around him from machine-gun fire, and then he somersaulted in the air and landed on his feet. The drawbridge made a boom that reverberated loudly.

Weremutants charged Hagen, and he brought up his lever-action rifle and defended himself. A nearby Nazi soldier fired his machine gun, and dirt sprayed up close to Hagen's face. Hagen fired one shot—the soldier's head jerked back, and he was down. Several Nazi soldiers rushed him along with weremutants. He fired his rifle over and over until the sound of the shots melded together and the enemy went down. He stood up then, amazed to see the entire sentry force decimated. A new group of weremutants and soldiers came around a corner, and this time, he was going to be overwhelmed.

Something jumped from behind him, over his head, and it bellowed an animalistic roar. Several wehrwolves landed in front of him and charged the weremutants and Nazi soldiers, and soon the enemy ranks were slaughtered.

Hagen stood up, touched his back, winced, then stared at the blood on his hand.

Roesia called to him, "*Hagen! You're shot!*"

Roesia was on her feet, carrying a bolt gun. She came up to his side, nodded to him, and stared up into the sky. "Go, Hagen. I'll wait for as long as we can."

Hagen cocked his head back, concentrating. Images flitted through his mind. He met her eyes. "They don't have much of a force in the dungeon. You should be okay."

She stepped backward and swallowed. "You see that?"

"Sense it."

She nodded, wheeled around, and trotted away. A few wehrwolves split off to follow her, including two with rucksacks on their backs, which contained the explosives.

Hagen waved Riesig over and leaned in to whisper into his ear. Riesig turned and disappeared around the gate wall with three wehrwolves following him.

Hagen stood up; his army waited for him, and he addressed them, "I know where Ivan is, and you can be sure, Adolf will be close by. We'll avoid the courtyard—they have their main force there."

Five minutes later, Hagen and his small army had moved outside the courtyard, staying away from the large garrison located there. They were inside the castle and snaked through the halls and into the ballroom that was now in shambles, paintings fallen to the floor and tables overturned. Hagen stepped from an archway into the vast room. Corpses lay in front of him, including the duchess whose neck was slashed open, a pool of dried blood creating a sheen on the floor around her. Pieces of shattered champagne bottles littered the floor. A skirt for a dining room table was stained red. A severed human arm inside a tuxedo sleeve was the centerpiece of one table.

He froze and his heart sank.

On the other side of the ballroom was Adolf. Weremutants flanked him on each side. Hagen walked forward, and his wehrwolves filed out of the hallway behind him and came to either side. Several Nazi soldiers stood to the sides of the room, their guns trained on him. A couple of soldiers were high up in balconies, pointing their guns down on him.

Adolf stepped up, a smile forming on his face—the chin with its rift, the pronounced crease lines in his forehead, and greased hair with strands of white transformed. The young Adolf from his childhood stood in front of him. He had soft-hued skin and a dark trimmed beard. His hair was no longer greased back, but disheveled. He indeed had powers to change the way he appeared, and he now looked the same as when Hagen had been ten.

A small man cowered close to Adolf, wearing a tuxedo and a pink bow tie. Hagen recognized the smell of lavender. Duke Waldo Jank.

Hagen twitched his head and sniffed the air. A strange sensation overcame him. His skin crawled, and he was nauseated. *Silver. Lots of it.*

Adolf and the soldiers were carrying silver bullets. Adolf's smile became smug, and he patted Duke Jank's shoulder. The man squealed in shock and terror.

Adolf bellowed, "Hagen. It is good to see you again. I believe you both have met."

Hagen raised his lever-action rifle up an inch.

"Duke Jank told me something interesting," Adolf said. "His home holds many precious articles, inanimate and...live rare species. He breeds these rare species. That fascinates me, and I entertained a new idea, Herr Hagen. Your life may still have merit. But what truly riveted me—the duke believes he has a scientist working for him who is close to a new science called cloning. You ever heard of such a thing?

"Basically, it means we'll duplicate you, Hagen Messer. And these, uh, clones, unlike you, will be trainable and obedient. Now, *that* sounds amazing."

Hagen took a deep breath; he had less than a second. He dusted the trigger with his finger. Just one round through Adolf's head. His mind pounded one message over and over. *Change! Become!* He couldn't do it. He might be lost to his new werewolf brain and unable to save his brother. He breathed.

Though Adolf's eyes barely moved, Hagen glanced upward and flinched as metallic nets plummeting down at his head. Nazi soldiers had opened panels in the ceiling above him and dropped several shiny gray metal nets. He fired off one shot aimed above him before a net nailed him; a body dropping from the ceiling. He was slammed down on his knees, in instant pain, and bared his teeth. Silver.

The wehrwolves around him charged; the room echoed with a thunderous roar of machine-gun fire. Wehrwolves close to him collapsed as he struggled in the net. The pain was sharp and agonizing. Nazi soldiers filed out of the hallway he and his small army had come from, and they threw a thicker silver chain link net over him. They started to pummel him with the butts of their rifles, and in his weakened state, the hits were jarring. A thick fluid ran down his throat. His rifle was snatched from his hands. He removed his revolver and fired; the aggressors who were struck fell back but then his gun clicked empty. A large force hit his head. He was dazed, and the pistol was taken from him.

Hagen pushed against his chains, but thick smoke drifted up from his hands and he shrieked out in pain.

High, shrill screams of soldiers and creatures came from Adolf's direction, and the scent of blood being spilt over the floor drifted to him—soldiers, weremutants, and wehrwolves were being killed, but his own army was about to be slaughtered. He had led them into a trap. He bared his teeth and pushed out against the net, but it was a dead weight and too heavy.

The machine-gun fire grew silent, and Hagen remained lying on the floor, struggling against his chain prison but unable to break from it. He shoved, and a growl escaped his mouth.

Adolf looked down at him and wagged his finger back and forth. "Too easy, Hagen. Come, witness the power of immortality, and oh, of course, watch your brother die." He waved to the guards, who bent down and dragged him along the ballroom, the chains scraping over the wooden floor.

Hagen stared around at him at the carcasses of wehrwolves, their eyes open and bodies shredded. Several bloodied severed limbs from fallen Nazi soldiers were spread over the floor. Then a wall blocked his view and he was being dragged down a hallway. Tendrils of smoke continued to lift from his body, burning as though he was being roasted from the inside. His energy waned, he wanted to vomit, and his head pounded with such pain that his vision blurred. He was pulled up a staircase, his side and head hitting each step, and then down another corridor. He lost track of time, whimpering mixed with growls and snarls coming from his mouth.

He was pulled inside a dim room and lay, staring up at the ceiling. It had a large aperture at the top; iron doors had been folded on top of one another, similar to an accordion. A switch undoubtedly closed them. Walkways were visible up at the ceiling section to allow easy access for necessary repairs to the overhead structure. A red-orange sky was visible, a faint full moon coming into light. He was in Wehr Wolff Castle's observatory room.

In the center of the room was a telescope. A cylindrical object constructed of web metal, it sat vertical and was fastened onto a horizontal beam, which allowed it to be swiveled for different vantage points. The structure was thirty feet in length, and even at a ninety-degree angle, the end of the telescope was far under the roof above them. A concrete staircase was flush to the telescope to allow a person to go below and presumably put their eye to an optical lens.

At the back of the room were obedient Nazi soldiers who were watching the spectacle. Duke Jank huddled near the door against the wall and shrank back from the number of weremutants that wandered into the room.

Hagen's eyes fell on the horizontal steel beam where the telescope was secured, his blurred vision clearing for a second, and he discerned a handful of names, but only one stood out. One was *Messer*. His father had helped design this for the Wehr Wolff family. Not far from the dug-out concrete staircase was his brother, who was trussed to a stake—silver chains wrapped tautly around his chest and abdomen, and thick shackles were over his wrists, which were behind his back.

Ivan turned his head toward Hagen, and croaked, "Hagen, remember what Mother kept closest to her heart."

Adolf strolled toward Hagen and snickered, then squatted down in front of him. A gold medallion was fastened around Adolf's neck which swung back and forth, mesmerizing Hagen. Light reflected off of it and shone in Hagen's eyes.

"Yes, dear Hagen," Adolf tittered. "Remember your loving whore of a mother. She'd be proud to watch your brother die like a stupid lamb." Different areas of Adolf's face were transforming in minute detail, disfiguring themselves into a beast, then back to human. He snarled, his voice husky. "I will take his heart as your brother lives and breathes, consume it, and bathe in his blood." He showed Hagen the antique curved knife he held. "Comes from Egypt, where I'm told we were born."

Hagen barely listened to Adolf's blather. His eyes were fastened on the object around Adolf's neck. Ivan's words echoed in Hagen's mind.

Hagen remembered his conversation with Justine. She had spoken of his mother and said she'd kept something closest to her heart.

He licked his cracked lips and spoke up to Adolf. "How powerful could you be? Why do you wear something that's supposed to bring protection when you know black magic?"

"Oh, this." Adolf placed the medallion in his palm and turned it back and forth. "Belongs to your old bitch of a ma, doesn't it?"

"Tell me," Hagen said, "does your heart beat in fear of separating from that relic of old?"

Adolf cocked his head and tittered. "My, my. I have my work cut out for me. I will need to break you." Adolf yanked on the medallion, and the chain snapped off his neck. "Here, let's start with this, boy. Let's see what protection this really brings you. I assure you, it's only gold." He dropped it on top of Hagen, and said, "Those hieroglyphics on the back—it's no magical spell. Just means *Salvation Lies Inside*. Your English friends would say it's a bunch of rubbish." He rose and sauntered toward Ivan.

Hagen stared at the stairwell adjacent to the telescope. Amber eyes peeked over the ledge and stared at him. Riesig. Hagen had known where his brother was and told Riesig to take another route in case he never made it. His hand grasped the medallion, his fingers rubbing the inscription his mother had learned and passed on to his brother. He gritted his teeth and pushed harder on the surface, praying his intuition was correct. The top part of the medallion slid open, and his fingers touched the grainy and coarse substance inside. A faint smile came over Hagen's face.

The light muted in the room, shadows grew longer, and Hagen stared above him. A bright midnight-blue moon was in full view; he glanced to Adolf, who had his arms extended out to his sides, the knife in one hand, his head bent back. He chanted in a language Hagen had never heard.

Hagen brought up the coarse grist to his nose, and though the silver made his sense of smell feeble, he recognized the scent. *Silvium.* The herb Justine had grown and told him about. His mother had always kept closest to her heart the one thing that would overcome the single weakness of the Wehr Wolff.

He pushed the grains into his mouth and the change was instant; his eyes dilated and his vision focused, and his thoughts churned from his comfortable humanness to something new—animalistic. The clothes on his body ripped and a guttural noise came forth.

A furious growl bellowed from him. He wanted to fully give in to the darkness, but he held back.

A soldier shouted from the back wall. Riesig and three other wehrwolves vaulted from their hiding place and stormed Adolf. Riesig jumped into the air, his claws extended in front of him. Adolf whirled around at the last second, his hands coming up defensively, and folded his arms around Riesig as the wolf plowed into him with substantial force. They rolled over the floor and hit the stake where Ivan was held so that it toppled over, taking Ivan to the floor. It made a loud clanging noise as it hit the stone. The three wehrwolves were on the offensive and gave Riesig their aid.

A renewed adrenaline pushed through Hagen, and with every ounce of effort, he thrust out against his restraints until there were definitive snaps of metal and he was no longer restricted.

Hagen was in partial werewolf form. His human hands had long thick nails extending from them, sparse hair had grown over his face and neck, and his ears had grown longer and more slender. The lustful urge to completely transform remained a sweetness he craved and wanted to devour, but he staved off that drive. He came up in a crouch. After shrugging off the broken chains, he charged toward the surprised Nazi soldiers on the back wall, who were watching in shock as their new leader was attacked. Hagen leaped in the air close to his brother, gripped the manacles over his brother's wrists, and pulled. They snapped under the strain, and Ivan's hands were free.

"The guards, Hagen!" Ivan shouted.

Hagen wheeled around and moved quickly. He clotheslined one guard's neck as he rushed him, and the man somersaulted three times in the air before landing on his head with a crunch. Hagen had already sprung close to another guard and gashed open the man's stomach with his brand-new gnarly claws. The man's innards flopped to the floor and he dropped the rifle, which Hagen caught with one hand. A third guard rushed him, raising his rifle to fire— Hagen acted on instincts, kicking out, surprised to see his foot had transformed to claws. He grasped the man's face with a clawed hand and flung him high.

Hagen picked up a second machine gun and bounded up into the air just as several guards got over their shock and began discharging their weapons at him. He twirled in the air over the men, shooting down on them, and then he pushed off the nearby wall and flipped backward, blasting away. The rounds annihilated the last standing Nazis. He came down in a crouch. Duke Jank ran to the door, and Hagen fired from his hip with both guns, but there were only dry clicks and the man was gone.

Hagen tossed the weapons to the ground, picked up a new rifle, and turned to face off with Adolf. Adolf had completely transformed and held a wounded Riesig in a viselike grip in his mouth. He threw him at Hagen. Riesig sailed across the room and slammed into Hagen. The rifle flew out of Hagen's hands, and he hit the far wall with a crash, pieces of wood and debris falling to the floor around him. Hagen thumped to the ground, Riesig on top of him. Hagen pushed the wounded Riesig off and climbed to his feet to square off with Adolf. Adolf stood up on his hind legs and roared in fury, the noise reverberating through the room. Three dead and bleeding wehrwolves lay at his feet.

Hagen glanced at his revolver on the floor and dashed to it. He fell on his knees in a slide, but Adolf cut off his path and swiped at him with one arm. Hagen rocketed sideways, and his back collided with the horizontal beam that anchored the telescope. Parts of the telescope crashed down on him. Adolf pounced on him, bit into his shoulder, and twisted to throw Hagen into the air. Hagen struck the floor, skimmed out of control, and smacked into a cabinet, bursting it into splinters. Adolf blitzed him and backhanded him with a thick forearm. Hagen hit a solid stone wall and dropped, only for Adolf to grip the back of Hagen's head and slam him headfirst into the floor.

Adolf grabbed Hagen's arm and wrested it hard in one direction, resulting in a loud snap. Hagen shrieked, but the sound came out as a deafening howl. Adolf raised his clawed fists over his head and battered Hagen's face. Hagen's vision grew blurry, and then he lost consciousness.

A SHARP PAIN spiked through his shoulder, and he opened his eyes. He was being dragged across the floor but could see the destroyed telescope lying on the floor. One of his arms hung loosely by his side. Adolf was in werewolf form, his jaw locked over Hagen's shoulder as he dragged him backward. Hagen tried to sit up when Adolf let him go, but Adolf returned to his human form in one second, put a knee on Hagen's one good arm, and held the sacrificial knife in his other hand. He lifted it over his head and chanted; his eyes turned bright yellow, and he stared down at Hagen as sharp teeth pushed out of his mouth. Adolf was ready to sacrifice Hagen.

A resounding explosion sounded out in the distance, and the entire room shuddered, debris falling from the ceiling. The distant noise of stone collapsing was audible. The entire floor trembled. Adolf's eyes widened, and he tilted his head to the side.

He muttered, "*Nooo...that lady.*"

Hagen looked past Adolf, up into the starlit sky, at the full sapphire moon. Memories reeled through his head. Liam smiling as he sat next to him in the nose of an airplane. He and Liam laughing while walking back to the base from an Irish pub. Liam staring from in front of a window at Wehr Wolff Castle, then turning to ask, "Do you fancy me?" Afterward, there was the dark passage.

A throaty growl came from Hagen's lips. Adolf turned to him and raised the knife again, but Hagen transformed there and then, fully, into a werewolf under the night's blue moon. A new dark energy pumped through Hagen and distracted him, overwhelming him. Hagen held onto his human mind, which wanted to slip away to be replaced with an animalistic one.

Adolf brought the knife down, but Hagen snapped and gripped Adolf's wrist with his entire jaw. Hagen wrenched, breaking the wrist and partially severing the hand from Adolf's body. Adolf staggered back and transformed once again. Hagen stood and brought one clawed fist up and back down, but Adolf was faster. He gripped the side of Hagen's head in his jaw and relentlessly slammed Hagen's head into the ground without stopping. A shadow flitted in Hagen's peripheral, and the vise grip of Adolf's jaw was off of him. Hagen continued to lay on the ground, unable to move, darkness coming yet again.

HAGEN STOOD ON a cliff, staring out into a rising sun. A crisp, cold wind blew in his face. A noise behind him made him turn, and the sergeant was standing close to him in complete uniform.

"Bloody hell, Kraut. What are you doing? Go kick his arse."

Hagen breathed in and sat up, noticing he was naked and coughing and wheezing. There were two fighting werewolves close to the wreckage of the telescope, exchanging blows. Ivan and Adolf.

In a flash, the floor underneath Ivan and Adolf crumpled away, and they both fell. Ivan shot his hand out and dug claws into the frayed ledge.

Hagen hurried to the gaping hole and stared down at his brother dangling in the air. Adolf had bitten down on Ivan's leg and swayed in the air below him. The entirety of the structure was giving out, and below them, the fall was not just a story's worth—it went down far into the depths of the castle. The floor crackled around Hagen, and a section tilted; the chain he had been imprisoned within, along with the metallic case that held an antidote and his revolver, slid over the floor in his direction. Hagen moved, but the revolver and metallic case flew past him too fast and went into the hole. He bent down, snagged up the thick chains, and pushed them away. He brought the silver net up, twirled it so it formed into a whip, and took one breath while smoke rose from his palm before snapping his wrist. The end wrapped neatly around Adolf's forepaw. Hagen faced away from the hole and tugged as hard as he could. A yowl erupted from inside the hole as the line grew taut, and then Hagen let it go and looked over the edge. Adolf was free-falling into the massive wreckage below. Hagen gripped Ivan's arm and pulled; another yank and Ivan came over the lip of the hole.

Hagen fell back. In one instant, Ivan changed and knelt down, several deep lacerations revealed on his body.

He grabbed Hagen's hand. "Hagen, you must change. We're stronger in werewolf form."

Hagen's vision was blurry, his head dizzy from the beating he had taken earlier, and the pain in his arm was unbearable. It swamped all of his senses.

He licked his lips and tears rolled from his eyes. He croaked, "I can't."

Ivan grabbed Hagen's arm. "Brace yourself—" Ivan yanked on Hagen's arm, there was a snap, and Hagen cried out.

Ivan picked Hagen up, cradled in his arms, and hurried forward, then slowed. A wounded Riesig had risen unsteadily to his feet. Ivan did not hesitate; he put Hagen over one of his shoulders, stepped closer, and gripped Riesig's neck. He got on his knee and pushed the beast to his other shoulder.

The floor began collapsing around them, and Ivan made a run for the far end of the room. Hagen stared around Ivan's hip. The ceiling with its iron doors plummeted down and the wall in front of them crumbled, but Ivan didn't hesitate. He hurdled high over the jagged wall ledge. Air rushed past Hagen as Ivan descended fast. A parapet walk came into view, and Ivan landed on it and sprinted forward. The walk crumbled away, and Ivan jumped toward a tower that had pitched at an angle and was falling. Hagen was free and slid along the surface of the tower, his brother in front of him, still holding Riesig. The top end of a giant wolf statue barreled into the tower, and pieces of stone showered him.

Ivan leaped off and yelled, "*Move, Hagen!*"

Hagen jumped up and followed his brother, bounding up in the air. He landed on a second outer surface of the castle wall, which tilted inward, the structure buckling, and they slid down. A fissure formed in front of them and caved in, and Ivan tried to push off but slipped and dropped Riesig. Hagen was there, and he caught the nape of Riesig's neck right before the creature fell through the hole.

"Jump!" Hagen yelled.

Ivan leaped, and they both crashed to the earth below. Riesig fell from Hagen's arms.

Hagen got up and looked around him.

Roesia was about twenty feet away on her hands and knees; she looked out of breath, her face bloodied. The wehrwolves that had gone with her were in a defensive position around her, and they all faced the courtyard, paying Hagen no attention. Roesia no longer had a rifle but instead the semiautomatic pistol that had been Wagner's. She stared at Hagen in shock. Ivan stepped up beside him. Riesig rose and limped in front of Hagen, then lowered, ready to strike.

A pounding noise came from the collapsing castle and tremors vibrated underneath Hagen. He tensed his shoulders and widened his stance, then glanced over his shoulder.

Suddenly, the walls of the Wehr Wolff Castle imploded. A tremendous roar resonated through the night, and a large gray cloud billowed into the air. As they stood in amazement, a shock wave blew thick and dusty debris over them. Hagen stared out at the courtyard. Uncountable pairs of tawny eyes glowed through the plume.

Before Hagen stood hundreds of strong weremutants, ready to massacre him and the others, their harsh snarls clear above the den.

"Brother," Ivan whispered, "now is—"

"I know," Hagen said, and stared through the dust, up into the night at the full moon. Electricity seemed to charge his body, and a sweetness filled him, the lustful urge to give in at hand. And he finally did. His breath grew heavy, his eyes dilated, and he extended his arms out. "It's so powerful. Ivan. Make sure I don't kill Roesia." He closed his eyes.

A ravaging hunger filled him, and when he opened his eyes, his senses were sharpened and he was no longer standing on two legs, but all four.

The presence of his human mind diminished, a new one holding sway.

He roared, spittle flying from his mouth, and that bellow resonated. He bolted forward, ripped into the first weremutant, and blood ran down his throat.

He killed and killed and knew no more.

Thirty-Three: Wehrmacht's Mutante Wolf

A distant voice called his name

HAGEN'S EYELIDS FLUTTERED open, his entire body aching. Roesia knelt a few feet away from him; her eyes held a hollowness and were fixed upon him. He sat up—in front of him was Wehr Wolff Castle's rubble, nothing left but piles of stones on top of more. His head throbbed, one eye stung, and his naked body was covered in sweat, blood, and dirt. The moon was still out, but time had elapsed and sunrise was a few short hours away. He touched his hip, and a stinging pain reverberated through his body. The arm that had been broken throbbed and was swollen. He could barely move it.

"W-what happened?" he rasped. He touched his side and winced, stroking the laceration over his ribs.

"Y-you were monstrous, Hagen."

"What?" He turned to her. "What happened, Roesia?"

"You won," Roesia whispered.

Hagen started to look behind him but stopped at seeing Ivan lying unconscious on the grass close to his feet. He, too, was buck naked. His entire body was covered in slimy blood, wounds blanketing his body.

"You carried him here during the fight after he was wounded. I thought you were going to kill me."

"I-I have no memory." Hagen knelt by his brother.

Ivan's back rose and fell at a steady pace.

"M-my God. What happened?" Hagen asked, and turned around to view the butchery inside the courtyard. He could find no words. The weremutants that had been previously poised to strike were now completely obliterated. Except for the few who had yet to die, the weremutants' bodies had transformed back to their human forms, and the carnage of dismembered bodies, all completely naked, was piled there, one on top of another with random limbs scattered over the grassy area.

Roesia touched his shoulder. "Hagen. We should go."

Hagen nodded, unable to speak.

A half hour later, after Hagen located a loose robe, he and Roesia found two vehicles, a jeep and a transport truck, near the guards' bunkhouse and drove them to load the wounded wehrwolves. Hagen picked up a lame Riesig and set him next to his brother in the back of the jeep. His brother's feet faced the back end, his head close to the driver seat, and Hagen placed blankets up to his neck.

Hagen turned the ignition and glanced in the rearview mirror; Roesia had both hands on the truck's wheel, ready to go.

And so they departed the ruins of Wehr Wolff Castle. Hagen's keen tracking sense led them down gravelly roads and through the forest, taking them back to Justine's.

Hagen sat up straight, his hackles raised. He could sense something dark in the air. Hagen braked and turned the engine off.

Roesia halted behind him and trotted up to his door. "What is it, Hagen?"

Hagen stared out into the dark forest, catching shadows moving in the trees. Roesia took out the Nazi semiautomatic pistol she had in a holster, the one that had been Wagner's. It contained silver rounds and was at least deadly to any weremutant.

She cocked it and whispered, "I-is it more of those m-mutants?"

Hagen shook his head. "I don't think so, but I smell death. And there's something new, but also a very familiar scent." He made fists, clenched his jaw, and uttered in a low voice. "*Liam*."

"Liam?" Roesia asked. "Is he hurt?"

"I-I don't think so," Hagen answered. "There's...something in the cabin."

Roesia stared out into the trees, squinted, and shivered. "How far is it?"

"Close."

"Can you even turn and fight, Hagen?"

Hagen stared through the branches of trees above him. The moon was fading but visible. "It's not a question of if I can, but whether I will turn back. I let go earlier, and fate had me knocked unconscious. Now..." Hagen looked up through the treetops and said, "Now that taste is on my tongue, Roesia. I want to give in to it so badly. I want to bathe in it."

"H-Hagen, can you control it at all?" Roesia's terror was palpable.

Hagen turned to her, and Roesia gasped and stepped back from him. He whispered, "No." He brought his attention back up to the moon. "The darkness wants me, Roesia. I don't think I have any control over it." He wanted to scream into the air—

No, he wanted to *howl*.

"Hagen," Ivan said in a weakened tone from the back of the jeep.

Hagen wheeled around and met Ivan's one eye. His brother smelled of death. Ivan brought his head up more and spoke in a raspy voice, "You've been learning to control this all your life. The time will come; just remember to breathe." Ivan's one good eye closed, and he was back out, as if he had never spoken.

Hagen got out, turned from the vehicles, and started toward Liam. He met Roesia's terrified gaze and said, "If I don't come back, you need to go somewhere far. The Nazis will send reinforcements. Justine said there's a safe house nearby, but I'm not sure how you would find it." He eyed the two vehicles and said, "You would have to take the weakest in one truck."

Roesia touched his hand. "H-Hagen, please come back, will you?"

Hagen did not answer but stepped away and headed into the forest. Branches snapped close to him, and he turned, the corner of his mouth curled up in a snarl. A figure came out from behind a tree. A stocky weremutant creature wearing a tattered Nazi uniform came out of the dark shadows. *Sgt. Collins.*

Hagen nodded. "I felt you following us. Be ready. The fireplace is done burning." He stepped forward and paused, then called over his shoulder. "Watch over them if I don't come back." Hagen pushed the robe off of his back. It fell to his feet, and he continued forward, stark naked. Darkness became his new cloak. He breathed in the air, letting it fill his lungs, then exhaled. He took three more steps and took in another breath. Hair grew on parts of his body, and half a snout grew in place of his nose. He was half-beast but continued to stand on hind legs, transformed only partially.

Hagen wanted to let everything go, though, and to give in to this lustful power, but he needed his mind. The handkerchief. He coveted that energy so much that he had not given Euan his last dying wish. Liam needed him. *I will see this to the end.*

He focused, breathed in and could taste the variety of smells surrounding him. A vile scent punched him hard, and a pure surge of adrenaline poured through him.

Liam! He's being hurt.

He was on all fours, making haste to Justine's cottage. He whisked by slender trees.

The clear scent of the wehrwolves that had remained with Justine was there, but they lay dead in front of him. He did not need to see them to know their bodies had been maimed beyond recognition by something that had gorged on them. A new horrific scent. *Justine. No.* She was dead.

What could beat that woman?

Justine's cottage was front and center. Hagen vaulted over a woodpile close to the house and headed toward a window. Glass exploded outward from the small room. He used his clawed feet to control his slide, went quickly through the doorway, and froze, staring at the ghastly figure who stood in front of the hearth where the flames had died.

A mutated George Martz stood close to the kitchen, near Liam's makeshift bed. He was no weremutant and certainly no recognizable human. Martz was a successful candidate for the Wehrmacht's Mutante Wolf Program; he had injected himself with Mengele's new serum.

Martz still had human skin, but Hagen sensed that it was dense, capable of thwarting bullets or at least slowing them down, and sharpened razors extended from his fingertips, his mouth filled with long needlelike teeth. His bald head along with his entire body had grown in size, and he had defined muscles everywhere. The clothes he'd been wearing had ripped off his arms and his chiseled chest was bare. Martz pushed down on Liam's chest, his nails dug into Liam's skin, and blood seeped out from under the pointy tips. Liam moaned in pain and squirmed.

"Herr Fluke, I've been waiting," Martz hissed. "You've missed the appetizer." He kicked at a severed arm that was close to a table leg and leered. "But I see you've made it for the main course." The limb flopped down by Hagen's left foot. He stared down at the grisly limb with its finger nubs, and on the forearm, the tattoo of a crescent moon, with a sword impaled through it, could still be made out. Justine's severed arm. Hagen snapped his head up and snarled.

Martz pressed his nails deeper into Liam, and he cried out in pain. "Oh, I figured it all out. I killed many to get out, and then I went on a hunt." He leered at Hagen. "You know what I hunted for?" Martz pointed his sharp nail at him. "You. We're not done." He laid his fingertips against Liam's abdomen and red fluid bubbled from around the claws. Liam moaned in pain. Martz bent down to Liam's sweaty forehead and an animalistic tongue came out of his mouth and licked Liam's cheek.

Liam cried, *"He has a gun!"*

Martz's eyes flashed with fury, his jaw opened wide, and before Hagen knew what was happening, Martz bit down hard on one side of Liam's face. Liam's scream jolted Hagen, and he charged from the doorway and across the room. Martz straightened and forcibly shoved the table Liam was on with one hand, then with his other brought up Justine's lever-action rifle that must have been fastened under the table. Liam and the table flew in the air and crashed into the far wall. Hagen barely registered this, though, and focused on closing the gap, but he was not going to be in time.

Hagen observed that Martz had retracted his nails, and he aimed the gun with a steady arm. A shadow moved close to Martz, and a wrathful howl erupted from Hagen as he madly charged. The shadow darted from the hearth and rammed into Martz. Martz stumbled forward, firing the gun. A piercing pain erupted in Hagen's shoulder, and he nosedived down onto the floorboard but was back up immediately.

Sgt. Collins was beside Martz. The sergeant threw a series of hooks with his clawed hands, and each made audible thumps as they connected, causing blood to splatter onto the fireplace. The rifle fell to the floor and skimmed across it until the weapon halted close to the hearth. Martz roared in fury and backhanded Sgt. Collins; he soared across the room, slammed into the wall, pulverizing it, and vanished from sight through a gaping hole he'd made.

Hagen leaped at that moment and slammed into Martz, knocking him off of his feet so that their tangled bodies splintered dining room chairs. They landed close to where Liam lay on the ground next to the rifle. Martz rolled to the gun, picked it up, and pointed it toward Hagen. Hagen was already up; he gripped the barrel with a clawed hand and bellowed as he bent the barrel down. Hagen's fist, clutching the gun barrel, punched straight out and thudded into Martz's face. Martz staggered backward, and Hagen thrust his claws into his chest and propelled him into the fireplace until Martz's back collided with the hearth. Brick debris toppled on both of them.

Martz pushed his gnarly nails into Hagen's wound, and he cried out, letting Martz go. Martz performed two hooks and one uppercut, all of them effective. Martz and Hagen spun over the cabin floor, hit the cabin window, and smashed through it to the ground outside.

Sgt. Collins's shadow charged and kicked Martz's abdomen as he tried to get up on his elbows. Martz flew in the air, slammed into the side of the cabin, and came back down on his face. He rose a moment later. Sgt. Collins executed several well-placed punches. Martz dipped under one and shoved him. Sgt. Collins skidded away and stopped close to Hagen.

He growled up to Hagen. "Kraut. Get fighting or get dying."

Hagen rushed forward; Martz was slower now, and Hagen slashed his claws out with all his might. He hit Martz's face and was rewarded by grisly gashes. Martz flipped in the air and came down hard several feet away.

Hagen charged for the coup de grâce. One of Martz's eyes dangled out of its socket, held by a thin cord. He rose to meet Hagen head-on and punched with fury, left and right, until the air was knocked out of Hagen. He staggered back and fell down.

Sgt. Collins attacked, and Martz picked the sergeant up and held him over his head. Then he flung him far out into the dark forest. Hagen struck, but Martz delivered two uppercut punches causing one of Hagen's broken fangs to soar through the air. Hagen fell to the ground, and was slow to get back up.

Martz grabbed Hagen by the scruff of his neck and used him as if he was a battering ram, taking him headfirst into a tree, over and over, until the trunk was broken and the tree keeled over. Hagen was thrown several feet, and he hit the ground, his breath raspy. He wanted to let go, but he held on. What happened if he lost all thought?

Wait. Wait.

He breathed and restrained himself from fully turning.

Martz sauntered up to him and wrenched an axe from a tree trunk. A smell came to Hagen—one he recognized—and a plan formed.

Martz raised the axe over his head and snickered. "Goodbye, Herr Fluke."

Martz swung down, and Hagen rolled to the right. The axe blade lodged in the ground. Hagen squatted back onto his palms, curled up in a seated position, and pistoned his legs out. His heels connected with Martz, who arced in the air and came down several feet away.

The ground crunched where Martz landed—Roesia stepped out from a large tree. Martz wheeled at the sound. She brought up a semiautomatic pistol and fired. Martz's body jerked. She continued to fire repeatedly, taking only moments to aim. Her gun clicked empty before she brought the gun down to her side, then dropped it.

An acrid scent reached Hagen. Martz continued to stand and brought his hands up and touched his chest and abdomen.

His gaze returned to her, and he guffawed. "I'm immune to silver, you idiot. Don't worry, precious, I'll consume you slowly, with that Irish twit."

Roesia shook her head. "I wasn't aiming at you." She pointed behind Martz.

Martz glanced over his shoulder. Behind Martz was the fuel truck Roesia had driven from the castle and Justine later parked away from the cabin. Several holes had been punctured into the metal tank, and caustic fluid now coursed from the breaches. Sgt. Collins stood close to it, a lighter held in his clawed hand. Martz started to turn, but he was too late. Hagen rushed him, giving everything he had in the charge.

Hagen rammed his shoulder into Martz's sternum. Martz was launched off his feet, flew into the truck, and hit the side of the tanker with a sharp ding, then fell to the ground face-first. Liquid poured over Martz's head, back, and legs, but he got back up. Hagen did not quit his run but pressed forward and held his hand up. Sgt. Collins threw the lighter, which Hagen deftly caught with one hand. He flicked the lid open, the flame flickered, and Hagen tossed it. He turned then, but not before making sure the lit lighter landed close to Martz's foot. There was an audible *whoosh*.

Hagen took two large strides and jumped toward Roesia. A sharp *boom* erupted behind him. Fire engulfed Hagen as he landed on top of Roesia. The ground shook, and a second fiery wave blasted out, igniting trees and one side of the cabin. Hagen's back was on fire. He rolled to snuff out the flames, then stopped. His smoldering back was excruciatingly painful. Hagen got onto his knees; he felt mortally wounded.

An inhuman cry came from the inferno. Martz's fiery figure rushed out of the flames, ran into a tree, fell, and rolled on the ground where he smothered portions of the fire even as others spread, spurred on by the fuel. A few flames continued to flare, and smoke drifted from his raw, burnt body as he crawled away from the burning wreck, deep moans coming from him.

Martz's entire body was blistered and blackened. But even so, Hagen had the feeling Martz would probably heal if given time and be ready for a new day on the battlefield sooner than later, but that would never happen.

Hagen staggered up to his feet and turned to Roesia. A trickle of blood came from her ear. Her hair was singed. She stared at Hagen with frightened eyes. Hagen guessed that part of his face was burned.

He pointed to the cabin, one side of it on fire. He rasped, "Get Liam. He's crawling to the front door."

She hesitated and looked back at Martz. "*Kill him.*"

Hagen stared up the moon; it was faint, and dusk was around the corner. He shook his head. *Feed.*

"I don't think werewolves like cooked meat." A leer etched its way over his face. Roesia recoiled and bumped into a tree. A fresh darkness engulfed Hagen, and he tittered, "But a medium rare, I think, is just fine. Roesia, I've waited so long for this." A laugh came from his mouth and turned to a ferocious snarl.

Roesia sprinted to the cabin.

Hagen extended his arms out, breathed, and transformed. His body grew immense in size, hair grew at a rapid rate over his body, sharpened nails extended out, and his human mind was going and going. He was barely aware that he crept up to Martz.

He bit into Martz's calf, and Hagen fed and fed until there was nothing left. He was barely aware of a woman with a wounded young man in her arms.

His mind shrieked.

Do not kill them!

Thirty-Four: Aoibhneas

May 14, 1940 through Early July, 1940
Wehr Forest, Nazi, Germany

HAGEN'S SOUL COMPLETELY surrendered to the werewolf brain, a sliver of his human mind tunneling somewhere deep in his consciousness, and several years later, he would recall bits and pieces of his forage in Wehr Forest during that time.

Hagen, though, on that night in May, while standing under a full moon that bathed the forest, became lost in a murky, blissful fog and embraced a lust he had longed for. Whatever he might have called a moral compass had died inside him and was now replaced with a dark hunger. His past as a human was almost forgotten. Almost.

Hagen did what came naturally. He hunted and he killed, mostly for meat, but sometimes, he killed for his dark pleasure. He ripped a bear to shreds, ate a pack of wolves.

And then there were the soldiers. His favorite hunt.

He snuck up on Nazi units and slaughtered them, devouring each soldier, flesh and bone. He fed and fed. A company of soldiers came in by boat from across the lake, and he ambushed them at night, slaughtering every one. They had set up traps, but he was not fooled by them, and killed them, then destroyed each trap.

One morning, he came across a strange scent, followed it, and found a pack of weremutants that scurried through the forest and fled from him. He greedily ate several and came to a narrow footbridge that spanned a canyon; his nose caught the scent. His werewolf brain knew the smell. It was instinctual. Another werewolf. On the other side of the canyon was a severely wounded Adolf Tabor Wehr Wolff, his prone body broken. He barely breathed and was in agony and unable to walk. Hagen felt Adolf's need to transform, but he wasn't able to. Adolf was being pulled by a couple of weremutants over the bridge, and they made it across.

Hagen snarled and decided to rip that werewolf to pulp and guzzle his blood. He started to cross the bridge but stopped. One weremutant let Adolf go and stepped up to the edge of the foot-walk on the other side. Its odor teased his nostrils, and a growl escaped from its mouth. The name General Wagner scrolled through his head. Hagen stared down at his four paws and a nagging memory tugged at him.

A human question developed in the far reaches of his animal mind, startling him. *Why does Wagner have four paws?*

A memory came of Wagner's severed hand lying on a floor, its fingers gripping a pistol. Ivan was speaking to him and told him that when one *Becomes* everything which was broken as a human becomes whole again. Hagen stared at the whole paw that should be a stub. Wagner had regrown a limb when he *Became* a weremutant. Extraordinary.

The creature once known as Wagner gripped a heavy rock, raised it over its head, and tossed it. The boulder smashed through the middle of the bridge. Other weremutants were doing the same, and the bridge collapsed under the pummeling.

Who is Wagner? Hagen's human mind wanted to come forth, and old memories started to return, but he pushed them down. Those memories felt like they would take him away from this new life he loved.

Two weremutants grabbed Adolf with their jaws and towed him away over the crest of a hill, and they were gone. The pack of weremutants vanished from sight, but one lingered back and stared at Hagen. The one named Wagner. Hagen wanted to hunt, to pursue, and to consume all of them, so he looked over the cliff, ready to scale down so that he could find his way across, when a horrid sensation came over him and he backed up. He wheeled around, sniffed the air, and his hackles raised. His darkness receded for a moment, and a new light came forth. A name resonated in his mind.

Liam.

A feeling of warmth came over him, and he went into a full sprint. After a couple of hours, he was at a ridge and looking down at a truck that drove at a low speed over a dirt road. He sensed the occupants' starvation. A werecreature trailed far behind the truck, and the scent told him of the useless name of this beast. Sgt. Collins.

A woman drove a transport truck. A young man who smelled of infection and death sat in the passenger seat. *Liam. Who's Liam?*

Hagen's mind felt the presence of another werewolf, and the name *Ivan* came to Hagen's mind. This Ivan was in the back of the truck, comatose. Hagen wanted to eat them and put the werewolf out of its misery, but the desire was pushed back in an instant. Something else held sway and the word *Aoibhneas* echoed in his mind.

Hagen decided to leave and hunt. These persons were not meant to be killed. He backed away but stopped at hearing a shriek. Liam shrieked and cried from his agonizing pain. He begged the woman to shoot him, to end his life.

Liam cried and pleaded. "Please. Hagen promised he would. But he left us. You have to do it, Roesia. Please."

Hagen's hearing pricked up at the name Hagen. Roesia leaned forward over the wheel, tears streaming from her eyes.

"I can't do it, Liam. I can't. Don't ask me to do that. Please."

"Just give me the rest of the morphine."

"Okay, Liam. If you still want me to, I will do it tonight."

It happened fast; the young man reached over, grabbed the pistol from Roesia's holster, and opened his passenger door. He tried his best jump, but he was feeble. His feet hit the ground, and he cried out in pain as he rolled over two times upon impact. The gun flew out of his hand.

The woman braked, and shouted, *"No, Liam! No!"*

Liam. That name again.

A comfort came over Hagen that was alien to his werewolf form. He inched forward. This young man known as Liam was crippled and barely able to move, let alone walk. It would be a mercy to kill him. Liam managed to get up on his hands and knees and crawl toward the gun. His face was swollen to balloon size, an ear partially severed, and splints covered some of his fingers.

Hagen advanced fast; he did not know why, but he did nevertheless. Liam crawled frantically to the pistol and picked it up. He fumbled with the weapon; he was trying to put a finger on the trigger but unable to. Liam shoved off splints, bared his teeth, bent a finger, and placed an injured and swollen digit on the trigger, then started to bring the gun up to his head.

Hagen trotted up at that moment and regarded this Liam. Liam smelled of death. He would be dead in a week, if that. Hagen's brother's voice whispered in his ear from years ago when he was a boy, *"Put it out of its misery. It's in pain."* Hagen shoved the voice down. *No. I cannot. I will not!*

Liam glanced up. His eyes widened at seeing Hagen, and he scooted back against a tree. Liam's survival instincts took over, his need to commit suicide forgotten, and he pointed the gun at Hagen. Hagen smelled silver in the gun, but still he did not react on instinct. He lowered himself to the ground and wriggled his way up to Liam.

The woman said from Hagen's side, her voice hoarse, "*My God, it's you!*"

Hagen glanced up to the woman, and she staggered backward, her mouth open in shock. Hagen gazed back to Liam, who half-lowered the pistol.

"*H-Hagen?*"

The gun's barrel now rested close to Hagen's snout. Hagen glanced up at Liam. A scene of beautiful roses came to Hagen, but what he saw was not beauty. Liam's eyes were bloodshot red, and he had a disfigured face that had partially turned black. Hagen smelled the sickness that effused Liam's pores, and pending death—but there was something else there, too.

A toxic venom meant to kill had been eating at Liam's body at an agonizingly slow pace. A memory of Martz biting Liam played in Hagen's human mind. Hagen breathed in through his nostrils, trying to keep that thread. Martz's bite was designed to kill, not transform people into beasts.

Liam should have been dead, but he wasn't.

Hagen straightened, and he did something unexpected, and confusing. He licked Liam's face.

Liam cried, and whispered, "H-Hagen, I can't... no more."

Hagen lowered his head. His teeth bit gently down on the top of the pistol and tugged on it.

Liam's hand gripped the pistol harder, and he whimpered, "*You promised.* Why did you leave me?"

Hagen tugged harder, and Liam relented, his fingers opening as he released the weapon, and Hagen stepped backward several feet, jerked his head, and flung the gun close to the truck.

Hagen picked up the scent of the bite on Liam's shoulder. Something had bitten him there, and it was not Martz. That bite was saving his life.

The woman spoke from his side, her tone fatigued and accusatory. "*He bit him.* I threatened to kill him, and he left us alone."

Who? An image of a weremutant was in his mind, wearing a Nazi officer uniform. The name Sgt. Collins flitted in his mind. *Martz's bite was meant to kill. Sgt. Collins's bite countered it, saving him.*

He stared up at the woman, and she came to Liam's side, squatted down, and stared at Hagen with terrified eyes. She narrowed her eyes at him. *"A-are you going to help us?"*

Hagen backed away. His senses surmised that whatever pain medication they'd had before was gone. They had no food and were hungry, at the borderline of starvation, and whatever gasoline they had used or found along the way was nearly used up. Hagen reached the edge of the worn dirt road.

It was a miracle they had not been re-captured by the enemy.

No, it's not. I've been killing any units close to them, haven't I?

Liam bawled to Roesia. "He's leaving us, he's leaving..."

Hagen left the area but turned once more as the woman carried Liam back to the passenger seat and sat him down. Something tugged on Hagen's mind; the woman's words were in his mind and the scent of Wagner was in his nose again. Hagen sprinted forward, returned to the truck, and went to the driver's seat.

Roesia came around the hood but fell back at seeing him. Her hands were held up in defense. Hagen stood up on his hind legs, towering over Roesia, and she stared up at him in horror.

Hagen snarled down at her, and she scurried back, fumbling with the gun at her side, and shrieked, "What are you doing? Get away from him!"

Liam's bloated face stared at him from the passenger seat; he cried and reached out to Hagen. "Help us. Please, don't leave."

Hagen's clawed hand grabbed a leather satchel near the driver's seat, and he put the strap in his mouth, then came down on all fours.

The woman had her gun out and pointed at him. Hagen backed away from her. She lowered her weapon to the ground and bent her head as she cried. Hagen turned and weaved through the thick forest. In a while, he came to a cottage nestled by a river. He dumped the satchel on the doorstep. A crystal ball came partially out of the opening. The door opened, and an old man stepped out of the door, looking both ways. He bent over, picked up the satchel, and peered inside.

"Justine?"

"Arthur," an elderly woman's terrified voice called. "Who is it?"

"I-I don't know." Arthur's gaze snapped up, and he stared at Hagen, who was several feet away, close to a tree.

The man's wife appeared at the door a second later; both of them stared but did not move. Hagen rose on his hind legs and bellowed out a howl. He then wheeled around and vanished into the darkened woods.

His sensitive ears picked up the man's words. "The crystal ball is showing us something—look. A truck."

Time moved neither fast nor slow, and Hagen fed on forest animals, but the joy of killing beasts had lost its pleasure. A week went by, a month passed, and time ticked on. He didn't care about time, though, and ate to feed his hunger. The hunting of the Nazis had at least not lost its thrill.

One day, he came upon a werecreature in the woods that had been wounded by a trap. Nazi soldiers were gleeful at having caught the creature and had started a fire pit. They planned to roast the creature alive. Hagen almost left it to be slaughtered by the Nazis, but stopped and sniffed the air. The word *Kraut* danced in his mind, and Hagen wheeled around and decimated the campsite. He dragged the wounded weremutant to a distant cave, killed a deer, and left the carcass for the beast. He returned to the cave over the next few days, until one night he found that the weremutant once known as Sgt. Collins was gone. He barely detected any trace of his scent. He had moved north.

Hagen forgot about this beast and instead grew aware that the pockets of troops in the area were growing in size.

They were sending sentries farther from the castle, trying to fortify the area. Hagen was lost to his animal life, only a memory of his previous life gnawing at him, but he was content. He had no desire to return to human form.

It was fate, perhaps, that he found the scent of lavender, which brought him to the outer ruins of Wehr Wolff Castle a couple of hours before dawn one night. He snuck past the sentries without any problems. The stench of death and rot in the far courtyard had begun to fade but still held sway. Human voices caught his attention. One voice in particular he focused on, and a memory of a pink tie popped in his mind.

A small Nazi unit of twenty military personnel was in front of him. They believed they were safe behind a strong line of defense. Hagen took his time killing soldiers one by one in the night without being heard or seen. He crept up to the remaining force of six men, who were studying the rubble. A man in a business suit was with them; he wore a pink tie, and the scent of lavender wafted from him.

An SS Nazi officer was standing close to the man in the pink tie and had his hands on his hips. He smelled vile and like one who needed to be put out of his misery.

He said, "Duke Jank, we will start digging tomorrow. You're certain the labs were on this side?"

Duke Jank fiddled with his tie, smiled, and said, "Yes, very certain. Straight down."

"I've heard rumors. This Dr. Mengele used the blood from creatures in the forest and a couple of prisoners to create a serum that could bear a, uh, a super-soldier?" The SS officer asked.

The duke stared out into the distance, over the lake, where the moon still hung in the sky. "It's true. But as brilliant as Mengele was, he could never have done such a feat by himself. I tell you this in secret. He had help from the ones who are paying for this excavation." The duke chuckled. "You could say that my investors, uh, prefer to stay out of the spotlight. Old enemies of the Wehr Wolff family from long ago." The duke lifted his arms up in the air, turned where he stood, and said, "After we unearth what we need, I will rebuild this and make it more grand."

Two soldiers stepped up from where they had been holding guard, smoking cigarettes, and one asked in a strained voice, "Is it true? You saw a werewolf?"

Hagen leaped, both arms extended out, and glided between the two closest men, his long claws slicing through their carotid arteries. The soldiers flopped to the ground. A couple of soldiers wheeled to him, but never had time to raise their rifles to fire. He swatted one backhanded, and the man was flung at an ungodly speed into a partially standing wall; the body stuck to it. Hagen's claws curved up, gashed deep lacerations from abdomen to chest in the next soldier, and this man fell back, one breath away from death.

The wide-eyed SS officer tugged at the pistol in his belt and got it out, but Hagen had already pounced and his claws blurred through the air. The man's severed arm, holding the gun, plopped to the ground. Hagen opened his jaw and bit hard into the man's face and torso, mouthwatering blood gushing down his throat, and then he dropped the limp dead body to the rocky ground.

Hagen crept close to the man dressed in the business suit who wore the peculiar pink tie. *Duke Jank.* The duke had fallen and held one hand up defensively as he stared at Hagen with awe and terror. Hagen did not strike but stared at the man.

A word spilled from the duke's mouth in a whisper. "*Atemberaubend.*"

Memories whirled in Hagen's mind. The German word bounced around in his head and the translation came through.

Breathtaking.

The word *Aoibhneas* echoed from deep in his consciousness. Hagen was no longer staring down at a terrified man.

Emerald eyes stared at him, and a feeling of completeness swelled over him. An old woman's voice spoke. "Willpower will bring you back. But it need be connected to something of worth in this world. Love is the best path."

Hagen was backing up at a slow pace. Forgetting the man in front of him, he wheeled around and bounded over the ruins.

He crawled over the castle rubble, pushed large stones out of the way, and burrowed down deep into the debris. Time ticked by. His nose led him downward on a path that seemed to have no end. He moved past bodies without much thought and finally came to a silver revolver inside a holster, silver rounds fastened into loops. An image of sitting by a young man with red hair and mesmerizing green eyes came to mind. He wound the belt around a clawed forearm, nauseated by the silver, but he pushed that sensation away. He moved several feet deeper and found what he was searching for, then climbed upward through the ruins. He reached the top. The afternoon had grown into early evening. He sniffed the air; there were multitudes of humans in the area who were frantic and hunting. Hunting for him. He moved furtively, avoiding the soldiers, and hurried through the forest.

Night came. A new full moon was out—a renewed sense of lust filled Hagen, and adrenaline pumped through his body. He was invigorated beyond belief, and he wanted to give in to this lust. The full moon was the best time to gorge himself. The gun belt wrapped over his arm burned and had already made a raw wound, but he did not push it off. He felt compelled to deliver his gifts. *Then, then...* he could continue his life as a hunter.

He inched toward a cottage, smoke rising from its chimney.

The strong odor of the wehrwolves guarding the home was heavy, and he stopped. Riesig came out from the shadows and crouched with a deep throaty snarl, ready to attack Hagen. Several other wehrwolves came out of their hiding places, growling, ready to tear Hagen apart or at least try. He was of a formidable size compared to them. It would be one-sided, and Hagen would likely come out as the victor.

Riesig sniffed the air, and his eyes lit up. He trotted to Hagen with a discernible limp and touched Hagen's muzzle with his own.

Riesig glanced behind him, and a beast whose fragrance was familiar came out from behind a tree. This was not a wehrwolf, but another weremutant, but it did not possess the vileness of so many he had killed. It had velvety brown felt fur, and soft sad amber eyes.

Hagen dropped the metal case clenched in his jaw and walked to the brown-furred creature. Hagen's nose touched the weremutant's muzzle. It licked Hagen's face. They both stood there for several moments, their heads pressed together.

Hagen backed away and stared up into the night sky. The moon called to him, beckoning him to hunt and hunt. A voice inside his head said, "Breathe." Hagen shut his eyes, inhaled, and for the first in a long time, he felt his body changing back to human form.

Hagen knelt on the ground; he rose and stared down at his stark-naked human body. He picked up the case from the ground and opened it.

Hagen petted the brown-furred weremutant's muzzle, knelt by him, and said, "Do you trust me?"

The weremutant pushed his muzzle against Hagen's face, and Hagen took out the vial, pushed the syringe's needle into the top, and withdrew the turquoise liquid. He pushed the needle into the weremutant's furry neck. It flinched but didn't pull away. Hagen took the needle out and stood, then stared down, waiting.

"Hagen?" Ivan's voice called from behind him.

Hagen turned; his brother was dressed in farm clothes, his face gaunt. A black patch was over one eye. Hagen's intuition told him that his brother had lost his ability to change. Ivan's scent, though, was full of vigor and life.

Ivan grinned, strode forward, and pulled Hagen into a hug, laughing into his neck. "Oh, thank God, you're alive. *Thank God*." Ivan laughed and cried. Hagen had tears streaming down his face. There were snaps of branches, signaling something coming closer to them, and they broke their embrace. Roesia poked her head out from behind an oak, and a hand went to her mouth.

"Hagen."

She ran up and embraced him, too, kissing his cheek and laughing.

She hugged his neck hard, and he whispered, "I think I saw Sergeant Collins a couple of weeks ago. My memory is fuzzy. I think he went north."

She nodded, wiped her eyes, and looked down. She appeared to notice his nudity for the first time. "Oh," she said, with a chuckle. "We should get you something to wear."

A hoarse voice called. "Bloody better make it for two."

Roesia snapped her head around, her eyes wide. Ivan stepped forward, a grin spreading over his face.

A nude Liam sat on the ground, dirt and grime plastered over his bare chest and legs. Hagen marveled at his beauty. Liam stared at his fingers, flexing them. They had no discernible disfigurement.

Hagen knelt beside Liam and stroked his face with his fingers, his cheeks wet. "I almost lost you."

Liam laughed, he turned his emerald gaze up to Hagen, and said, "Don't be a complete muppet. I was here the whole bloody time, waiting. I knew you would come."

Hagen kissed his cheek, put his nose against his neck, and breathed, "I love you, Liam O'Malley."

Epilogue

ONE SUMMER DAY in August 1940, three survivors of the Night Angel returned to Shoreham Royal Air Force Base. The three members included Private Hagen Messer, Second Class Airman Liam O'Malley, and Professor Roesia Caron. Each of them were debriefed, and though their reports were classified as Top Secret, rumors came to light that they had infiltrated, then were captured inside a major Nazi hideout where hideous experimentations were being conducted. Diabolical procedures that attempted to mutate human beings into horrid monsters.

Outlandish rumors surfaced about the creature they brought back with them. Some said it was a new wolf species found in the Bavarian Forest, others said it had once been a man and turned into beast by the Nazis, and even some said the wolf had actually been a member of the Night Angel, Sergeant Brady Collins. This information of course was dismissed as mere hearsay, sparked by news stories trickling into England about abominable human experiments carried out by the Nazis. One consistently reported piece of information, though, regarded Liam O'Malley. His peers reportedly never considered him to be a strapping lad or extremely athletic. In fact, what they said was that he was lean and fit, though not much into sports as he was a bit uncoordinated. Yet, this young man had been seen demonstrating unheard of feats. He had the speed of an Olympic sprinter, agility of an acrobat, and the strength of three brawny men. That story came with many explanations too. One popular story was that he had been turned into a mutant wolf, and after given an antidote, he'd returned to human form—but with nimble feet and prowess never seen before in such a small-framed person.

The one folklore that continues to this day and sometimes can still be heard in pubs from Ireland to Scotland to England is of the American named Hagen Messer, who volunteered for the Royal Air

Force. It is said he was born from a German family with werewolf lineage and he could turn from man to beast at will. Accounts go on to say that Hagen carried out secret missions for England against a vampire clan aiding the Nazis.

Now that tale is an interesting one to hear.

About the Author

Bryce is professionally a psychologist who has worked mainly with veterans and provides LGBT consultation. He writes across multiple genres in both YA and Adult, his works including Sci-Fi, Dark Fantasy, Horror, and even Romance. For those individuals seeking a niche with extra spice and erotica, Bryce also writes gay fiction romances that range in levels of darkness. Merlin's Rogues: The Permesis Magician, a gay romance and dark fantasy novel, was published by Siren Publishing Allure ManLove April 2017. His *Wehr Wolff Castle: The Werhmacht's Mutante Wolf Project* (Horror/Gay Romance/Spy Thriller) will be published by NineStar Press in 2017. His nonfiction book, *Queer Sense*—a work that describes how culture shapes attitudes towards LGBTQA+ individuals—is scheduled to be published in 2018. Bryce has self-published *Rotville*, *The Zombie Squad*, and *The Flesh Stalker Series: Tales of Daemon the Demon Boy*. His early works include *Amen to Rot* and *Fresh Meat*. Bryce was the winner of the 2015 Dan Poynter Global eBook Award for Gay Fiction for his novel *Fresh Meat*. His Sci-Fi novel, *Rotville*, was a 2015 U.S. Book News Finalist and took first place for best unpublished manuscript at the 2015 Hollywood Book Festival. Additionally, *The Zombie Squad* was a 2016 Readers Favorite finalist for YA Horror.

Email: brycesummerstheauthor@gmail.com

Facebook: https://www.facebook.com/brycebentleysummers

Twitter: @Rotville